THE Marrying Game

Kate Saunders

 St. Martin's Griffin ✿ New York

www.stmartins.com

Library of Congress Cataloging-in-Publication Data

Saunders, Kate.
    The marrying game / Kate Saunders.—1st St. Martin's Griffin ed.
        p. cm.
    ISBN 0-312-31043-9 (hc)
    ISBN 0-312-31044-7 (pbk)
    EAN 978-0312-31044-8
    1. Aristocracy (Social class)—Fiction. 2. Fatherless families—Fiction. 3. London (England)—Fiction. 4. Mate selection—Fiction. 5. Home ownership—Fiction. 6. Poor families—Fiction. 7. Poor women—Fiction. 8. Sisters—Fiction. I. Title.

PR6069.A915M37 2004
823'.914—dc22   2004046707

First St. Martin's Griffin Edition: August 2004

10 9 8 7 6 5 4 3 2 1

Acknowledgments

I am grateful to everyone who helped with the writing of this book, particularly to Philip Wells, for translating the Hasty family motto into medieval French, and to Felix Wells, who first dreamed up the Ressany saga. Thanks are also due to Amanda Craig, Joanna Briscoe, Charlotte Mendelssohn, Louisa Saunders, Bill Saunders, and Charlotte Saunders.

Part One

Chapter One

This one is the set of Narnia books, from Roger," Nancy said. "This one is Barbie and her strangely enormous pony, which looks more like a dray horse—that's from Mum." She held the gaudy parcels up before her sister's dazed, melancholy face. "And mine's coming later. That's at least three more presents than we thought."

"Four," Selena said, from the depths of her book. Her obsessive reading never stopped her joining in the conversation. "I made her some chocolate fudge, and I thought I'd put it in my painted box—she's always fancied it. Has anyone got any spare wrapping paper?"

"I have," Rufa murmured. "Leave it on my bed, and I'll do it when I wrap mine."

Lydia was smiling mistily, like sun breaking through cloud. "It's going to be all right, isn't it? I can stand anything, as long as Linnet has enough presents. You're all wonderful—I don't know how to thank you."

"You can stop her getting up at dawn," Nancy suggested. "It's so fiendishly cold, I need at least an hour's notice before I leave my virgin couch."

Rufa laughed softly. "You'll be lucky. Linnet told me she's going to borrow my alarm clock and set it for five." She was stretched out on the sofa, exhausted and reeking of nutmeg after weeks of Christmas cooking. Her long auburn hair, the color of garnets, poured over the hideous orange tweed cushions. Her three younger sisters sprawled on the floor, their long ropes of hair brushing the ashy carpet. Each had a slice of herself wedged against the fender, exposed to the tiny fire.

"Liddy," Nancy said, "get that monstrous great bum of yours out of the way."

"Monstrous bum—look who's talking." Lydia's soft voice was gently steeped in complaint. "I need more heat than you do. I'm thinner, and my surface area is greater in relation to my volume." She wrestled the cork from a bottle of cheap red wine.

Selena finally raised her head from the pages of *Paradise Lost*. "Biscuit, anyone?" From the darned folds of her huge jersey, she produced a packet of chocolate digestives.

"My God," Nancy exclaimed. "Where on earth did you get those?"

"Brian gave them to me. I think he's sorry for us."

Brian was the sweaty young man from the auctioneers, currently estimating the value of the ancient house and its dilapidated contents. Melismate, home of the Hasty family for nearly a thousand years, was about to go under the hammer.

Selena tore the packet open, and her sisters shot out begging hands. The appalling lack of money, further beyond a joke than it had ever been, made chocolate biscuits seem as exotic as caviar. They had been living on their mother's meager leek soup for several weeks, hoarding every penny for the last Christmas at Melismate.

"That was nice of him," Rufa said, with her mouth full. She felt it was important to notice when people were being nice.

"Hmmm." Absently, Selena turned a page.

"He's rather odious sometimes, but it's not his fault we're ruined."

"Don't say 'ruined' like that," Lydia murmured. She poured the wine into four mismatched teacups, and handed them round. "Every time I think about the future, I just feel sick."

It was Christmas Eve. The Zed was enjoying his first Christmas in heaven. The house he had left was freezing. Under the hammer, his family were being beaten to smithereens. Next day's lunch, a supermarket chicken the size of a canary, sat in the echoing fridge, ready for cooking. Rufa had spent her last reserves of energy scrubbing and peeling the mountain of potatoes that would have to fill seven empty stomachs. Now, they had reached the point where there was nothing left to do. The pies and cakes, which would have occupied her in the days of relative plenty, did not exist this year. Their mother was downstairs, with Lydia's little daughter. The Hasty girls had gathered, as they often did, in the old nursery.

The nursery consisted of two garrets in the sloping roof, knocked into one large room. It was as drafty as the deck of the *Cutty Sark* and crammed with lumber. Brian had valued the lumber, in its entirety, at forty pounds. He could not be expected to see that its true value went beyond money. The nursery was a mille-feuille of family history; layer upon layer, like the rings of a tree.

The scrap screen, covered with yellowed pictures of cherubic children in sailor suits, was a relic of some Victorian Hasty. The formidable Silver Cross pram, now dented and lame, dated from The Zed's postwar infancy. The orange sofa, disfigured by a huge burn, was part of the girls own history. They all remembered the famous bonfire night in the 1980s, when The Zed had painfully learned the difference between outdoor and indoor fireworks.

The Zed was their late father. He had flown out of the world six months before, leaving the rest of them to drop to earth like so many spent rockets. The Zed had been divinely handsome, dazzlingly autocratic, royally eccentric, and utterly charming. He could carry a ridiculous gesture far beyond comedy, and invest it with grandeur. On his honeymoon in Antibes, he had rushed out during an argument and tried to join the Foreign Legion. He had once daubed his naked body with blue powder paint and attended a children's fancy dress party as an Ancient Briton. The Zed had loved parties, he had virtually lived at a party. He liked his house teeming with people and ringing with laughter. He had loved to lose his heart, and his wife and daughters had nursed him tenderly through his many infidelities, when that susceptible organ was sent back in pieces—somehow, even his adultery was different, and did not count as betrayal. It was godlike, Olympian adultery—like the King of the Gods, he always returned to his wife and his mountain afterward.

Nobody could remember exactly when they had started to think of him as The Zed. Someone had called him "Zeus" when the girls were babies, and the nickname had stuck because its mixture of the majestic and the faintly loopy seemed to suit him. Gradually, familiarity had rubbed "Zeus" down to "Zoozy," then "Zeddy," then (he seemed to need the gravitas of the definite article) it wound through "El Zeddo" and "Le Zee," until it settled into The Zed; the title of the Alpha Male who was also the Omega. He had surrounded himself—and them—with an atmosphere of excitement and glamour. When he died, all the color had bled out of the world.

Rufa struggled into a sitting position to sip her wine. She had adored her father, but was beginning to admit that The Zed's highly individual morals had had a blighting effect on the romantic lives of his daughters. He had given them their fatal preference for the ornamental over the practical.

The problem was not that there were no men like him. On the contrary, the world positively seethed with charming eccentrics who never got up in the mornings. They were easier to catch than the flu, and always disappointing. Their charming ineffectiveness could never compare with the epic, sweet uselessness of Rufus Hasty.

Rufa's first romantic disappointment had been a major one; so heartbreaking and humiliating that, even three years later, she wanted nothing more to do with love.

And it's not just me, she thought—look at the others.

Lydia had come home, with her little girl, after the failure of her ludicrous marriage. Nancy was currently madly in love with the doctor's son, who lived in a caravan at the bottom of his parents' garden. Selena was still at school, and too young for really deep disappointment, but she already had an instinctive taste for a good-looking loser. It was only a matter of time.

Lydia said, as someone was always saying, "If only there was something we could do!"

Nancy helped herself to another biscuit. "Well, there isn't. Unless we all marry money."

"We might," Selena pointed out.

"What, before the auction?" Rufa laughed. "We don't even know anybody rich. Let alone anybody rich enough to pay The Zed's debts and save the house."

Selena put down her book. "But it's still a possibility."

"I got the only available man for miles around," Lydia said wistfully, "and just look at him. We never meet anyone."

"You can say that again," Nancy agreed. "This place is like Brigadoon—God knows what century it is out there. I must take a peek sometime, and see if they've repealed those awful Corn Laws."

"Actually—" Rufa began. Her eyes were fixed thoughtfully on a snake's tongue of flame that had shot out of the red embers. "Actually, Selena's right. If we could meet the rich men, it ought to be perfectly possible to marry one."

"I've got a better idea," Nancy said disconsolately. "Let's rub all the lamps, and see if a fucking genie pops out."

"I'd happily work for the money," Rufa said, "if I knew how to earn enough. Unfortunately, making jam, at a clear profit of sixty-two pence per jar, is never going to get us millions of pounds by the end of March."

"Well, don't look at me," Nancy said. "My tips barely keep me in cigs as it is."

Rufa had shaken off her exhaustion. She was looking narrowly at their faces. "You're all lovely looking girls, you know. And I'm not bad, when I don't smell like a mince pie. Now, there's an asset—it's almost a shame Brian can't put us up for auction along with the furniture."

There was a silence, as the four of them considered the unarguable, taken-for-granted beauty that was a fact of being a Hasty. It had never occurred to them that this beauty might do more than give them first pick of the local talent. And they could not think of their looks without hearing the rapturous voice of The Zed—"My seraglio, my genetic miracles, my peerless princesses—"

Rufa, at twenty-seven, was a Burne-Jones nymph in jeans and Timberlands. Her skin was transparently soft and white, against the royal burgundy of her splendid hair (all the girls had fathoms of hair, because The Zed had insisted that his lambs should never be shorn). Rufa's eyes were of a rare dark blue, that could blacken in shadow and suddenly blaze sapphire. She was as tall as The Zed had been, and very thin. A woman from a model agency had "discovered" her while she was in the Fifth Form at Saint Hildegard's, and begged her to come to London.

The Zed had laughed and laughed, at the bare idea of exposing his firstborn and favorite to the vulgar gaze of the public. It had never been mentioned again.

Nancy, at twenty-six, was a Renoir in everything but flesh. Her curves were slender, her voluptuousness spiritual rather than physical. She was a kind of alternative, X-rated version of Rufa—less gaspingly beautiful, more absolutely sexy. Nancy's hair was decidedly red. Her large, firm breasts were the envy of her skinny sisters. Her eyes were sleepy and mocking, her lips generous and wanton. She was an orchid among lilies of the valley.

Twenty-four-year-old Lydia was more like their mother than The Zed. Her style was delicate fragility, exquisite in the detail. She was smaller than Rufa and Nancy. Her eyes were of a lighter, brighter blue, and her billows of curly hair were golden-brown. At her best she was a Hilliard miniature,

7

executed with the finest of fine brushwork. These days, unkempt and unplucked, she had the wistful appeal of a mossy stone angel in a secret garden.

Selena, The Zed's afterthought, was seventeen. She was very tall and lanky, but it was difficult to tell exactly what she looked like. Her hair, the same color as Lydia's, was worn in matted dreadlocks. She was further disguised by small round glasses and studs in her nose, lower lip, and tongue.

Regretfully, Selena said, "Nobody marries for money anymore."

"People have always married for money," Rufa returned, "and they always will. Most of our ancestors did. Nobody bothered about romance in those days."

The others furtively exchanged significant looks. They all knew she was thinking of Jonathan, the man who had broken her heart.

"Marriage without love is totally pointless." Lydia, the passive and retiring, spoke with unaccustomed authority. She was the only one of them who had ever been married. "It's total agony anyway. I could only leave Ran when I stopped being in love with him."

This time, Rufa joined in the significant looks. Lydia's sisters did not believe she had ever stopped loving her hopeless young husband.

"There would have been a point, if Ran had loads of money," Selena said.

Rufa tipped more wine into her teacup. "In this family, we've always made love far too important. It's only ever brought us trouble."

"I did have Linnet because of love," Lydia pointed out.

"Apart from Linnet." Rufa crossed her long legs, and pushed her hair impatiently over her shoulder. "Maybe we should think about marrying money. A hundred years ago, it would have been the sensible thing to do."

Very unwillingly, the other three drew the real, outside world into focus.

"I suppose I could just about marry a man I don't love," Nancy said thoughtfully. "But I draw the line at someone I don't fancy."

"I'm sure you could make the effort," Rufa said, "since you seem to fancy just about anything with a backbone."

Nancy smiled, not displeased. "If I was as fussy as you are, I'd never have any fun at all."

Rufa sighed. "Being fussy didn't do me much good, did it?"

She did not often talk about this episode in her life—the one time she had been at odds with The Zed. He had teased her relentlessly about the affair with Jonathan. He had entertained the family with such marvelous imitations of Jonathan that even Rufa had been forced to laugh. The seriousness of Rufa in love had alarmed him. For once in his life, The Zed had found himself sharing his throne.

"It was like a tasteful film on Channel Four," he used to say, smiling down the dinner table, over Rufa's bowed auburn head. "Tonight, after the news, poncey London novelist rents country cottage, falls for local redhead—then rushes home to his wife, to write it all down."

That had been more or less it, in a nutshell. At the time, three summers ago, Rufa had not known that losing her heart to Jonathan Wilby was a cliché. She had been ready to give him her body and soul—and he had not been able to cope with the intensity of his village-born beauty, nor the antics of her barking upper-class family. Rufa had never found out why Jonathan took fright so suddenly. She suspected The Zed—of what, she did not know; but it was the one canker in her memories of him.

"If you ask me," Nancy said, snatching the wine bottle, "falling in love is the only thing that makes life on earth worth living. But I'm not sure about marriage. I mean, look at Liddy."

"God, yes," Lydia sighed, "look at me."

Ten years ago, the teenage Lydia had fallen wildly in love with Randolph Verrall, who raised goats on a neighboring smallholding, and believed that keeping a crystal in your pants drawer could increase your sexual potency. Ran's mother lived in a ruined Scottish castle, which she had turned into a commune. His father, long dead, had left him a Georgian farmhouse, squatting on a few scrubby acres. It was here that Ran tended his goats, hosted fire-walking weekends, and meditated naked.

Ran's extraordinary dark beauty had blinded Lydia to his absurdity. Like The Zed, he was an Old Etonian of the purely ornamental kind. Lydia had married him in a meadow, wearing Indian cotton and a wreath of buttercups.

As The Zed had cheerfully predicted from Day One, the marriage ended in a mire of droppings and disillusion. Ran's incompetence was spectacular. After the goats caught something and died, he had tried various methods of making money without doing too much actual work. Everything he touched reeked of doom.

Lydia was used to financial doom. It was the adultery she could not bear. Also like The Zed, Ran was prodigiously unfaithful. Lydia had finally despaired of him, and crept home to Melismate. The family had been overjoyed to have her back—The Zed had swapped a china footbath for two bottles of champagne, to celebrate. It meant that they had Linnet, and they all adored Lydia's little girl.

Because Ran was the father of the blessed Linnet, and because he was an amiable soul, the sisters were fond of him. He was a loving father and a kind neighbor—but you could not call him an advertisement for marriage. Or, for that matter, love.

"Falling in love," Rufa announced, "is overrated."

Nancy shrieked at this dismissal of her raison d'être. "Oh, yes. Vastly overrated, by millions of people. But we're all wrong. Don't listen to us."

"Tim Dent is that great, is he?"

"Tim's fabulous," Nancy said staunchly. "You should just hear some of his poems."

"Seriously." Rufa refused to be distracted. "Looking for a rich husband has got to be better than shagging in a caravan."

Nancy groaned softly. "So what? I might be grateful for that caravan soon. When this place is sold, we won't have time to chase rich men. We'll be too busy earning a crust, and finding somewhere to live."

"I won't," Selena put in sulkily. "I have to live in that shitty cottage in Bangham, with Mum and Roger. She says I've got to finish my exams."

"So you have," Rufa said.

"I am not going to university, okay?"

"Shut up. Yes you are."

Lydia was frowning anxiously. "Mummy said she'd always find space for Linnet, but there won't be room for me. And I could never live apart from her, anyway. So it looks as if I'll end up camping in Ran's barn—with a chemical loo and that horrible girlfriend of his over in the farmhouse."

"That leaves you and me, Ru," Nancy said. "And I'm not as lacking in ambition as you seem to think. I have made plans for the future, you know. When the time comes, I shall do extra shifts at the pub."

Rufa laughed. "That's ambition, is it?"

"And I'll completely stop taking tips in the form of drink."

The State, thankfully, recognized no difference between decayed gentility and ordinary poverty. Lydia, as a single mother with a penniless ex-husband, received some State benefits—she called them her "houndstooth checks," because they were very small. Selena intended to go on the dole the second she left Saint Hildegard's, whatever Rufa said.

Nancy, who had achieved neither A levels nor university, did her bit for the family finances by working as a barmaid in the village pub. It was called the Hasty Arms, and when The Zed heard that she had got herself a job there, he had not known whether to laugh or cry. His own coat of arms decorated the creaking pub sign, with its family motto, *Evite La Pesne*. The Zed said this meant "Avoid Fatigue," and it was not appropriate to find a genuine, Norman-blooded Hasty pulling pints and calling time. He had been rather touchy about the quality of the family blood—all the more so since he had married out of his class to produce his genetic miracles. Nancy had won him round, however, by giving him free drinks—and reminding him how much they needed the cash. The Zed had said oh well, he always hoped to have a daughter called to the bar.

Nancy enjoyed her work. She was good at it, and had no ambitions beyond persuading the landlord to drum up more trade with a karaoke machine. You could be sure of congenial company in a pub—as Nancy had always pointed out to The Zed, "I'd be in there anyway, so I might as well get paid for it." There were endless opportunities to fall in love. Nancy had been desperately in love any number of times. She said her heart was a mass of cracks, where it had been broken and glued together. Rufa, who suspected that her favorite sister was the cleverest of all of them, some-times wished she had done something a little more elevated with her life. When she expressed this regret, Nancy replied, "What, for instance? There aren't that many openings for a good-natured rural slut. I'd only be on the dole."

Rufa had never been on the dole. She had the family's only A levels (En-glish, Latin, History of Art), and would have gone to university, if The Zed had not been so vehemently against it. With tears dripping from his heav-enly eyes, he had begged Rufa never to leave him. He needed all his people around him at all times.

Staying at Melismate, however, had not dimmed Rufa's natural capacity for earning money. By some genetic quirk, the daughter who most resem-bled The Zed brimmed with energy and enterprise. A freakish little piece of her DNA urged her toward normality, like a compass needle yearning for the North. She was the only sister to have taken and passed a driving test. She had spent her hoarded savings on an old blue Volvo—and The Zed had been very cross when he realized there had been such a sum of ready money in the family.

In the fruit season, Rufa made tons of excellent jam, and drove around the Cotswolds selling it to tourist shops. For the past six weeks she had been making mincemeat, and little crocks of brandy butter, decorated with pretty labels she had drawn herself (hiding the brandy from her relations had been harder than splitting the atom). She also cooked for local dinner parties, and

11

did fancy knitting for a London designer. The sums of money were small, and won with backbreaking toil, but they helped.

"I must admit," The Zed had once said, "your middle-class antics do keep the wolf from the door."

The Zed's teasing about work had been relentless. Though very funny, it had been an expression of opposition or hostility. He had found it too hilarious when a Norman-blooded Hasty cooked for people who could not trace their ancestors back to William Rufus.

He had accepted Nancy's bar-work by turning it into a joke, but Rufa was different. He bracketed her with his dead mother, who had been the most beautiful debutante of her generation. He could stand knuckle-headed locals calling Nancy "love" and demanding vodka and Red Bull, yet he hated Rufa taking orders from the neighboring gentry. The Zed had not considered himself a snob. He had defined snobs as people unreasonably obsessed with keeping their houses and families clean. In his book, only those who remembered the gutter cared about hygiene, and he did not need to prove his gentility with any outward show. The Zed had followed a long line of handsome, russet-headed forebears to Eton, and inherited a house that was listed Grade One. It had taken him years to realize this did not entitle him to any special protection.

Rufa, deeply as she had loved The Zed, was under no such illusion. Firmly, unwillingly slotted into the real world, she was the Little Dorrit of the family, slaving to finance a fantasy she could not share. Sometimes she envied Lydia and Selena, for their ability to float through the world without truly seeing it.

Nancy, whose refusal to be upper class had a certain stubborn energy, was another matter. It was to Nancy Rufa addressed herself now.

"All right, look at the available choices. You could go on working as a barmaid, and living in Tim's caravan—knowing that Mum, Roger, and Selena are crammed into a nasty cottage next to a garden center. Knowing also that Liddy and Linnet have to doss down in Ran's barn—next door to that strumpet from the bookshop, who's forever nibbling his ear in public." Rufa paused, to subdue the rising indignation in her voice. "Or you could take a mad stab at marrying money, bearing in mind that it'll mean a lot of hard work, and a fair amount of behaving like a lady."

"A what?" Nancy murmured. "God, she's serious!"

"I am, actually." Rufa listened to herself saying it, with amazement. "I think it can be done. There must be rich men ready to fall in love with looks and breeding. Both of which we have in abundance."

Selena, who had been gradually sinking back into her book, suddenly resurfaced. "You could always divorce them, once you'd got your hands on the cash."

Nancy could not help showing she was interested. "Well, find me a rich man, and I'll be happy to consider it."

"I could never go down on a guy with a paunch," declared Selena.

"Excuse me, madam," Nancy said, with mock severity, "you're not supposed to know about 'going down' on anything but a staircase."

She reached out, bracelets jangling, to pull Rufa's watch toward her. "Bags I the bath. I'm going out to dinner at the Dents."

"They're letting you inside the house now, are they?" Rufa asked.

Nancy stood up on the ragged hearthrug, and stretched luxuriously. Her tight black jersey strained across her chest, and rode up to reveal her navel. Nancy's clothes often seemed on the point of falling off.

"It'll be incredibly dull, but I have some important business. Thanks to my tireless efforts, there's a fab present waiting for me under the Dents' tree."

"Lucky cow," muttered Selena. "What is it?"

"Ma Dent asked if there was any special treat I'd like. I said there certainly was, and I told her exactly where to get one." She smiled down at her sisters, enjoying their suspense. "It's a fairy outfit, in rainbow tulle—"

"Oh, Nancy!" Lydia cried, in ecstasy.

"—comprising sticky-out skirt, wings, twinkly wand, and tiara."

"You total darling." Lydia was almost in tears. "She'll be in seventh heaven."

Rufa beamed. "It'll make Linnet's day. You are a love, Nance."

"I just wish they made them in a size twelve," Nancy said. "Then I could wave my magic wand, and make the Dents interesting. In the name of humanity, don't drink all the wine while I'm out—the doctor's house is as dry as a fucking bone." She shot a calculating glance at Rufa. "May I borrow the car?"

"No, you may not," Rufa said sharply. "For the last time, not till you get a driving license. And anyway, Roger's got it."

"Oh well, worth a try." Halfway round the edge of the scrap screen, Nancy turned back to add, "Which is exactly my position regarding your idea, darling. I have a feeling I'd be terrifically good at the Marrying Game."

Chapter Two

A nd it was always said of him that he knew how to keep Christmas well, if any man alive possessed the knowledge . . . ' "

Rufa heard the low, tearful voice of her mother, as she went into the cavernous kitchen. Rose Hasty sat beside the ash-caked range, with her Sellotaped reading glasses low on her nose, a battered paperback in her hand, and Linnet on her knee.

" 'May that be truly said of us, and all of us! And so, as Tiny Tim observed—' "

Her voice wobbled, and failed.

Linnet finished for her. " 'God Bless Us, Every One!' " She squirmed off Rose's knee. " 'The End.' "

Rose closed the book, and leaned back in her chair with a loud sniff. "My God, the emotional drainage!"

"Well, if you will read Dickens," Rufa said.

"I know. I must be mad."

Rose was fifty: an ex-beauty not so much running as dashing to seed. The fair skin around her eyes was curdling into a network of lines. The soft flesh sagged away from her jaw, and her wild curls were degenerating into a frowsty puff of pepper-and-salt. It was still possible, however, to trace the outlines of the exquisite flower child who had captivated The Zed thirty years before, at a muddy rock festival down in the West Country.

"Kettle's on," she said. "Get us some tea, there's a love."

Rufa was the only member of the family who could be asked for tea without arguing or making elaborate excuses. She stuffed two tea bags into two mugs, and filled them from the heavy kettle on the range.

"Roger not back yet?"

Roger was Rose's lover, and the Useless Man of the house, now that The Zed himself had gone. He had arrived at Melismate, by accident, ten years before, and shared Rose's bed ever since. The Zed, glad to have his wife's bed decently occupied, had grown fond of him. And they had all benefited from his minuscule private income.

"He went over to Ran's," Rose said. "There's a crisis, apparently."

Linnet's voice floated up at them, from under the huge and ancient kitchen table. "The old tart from the bookshop left him. He rang up crying, and I said I wasn't sorry."

Rufa's convention gene twitched disagreeably. It was absolutely no use reminding anyone here that little pitchers had big ears. They were all strangers to embarrassment.

"Twenty minutes to bedtime, plum," she said.

Linnet growled irritably. "Can't you see? I'm busy in my house."

She was five, and as beautiful as a child could be. Her mother's porcelain features and blue eyes had gone into the genetic mixer with Ran's glossy, dead-straight black hair, and the result was a pale, grave little Rapunzel. She wore a bright green jersey, with a yellow jersey showing underneath through the holes, and somehow radiated dignity.

Sipping her tea, Rufa knelt on the stone floor beside the table. Linnet had furnished her house with a very dirty cushion, and a bald twig supposed to represent a Christmas tree. Her two brown bears, the Ressany Brothers, lay at drunken angles upon a towel. Two of Linnet's socks were tacked to the table leg, at bear height.

"This is their fireplace," she explained. "They've just hung up their stockings."

Rufa took her mention of stockings as a hopeful sign. Some weeks earlier, Linnet had found her grandmother sobbing over a gigantic electricity bill. Because nobody ever thought of being discreet in front of the little girl, she had heard loud disputes about whether they should have electricity or alcohol for their last Christmas at Melismate.

A little later, she had said to Rufa, with studied casualness, "There probably won't be many presents this year, I should think."

The bravery of this had hurt the sisters indescribably. The idea of Linnet being disappointed on Christmas morning had startled them all out of the general, despairing chaos. Even Selena, who rarely lifted her head from the page long enough to grunt, had managed to scrape together the wherewithal for her chocolate fudge. Nancy had grandly declared that she would get Linnet a present if she had to sleep with an entire Welsh Male Voice Choir, all singing "Myfanwy," to do it (luckily this had not been necessary). Rufa had burned quarts of midnight oil, stretching the money that had not been swallowed up by the Electricity Board.

Now, giddy with the realization that it was going to be all right—that Linnet's delight would make a window of all-rightness in the pervading depression—Rufa was almost happy. She had knitted a brilliant jersey, from Technicolor scraps. She had made two tiny Pierrot costumes for the Ressany Brothers, and illustrated a story of Nancy's called "Trouble at Ressany Hall."

The spirit of The Zed was in me, she thought, making magic out of nothing.

There was not a drop of gin in the house, and other basic necessities were down to a minimum, but the sacrifices had been worth it. Tomorrow morning, at the foot of the bed she shared with her mother, Linnet would find a stocking bulging with presents.

Under the table, Linnet was wrapping two wrinkled conkers and a tarnished brass doorknob in tinfoil.

"Bless them," she said indulgently, nodding toward her bears. "They're so excited. Calm down, boys."

"It's nearly time to hang up your own stocking," Rufa said. "And we mustn't forget to leave a little something for Father Christmas."

It hurt her to see the shrewd, cautious look cross Linnet's face. The Zed had always left a snack for the overworked saint on Christmas Eve. But The Zed was dead, and everything was horribly changed.

Linnet emerged from her house on all fours. "We gave him gin and tonic last time."

"No gin," Rose sighed.

"A cup of tea and a biscuit," Rufa suggested. "It's what I'd fancy myself, on a night like this."

Linnet nodded, satisfied. "And some grass."

"Oh no, darling," Rose said, "I don't think Father Christmas smokes."

"Not THAT kind of grass, silly. I meant for the reindeer to eat."

Rufa swallowed an unholy snort of laughter—Linnet hated any laughing that seemed to be connected with her. "It's too cold to go outside. How about sugar lumps?"

"Okay."

Rufa kissed the top of Linnet's head, which smelled of wood smoke, and went to find sugar lumps and a saucer. The sugar lumps were elderly, and stained a rather sinister brown color.

Linnet giggled. "They look like little poohs."

The door flew open, and Nancy blew in on the draft. "Miss Linnet, your mother wants you upstairs."

She was fresh from the bath, in a cloud of glorious hair and unidentifiable perfume. She had changed into a black knitted dress that showed the outlines of her nipples and hugged her braless breasts.

"Ow, not yet!" Linnet protested.

Nancy said, in a pert, squeaky voice, "Come on, Linnet, I'm sleepy." In a deep, gruff voice, she added, "It'll make Christmas come quicker!" Nancy, not to be relied upon for serious child care, was a Mel Blanc of vocal characterization. She had invented voices for all Linnet's principal toys, and could "do" the Ressany Brothers for hours at a time.

"Come up with me," Linnet ordered.

"All right."

"That dress looks nice on you," Rufa said.

"Doesn't it? Sorry I didn't ask. But you don't mind, do you?"

"No. I only wish I filled it out in the same places."

"Thanks." Nancy picked up Rufa's cup of tea, and dropped in three of the discolored sugar lumps.

Linnet gave her good-night kisses, and the two of them departed, in a cloud of witnesses—the Ressany Brothers could be heard arguing, all the way up the stairs.

Rufa moved to the range, to make herself another cup of tea. Nancy really could look absolutely stunning, she thought—if she would dress like a lady, instead of like Posh Spice crossed with an amorous milkmaid. The notion of marrying money was hardening in Rufa's mind.

While she waited for the kettle to come back to the boil, she looked around the room. This enormous kitchen, and the vaulted Great Hall that adjoined it, were the oldest parts of Melismate. They had been built in the fourteenth century, and their massive walls had sunk deep, immovable roots into the Gloucestershire earth. Now that she was about to lose her home, Rufa ached for all the lost opportunities. What a house it might have been, if there had been enough money to restore its diaphanous roof and sagging timbers. She hated the waste of so much beauty.

She made her tea, in a mug with I'VE SEEN THE PIGS AT SEMPLE FARM! printed on its side. Semple Farm was where Ran lived, and there had never been any pigs. The mugs were all that remained of that particular doomed project.

She asked, "Has Ran's girlfriend really left him?"

Rose stretched out her legs in their faded blue corduroys. "I knew it couldn't last. She was far too clean."

Rufa laughed. "When she came to supper here, I swear she wiped her feet on the way out." She sat down at the kitchen table. "I bet Linnet's pleased, anyway."

"So is Lydia, no doubt," Rose said sagely. "That idiotic girl is still in love with Ran."

Rufa sighed. "She says she dreads having to live on the farm again—but only because she can't bear the jealousy."

Rose sighed too, and they sat in peaceful agreement. Rose had not always got on with her eldest daughter, despite her relentless efforts to please. Rufa's normality had grated on her. As a teenager, Rose had run away from a sweetshop in Falmouth to escape normality. She had fallen in love with Rufus Hasty because he was the exact opposite of normal. Rose had chosen to be different, and Rufa's inbuilt normality had sometimes seemed like a reproach.

The arrival of Linnet, however, had awakened Rose's dormant bourgeois values. As a mother, she had cultivated eccentricity. As a grandmother, she wanted Linnet to have all the good, solid, dull things that other little girls had. Rufa, who all but worshiped Linnet, wanted it too. Rose had suddenly found she had a lot in common with her firstborn. She leaned on Rufa these days, as she had never leaned on The Zed, or Roger. You could throw a normal sentiment out at Rufa, without risking a barmy response.

"Mum," Rufa said, "what do you think about marrying for money?"

"Seriously? Oh, of course you're serious—you're never anything else. Have you met someone rich?"

"No. I'm theorizing, at the moment. What would you think if I married a very rich man, without necessarily being in love with him?"

Rose narrowed her eyes thoughtfully. "I'd think," she said slowly, "that you were either very cynical, or very naive. Cynical to marry without love. And naive, to imagine you can live without it."

"I can," Rufa said dismissively.

"You will get over Jonathan, you know. You can't marry without love, Ru. You'd have a nervous breakdown. Nancy would get by—she can persuade herself to fall in love at the drop of a hat—but not you. Strange as it seems for any daughter of mine, you're too refined." Rose leaned forward, to put her crowning point more forcefully. "You'd have to sleep with this rich husband of yours, I presume."

There was a pause, during which Rufa stared at the fire, through the open door of the range. She said, "I'd sleep with Godzilla, to get us all out of this mess."

Rose winced at this naked reminder of the "mess" they were trying to ignore. "Darling, we will make out, you know. It won't be such a tragedy. The Zed went on about the house, and the family history—but nobody can take away the history, and we'll only be living like millions of others."

Rufa's blue gaze did not waver. "It means too much to let go. I can't do it."

"You're young," Rose said. "Don't set out to bugger up your life." She stood up, and took a bottle of red wine off the dresser. Deftly, she plucked out the cork and found two bleary glasses. "Apart from anything else, you'd have to meet some rich men first."

"We'd need to be in London," Rufa murmured. "We must get to London."

"Oh, God—is Chekhov writing our scripts again? I preferred Benny Hill." Rose took a deep gulp of wine, like a dose of medicine.

"And we'd need to buy some decent clothes."

"Wake up, lovey. With what? Not one of us has a bean."

"Nancy and I could be the first wave," Rufa went on. "We'd think of it as one of The Zed's games—the Marrying Game."

"Marriage is not a game."

"And we could stay with Wendy. I'm sure she'd have us."

Wendy Withers had been their nanny. She had put up with the state of the house, and the irregularity of her wages, because she had been hopelessly in love with The Zed. They had enjoyed one of his brief, intense affairs, and she had followed him home on the strength of it. The girls had loved her, and Rose had become very fond of her. When, after five years, Wendy had left to make room for some Balinese dancers, both women had wept. Rose was impressed that Rufa had carried her idea this far.

"You're right, she'd be thrilled to have you."

Rufa was planning. "I can get a few thousand for the car, and we might squeak by." Her forehead wrinkled anxiously. "Linnet would have to walk to school, though. And how would you get to the shops? Perhaps it isn't worth the risk."

The fire, sunk into sullen red embers, turned her auburn hair the color of the wine. Its light fell golden against her cheek. She was so beautiful, Rose thought. And she was wasting her life here, because The Zed had made her promise to stay forever.

"Take a risk," she said impulsively. "For once in your life, do something silly. I'd hate you to be unhappy, darling—but your Marrying Game is the soundest bloody idea I've heard in ages."

Rufa was startled. The two women stared at each other, intrigued.

The moment of unexpected intimacy was broken by the sound of the front door opening ponderously, with a creak like Dracula's coffin lid. A tuneless tenor voice sang out:

We are not daily beggars,
That come from door to door;
We are your neighbors' children,
Whom you have seen before!

"Oh, it's Ran," Rose said, smiling and rolling her eyes. "Quick, think of something else to throw in the soup, or it'll never stretch."

Rufa stood up, mentally shelving her Marrying Game. "A plimsoll?"

"Can't you spare a potato?"

"You were telling me to get real a second ago," Rufa said. "There's no such thing as a spare potato round here."

The massive, veined door that joined the Great Hall to the kitchen opened, and frigid air whipped into the smoky warmth. Roger came in, unzipping The Zed's old Barbour. He was a pale, weedy man of thirty-five. His hairline was in fluffy retreat on the dome of his forehead, and a thin brown ponytail hung between his shoulder blades. The main fact of Roger's life—all you needed to know about him—was that he had loved Rose for ten years, and would love her devotedly until he died. He exuded benign calm, and brought an exotic tang of common sense into the household. Despite his surroundings, Roger was quietly and persistently normal.

"Sorry I'm late," he said affably. "Ran wouldn't let me leave him on his own, so I brought him with me."

"Another mouth to feed," Rose said, "but I can't find it in my heart to protest. That boy's love life is as good as the telly."

Ran sprang into the room, jostling Roger aside. "Merry Christmas, girls." He dropped a damp sack on the table, and darted forward to kiss Rose and Rufa. "God, it's cold. Give me a drink."

"You'll be lucky," Rose said. "There's a long waiting list for this wine."

Ran was another one, she thought, who was allowing outrageous good looks to rust away in this rural backwater. He was wearing a tie-dyed waistcoat and silly embroidered hat, but his beauty shone through them. His eyes and his thick, shoulder-length hair were dark and lustrous against his parchment skin. Linnet's batty young father had the face of a Renaissance angel.

"It's really nice of you to have me," he said, fixing Rose and Rufa with his poignant gaze. "I know how tight things are, so I didn't come empty-handed. I brought a carload of logs, plus the onions I couldn't shift at the Farmers' Market."

Rufa examined the sack on the table. "Brilliant. The soup now has stretching possibilities." Ran was looking around hopefully. "Where's Linnet?"

"Upstairs. Liddy's putting her to bed."

"And if you get her into one of her states," Rose put in sternly, "you'll be the one responsible for getting her to sleep."

Ran asked, "Couldn't she stay up for supper?"

"No, we're far too knackered. Roger, make yourself useful. Roll us a joint."

"Hmmm. Better not," Roger said. He lowered his voice. "We've got Edward with us."

Rose groaned softly. "Can't he find someone else to lecture?"

Rufa glanced up from the onions she was slicing. "Don't, Mum. He's only trying to be kind."

"I suppose so. But if only he could unclench himself, just for one evening."

Edward Reculver, whose farm abutted Ran's doomed acres, was Rufa's godfather, and the family's most persevering friend. The Reculvers had farmed this corner of Gloucestershire for centuries, and had fallen out with the Hastys at the time of the Civil War. The Hastys had been Royalists, while the Reculvers were for Parliament. Though the ancient quarrel was only a historical curiosity when Edward Reculver was growing up beside

The Zed, he still looked like a grizzled Leveller beside Hasty's curled cavalier. Curiously, this Roundhead had been The Zed's closest male friend.

He had criticized The Zed without mercy, but The Zed had respected him as a kind of offshore conscience, and listened to his straitlaced views with detached interest. Reculver inhabited a solitary, misanthropic world of speckless neatness and austerity. He grew herbs, recycled every scrap, and was the last being on earth to darn without irony. All kinds of abundance made him suspicious.

He had not always been like this. Until six years ago, he had been an officer in the army. His farm had been let, and he had made occasional, dramatic drops into the lives of the Hasty children, to treat them to a circus or pantomime. Rufa vividly remembered, throughout her childhood, Edward's returns, tanned and inscrutable, from various exotic hot spots. He had been decorated after the Falklands War, and had a small scar on his upper arm, where a sniper's bullet had nicked him in Bosnia.

Rufa admired Edward, and had always been slightly in awe of him. She had assumed, as everyone did, that he was a soldier to the ends of his fingers. It had felt strange at first, when he left the army, to have him nearby all the time. The Zed had often wondered what made him leave. When feeling uncharitable, he would say, "Edward knew he'd never make colonel. He's too bolshy for his own good." In a kinder frame of mind, however, he would sigh, and say, "Poor old Edward, he left the army because his heart was broken. He still can't live without her."

In the fifteen years since the death of his wife, Edward had been in gradual retreat from the world. Rufa vaguely remembered Alice: a quiet, fair woman who had looked slightly away in photographs, so that she could never be recalled completely. They had been childless, and Edward had made no move to marry again. Unlike The Zed, he could apparently live without romance. His life seemed to have left the road and run aground.

After the death of The Zed, Edward had taken a dim view of the continued chaos and squalor at Melismate. Between lectures, however, he showered the Hastys with kindness. The Zed had died owing him large sums of money, which he never mentioned. He had done the clearing up after The Zed's death, when no one else could bear to. When Selena broke her ankle falling off her bicycle, he had driven her to school every morning in his Land Rover. Selena had not been grateful. As Rose said, there was something faintly punitive about Edward's favors. He wanted them to face reality, and they had different ideas about what reality actually was.

Rose stood up crossly. "I know he's only trying to be kind," she muttered, refilling her wineglass. "That's the awful part—why is it so easy to resent someone who's trying to be kind? And the poor soul won't see much Christmas cheer round at his place."

She stopped abruptly. Reculver was in the doorway. He looked gravely at Rufa and Rose, then gazed around the room. His gaze seemed to throw a lurid, pitiless light upon saucers brimming with dog-ends, pooh-colored sugar lumps, and the anemic pan of soup on the range.

"Hello," he said.

He never kissed anyone, but Rufa made a point of crossing the room to kiss his cheek. He was her godfather, after all; and she minded more than the others about not being grateful enough. Reculver was a tall, lean man aged somewhere in the forties. Officially he had been a good few years younger than The Zed, but age is a state of mind, and Edward had allowed his flamboyant neighbor to treat him as an elder statesman. He had a close-cropped beard of iron gray. His thick hair was also iron gray; he had it mowed short at the barber's every market day. He was very handsome, though this was never what people noticed first.

"Edward," Rose said wearily, "what a nice surprise."

Reculver did not waste words. "Find some dry clothes, or that man will die of pneumonia."

"Man?" Rose echoed, "what man?"

Reculver looked over his shoulder. "Come in—it's marginally warmer."

He stood aside, to admit a stranger. The stranger wore a suit and tie, and city shoes. He was soaking wet, and plastered with stiffening mud.

"Oh yes, this is Berry," Ran said carelessly. "He was at school with me."

Berry was a round, rosy young man, with startled deer's eyes behind designer glasses.

"Hector Berowne," he said. And, as an afterthought, "Hello."

Chapter Three

Hector Berowne had no idea, as he drove his new BMW through the frost-bound lanes, that he was about to slip into another dimension. He had assumed that he was heading for a mellow farmhouse—all inglenooks and golden stone—that he and his fiancée, Polly, had rented for the holiday at huge expense.

"Good King Whatsit pom-pom-pom," he sang to himself.

Berry had a gift for contentment. The vexations of work fell away from him, as he dwelt on the delights to come. His parents, with whom he would normally have spent the holiday, were away visiting diplomatic friends in Bermuda. His City office was behind him, for two whole weeks. No more getting up at a quarter to six. No more being too exhausted for sex. And he still loved the anticipation of Christmas Eve. Log fires and claret—the whole world holding its breath at midnight—he knew for a fact it would be perfect.

Polly had started drawing circles round country lets in September, and had spent the past six weeks ordering hams, ironing sheets, and breaking in new corduroys. Polly, whom Berry had loved comfortably since their final year at Oxford, was very big on the Correct Thing—drawing rooms and napkins, circling port and no yellow flowers in the garden. She tended to be a little neurotic about the social face she presented to the world. Her obsession with the Edwardian trappings of perfect gentility was too ironclad to be dismissed as mere snobbery. She marinaded herself in graciousness, to obscure the regrettable fact that her parents were Australian. You could talk of high-bred diggers and colonial aristocracy, but, to Polly, it was almost as bad as being secretly Welsh.

Berry knew, from past experience, that his Christmas would resemble a spread in *Harpers*—the kind of Christmas nobody, except a Secret Australian, would attempt in real life. Wreath on the door, ivy round the pictures, and so forth. There would be an atmosphere of wood smoke, potpourri, lavender, and beeswax—Polly had even planned the smells.

Some people, for instance his sister Annabel, had accused Berry of being scared of Polly. What nonsense. He was only rather in awe of his own good luck, that he had landed a woman so conspicuously pretty and charming.

"Sire, the night is darker now," sang Berry.

Actually, the night did seem to be getting darker. Berry slowed the BMW to a crawl, then halted. The only light showing for miles blazed from a Volvo, entirely blocking the narrow lane. Its two front doors stood open. Berry waited for a long moment, listening to the immensity of the surrounding silence. Nobody came. The deserted Volvo blazed on, like the *Mary Celeste*.

He switched off, pulled out the key, and got out of the car. The shock of the cold took his breath away. Shivering in his navy suit and thin city shoes, Berry advanced toward a tangle of spiked bare boughs, five yards or so from the side of the road. Behind this thorny screen the light from the Volvo was dimmed, and laced with shadows. Through the fog of his own breath Berry made out two figures, at the edge of what appeared to be a small pond.

A lifeless pheasant lay upon the frozen turf. One of the figures knelt beside it. In a wretched voice, he said, "I'll never stop blaming myself. I made you take the short cut, and I destroyed this life. Everything I touch turns to ashes."

Another voice said, "I'm freezing my bollocks off here. Bury it, or give it mouth-to-mouth, then we can go home."

Sobs broke from the kneeling man. He turned his head toward Berry. The light made diamonds of the tears in his beautiful dark eyes.

They stared at each other. The meeting was so unexpected, it was beyond surprising. "Ran?" Berry hazarded. "It is Ran Verrall, isn't it? From school?"

Ran sprang up, dragging a sleeve across his face. "Shit, I don't believe it—Hector Berowne."

"Well, hello," Berry said. "I was just wondering whose car—"

"My leading man from *The Mikado*," Ran said, grinning suddenly. He gestured at the shadow-striped figure of the other man. "This is Roger."

Berry and Roger exchanged uncertain smiles, not knowing whether to shake hands.

"This is incredible," Ran said happily. "Berry and I were at school together, Rodge. I was Yum-Yum to his Nanki-Poo. I had to kiss him on the lips, and that's not something you forget easily."

Berry had made himself forget. He remembered now, and was glad he was too cold to blush. At the time, knowing he was the envy of half the school had almost disabled him with embarrassment.

"He had a gorgeous voice," Ran went on, seemingly oblivious to the bitter cold. "I was only chosen because I looked sweet in a kimono. Well, well. How are you, you old Wandering Minstrel?"

"Oh, absolutely fine," Berry said. "Er—could you possibly move your car? It's blocking the lane rather."

"It must be ten years, at least," Ran said.

"Yes." Berry had a general feeling of losing his grip on the conversation. "If you could let me through—"

"Let the man through," said Roger. "I want to get home—Rose will be worried."

"I've got a daughter," Ran announced. "Her name's Linnet. She's five. Have you reproduced yet?"

"Not yet. I'm getting married next summer." How absurd, Berry thought, to be having a cocktail-party conversation out here.

"Have lots of children," Ran said. "They're the only things that make any sense in this life." He looked down at the pheasant, cold on the cold ground. "My Linnet would have loved this bird. She has such an affinity with all living things. I'm giving her a guinea pig."

"Rose will go mad," Roger predicted. "Don't be surprised if she cooks it."

Mournfully, Ran contemplated the dead pheasant. Despite the cold, he seemed about to launch into a funeral oration.

"We knocked it over. I made Roger stop, but there was nothing I could do. It was too late." A sob shook him.

Ran had been famous for this sort of thing at school. Berry remembered him being led out of exams and chapel services, in floods of tears. He watched helplessly, wishing he could get up the nerve to mention his car again. Polly would be waiting, and her dinners were the sort that spoiled.

"His girlfriend left him," Roger explained.

"Oh."

"Come on, Saint Francis. Let's get back to Assisi."

"I have to follow his spirit," Ran said. "It's still hovering."

With horrible suddenness, the pheasant twitched back to life. In a great flap of wings, it rose from the ground and fluttered drunkenly into Berry's face. His hand-stitched leather soles slithered on clods of frozen earth.

The next few seconds unfolded as if in slow motion. Berry had one moment of still, isolated despair, before he toppled forward. Very fast, but in minute detail, he saw the black pond rushing to meet him. He crashed through a layer of ice, into two feet of freezing water. Knife-blades of iciness sliced through his clothes. The thunderclap of cold silenced Berry's scream of anguish. Cold bit into his belly, and sent his testicles into the Retreat from Moscow.

The reeking embarrassment added to the horror. Berry struggled upright, trailing glutinous strands of weed. He managed to grab Roger's outstretched hand, and staggered back to the bank. His glasses were speckled with mud. Gasping for breath, he took them off, and automatically groped in his wet pockets for a handkerchief.

"Here." Roger handed him a tissue.

"Th-thanks—"

"You all right?"

"Think so—"

"I didn't kill him," Ran said jubilantly. He pointed to the pheasant, scuttling away into the bushes. "There is no blood on my hands."

It was at this moment Berry realized, with the bottom falling out of his stomach, that he was no longer holding his car keys.

"I dropped my keys!" he croaked. "Oh, God in heaven!"

Not that he was in any way scared of Polly, but she would kill him for this. And—God! God!—the number of the farmhouse was locked in the boot! Until he could get into his car, he could not telephone Polly, to let her know he was not dead.

He stood groaning on the bank, in an ecstasy of shivers. Roger rolled up his sleeves, lay down on the ground, and began feeling about in the congealing water. Ran shrugged off his donkey jacket, draped it round Berry's shoulders, and lay down beside him. The two of them splashed and swore.

Roger cut his finger on a broken beer bottle. Berry fought a deadening sensation of creeping unreality. How on earth had he got himself into this ghastly situation?

Another car was coming along the lane. They heard it braking sharply behind the Volvo. There was an irritable blast of horn.

"Great," muttered Roger.

A car door slammed. A tall man stepped into the silver glare of the headlights. He saw Ran, and snapped, "I might have known. What's going on?"

He was very handsome, in a wrathful, bearded, Old Testament fashion. He listened, in silence, to the garbled explanations. Ran introduced him as Edward Reculver. He frowned when he took Berry's hand.

"You're perished," he said. "Where's your house?"

"I don't know—about twenty miles—"

"We'd better take you to Melismate."

"I c-can't leave my—"

"Don't worry about the car. I'll come back with a net, and drag the pond properly. It's not deep."

Through his Saint Vitus' dance of shivers, Berry was aware of Reculver introducing some good sense into this nightmare. The door of the BMW was unlocked. Reculver got in, released the hand brake, and ordered Ran and Roger to push it off the road.

"We can't take him in the Volvo, I'm afraid," Roger said. "The back's full of logs."

Reculver asked, "Are you short of fuel? You should have told me. I'll take Berowne." He had got Berry's name already.

Berry had lost all power of movement. Reculver had to almost lift him into the passenger seat of his Land Rover. It was deliciously warm. The warmth made his hands hurt. His ears felt as if they had been nailed to the sides of his head. Reculver waved off the Volvo, containing Roger and Ran. He climbed into the Land Rover, and they roared off down the lane.

Berry glanced aside, at his implacable, righteous profile. Reculver was a younger-looking man than he had assumed at first. "This is really good of you."

"Not at all," Reculver said.

"Wh-where did you say you were taking me?"

"Melismate. The old manor, where Roger lives. Just a couple of miles away."

Hugging his hands under his armpits, Berry began to feel a little less ghastly. Polly would not be too angry, if he eventually rang her from a real manor house. He could borrow some clothes, and the rational Mr. Reculver would reunite him with his stranded BMW. Then he could escape from bonkers Ran Verrall, and not see him again for another ten years.

"God knows what they'll think of me," he said. "I can't believe I've got myself into this ludicrous mess."

"Yes," Reculver said. "Randolph often has that effect."

"I know. I should have remembered, from school."

"Ah, so that's how you were dragged into his orbit, Well, don't worry. I can tell you're basically normal. You didn't choose to get entangled again."

"God, no," Berry said, thinking wistfully of Polly and her warm farmhouse.

"Ran used to be married to one of the girls at Melismate," Reculver said. "I really ought to warn you about the house. It's a dreadful mess. They're about to sell up. They haven't a penny." He frowned at the ribbon of Catseyes in front of him. "This will be their first Christmas without their father. He died last June."

"Oh," Berry said, "how awful."

"It was," Reculver said. "None of us have come to terms with it yet, whatever that means. He made a terrific thing of Christmas. They must miss him cruelly." He slid a speculative glance at Berry. "I know I do. I grew up with him. And I've known the girls since they were babies. He would have expected me to look out for them."

"You're fond of them," Berry observed.

"Yes," Reculver said. "Are you thawing?"

"A bit."

"We'll get some tea down you, and a slug of brandy."

Berry found that he was comforted. Reculver must have sensed that talking about death was making him colder. He fastened his imagination to the proposed tea and alcohol. His teeth had stopped rattling, and he was desperately tired.

He did not realize he had dropped into a doze, until he woke. The car had stopped, and Reculver was gently shaking his shoulder.

"Out you get. We're here."

Impressions loomed at Berry out of the darkness, like the disjointed fragments of some crazed dream. There was a great doorway, with words carved in stone above it, and a weatherworn coat of arms.

"Be nice to them," Reculver said. "They're all more or less dotty. But they

have an excuse. They'll do anything to avoid the truth about their father."
He helped Berry out of the car. "The fact is, he blew his brains out—sprayed
them all over the downstairs sitting room. Do bear that in mind, if they start
spouting nonsense at you."

Chapter Four

Rufa showed the shivering stranger into the only working bathroom: a dank and echoing tunnel on the first floor. Berry, when he entered, visibly struggled to contain his horror. Rufa was ashamed. The bathroom was a slum. For some reason she could not now remember, it was full of old bicycles. The huge, cast-iron tub had a greenish patch breaking through at one end, where generations of bottoms had worn away the enamel. The geyser, which clung to the wall like a malevolent insect, yielded a stingy trickle of tepid water.

It was evident to Rufa that Berry was not used to thinking of hot water as a luxury. He said nothing, but behaved as if he had arrived in a shanty town and was too riven with compassion to dream of criticizing. Avoiding his stunned, innocent brown eyes, Rufa presented him with a towel—hard and bald, but clean. Both she and Berry studiously ignored the degraded heap of dry clothes unearthed by Roger.

On her way downstairs, Rufa imagined Berry's bathroom—tropically warm, thickly carpeted, with heaps of fluffy towels in tasteful colors. Perhaps tall jars of colored soaps, like you saw in magazines. She yearned for such a bathroom, though she knew The Zed would have laughed at her. Why was it so wrong?

Edward met her at the bottom of the stairs. He was still in his outdoor clothes, and carrying a ragged fishing net. "Look what I've found. Just the thing."

"You're not going straight out again?"

He laughed. "Roger and I have to trawl for that poor chap's car keys. And like Captain Oates, we may be some time."

"It's awfully good of you." Rufa felt this was not said to Edward often enough. His goodness was shamefully taken for granted.

"I don't mind," Edward said dismissively. "He seems like a nice boy."

"Well, don't die of exposure."

"Wait a minute—" He put a hand on her arm, to stop her going into the kitchen. "I never get a chance to talk to you alone. Are you—all right?"

"Me? Of course I am. I'm fine."

"You look exhausted. Everywhere I go these days, I'm confronted by your jars of mincemeat."

"I hope you've bought some."

He was serious, and would not let her lighten the tone. "You've been working like a slave. It won't do, Rufa. You shouldn't be spending your days flogging mincemeat."

Rufa sighed. She dearly loved poetry, but Edward's plain prose could be very comforting, like dry bread after tons of chocolate mousse. "The hardest part wasn't the work," she said. "I don't mind raising a few blisters. The hardest part was persuading them all to pay the electricity bill, instead of buying gin."

He let out a grim bark of laughter. "They are a lot of lazy bastards."

"Oh, they're not that bad. Nancy's done loads of overtime. She wore one of her bosomy shirts last night, and came home with a fortune in tips."

"Nancy's a career barmaid," Edward said. "With her, it's a vocation. But you're a clever girl, and I wish to God you'd make something of your life. I always told your father he was disgustingly selfish, talking you out of university. You're still young enough to do it, you know."

"You think I should have ignored him," Rufa said, without rancor.

"You spoiled him. I mean, we all did." Edward sighed. "God knows, I couldn't refuse him anything either."

"If you're pushing university, I wish you'd work on Selena."

Edward knew she wanted to change the subject. "Hmm."

"You don't believe me, but she's terribly bright. A girl who reads Milton and Spenser for fun should be doing Eng. Lit. at university."

"I'm talking about you," Edward said. He took a step back, so that he could look into her face. "I'd be a rotten sort of godfather, if I let you throw yourself away."

Rufa knew, absolutely, that Edward would be dead against the Marrying Game. The bare idea would make him furious—she might as well tell him she was going on the other sort of game. She wanted to get him off the subject of the future.

"I don't think The Zed meant godfathering to be such hard work," she said, smiling. Edward had been a boy of seventeen when The Zed selected him for the honor, and from the first (totally unlike every other godparent haphazardly chosen to sponsor the girls), he had done his duty with high seriousness.

He gave her one of his rarer smiles, grave and tender. "I don't think of it as work. And I think I'd worry about you, whether you were my godchild or not."

Rufa was touched. She forgot, for long periods, that Edward was such a handsome man. It struck her again now, seeing his face in the half-light, and made her feel suddenly awkward—handsomeness had never been part of Edward's job description. "You really mustn't."

"It's dirty work, but someone has to do it."

"Things will get better. They have to."

Edward said, "Losing Melismate could be the best thing that's ever happened to you."

She drew in her breath sharply. This was heresy.

"No, listen to me. I don't mean The Zed dying, of course not. But his death might have the positive side effect of setting you free. I cared deeply for your father, and I care for his family. But I care for you most. You're worth the lot of them put together." *Care for* was Edwardish for "love." "At least this way, I won't have to stand by and watch you falling into the same trap—the fantasy that inheriting a pile of old bricks somehow cuts you off from ordinary life. That's what killed your father."

He would not allow her to protest.

"Once this house is sold, I want you to join the real world. I don't care what you do, as long as it's more constructive than skivvying for your hopeless relations."

This was a very long and very revealing speech for Edward to make—and he had not finished. He pulled something out of his jacket pocket. "I want you to have this. It belonged to my mother."

He put a small box of worn leather into Rufa's hand. Surprised to get a present from Edward that was not a Boots token, she opened it. Inside, on a faded velvet bed, was a Victorian brooch of thick gold, set with large, dingy jewels.

"Diamonds and sapphires," Edward said.

"It's lovely—but I couldn't—" Rufa stammered.

"She would have wanted you to have it, as a matter of fact. You always were her favorite." He chuckled softly. "And she would have expected you to sell it. I'm told it's worth a few bob."

"Oh, Edward—" Rufa's mind had flown straight back to the Marrying Game. The brooch might be worth enough to bankroll her assault on London, without her having to sell the car. Edward needn't know how his gift had been invested, until he got the engraved wedding invitation.

She sidestepped her guilt by telling herself that his mother would have supported her. She had liked old Mrs. Reculver—a brisk, horsy lady, who had died five years before. Edward's mother would have considered marrying money a positive duty for a well-born but impoverished gel. She had not shared her son's Roundhead views of class and inheritance.

She smiled at him. "Thank you."

Edward kissed her forehead. "Merry Christmas." He tweaked her nose, as he used to do when she was a small child. "And don't you dare tell the others."

Before he left, with Roger, to drag the pond for Berry's keys, Edward carried in his official Christmas gift to the family—a large box of assorted bottles. Rose yodeled with joy and gave him a stifling hug. After he had gone, however, she did remark that it was like being rewarded by God for self-denial.

"He set unto them a test, and they failed it not—yea, they bought not gin, and they were pleasant in his sight." She poured a handsome shot of Gordon's into the nearest glass.

Lydia and Selena had come down to the kitchen, lured by the sound of company and the smell of onions. Lydia was radiant, because Linnet was asleep and Ran's latest girlfriend had left him. She organized more glasses, while Selena put her book down long enough to uncork a bottle of Barolo.

The door opened. Very slowly and cautiously, Berry crept in. He was tall, with an ample stomach. His borrowed brown corduroys did not do up at the waist, and the gaping flies were only partly covered by a billowing pink jersey. His brown hair had dried into a hearth brush, and the seam of the trousers went right up his crack.

They all collapsed in howls and screams of laughter. As Rufa said later, it might have been sticky, if Berry had not been such a good sport. After a moment of amazement, he grinned, and hitched up the trouser-legs, to heighten the comic effect.

Suddenly, miraculously, it felt like a real Christmas. The kitchen was crowded with laughing people, as it had not been since the death of The Zed. Berry had stopped being startled by this peculiar family. Now, he remembered only that they had lost their father—in horrible circumstances—and were about to lose their home. The girls were eye-poppingly gorgeous, but there was no self-interest in Berry's longing to comfort them. He even decided that he felt fond of Ran.

The soup, plentifully peppered and onioned by Rufa, made the room dim with its savory steamings. Berry helped to lay the table with bowls and bread board, and his high spirits had quite a loaves-and-fishes effect on the quantities. He discovered none of the family liked dry sherry, and poured half of Reculver's bottle of Tio Pepe into the soup.

Warmed by the alcohol, which they were hoovering up at an incredible rate, they began to sing carols. At some point, after they had seen off all the soup and two loaves of bread, a piece of paper appeared under the door to the stairs.

"Oh God, it's Linnet," Rose said. "We've woken her up, and now she's dropping leaflets."

The note said: "WAT IS THAT OPORLING RAKET?"

Lydia, dreamily sozzled, leaning against her ex-husband, sighed. "Mummy, couldn't she—?"

"Go on, then." Rose was full of gin-flavored indulgence. "Go and let the little blighter in. It is Christmas Eve, after all."

Ran leaped up to open the door, and returned to the table with his daughter in his arms. She wore her blue duffel coat over Barbie pajamas, and carried a Ressany under each arm. She settled on Ran's knee, a starchy little infanta.

"Who's that man in Granny's jersey?"

Berry got on famously with Linnet, because he did not make the fatal mistake of altering his manner when he talked to her. He related the story of his lost car keys as if she had been one of his colleagues at the bank, and she listened enraptured. Rufa, who judged everyone by the way Linnet reacted to them, rewarded Berry with an unsolicited cup of tea.

35

She was arguing with the others about opening the brandy, which she wanted for tomorrow's pudding, when Nancy returned from the Dents. She rushed straight to the range, wriggling out of her coat.

"It's bloody freezing out there. Look at my nipples—standing out like a couple of bottletops."

She thrust out her chest, and everyone looked at her nipples.

Rufa said, "You're back early."

"Yes, thank God. The Dents are driving to some posh Midnight Mass, absolutely miles away. I escaped before they could make me go with them."

She noticed Berry. Her lips curved into a lush smile. "Hello. I'm Nancy. You must be my Christmas present—oh girls, you shouldn't have."

"Shut up, don't tease him," Rufa said, laughing. "His name's Berry. He was at school with Ran."

"And he's really nice," Linnet said. "He whispered in my ear that while he was in the pond, he did a wee."

There was a great shout of laughter. Berry's round face flushed puce.

In a slow, puzzled voice, Nancy asked, "Why can't we deliver presents at Melismate, Father Christmas?"

And in a deep, plummy voice, she said, "Sorry, reindeer—there's a naughty little girl who won't go to sleep."

Linnet commanded, "Make the Ressanys say it's all their fault."

Deep voice: "How dare you cast aspersions on those innocent bears? Off to bed with you!"

Ran stood up, squeezing Lydia's shoulder with one hand. "I'll take her up, darling."

"Well, I'm not going," Linnet said testily. "Why this fixation with going to bed? What's the point, if I'm not even tired?"

"Come on, madam. You've had a good innings." Ran gathered his daughter into his arms. "Kiss your hand to everyone, and say Happy Christmas."

"Happy Christmas." Linnet kissed her starfish hand, then added, "Wait— I'd very much like to actually kiss the man who weed in the pond."

Ran carried her over to Berry. Everyone tried hard to contain any insulting laughter, but Linnet was very much on her dignity as she dropped a queenly kiss on Berry's cheek. Ran had made one of his sudden transformations. The deserted lover was now, magically, a considerate husband and father. After he had sweetly borne the child out of the room, Rose and Rufa exchanged glances of deep skepticism.

Nancy said, "Ma Dent saw the bookshop woman crying in a wine bar. Do I take it she's left him?"

"You missed his suicidal grief," said Rose.

"What a shame. I always enjoy that."

"Never mind," Selena said. "There'll be another one along in a minute."

"Bitches." Lydia was plaintive. "He's trying to be cheerful, and it's all for Linnet's sake. So you shouldn't be so mean."

Nancy tipped another friendly smile at Berry. "I wonder who'll be next? The field is narrowing somewhat."

"That old hippy in Bangham, who sells crystals," predicted Selena. "I swear she fancies Ran."

"You utter bitches!"

Rose was laughing so hard that she was sliding off her chair. She collected herself, with a boozy sigh. "Don't be silly, you know we all adore the Village Idiot. I'm going to nominate him for Village Idiot of the Year."

At a quarter to eleven, Edward and Roger returned, in triumph.

"I've driven a new BMW, I can die happy," Edward said, holding up Berry's keys. "And I filled your car with petrol, Rufa—you mustn't let it get so low."

Unseen by him, Rose made a gargoyle face.

"Thanks," Rufa said mildly. She touched Berry's arm. "Look—you're free."

Berry tore his eyes off Nancy with such an effort, you could almost hear it. "Sorry?"

"Your keys." Edward forced them into his hand. "You can go."

"Oh, don't!" Selena cried.

Berry said, "I've no intention of going. I just need to fetch something from the boot."

The cold cleared his head but did not bring him back to his senses. He had lost those the moment he saw Nancy. He was elated, terrified, newborn. She was a red-headed goddess, with breasts he wanted to lick. He had never realized sexual desire could be so urgent, or so specific. He had fancied women before, naturally. But this was beyond fancying. Within seconds of seeing Nancy, Berry knew exactly how he would make love to her.

Good God, what had she thought of him? One glimpse of her hard nipples, under that clinging black dress, and he was burbling as if he had just come out of the dentist's.

He opened the boot of his car. His address book, containing the number of Polly's farmhouse, lay on top of a wicker hamper. Berry thrust the book aside impatiently. The hamper was filled with luxurious jars and tins, and an enormous turkey. A client had sent it to him that morning, and Polly need never know—it wasn't her sort of thing, anyway. He hefted it out on the cobbles, grinning to himself at its weight. This had been sent by heaven, he decided, to lay at the feet of the foodless, fatherless Hastys.

Chapter Five

Berry departed, in a sudden, guilty flurry, an hour after midnight—diffidently pressing into Ran's hand his phone number, which Ran immediately lost. Thanks to Berry's hamper, Christmas at Melismate was celebrated in a style that had not been seen since The Zed's last store card bit the dust. The turkey was a sumo wrestler of a beast. Rose kissed it drunkenly before she shut it in the oven—"It's twice the size of Tiny Tim!" With a great collective suspension of disbelief, they managed to take a few days' holiday from grieving.

Rufa performed miracles of stretching with the food. She made turkey pie, turkey curry, and turkey risotto—not one atom of that bird was to be wasted. Finally, on New Year's Eve, she boiled up the picked bones to make a rich turkey broth. She stood patiently over the simmering pan, neatly skimming off the fat. Her spirits had dwindled along with the bird. The wolf was still lounging at the door. The Zed was still dead.

This, she could not help thinking, is the last day of the worst year of our lives.

She would have given anything—really anything—to fly back in time, just to see him once more and hear his voice. On this day last year, The Zed had found a suitcase full of ancient clothes. He and Rose had dressed up as their youthful selves, and done a demonstration of Seventies dancing that had made them all weep with laughter. Rose's ethnic robe had been ravaged by moths, and one sleeve had suddenly fallen off midgroove. The Zed's stomach had strained against the waistband of his purple velvet loon pants. He and Roger had fetched their guitars, and strummed embarrassing old hits by Mott the Hoople and Fleetwood Mac. Edward, who had seen in every New Year at Melismate since leaving the army, had said, "Think what I missed, by spending those far-out years at Sandhurst—the only place on earth where short hair and straight trousers stubbornly hung on."

The Zed had said, "You've got some catching up to do, Ed—but it's never too late to drop out."

He had been in high spirits that evening, welcoming the unseeable New Year like an immortal boy of twenty.

Rufa half-closed her eyes, to conjure a picture of The Zed under the dim kitchen bulb. There had been scarcely a thread of gray in his thick auburn hair. At midnight, he had taken Rose into his arms, and for a moment—as they had always done—they gazed at each other as if the rest of the world did not exist. Their love, unshaken by age or infidelity, had been the rock that sheltered them all.

Then—as they had always done—Rose and The Zed had held out their arms, to embrace all four daughters at once.

"My silk princesses—my butterflies—my orchids! Who needs sons?" He never would accept that he ought to have wanted a son to carry on the venerable Hasty name. He had roused a cross, sleepy Linnet, to give her a sip of wine, just as he had done when his own girls were little. He had delighted Linnet by pretending to give some to the Ressany Brothers, and then fining them a penny each for being drunk and disorderly. He had embraced Roger and kissed Edward, mainly to annoy him. Lastly, according to tradition, he had raised his glass and, with tears in his beautiful eyes, he had murmured, "Absent friends."

Rufa blinked away the tears smarting behind her own eyes. He had meant his adored mother, dead since his adolescence. And now the absent friend was him. She had been over and over every memory, searching for clues. Later, there had been shadows, but last Christmas had been without a cloud. The Zed had been celebrating a small victory against "the Abominable Dr. Phibes," also known as Sir Gerald Bute, master of the local hunt. The Zed had stopped hunting when he fell behind with his subscription and grew too stout for his father's old pink coat. Typically, he had then decided all hunting was wrong, and banned the hunt from his land.

That had been the year of Edward's return, and to the fury of the Abominable Dr. Phibes, Edward had taken up The Zed's battle against cruelty to foxes. Every year since then, the two of them had joined the protest at the Boxing Day meet. The other protesters were mainly what Sir Gerald called "wholemeal City types," and he regarded his neighbors as traitors—especially Edward, who had once been an officer and a gentleman, and a fearless rider to hounds. Edward had followed the hunt in his Land Rover, with The Zed hanging over the side, scattering anti-blood-sport leaflets and yelling rude things through a loud-hailer. Rufa warmed herself with the memory of them coming home after dark, plastered with mud and sometimes carrying a bewildered, ungrateful fox. These were the only times they had seen Edward drunk. He and The Zed knocked back his searing homemade sloe gin all day, and you could hear them singing up the road for miles. It had been a poor New Year that was not seen in with an angry letter from Sir Gerald.

Rufa paused in her skimming, to wipe her eyes. Sir Gerald Bute had not written a line when The Zed died, and Edward had fiercely denounced him as a "shit." This Boxing Day had been very hard for Edward. Everyone had times and places where The Zed's absence was insupportable. Edward had taken refuge at Melismate because he could not even bear to hear the barking of the hounds on the road beside his farm.

Roger ambled into the kitchen. "Still at it?"

"Not long now." She kept her face turned toward the pan, so he would not see she was crying.

He briefly squeezed her shoulder. "You've been standing there for hours. Give yourself a break."

"Oh, I've nearly finished."

"Here. Let me do it." Roger took the spoon out of her hand, and gently nudged her away from the range. "You can trust me. I'm famed for my patience."

This was true, and Rufa felt a surge of fondness for him. Good old Roger. His patience and his unshowy, unstinting devotion had kept Rose from losing her head in the days after it happened.

"Thanks, Rodge. It needs to reduce about another half inch."

"Righto."

Rufa made herself a mug of tea, and climbed the rickety stairs up to the old nursery. The gray countryside had fought off the intense cold, and heavy rain hammered against the leads. Water dripped through the holes in the ceiling, pinging discordantly into an enamel bucket and two chamber pots. Nancy lay on the sofa, nursing a tiny fire and reading a ragged *Woman's Weekly* that she had found in one of the heaps of lumber.

"Hello," she said. "Is the soup ready?"

"Nearly."

"Can I have some before I go to the pub? I'm on at six."

Rufa said, "It seems a shame, working on New Year's Eve."

Nancy, without raising her eyes, said, "The money's good, and heaven knows, we need it." She looked up. "I didn't want to stay here. The memories would choke me."

"I know. I'll miss you, though."

"Don't, Ru. I'm sorry." Nancy frowned. "What a ghastly bloody day. Water coming through the ceiling is only amusing in novels about lovable madcap families. In real life it's just depressing."

"Move your butt," Rufa said. "I want the sofa. I feel as if I'd just eaten that entire seventeen-pound turkey single-handed."

Nancy sat up against one of the arms, making room for Rufa. "There's a great story in here. It's about this secretary who marries her boss. She tries to look plain, so he'll admire her efficiency. Then a big gust of wind comes along, knocks off her glasses and blows down her hair, and he suddenly notices she's pretty. A man that thick should be in a home."

"The Zed said men were pathetically suggestible. He said if a plain woman with reasonable legs wears a garter belt, it takes the average male several hours to realize she's not gorgeous." They laughed. Repeating The Zed's sayings to each other made him seem nearer for a second, then even further away.

"Oh, I wish we knew why," Rufa sighed out. "What made him do it, Nance?"

"We'll never know," Nancy said sadly. "So we might as well stop asking, and try to let him go."

Rufa was shaking her head. She would not hear of letting The Zed go. "There should have been a note. You know he never could do anything without a fanfare. Why didn't he at least leave us a note?"

Nancy leaned across the rug to put a cobwebbed log on the fire. "It could never have said enough for us. We would always have wanted more."

"Just 'Good-bye' would have been enough," Rufa said. " 'Good-bye and I love you.' "

"Stop beating yourself up." Nancy's face was gentle, but she made her voice bracing. "This is a new year, and we've got to stop acting as if it happened yesterday—Edward's certainly right about that. We should be doing something about the future."

"I won't give in, Nance."

"What are you talking about?"

"I'm not going down without a fight." Pale and determined, her hands clenched with excitement, Rufa told Nancy about Edward's brooch. "He says he'll help me to get a good price for it, if I promise to do something constructive with the money."

"Like getting your tits enlarged," Nancy suggested.

"Oh, ha ha. I'm trying to be serious."

Nancy leaned forward. "Why couldn't Edward just give you the money, instead of going through all this rigmarole?"

Rufa was patient. This had also occurred to her, and she had prepared an answer. "You know how odd he is about actual cash—he doesn't like anything to do with it. You certainly can't call him mean, though."

"No, but I can call him a control freak. He basically won't give you a penny, unless you carry out his orders."

"He trusts me," Rufa said. "If I say I'm using the brooch money to pay for a course, or start a business, he'll believe me."

Nancy missed the significance of her tone. "Of course he will—he knows you can't lie to save your life."

"I've broken one promise to him already. I said I wouldn't tell any of you about the brooch."

"Miserable old sod, he obviously thought we'd fleece you." Nancy did not always see eye to eye with Edward. The Zed had said they were polar opposites—hot and cold, loose and tight, oral and anal. "Why are you telling me, by the way?"

"I wanted to ask you something."

Nancy threw down her magazine and leaned closer to Rufa. "Darling, tell me you're not still thinking about that cock-eyed Marrying Game!"

"I can't get it out of my mind," Rufa said earnestly.

"Oh God, I might have known. You're that bloody desperate."

"You realize it's theoretically possible, now we have some money," Rufa went on stubbornly. "We can invest in the right clothes, go to the right places—"

"And what if we fail? I'm not having Edward accusing me of leading you astray."

Rufa had not thought of this, and had to admit it was exactly what Edward would do. "If we fail, I'll confess. I'll take all the blame."

"Well," Nancy said. "I don't know." She was silent, looking thoughtfully at Rufa, weighing up their chances. "What will you do if I say no?"

"I don't know." Rufa was silent for a few seconds, then said in a rush, "Go by myself."

Nancy laughed suddenly. "I was afraid you'd say that. You know I'd never let you go to London alone."

"Why? I'm not a half-wit." Rufa was nettled. "I can look after myself."

"You won't have to. I'm coming too."

"Does that mean you'll do it? The Marrying Game?"

Nancy sighed, pensively gazing into the fire. "Yes, I suppose it does. Actually, it's come at rather a good time. Things with Tim—well, he isn't the man I took him for. His mother keeps hinting that he'll go back to college if I'm off the scene. I need to broaden my horizons."

The Marrying Game had rooted stubbornly in Rufa's mind. From her position of having nothing and knowing no one, she had spent Christmas building an airy scaffold of hope. "The men—our potential husbands— would have to be very, very rich," she said. "Not just what old Mrs. Reculver used to call 'well-orf.' We're faced with a ruined house and an absolute mountain of debts. It would take a tycoon to help us without feeling any pain. A billionaire rock star is the sort of thing we have to look for."

"All right," Nancy said, "as long as we can find a couple who aren't fat old trolls."

Rufa was stern. "Fat trolls if necessary. We're not doing this for fun. Our mission is simply to find some very rich men, and make them fall in love with us. Whatever they look like."

Nancy groaned. "Don't—you're scaring me. There must be some rich men who don't have to go out with a Gucci bag over their heads."

"Nance, please be serious!"

"I'm sorry." Nancy's expression softened, as she saw how much the Marrying Game had come to mean to Rufa. "I'm just not used to you being so barmy—you're supposed to be the sensible one. I mean, this has virtually no chance of working."

44

"A tiny chance, and that's enough. The question is, are you up for it?"

"I think so," Nancy said. "I'd love to go to London. I don't feel I'm ful-filling my potential here. I'm so starved of love."

Rufa laughed softly. "Berry fancied you."

"Didn't he just? But I don't think he's quite my type. He's got that paunch, and hair like a bog brush." She sat up briskly. "So, when do we leave the Cherry Orchard and make for Moscow?"

"As soon as I've got the brooch money, and told Edward a pack of lies, I'll call Wendy. But Nance—" Rufa's usually reserved face was nakedly plead-ing. "You will do it properly, won't you? I keep calling it a game, but it's not a game. I couldn't bear it if you were treating it as a joke."

Nancy smiled, and nudged her favorite sister affectionately with her foot. "Don't worry, I won't subvert it. I'll be incredibly serious. And I bet I score first."

"Oh, I don't doubt it," Rufa said. "But I bet I get the first proposal that isn't indecent."

❋ ❋ ❋

Wendy Withers had just retreated from a vigorous argument with her fas-tidious gay lodger (as opposed to her uncouth straight lodger) when Rufa's phone call came. It irradiated the January morning like a bolt of lightning. Afterward, Wendy was in such a flutter that she cracked open a packet of Mr. Kipling's Almond Slices. To hell with the calories. Rufa and Nancy were coming to London, and a celebration was called for.

Wendy was a large woman, who had stopped reckoning her age a few years before, when she turned fifty. Since her exile from Melismate, her life had been a tedious struggle against penury and encroaching middle age. She dressed her soft, bulky body in the flimsy Indian cottons that had been fash-ionable in the 1970s, which she regarded as her heyday. She wore her hennaed hair long, because The Zed had once said it was her best feature. Her tallow cheeks were always slathered with blusher, even when she was stuck in the basement all day with her reflexology clients—alternative therapies had been a great boon, she often thought, to women like her, without family, qualifica-tions, or talent. Melismate and its inhabitants had been the romance of her life.

"We insist on paying you," Rufa had said. "Or we won't come. I've just sold something, so we're not as skint as usual."

"Just a token, then," Wendy had agreed. Privately, she congratulated Rufa for having found a piece of portable property. During her time at

Melismate, there had been a constant exodus of silver, china, furniture, and everything else that was not nailed down.

"We don't want to take up valuable space," Rufa had said. "Just stick us in the attic, or something."

Wendy would not have dreamed of it. God knew, there was enough room in this dingy old house. It had five bedrooms, and besides herself, there were only her two lodgers, Max and Roshan. They lived on the top floor. Her beloved girls could have the large room at the front of the first floor.

Arming herself with another almond slice, Wendy went upstairs to inspect it. Look on the positive side, she thought; it was a little sparsely furnished, and some people might have considered it depressing. But it was near the bathroom, and there was a fine bay window, with quite a cheerful view of Tufnell Park Road.

It was furnished with two single divans, a dressing table with drawers, and a wardrobe. When you walked past the wardrobe, the metal hangers inside set up a ghostly clatter. Wendy decided to cheer the room up with a framed poster of Gandalf, now hanging in the basement.

The girls would be next to her, and what fun they would all have—chats and confidences, and little sinful snacks at odd hours. At last she would have someone to share the small treats she awarded herself, to keep herself going. Max and Roshan sometimes deigned to eat a take-away with her, but there was nothing like the company of girls. "Other girls," as she would have said, until only a few years ago.

A great-aunt had left Wendy the house in Tufnell Park. It was full of swirly pub carpets and sad Formica things from the Sixties, with legs like a sputnik. Wendy was very grateful to have a solid roof over her head, but the place made her feel defeated and helpless. She had not chosen the decor, and had no power to impose herself upon her own surroundings. There was never enough money to do more than put down a few Indian rugs. Nothing could erase the stubborn reek of Auntie Barbara. The narrow, four-story semi cried out for the youth and energy of the Hasty girls.

Rufa and Nancy arrived the following afternoon. Roger had driven them to the station, and Nancy was still annoyed with Rufa for leaving her Volvo at Melismate.

Rufa had said, "Mummy needs it, whatever she says. And being seen in a dowdy old banger is worse than not having a car at all."

She had wanted to save money by taking the tube, but Nancy insisted on a taxi. Wendy met them on the front steps, with a shriek of joy and a damp explosion of tears. She had not seen the girls since The Zed's funeral, and could not help weeping over them again.

Kind, patient Rufa patted her and soothed her, and made them all mugs of tea in the cramped kitchen behind the consulting room. Nancy sat at the table, finishing the almond slices, while poor Wendy sobbed for the love of her life. At the funeral, she had been one of a dozen inconsolable women. Rufa felt it was only fair to let her luxuriate in her sorrow, away from the competition.

Two mugs of tea and one packet of Maryland cookies later, Wendy blew her red nose and led them upstairs. The two girls were thrilled with their room.

"Isn't it clean?" Rufa sighed.

"Isn't it divinely warm?" exclaimed Nancy. She dropped her rucksack on one of the beds, and nodded toward the poster of Gandalf. "Some elderly relation of yours?"

Wendy giggled delightedly. The Zed had teased her like this. "The bathroom's on the landing, and there's another loo downstairs. I'm afraid you'll have to share with my lodgers."

Nancy asked, "How many lodgers?"

"Just the two."

"Sex?"

"Not on the premises," Wendy said solemnly. "It creates too much upheaval."

Nancy snorted with laughter. "I meant, are they male or female?"

"Both male." Wendy's lodgers were her great subject, and she did not register the gleam of interest in Nancy's eyes. "Roshan has my top-floor front. He's an Indian from Leicester, and he's a journalist. And he's gay."

"Oh." Nancy's interest faded. "I suppose the other one's his boyfriend."

Wendy became more solemn. "I don't in the least mind Roshan being gay. My only prejudice is against people who hog shared bathrooms—he's forever waxing his chest in there. And once he's been at the hot water, the boiler has to start again from scratch."

"Perhaps we should draw up a rota," offered Rufa.

"Oh, I've tried. He didn't take the slightest notice. Neither did Max—who's not his boyfriend, by the way."

Nancy, beady again, asked, "Isn't he gay too?"

"Quite the opposite," Wendy said primly. "I had to make my No Sex rule when I kept meeting different girls in the kitchen. He works at the BBC, and he claims to be writing a novel."

Nancy raised her eyebrows at Rufa. "More your type, possibly."

"He can be quite nice," Wendy rattled on innocently, "except that he leaves the sink full of little black dots when he shaves, which isn't often. And Max is the one to watch if you've left anything in the fridge—don't imagine labeling it will put him off. Roshan, on the other hand, wouldn't touch anything in my kitchen with a barge pole. Oh, no. Perish the thought. He has his own fridge, if you please, and a microwave."

Rufa was not attending to this barrage of pent-up grievances. She faced Nancy sternly. "You're not to fall in love with either of them. I forbid it."

"The wind bloweth where it listeth, darling, as The Zed always used to say. I'll do my best, but I can't help my heart."

"Well, you'll have to get that heart of yours under control, or we'll get nowhere."

Nancy sighed, and rolled her eyes. "You're a hard woman. First you leave the car, then you make me wear knickers, and now you say I can't fall in love."

Rufa opened her mouth to argue further, but caught sight of Wendy's baffled face. "I'm starving," she said quickly. "Shall we order a pizza for supper?"

She was not starving, but hoped the pizza would take Nancy's mind off non-profit-making romance. It did—next to love, food was Nancy's favorite thing. She devoured slices of ham and pineapple pizza with groans of joy, while Rufa told Wendy about the Marrying Game.

Wendy asked, "Isn't it rather rash, coming to London to marry these men, when they haven't even proposed?"

"That's the whole point," Nancy said, businesslike again. "We've never met our husbands. We don't even know who they are."

"Oh—I see—" faltered Wendy.

"Identifying our targets will be the hardest part," Rufa said. "But once we have, we'll get ourselves into the places where they hang out. It can't be impossible. We'll need new clothes, of course. The Zed said you could crash in anywhere by simply looking as if you belonged."

Wendy looked at the girls. They were both wearing jeans and jerseys, and managing to make them utterly different. Nancy's blazing hair was loose. Despite the January cold, her tight black sweater had a plunging neckline.

Rufa's hair was neatly plaited. Her jeans had been ironed, and her sweater was a navy guernsey. They were ravishing, but it was a struggle to imagine them in one of the high-society gatherings Wendy saw in her newspaper. "Won't it be terribly pricey?"

Mention of money made Rufa uncomfortable. She spoke irritably. "We haven't got much—we'll have to stick to the essentials."

"Underwear," announced Nancy, "is not an essential."

"Yes it is. Try to grasp this difficult concept—you have to look like a lady. And behave like one."

"Listen to her," Nancy said, through drooping strings of mozzarella. "She's sure I'll use the wrong fork at dinner, and scratch my fanny before they've toasted the Queen. Lighten up, old girl."

Rufa, however, was determined to make Nancy play by strict rules. The moment they were alone, she said, "I meant it about falling for the lodger."

"Oh, all right. Keep your hair on. If he's writing a novel, he's probably far too much like that drip Jonathan."

"You have to swear."

"For God's sake!"

"Repeat after me—I, Nancy Veronica Hasty—"

"I swear, OK?" Nancy slipped into a perfect imitation of Wendy. "I won't even look at him—perish the thought."

Rufa snorted with laughter. "Bitch. You've got your fingers crossed."

Roshan Lal was a slight and delicate young man, with skin the color of strong tea. Wendy found him waspish and complaining, and thought he expected far too much in exchange for his rent. He was a reliable tenant, however, and she hoped he would not be annoyed by the invasion of Hastys.

She need not have worried. When Roshan entered the unlocked bathroom next morning, he found Nancy lying in the bath, smoking and reading *Private Eye*.

"Hello," she said. "You must be the gay one. Could you pass me a washcloth?"

Within minutes he was perched on the lavatory seat, shrieking with laughter, and promising to take Nancy round all the gay pubs in Camden Town. When he met Rufa, slender and aloof as a lily, he fell into absolute worship.

Before Rufa could stop her, Nancy told Roshan about the Marrying

Game. He was captivated, and immediately voted himself onto the committee. "I'm exactly the person you need. I read every magazine in the world, and I can tell you who's really gay. You'd be amazed."

Looking reverently at Rufa, he invited the sisters to breakfast in his top-floor bedroom. It was exquisitely tidy, as crammed with comforts and luxuries as a pharaoh's tomb. A very clean Apple Mac stood on a dustless desk. The walls were painted white. He had a microwave, a steam iron, and a hissing coffee machine. Nancy, wrapped in a shocking pink bathrobe that clashed outrageously with her hair, lay down on the double bed.

Roshan poured coffee, in thin Conran mugs. He put chocolate croissants into his microwave.

"It's heaven to meet you two in the flesh," he said. "Wendy never stops talking about you. Her bedroom's plastered with pictures of your father."

"I can't get over the two of you living together," Nancy said. "How on earth did you find each other?"

"At a yoga class in Highgate. We got chatting one day, and she mentioned she had a room going. I can't tell you what she looks like in a leotard. Poor old sausage, I think living with us makes her feel her age. Max and I are about thirty years younger than she is, after all. We don't think *Tubular Bells* is deep, and we weren't even born when Dylan went electric."

"She's frozen in the time she fell in love with our father," Nancy explained. "Like a sort of Seventies Miss Havisham."

Roshan handed round the croissants. He pecked at his like a bird. "I'm relying on you two to settle an argument. Max and I are desperate to know if your sex-god father really slept with Wendy. Max has bet me ten pounds he didn't. I'm sure he did."

Nancy was chuckling, not unkindly. "You win. He definitely did."

"He was very fond of her," Rufa felt she should say.

"Oh, yes," Nancy agreed. "The Zed could only sleep with someone if he loved them. And he usually stayed a bit in love with them afterward."

Roshan's large, liquid brown eyes were wistful. "Oh, God. He sounds absolutely divine."

"Well, he was," Nancy said. "Though as a general rule, it wasn't a particularly good idea to fall in love with him."

"Nance!" Rufa was shocked. This was blasphemy.

"He was the greatest darling in the world," Nancy said calmly. "But he never let people go. To the naked eye, he could seem like a bit of a bastard."

Rufa had never allowed herself to consider The Zed in this unflattering light, and she refused to do it now. She finished her coffee in silence. Her father's heart had been as lovely as his face. Nothing he did could spoil its sweetness.

Roshan and Nancy were attacking a pile of glossy magazines, hooting with laughter. They were searching for suitable husbands, but, according to Roshan, everyone except the Archbishop of Canterbury was a closet gay. Rufa left them to it, and went downstairs to take her washing out of Wendy's machine.

While she was folding Nancy's collection of very small T-shirts and her own seemly knickers, Rufa met the other lodger. Max Zangwill dived into the kitchen, banged down a bunch of keys, and wrenched open the fridge. After grabbing the milk, he took a proper look at Rufa, and realized she was probably not one of Wendy's lentil-scoffing clients.

Rufa introduced herself, with sinking spirits. She would never keep Nancy away from this man. He was gorgeous—tall and brawny, with wicked, almond-shaped black eyes and thick black hair. His ripped jeans and faded plaid shirt marked him out as another impoverished beauty, of the type Rufa knew only too well.

Max made Rufa a cup of tea, and put four of Wendy's crumpets under the grill.

"I'm ravenous," he said. "I've driven all the way from Sevenoaks. You know about Wendy's No Sex on the Premises rule, I take it?"

Reluctantly, Rufa laughed. "She says it's your fault."

"She likes to paint me as a promiscuous swine because I'm the only person in this house with a normal sex drive."

From the top of the house, they heard a loud scream from Nancy, ending in a burst of laughter. Max glanced up curiously.

"Ru!" There was a sound of bare feet pounding downstairs. Nancy flew into the kitchen, clutching a glossy magazine. "Ru—oh, sorry—" Her white, redhead's skin flushed becomingly. She tightened the belt of her dressing gown, which Max's ruthlessly admiring gaze seemed to strip right off her.

"This is Max," Rufa said resignedly. There were enough plain men in the world, God knew—why couldn't Wendy have chosen one of them as her lodger? Nancy managed to look so fabulous in a state of *déshabillé*.

"Hi." She smiled into his bold dark eyes. "I'm Nancy. Ru's sister."

"Yes, I can see the resemblance. I'm Max—the straight lodger, horribly affected by the sight of beautiful, scantily clad young ladies. I don't hold out much hope for my blood pressure with you two around."

Roshan entered the crowded kitchen in time to hear this. "Morning, Max. I see you've started already."

"Started what?" Max asked, still staring at Nancy.

"I ought to sing a chorus of 'The Gypsy's Warning,'" Roshan said. "Ignore him, girls. He has a Ph.D. in corny pickup lines."

Max laughed. "I was at Cambridge with this dear little brown man. He loves me really—it's sweet, and rather sad. We're like A. E. Housman and Moses Jackson."

Nancy asked, "Who?"

"A. E. Housman was a poet," Rufa said, willing Nancy to look at her, so she could signal a warning not to flirt.

Max tore his gaze off Nancy, and turned to Rufa. "So you're the brainy one?"

"Not necessarily," Nancy said. "People just think she's brainier because she has smaller bosoms."

Rufa, though still annoyed by the inconvenient attractiveness of Wendy's lodger, could not help laughing. "Just in case you hadn't noticed."

Nancy, remembering why she had come down, pushed the glossy magazine at Rufa. "You have to look at this, Ru—it's too hilarious."

It was folded open at a page of society photographs, taken at a charity ball in aid of leukemia research. Rufa looked at it blankly, until Nancy pointed out a picture at the top. It was of two people in evening dress, standing on either side of the Duchess of Gloucester. One was a slender, fair-haired, elegant woman in dark blue velvet, and the other—

"Oh my God," Rufa gasped. "It's Edward!"

He was straight-backed and stern, his cropped hair and close beard incongruous above a dinner jacket they had not known he owned.

"The secret life of Major Edward Reculver," Nancy said. "By day, he wears wellies and cleans the nuts on his tractor. By night, he rubs shoulders with royalty."

"Rather gorgeous, in my opinion," Roshan said. "I love the designer stubble."

Nancy and Rufa both laughed, at the idea of Edward's stubble having anything to do with design.

"Sorry," Nancy said. "He's about as straight as they come."

"He does look handsome, though," Rufa said. "Don't you think?"

Nancy stole another glance at Max. "Oh, everyone looks more or less tasty in a dinner jacket."

"I don't remember Edward saying anything about this," Rufa remarked, studying the page curiously. "It says here that he's a patron of the Fox Trust, whatever that is. Oh, hang on—it's something to do with leukemia, and that's what Alice died of, poor thing. It's family stuff, and you know how buttoned-up Edward is about his family. I think the other woman must be Prudence, Alice's half sister." She gave the magazine back to Nancy. "He never talks about her. I think he rather disapproves of her."

"She keeps getting married," Nancy explained to Max and Roshan. She favored them both with a brilliant smile. "She ought to be our role model. We're just starting careers in marriage ourselves."

Chapter Six

They held their first committee meeting the following evening. Max insisted on joining them. He could not decide whether the Marrying Game was hilariously funny or a monstrous insult to his socialist principles, but was too fascinated by the Hasty girls to keep away. He brought two bottles of champagne, and placed himself where he could exchange smoldering looks with Nancy. Roshan provided Thai take-away and a towering pile of glossy magazines: *Harpers, Tatler, Vogue, Hello!, OK!.* They sat on the floor of Wendy's sitting room, around the ugly but comfortable log-effect gas fire. Wendy handed round Woolworths notebooks and biros, seeing the crazy optimism of The Zed in the whole daft enterprise, and thinking she had not had such fun in years.

Rufa had begged Nancy not to ruin everything by laughing, but she need not have worried. They were all serious; rather ludicrously like a real committee meeting. "Right," Rufa said, aware that everyone was looking at her expectantly. "First of all, we have to find our targets."

"Targets!" Max protested. "Is that what you call these poor, hapless fools?"

"Our future husbands, I mean," Rufa said quickly. "I propose we make a list of suitable candidates, which we can then narrow down to two—one each." She divided the tower of magazines into five smaller piles, and pushed one to each person across the rug. Roshan immediately set to work riffling through his pile, as brisk and businesslike as a bank clerk.

Max asked, "Are we looking for rich and sexy, or just rich?"

"Just rich," Rufa said. "Once we've got our first list of rich men, we can decide who's sexy."

"What if none of them are?"

"You're missing the point," Nancy said, rather sharply. Max had cast himself as devil's advocate, but she was not going to let him agitate Rufa. "A big bank balance is like a big willy—if a man's got one, you can always find something sweet to say about him."

Max snatched a copy of *OK!* from the top of his pile of magazines, and began to flick through its gaudy pages. "You don't seem to realize what you're getting into. For instance, find something sweet to say about this one."

He slapped down a photograph of a particularly silly old rock star, and they all—even Rufa—exploded into laughter.

"His teeth are in quite good shape," Wendy said. This made them laugh harder.

"It's a serious test," Max said, looking at Nancy. "Could you marry a guy like this?"

"He's not rich enough," Nancy told him airily. "It's as simple as that. Personally, I think he's an absolute Adonis, but we're not playing this Game for fun."

Roshan, shaking with giggles, was turning the pages of a *Tatler*. "I've got another test. Ah, here he is, the pouting devil." He displayed a photograph of a good-looking young man in a dinner jacket, covering the caption with his hand. "Would you throw this one out of bed for making crumbs? I think not. A foolish virgin would marry him without a penny."

"That's more like it," Nancy declared. "What do you think, Ru?"

"I don't know. Quite handsome, I suppose." Rufa, her heart thoroughly shredded by Jonathan, was not used to weighing up the merits of other men. "What's the point of this test?"

"We have to either stop Max being a smart-ass, or throw him off the committee," Roshan told her. "Come on, smart-ass—what do you make of this one?"

Max shrugged. "He looks like a croupier. But you're going to tell me he's someone posh."

"He is indeed—a marquess, and single, and one of the richest men in Britain."

"We'd better put him on our list," Rufa said.

Max poured himself more champagne, and leaned back against the Dralon sofa. "Why not just stop at him? Then you'll only need to find one more, and we can finish in time to watch *Frasier*."

"Obviously," Rufa said patiently, "it's not as simple as that. Once we've made a list of rich men, we'll make another list of the ones who'll be easiest for us to find and approach. At this stage, it's pure science. Personal liking only comes into it when we've found the men who score most for money and approachability. Then we plan our campaign in detail."

There was a silence. Max lounged against the cushions, his wicked black eyes mocking Rufa. "You've got it all worked out, haven't you?"

She was defensive. "Yes. As far as possible."

"So we're considering first money, then approachability. Then personal preference."

"That's right," Wendy said. "Should I put the Prince of Wales, Rufa? Or does his lack of availability cancel out the money?"

"Those ears cancel out the money," Nancy said. "Never mind the little problem of his girlfriend."

Rufa was stiff and self-conscious, aware that Max was still looking at her, waiting for an answer. "Yes, leave him out. We have to be a bit realistic."

"Anyway," Nancy said, "the prince couldn't save Melismate, unless he persuaded the government to vote for it."

"And there might be a revolution," Max said, his eyes still laughing at Rufa. "You don't want to lose your head."

Roshan threw aside one magazine, and reached for a fresh one. "Max, stop trying to subvert the Marrying Game. We know it's against your principles, all right?"

"I just don't get it," Max said. He looked at Nancy now, and suddenly sat up, full of energy. "You talk about sacrifice, and not putting yourselves first—as if you were doing something virtuous. As if you're so addicted to being posh, you'll sell yourselves to men you don't even fancy!"

Rufa's lips were pale. She did not know how to begin to reply. Max had accused her of the worst kind of hypocrisy. He refused to see that they were playing the Marrying Game for a reward that was worth a real sacrifice.

Nancy, glancing at her, quickly said, "It's not because we want to be posh. It's about saving a family home that means a lot to all of us—and meant everything to our father. We have to do this. We owe it to his memory."

"His spirit's in every stone of the place," Wendy said, her eyes brimming.

Rufa said, "You didn't know him, Max. I couldn't explain it to you, unless I could find a way of making you see The Zed. And how absolutely wonderful he was." She was calm, but her voice shook a little.

Max softened. "I'm sorry. But there's something so bloody sad about it. You're both sublime. You were made to be adored. And you're denying yourselves the chance to fall in love properly."

There was another silence. Nancy could see that Rufa was shrinking away from a wave of desolation. It had all got far too heavy.

"How do you know we won't fall in love?" she demanded. "If you don't want to help us, go and make a round of tea."

"Max never makes tea," Wendy said. She looked up from her magazine at Rufa. "Is Harold Pinter rich enough?"

"Probably not," Nancy said. "And I can't see him divorcing Antonia Fraser. Anyway, think of the conversation—all those pauses."

Roshan jumped gracefully to his feet. "I'm miles ahead of you all, so I'll make the tea. Max—are you with us, or against us?"

Max, glancing at Nancy, pulled his pile of magazines toward him. "With you. I think it's crazy, but you need me."

❅ ❅ ❅

After hours of wading giddily through parties, film premieres, and race meetings, they had penciled in their first two targets. They had argued fiercely, scribbling names and crossing them out. Balls of discarded paper lay among the mugs, biscuit wrappers, and ramparts of glossy magazines. Max, who did not seem to be able to do anything less than passionately, had now thrown all his energy into the Marrying Game. He had been very useful. He cut through flights of fantasy, and isolated the men who would be easiest to approach.

"Well, I think we can declare the meeting over," he announced, at half past one in the morning. "Roshan and I can ransack the cuttings libraries at work, to compile proper dossiers." Max was a trainee arts producer at BBC Radio Four, and Roshan was the assistant deputy style editor of a Sunday newspaper. Rufa was now thanking heaven for the usefulness of Wendy's lodgers. "Nancy's target will be pretty easy," Max went on, "though we'll need a sick-bag when we're going through his cuttings. Rufa's will be a shade more tricky, but at least he ventures out to the opera occasionally. You can always trail him to Glyndebourne and throw a faint at his feet."

Roshan was not entirely satisfied. "I still think Rufa should have gone for the marquess. They'd make such a heavenly couple."

"We could spend years trying to get near him. Let's at least use the contacts we already have." Max yawned noisily, stretching and showing perfect white teeth. "Though I must say, I'm disappointed you girls don't have more contacts of your own. I thought you upper-class types all knew each other, and married your cousins."

"The Zed didn't like conventional upper-class society," Rufa said. "He dropped out when he fell in love with our mother. She's from a different sort of world."

Max was intrigued. "He married out, did he? That explains a lot. I have an uncle who married out, and nobody's spoken to him for years. English-gentry types and posh Jewish types evidently have bags in common."

"It wasn't that people didn't approve of our mother," Rufa added quickly. "He didn't introduce her to anyone, that's all, because nobody was good enough. And her parents weren't remotely posh. They ran a shop."

"A newsagents, tobacconists, and confectioners," Nancy said, enunciating each word in an immaculate upper-class accent. "They're both dead now. Our mother always says they came from another planet—they stopped speaking to her when she ran away and got knocked up with Ru. I wish I'd met them, though. I often think I must be rather like them."

Rufa laughed softly. "The Zed said I was the one with the shopkeeping streak."

Nancy, pleased that she had been able to make Rufa smile, leaned over to nudge her affectionately. "No, darling, you take after the blue-blooded side of the family. I'm sure you got more of it than I did. The fact is, we're hybrids—half landed gentry, with a bloodline stretching back to William the Conqueror. And half corner-shop, closed Wednesday afternoons. That's why we don't know anybody. The Zed was rejected by most of his friends—"

"Except the Reculvers," Rufa put in.

"—and he annoyed most of the neighbors. They used to call us 'those poor little hippy girls from the manor.'"

Max and Roshan had been listening with intense interest.

Max asked, "Do people really care that much about class these days?"

Roshan sighed, and said, "God, how romantic—love across the social divide!"

"The Zed was the most romantic man in the world," Wendy said solemnly. "That's all you had to understand about him. The normal barriers were simply invisible to him. For instance, I remember a Bath and West

County Show, back in—sometime in the late Eighties, anyway—when he made Lady Garber give up her seat for me because a pig had trodden on my foot—"

Nancy and Max and Roshan snorted with laughter. Rufa's lips twitched, but she managed to sound sober. "Max, didn't you say you had an interview tomorrow morning? I think we'd better go to bed, or we'll be here till dawn."

Wendy beamed around at them all—she had had an entirely wonderful evening. Nancy and Rufa had all their father's gift for creating an instant party. She felt ten years younger. "All right. But do let's have one last reading out of the notes. I keep getting them mixed up."

Max had written down basic details of the two targets, on separate sheets of paper. To each sheet, he had clipped relevant articles and photographs cut from the magazines. He read out the notes he had made, in an insolent, challenging drawl, mostly directed at Nancy.

"1. George Hyssop, Earl Sheringham of Sheringham
Age: 32
Marital Status: Single
Financial Status: Seriously rich. Owns several London districts and a large slice of Canada.
Address: Lynn Castle, Sheringham, Norfolk
Personal Telephone Number: Not known
Remarks: Linked with several women, nothing long-lasting. Seldom photographed or written about. Sometimes turns out for charity events, classical concerts, and opera. Known to be classically stuck-up and operatically refined. May be a tad hard to approach at first, but committee feels he would be so ideal for Rufa that this does not matter. We believe he is drawn to very highborn ladies. Committee feels Rufa should play up the Norman blood for all it's worth, and make out his lot are parvenus. We feel that the novel experience of being looked down on may give him a kinky thrill.

"2. Timothy 'Tiger' Durward
Age: 29
Marital Status: Divorced. No children.
Financial Status: Vast fortune from great-grandpa's chain of supermarkets. His mother is an earl's daughter.

Address: Hooper Park, Wooton, Wilts

Personal Telephone Number: Not known

Remarks: If anything, Tiger is too easy to bump into—regularly all over the tabloids like a rash. His hobbies are fighting, getting drunk, and chasing totty. He is as noisy, dissolute, and useless as a Regency buck. Likes games with hard balls, ladies with large breasts. Shot to fame after streaking at Twickenham—a fool and his underpants are soon parted. Married a Page Three model when he was 21. Divorced and paid her off two years later, but not before he was arrested for shouting obscenities through her letter box. Several dalliances with topless models since then, nothing lasting. The committee regards this big lummox as beneath contempt, but Nancy is stubborn and insists she can handle him."

The others had been laughing and catcalling all the way through, and "big lummox" made them howl.

"Of course I can handle him," Nancy declared, wiping her eyes. "I regularly chuck out two or three like him from the Hasty Arms every Friday—we get them from the agricultural college in Cirencester. Their idea of foreplay is grunting 'Hellair' before they grab your tit."

Rufa looked down at the photographs Max had fastened to each page. Chasing a man like Earl Sheringham would certainly be a challenge. He was tall and thin, of a white-blondness that seemed to give him a silvery aura. Every line of him was bred to its ultimate refinement. He had pale blue eyes and thin blue blood. He looked as if a gust of strong wind would wither him like an orchid. Rufa knew she could respect the sheer exquisiteness of such a man. She could cast him as the Handsome Prince destined to save her father's kingdom.

It was a shame they had to chase a man like Tiger Durward at the same time. Rufa only saw tabloid newspapers when they were wrapped around vegetables, but even she had heard of him. His beefy, loose-limbed body and ruddy, guffawing face were a familiar sight, attached to headlines like "Savesmart Heir Asks for Time to Pay Speeding Fine" and "Exclusive—My Jacuzzi Love-Romps with Tiger." Still, perhaps he was not as bad as he was painted.

Wendy, with much huffing and groaning, began to heave herself off the floor. "I'm off to bed. Don't leave the kitchen in a mess."

"We won't." Rufa knelt to gather mugs and plates. "Tomorrow, we'll plan the first moves."

"I beg your pardon," Roshan said. "Tomorrow we're buying you some decent clothes."

❊ ❊ ❊

Ignoring Rufa's pained expression, Roshan interrogated her about the exact amount of money in her bank account, and dismayed her by earmarking the whole lot for shopping.

"I refuse to let you do this in a halfhearted manner. You're both stunning, but that isn't enough. I'm afraid you look like two little girls from the country, and you won't fetch your asking price."

Fashion was his religion and his livelihood. He escorted Rufa and Nancy along Bond Street with the businesslike reverence of a verger showing visitors round a cathedral.

"If you girls really want to marry serious money, clothes are going to be your biggest investment. I'll quote your own sainted father back at you—you have to look as if you belong. Rich men dally with all sorts of people, but they're dynasts at heart and they tend to marry their own."

"Surely it doesn't have to be this expensive?" Rufa pleaded. "I can't believe how much I've just spent on four pairs of shoes and two handbags." They had started the morning by making a huge crater in Edward's brooch money. Her lips were white with shock.

"*Prada* shoes and handbags," Roshan said, with exaggerated patience. "But if you want to marry a dustman, go ahead—get the rest at British Home Stores. If you're not prepared to deal in thousands, you're wasting your time."

"He's right, and you know it," Nancy said, giving Rufa a friendly nudge. "So don't be a drip." She halted suddenly, in front of a gleaming shop window. It displayed a single mannequin, dressed in a scrap of lime velvet. "Isn't that divine?"

"Moschino? Forget it." Roshan tugged at her sleeve, to pull her away. "It is lovely, and you'd probably stop the traffic in it. But it's completely off-message."

"Well, what do you suggest, then?" Nancy could not see the point in buying expensive clothes if they made no impact. "Twinset and pearls?"

"Yes," Rufa said. "We need to look posh."

"You need to look *stylish*," Roshan corrected her. "You need Chanel (though not the accessories), Jil Sander, Armani, Miu Miu, and God knows what else. For the last time, leave it to me."

Nancy smiled insolently. "All right. Where to next?"

"Rigby and Peller."

"God, what's that? It sounds like a firm of undertakers."

"They're corsetieres to the Queen," Roshan said loftily. "Bra-makers, to you."

"Oh, we won't bother with underwear," Rufa said. "Nobody will see it."

Roshan sighed. "Will you two cooperate? Style begins at the foundations. A proper bra is vital to the image I'm building for you."

"But I've got loads of bloody bras," Nancy complained.

"Yes, Wonderbras and Balconettes, and nylon whatsits that squash those lavish breasts of yours right under your chin. Real ladies sling them lower."

She laughed. "Aren't I meant to look sexy?"

"Only up to a point," Roshan said. "You need less sex. And Rufa, frankly, could do with a bit more—what *are* you wearing under that hideous guernsey?"

"Nothing, actually—"

"And your chest looks like an ironing board. You mustn't hide your assets." Taking her hand, looking deep into her eyes, he added, "Trust me."

Roshan had liked Nancy on sight, and they were already soul mates. Rufa was different, however. He loved Rufa with the sexless passion of a medieval knight, and had vowed to himself that she should be launched into society dressed like a princess. He dragged them from shop to shop, until they were laden with gilded bags and boxes. The short January day was darkening by the time he hailed a taxi.

"Not that we've finished—we need at least another week to sort out some evening dresses."

Rufa could not bring herself to think about the evening dresses. Her stomach clenched with anxiety every time she remembered the money she had spent, and where it had come from. Her deep pleasure in the beautiful clothes—the dull sheen of thick silk, the buttery softness of fine leather—made it seem worse. Luxury and frivolity on this scale were wickedly intoxicating. She had met the White Witch, and eaten her enchanted Turkish delight—now all she wanted in the world was more. Edward would have been horrified.

There's no going back, she thought; we have to succeed.

Nancy wanted to sit down with a cup of tea when they got home, but no one else would hear of it. Roshan marched the sisters straight upstairs, to transform the two country girls into blue-blooded belles destined to make dazzling marriages.

Wendy and Max were the audience, waiting in the kitchen. Wendy was a little surprised that Max was taking this much interest. The arrival of Nancy and Rufa had made him irritable and abstracted, but he was more absolutely there than he had ever been. Usually, he made a great show of treating Wendy's house as the temporary stopping place of a rising genius. Today, however, he had come home early, and every time Wendy had emerged from her consulting room, she found him prowling.

"The suspense is killing me," he said. "Do you fancy a cup of tea, Wend?"

She was on her guard. "Are you offering to make one?"

"No. I just thought, if you were having some anyway—"

"Well, you can think again," Wendy said. "I'm not a servant."

"Okay, okay." He grabbed the kettle aggressively. "I suppose it'll give me something to do."

"You really are in suspense, aren't you?" Wendy watched her handsome lodger thoughtfully. "It's Nancy, isn't it? I might have known you'd fancy her."

Max was nettled, but did his best to laugh it off. "She's ravishing. So's Rufa. I had noticed, actually."

"Don't you go spoiling things."

"For God's sake, Wendy, give me a break," Max snapped. "What do you expect, when you bring two flame-haired goddesses into the house? Are you going to evict me for drooling?"

"You know what I mean. They're here to marry money."

"Am I stopping them?"

Wendy smiled. The effortless strength of Max's sexuality reminded her of the atmosphere around The Zed. "It wouldn't be a problem, if Nancy didn't like you so much."

He grinned. "You reckon?"

"She only needs a tiny bit of encouragement to fall madly in love with you."

"A tiny bit, eh? Thanks, Wendy."

Reluctantly, she laughed. "You're terrible. I was only trying to say, don't go distracting her if you're not—you know—serious."

Max handed her a cup of gray, inadequately squeezed tea, and threw himself into a chair. It creaked alarmingly. He was not a particularly large man, but seemed too big for any room he was in. "Are they serious about this marrying thing?"

Wendy sipped her tea. "They are, and I can't say I like it. The whole family's desperate for money. But I'd far rather see them marrying for love."

"Why can't they just fall in love? Why does it have to be bloody marriage?"

"The Zed was a big fan of marriage."

Max snorted. "By the sound of it, because it gave him a fine excuse not to commit to any of his girlfriends."

She had to admit there was an element of truth in this. She could not allow Max to think it was the whole picture. "No, he truly believed in a lifelong commitment to one person. And Rose was that person. I always knew that."

"Then what was in it for you?" Max demanded. "How could you go and fall in love with him, knowing he'd end up dumping you?"

"The Zed never dumped me," Wendy said. Her lips curved around the rim of her cup, in a dreamy, wistful smile. "He didn't do that to anyone. He just had such a wonderful take on life."

She knew this sounded inadequate; knew she could never make Max understand. In her mind she conjured up one of the sealed memories she had never shared with anyone.

The Zed lay on his back in the water meadow, beside the little river at Melismate, on a balmy afternoon in late spring. If she half-closed her eyes, she could absolutely see him—arms behind his head, his beautiful profile tilted toward the smiling blue sky.

He said, "You have a longing for the poetic, Wendy. You'll never be happy, unless you keep that scrap of poetry alive."

She was sitting beside him in the long grass. "What do you mean? How do I do it?"

"Just settle as near as possible to the place where you really want to be."

"Oh." This was where she wanted to be, for all time, in this bubble of sun and serenity.

The Zed said, "I mean it, darling. People are wrong to be disappointed with life when they feel they haven't had enough of something. Even twenty-five percent of what you really want is better than one hundred percent of what you never wanted in the first place."

It was a difficult philosophy to explain—something along the lines of being better to have loved and lost than never to have loved at all. People did not always agree with that. Wendy, however, had found it sustaining. If she had been given a choice between marriage to an ordinary man, or her fraction of the ultimate man, she would have chosen the fraction every time. Loving The Zed had burned her wings, but it was better to be a middle-aged reflexologist with burned wings than an ordinary wife with no wings at all.

She turned her attention back to Max. "I don't know what you've got against marriage. Don't you want to get married someday?"

He shrugged. "Someday. I won't be in any danger until I meet someone Jewish."

"Why?"

"Have a little think," Max suggested testily.

"Oh, of course. Because you're Jewish yourself."

"Yes, Einstein. And if I marry out, my mother will have a nervous breakdown." He smiled sourly. "So you don't have to worry that I'll ruin the Marrying Game of the waspy Hastys. All right?"

"I'm only trying to look after them." Wendy wondered why he was so cross.

"Quiet in the cheap seats!" Roshan sprang dramatically into the room. "It's time for you to gasp at my artistry." He stood aside for Nancy and Rufa.

They were smiling, laughing whenever they met each other's eyes, exulting in their transformation.

Max and Wendy stared in silence.

Wendy exhaled tremulously. "You're both fabulous. Oh, if The Zed could only see you now—his silk princesses—"

Rufa wore a loosely cut black suit, over a thin cream silk jersey. Her hair was unbound. She looked flawlessly beautiful, breathtakingly expensive, and somehow softer all over—less scrubbed and angular, more gentle and seraphic. The real revelation, however, was Nancy. She wore a fitted taupe jacket and long black skirt. No more tits and tresses—the new Nancy had breasts that did not move, and her shameless riot of red hair was neatly contained in a French plait. She was still vivid and voluptuous, but no longer had *strumpet* tattooed all over her. Incredibly, she was a perfect lady.

Max, staring at her with faint indignation, stood up. "God, what's he done to you?"

"Don't you like it?" Nancy asked.

"Of course he does." Rufa was beaming, almost reconciled to the chasm in her bank account. "You're sensational. Princes and dukes will fall over each other to marry you."

"I can't take all the credit," Roshan said. "Blood will out. I only had to rub off a bit of the tarnish."

Nancy laughed. "Charming." Her gaze was locked into Max's, and it was obvious that he was mesmerized.

"Well, I believe it now," Wendy announced. "I had my doubts when I first heard about it, but I really believe I'm looking at Lady Sheringham and Mrs. Durward."

Nancy grinned at Rufa. "Don't worry, your ladyship. When we come to stay at your castle, I'll make Tiger sleep out in the kennels."

Chapter Seven

Roshan swept straight into the kitchen to tell them the great news, without stopping to remove his gray herringbone Paul Smith overcoat—barely one week after the selection of the targets, he had found their opening event. The pianist Radu Lupu was giving a recital at Sheringham House, in aid of the Rheumatoid Arthritis Fellowship. Sheringham House, in Kensington, was the London residence of the Earls Sheringham. The tickets were prohibitively expensive, and had been sold out for months, to friends and relations of the committee. Roshan had managed to wangle himself a rare press pass.

"Fortunately, I knew the PR from college," he said gleefully. To Max, he added, "It was Hermione Porter, of all the useful people."

Max nodded. "Rich and thick. It figures."

"She's thick, all right. She believed me when I said I was a music critic. I'm taking her out to lunch the day before the concert. I pray to heaven she doesn't check up on me and find out I'm a hack from the Style pages—just the type of riffraff she's employed to keep out." Roshan darted out of the room, to place his valuable coat carefully on a padded hanger. He darted back in again, and exclaimed, "Oh God, what's this? Can I believe my eyes? Nancy cooking?"

Max and Rufa were sitting at the table, watching the novel spectacle. Rufa looked uncomfortable, clutching but not drinking a cup of peppermint tea. Max was grinning, entranced by the way Nancy's hips moved as she hacked an onion on the counter. She labored under the delusion that she could cook spaghetti bolognese. With tremendous fanfare, she and Max had made a special expedition to Sainsbury's to buy the ingredients. These mostly seemed to consist of bottles of Barolo. Nancy was treating the rest—cheap meat, tinned tomatoes, dried herbs—with a careless brutality that made Rufa wince.

"I can't leave Ru to make a martyr of herself," she said cheerfully. "She's always lumbered with the cooking, and it's just not fair."

"I'm not being a martyr," Rufa protested. "Honestly, I love cooking. I'm better at it than you are."

"You're a famous cook, darling, but you hate competition. I think my sauce will surprise you."

Rufa's lips twitched. "It's already astonished me, thanks."

"You relax, Ru. For once in your life, lie back and take it easy."

Roshan looked into the heaving swamp on the stove, and made a gargoyle face at Rufa behind Nancy's back. Rufa snorted with guilty laughter. "That's brilliant news about the concert," she said quickly. "It's exactly the sort of thing we need."

"You'll be able to size up your future home," Nancy said, shaking out half a drum of dried oregano, "and decide where to put the new conservatory."

"Radu Lupu's terrific," Rufa said. "The Zed took me to Cheltenham to hear him. Do you know what he's playing?"

Nancy said, "I don't care if he plays chopsticks. What do we wear, and how do you get us in?"

Roshan, his movements neat and unhurried, uncorked one of the bottles of wine and took four glasses from the cupboard. "It's black tie, so you absolutely must have really *profound* evening dresses."

The whole question of evening dresses had been troubling Rufa. On the one hand, she yearned for a beautiful dress as ardently as Cinderella. On the other hand, there was the ever-present problem of money. Rufa lay awake every night, watching the orange lozenges of light on the ceiling from the streetlamps outside, agonizing about money, money, money. It was like living in chains.

"Couldn't we hire them?" she asked wistfully.

"No," Roshan snapped. "I'm not taking you to Sheringham House covered with someone else's soup stains. If the hire shop is even halfway decent, the frocks will all be notorious. You can't risk standing out in the wrong way—you have to look *divine*." He plucked the cup of peppermint tea from Rufa's hand, and replaced it with a glass of red wine.

She smiled. "You're right. There's no point, unless we give it all we've got. I'll try to think of it as an investment."

"I'm looking forward to the gate-crashing part," Nancy said. "I always did love breaking and entering."

Rufa said, "I hope this isn't going to be too difficult. I'm not going to bother with an expensive dress if I have to squeeze in through some lavatory window."

"We can't afford to mess up our hair or ladder our tights," Nancy pointed out.

Roshan filled his own glass with wine, and sat down. "Don't worry. Once I'm inside, there's bound to be a way I can let you in—a staff entrance, or a back door."

"This is as good as a bank heist," Max said, chuckling. "We should try to case the joint beforehand. Even from the outside, it should be possible to mark where doors and windows are." He leaned forward energetically. "Then—tell you what—I'll ring the house from work, saying I'm something to do with the caterer, double-checking details of delivery. I'll invent some immensely plausible reason for needing to know about all the doors and windows."

"That would be excellent," Rufa said. "And awfully nice of you—"

"I've always wanted to play at being a gumshoe. I'm in the Marrying Game for the sport."

Rufa thought, he's after Nancy, he's smart enough to sabotage the Game from the inside; and if she goes and falls in love with him, I'll be left to do it all myself.

It was not a noble line of thought, and she knew she ought to have been ashamed—she wasn't sure The Zed would have approved of her standing in the way of Nancy's happiness. Suppose Max turned out to be the great love of her life: the one Nancy was always going on about and never meeting?

But it had not happened yet, and, in the meantime, all this tiresome amatory energy could be channeled into something useful. Rufa smiled at Max. "I think we can promise you some reasonable sport." She smiled round at them all. "Do you know, I really think this might work?"

Max lifted his glass. "Watson, the Game's afoot."

Though she still smiled, Rufa was slightly annoyed. Watson, indeed. She was the one in the deerstalker, and he'd better not forget it.

Roshan said he would escort the girls to Harvey Nichols the following Saturday. On Thursday evening, Rufa made her usual call to Melismate. Either she or Nancy called every night, on Wendy's phone to save the bill at home (Rufa kept a scrupulous record of what was owed to Wendy).

This call began, as they mostly did, with the breathless voice of Linnet. "Hello? Hello?" Rufa settled comfortably against the kitchen counter, half-closing her eyes to summon a picture of Linnet in the kitchen at Melismate. Both sisters missed Linnet cruelly—a house without a five-year-old child seemed creepily still. Nearly every day, Nancy begged Rufa to squander some precious money on treats to send to Linnet. And more often than not, Rufa agreed—only that morning, she had found herself stuffing a furry Pikachu rucksack into a Jiffy bag.

"Hi, darling. It's Ru."

"Hello, Ru. What are you doing?"

"I'm having a cup of tea. Nancy's out, and Wendy's watching *Animal Hospital*."

Linnet had to know exactly where everyone was. She asked, "And where are those men?"

Regretfully, thinking it must be genetic, Rufa noted her niece's intense interest in the opposite sex. "Well, Max and Roshan are out with Nancy. I didn't feel like going with them. What about you? What are you doing?"

"Oh, just standing here in some new pink slippers Daddy gave me."

Rufa smiled. The picture this conjured up was delicious. She ached to hug the airy, wriggling, dignified little figure. "New slippers? They sound smart. Poor Nancy, she will be jealous."

This was a game Nancy had with Linnet. She would pretend to steal the child's new clothes, and weep with chagrin when they did not fit her. Linnet giggled, then there was a long pause.

Rufa prompted: "How are Mummy and Daddy?" She always had to check the state of Ran's love life. "Are they well?"

"Yes," Linnet said. She had to think about how they were. "Daddy comes to see us a lot. I think it's because he can't get another girlfriend."

Good, Rufa thought; that means Liddy's holding together. "How's Trotsky?"

Trotsky was the guinea pig Ran had given Linnet for Christmas.

She giggled delightedly. "Granny let him run on the table, and—he—he—" A storm of hilarity possessed her. Rufa laughed too; the sound was so beautiful. "He—he *did a pooh in the butter!*"

"Oh, yuck. Poor Granny. Was she cross?"

"Yes—she gave Trotsky a tiny smack on his bottom. She said next time it's an ice pick, but she didn't really mean it, she and Roger were laughing just as much as me. I'm going to write about it in my news book tomorrow."

"I can't wait to read it," Rufa said. "Is Granny about?"

"Yes. She wants to talk to you when I've finished."

"All right. Bye-bye, then."

Linnet was annoyed. "I didn't say I'd finished yet."

"Sorry." Rufa wondered uneasily why Rose wanted to talk to her. "Er—how are the Ressany Brothers?"

"I really need Nancy to do the voices." Linnet was plaintive, and faintly accusing. "It's not the same without her."

The drama of the Ressany Brothers was the joint creation of Nancy and The Zed. A few days after The Zed's death, unable to bear Linnet's bewilderment, Nancy had gamely picked up the threads of the saga and carried it on alone. "It's a way of keeping part of him," she had told Rufa later. "I couldn't let them die too."

Linnet went on, "When Roger does their voices, they're never naughty and they never do anything interesting. What? What?" In the background, Rufa heard Roger's voice, saying something indistinct. "WHAT? I CAN'T HEAR?"

Roger came closer to the telephone, and could be heard saying, "—but you'll have to come now if you want a piggyback."

Linnet said, "I do! I'm going now—good-night—"

A sound of scuffling, then Rose took the receiver. "Ru? Darling, I'm so sorry, but I won't fart about—there's been another slight disaster."

The shock was like being doused in cold water. Another disaster, in the Melismate minefield of disasters. You could not turn your back on them for a minute. "Oh God—what's happened now?"

Rose's curt voice softened. "Nobody's died, not that sort of disaster."

"It's money, then," Rufa said resignedly. "What for and how much?"

"I hate laying this on you, love, but I'm at my wits' end. The council have unearthed some sort of irregularity with the rates. They're demanding nearly five thousand pounds."

Rufa's knuckles whitened round the receiver. "Oh God almighty—what a time for them to discover one of The Zed's pathetic fiddles!"

"He should have roped you in on it," Rose said dryly. "I'm sure you would have fiddled the council far more efficiently."

"No, I didn't mean—but what the hell are we going to do? Five thousand pounds!" Rufa massaged her forehead, desperately trying to think. "Couldn't you ask the bank to extend your overdraft till after the sale?"

"You must be kidding," Rose said. "I light the fire with threatening letters from that bank."

"Oh. Well, you'll have to do what The Zed would have done, and let it ride until you get a summons."

"My darling, the summons came this morning."

They were both silent. Then Rufa let out a shaky, defeated sigh. "There's nothing else for it. We'll have to ask Edward."

"I've asked him."

"What? And he refused?"

"He hasn't a penny to spare until after the harvest." Rose laughed, without mirth. "He had the decency to interrupt me before I went down on my knees, I'm grateful for that at least. And then he reminded me about the brooch he gave you, and said you'd have something left after you'd paid for your course."

"Oh—shit."

"Yes, quite. Edward said you could pay the bill now, and he'd make up the money later. It was enormously generous of him—I had a terrible time dredging up the appreciation. I deserve an Oscar. I couldn't remember what bloody course you were meant to be on."

"Prue Leith's," Rufa said dully.

"That's it, I knew it was something to do with food. Anyway, I couldn't possibly tell him you'd spent all his money on mantraps. I just mumbled something in the way of thanks, and buggered off."

"We haven't spent it all," Rufa said. Through the fog of bleakness, she knew what had to be done. The Zed's enterprising fiddle (please God, the last to come to light) would have to be paid for out of Edward's brooch money. And Edward thought she had used it to pay for a course. He assumed that there would be enough left over, once the fictitious course was paid for, to fund a frugal student lifestyle until she found herself a job. He had no idea how much had been squandered on frivolities, and he must never, ever find out. Evening dresses were laughably out of the question now. So was everything else.

Her eyes smarted with disappointment. Just when it had started to look promising, the Marrying Game was, apparently, stone dead.

❄ ❄ ❄

"So we won't be going to Sheringham House. Once I've settled that bloody bill, we'll have barely enough change to buy ourselves a couple of bin bags. It's incredibly frustrating, and I should have expected it. When I made my plans, I didn't allow for the Melismate Effect."

Rufa leaned back against the plush banquette, which was pocked with cigarette burns. She had taken the unprecedented step of coming to find the others at the Duke of Clarence, two streets away from Wendy's house. She hated pubs, but she could not bear the death of hope without Nancy. The others listened to the bad news in sober silence.

Roshan squeezed her hand sympathetically. "What will you do?"

She tried to laugh. "I don't know. Go out as a governess."

"You can't give it up," he said, frowning. "I won't allow it. You've invested far too much. There must be ways to scale it down."

"We're already operating on a shoestring. If we scale down any more, we'll disappear."

Max stood up. "You need a drink."

"Yes, I think I do," Rufa said gratefully. "A white wine and soda, please."

The Duke of Clarence was echoing and ashy, throbbing with self-pitying country and western music. The new style of London pub, all chalked menus and bentwood chairs, had not yet penetrated the side streets of Tufnell Park. The Clarence had an authentic seediness and air of defeat. Silent men in denim and jewelry squashed their enormous stomachs against the bar. A party of girls drinking vodka and Red Bull shrieked around a large table in one corner.

Max went to the bar. Nancy watched him for a moment, then jumped up. "You can't drink wine in a place like this, darling—it'll taste like Windolene. I'll get you a proper drink."

Nancy remembered that her sister had led a ridiculously sheltered life, and knew next to nothing about public drinking, but her motives were not entirely pure. Changing the order gave her a fine excuse to sidle up against Max at the crowded bar. Dear God, he was sexy—and he knew it. Ru was watching her like a hawk, or Nancy would have swooned into his arms ten minutes after meeting him. No matter how often she ordered herself to be strong, she was falling for him with a mighty great wallop.

She squeezed herself against Max's shoulder. "Could you change Ru's to a gin and tonic?"

Max laughed. "God, you're expensive dates, you two."

"Didn't you hear? We've had a shock."

Max, with difficulty, turned to face Nancy, pressing his rib cage against her breasts. "You seem to be bearing up all right."

She smiled up into his face. "I take a more relaxed view of the world."

"Yes, you do, don't you? So why are you going along with this Marrying Game?"

"Because," Nancy said firmly, "it's a very good idea."

Max lowered his voice. "No it's not. It's a crap idea. Good for a laugh—unless it gets in the way of the real thing." He was daring her to bring their mutual fascination into the open. They had been exchanging signals for days. The warmth and solidity of his body made Nancy weak with desire. She allowed herself one luxurious moment of inhaling his musky, spicy smell, then firmly prized herself away and took Rufa's tumbler of gin and tonic back to the table.

"Think of it as a setback," Roshan was saying. "Your main asset in this game was always your beauty, and that's something nobody can take away."

Max, following Nancy through the crush as if glued to her, put down three pints of lager (Nancy, to Rufa's dismay, had a fondness for the stuff). "Will you have anything left to live on, when you've paid the council?"

"Not really," Rufa said, frowning. "I'm going to have to find some work sooner than I thought. The trouble is, most of my contacts are in the country."

Nancy had already decided that she had no intention of returning to the country. She loved London. "Don't worry, old thing. I'll get myself a job—you don't need posh contacts to pull pints."

"I didn't come all this way so you could slave in a pub," Rufa said crossly. "I mean, suppose one of the targets saw you?"

"With that cleavage," Max said, "he'd be enslaved."

"It depends on the pub," Nancy said. "They're looking for a part-timer here."

"Here? You couldn't!" Rufa was dismayed.

"What's wrong with it?"

"Wendy says there's a fight here every Friday night—"

"So? All decent pubs feature a Friday night fight. It's no big deal. You simply bang a few heads together and call the police."

"You never had to do anything like that at the Hasty Arms!" Rufa protested.

Nancy started laughing. "Of course I did. Pubs and human nature are the same the world over. Why do you think I number two policemen among my great loves? When we had the Bangham rugger team in, I regularly swept up enough broken glass to rebuild the Crystal Palace."

"You never said anything—"

"The Zed told me not to. He said you'd be worried."

"My God, he was right," Rufa said, shaken and not entirely believing. "You're not doing anything like that here."

"You need the money," Max reminded her. "It's only incompatible with the Marrying Game if someone spots you—and I can't exactly see that earl turning up for karaoke night at the Duke of Clarence."

Roshan placed a beer mat underneath Max's glass. "Rufa's absolutely right, it would be far too risky." He was looking thoughtful. "Let's be creative here. You can't make your raid on Sheringham House because you lack evening dresses. What if I could get you a couple of frocks for nothing?"

"Where from?" Nancy demanded. "Oxfam? Why should anyone give us evening dresses out of charity?"

"I don't think he's talking about charity," Max said. "Watch him, girls. He's playing an angle."

"I am not! I was only thinking of using one of my professional contacts." Roshan was excited. He addressed himself to Rufa. "My editor is obsessed with class, but he's as common as muck. And so is his paper, whatever he thinks. We can never get ourselves invited to any decent society event. If we do manage to blag our way into something, we can never find anyone posh enough—or pretty enough—to photograph. Frankly, he'd commit murder to have pictures of a couple of highbred doxies like you two spread all over his Style pages. Especially if we could snap you whooping it up at Sheringham House."

"Told you," Max said. "The little brown man wants to put your Marrying Game in his newspaper. Why don't you go the whole hog, and advertise?"

"Shut up!" snapped Roshan. "Who said anything about the Game? If I were writing the piece, it would be in my interest to play up the Norman blood like mad and make you look as if you'd been properly invited—nobody's going to check."

"Maybe not," Max said, "but how are you going to get your photographer in?"

"There's a reception before the concert. Hermione mentioned that they're letting in a few snappers then. They'll be the smarter ones, of course—from the likes of *Vogue* and 'Jennifer's Diary.' I'm sure I can sneak one past her, as long as the picture desk doesn't send one of their usual baboons."

Nancy and Rufa looked at each other. Rufa was cautious. "You're saying someone would give us free dresses, just to get them in the paper?"

"Certainly—once they see how gorgeous you make them look," Roshan said, utterly confident. "One tiny mention in the copy, and they'll be inundated with rich old bags begging to look the same."

Rufa said, "I don't know."

"You're thinking of Edward," Nancy said. She leaned closer to her sister. "Relax. He's too mean to buy a newspaper—he gets all his news from Radio Four."

"Suppose he buys some chips, or—or reads what's round the potatoes?"

Nancy hooted with laughter. "When has Edward ever bought chips? And he grows his own potatoes. We could be spread all over Page Three jumping naked out of a pie, and he'd never know."

This was perfectly true. Rufa joined in the laughter. "Well, if you really think we could carry it off—but won't your editor mind that we're not genuine society girls?"

Roshan smiled wickedly. "Not unless he knows about it. All he cares about is the end result. If in doubt, remember the first rule of journalism—"

Together, he and Max chanted: "Make it up!"

Chapter Eight

Sheringham House took up one side of a three-sided square facing Kensington Gardens. It was a flat Georgian building of yellowed stucco, with immense oblong windows that were lighted theaters of opulence. A long line of cars and taxis inched slowly toward the handsome, pillared front door. Two policemen stood beside the pillars like caryatids, watching men in dinner jackets and women in furs climb out onto the chilly pavement.

Rufa stared out of the taxi window at the line snaking round the square. She was magnificently calm, but her eyes were feverish with excitement. "How amazing," she murmured, "to think of all this just—just going on. I mean, in the same city as Tufnell Park. It's another world, isn't it?"

"Another dimension," Roshan said, fingering his bow tie nervously. He was on the tip-up seat behind the driver, the silk skirts of the girls lapping round his ankles.

"Rather scandalous really," Nancy commented amiably. "I've counted three Rollers and four Bentleys, and any amount of endangered species. We ought to string them all up from the nearest lamppost."

Rufa laughed. "What a time to turn socialist."

"Well, I'm beginning to think there's a lot to be said for socialism," Nancy said. "At least it's cheap and easy to join."

"Yes, but think of the *clothes*," Roshan said, shuddering. "They look worse than Christians."

"I don't care. I'm sure it's a lot more fun out on the barricades, in comfy shoes. I wish I'd done the outside surveillance with Max now. Aren't you scared, Ru?"

"Certainly not," Rufa said briskly. "This is everything we've been working for since Christmas, and we both look terrific. If we get scared now, we might as well go straight home to Melismate." The richness of this world intoxicated her. It was so ultimately safe; all danger and ugliness filtered out by a great mesh of old money. As the taxi crawled forward, she looked into rooms filled with gilt and damask and oil paintings, and felt like the Peri at the Gates of Paradise.

Roshan checked his watch, for the hundredth time. "Why is this taking so long? It's only an earl, even if he is stuck-up. What the hell are those policemen for? I don't like the look of them at all."

"Oh, I don't know," Nancy said, with a luscious smile, "the black one's not bad."

"I'm serious," he snapped. "Hermione didn't tell me it would be like breaking into the Kremlin. Let's go through it one more time—" Both sisters sighed and rolled their eyes, but he persisted. "Please, we can't afford to be careless, when we're poised above an absolute vortex of humiliation. I'll have my invitation ready, and I'll just flash it at them quickly as I'm rushing in. I'll stick as close as possible to the people in front of me, and you two must stick to me—acting as if you owned the place." The anxiety melted from his face as he surveyed them. "It shouldn't be too hard, when you both look like angels. Clare should be paying you to wear those dresses."

From his packed Rolodex of contacts, Roshan had unearthed a pearl: an ambitious young designer named Clare Seal. Clare earned her bread designing the Larger Than Life range of a well-known chain store, but she saw herself as the Madame Grès of the twenty-first century. To Roshan, this vision was as sacred as a vocation to the ministry. He had written an article about her graduation show at Saint Martin's. That had been helpful, but her dresses needed to be seen on the backs of the beautiful and privileged. In Roshan's opinion, fashion editors ignored real quality at the expense of the gimmicky and crass.

"Clare suffers," he had told Rufa, "because she chooses to work with silks and velvets, instead of barbed wire and traffic cones."

He had taken Rufa and Nancy to Clare's dusty loft, at the Hoxton end of the City Road. She was a short, stout woman, wearing Doc Marten boots and a black jersey tent, but she had wheeled out a rack full of exquisite gowns fashioned for swans. When she saw Nancy and Rufa, and realized Roshan had not been exaggerating about their looks, she offered to lend them as many gowns as they needed, in return for photographs on Roshan's Style pages and a credit in the copy. It had been that easy.

Rufa had worried that they were taking advantage of Clare, and was not sure that she would have chosen a dress like this for herself. Clare and Roshan had insisted on a long, plain sheath of heavy bronze silk velvet. It had a peculiar cut, a little like a medieval robe. She had to admit, however, that the color was wonderful with her hair, which Roshan had made her wear loose and unadorned.

He had brushed Nancy's long, wild red curls into a smooth knot at the nape of her white neck. Her dress was deep yellow silk crepe, with a low neck and 1930s fishtail skirt. Rufa thought she looked sensational—she was constantly surprised by Nancy's potential as a serious beauty. Perhaps, she thought, the stuck-up earl would prefer to make a countess of her sister. She hoped this did not mean she would be lumbered with Tiger Durward.

Clare had thrown in two taffeta evening coats, lined with velvet—dark brown for Rufa, black for Nancy—and Roshan had contributed two pairs of satin pumps, dyed to match at Anello and Davide.

Rufa smiled at him affectionately. "You've been so nice to us, Roshan. We couldn't have done any of this without you."

"God, no," Nancy said. "We're just two provincial maidens without a clue. It was a lucky day for us when Wendy took up yoga."

Roshan beamed. "You don't have to thank me—you two fulfill all the doll-dressing fantasies I had to suppress when I was a child."

Nancy took a tube of Polo mints from her otherwise empty evening purse. "Wouldn't it be perfect, if we could find a little romance for you along the way?"

His smile became mournful. "I've given up on romance. Rufa's approach is the right one—a sensible alliance, or nothing." He looked meaningfully at Rufa. They had both had their hearts broken by married men. Roshan had heard the sorry tale of Jonathan, and told his own tale of the solicitor from Epsom who had decided to stay in his comfortable suburban closet. They had agreed that the brokenhearted had an excuse to avoid passion.

The taxi swung round the corner of the square. They were moving closer to the front door. Rufa watched the people from the cars ahead emerging onto the pavement, standing about in convivial knots beside the railings, then drifting into the house. "Let's get out and mill about—we ought to practice belonging."

Roshan paid the driver, and gallantly helped out the two girls. It was cold, and their evening coats were thin. Rufa, seeing an elderly, fur-clad woman eyeing her curiously, made an effort to look warm. Roshan trotted ahead, toward the press of people in the porch, to spy out the land. He ran back in a state of agitation.

"This is ghastly—oh, God—let's not panic—"

Nancy patted his shoulder. "Calm down, darling. What's the problem?"

"They're checking invitations, just past the two rozzers with flaming swords." Roshan pulled his mobile phone from his pocket, and began punching numbers. "Why didn't that imbecile Hermione mention it? I'll be all right, but you two—hello, Max?" Max, in plain clothes, had been posted to spy out the area. "Where are you? We've hit a snag—"

A large group of people, all middle-aged or elderly, were drifting toward the gates of paradise with enviable ease. Rufa and Nancy, doing their best to imitate the ease, strolled as near to the front door as they dared.

Nancy was trying not to giggle. "Why are they all staring?"

"Because you look wonderful," Rufa said. She stated this as a plain fact.

"Thanks, but aren't we supposed to be blending?"

"If we blend too much, who'll notice us?"

"Hmmm. It's a pity we can't wear price tags. Let's hope someone decides to marry us before we get chucked out."

Rufa assessed the situation. Beyond the two policemen, the heavy front door stood open. Beyond that was a pair of glass doors. Behind the glass doors was a large entrance hall, with a black-and-white marble floor. A young woman in a black dress, flanked by two men in dinner jackets, sat at a small table, scrutinizing each invitation and checking names on a typed list. She guessed this was Hermione.

"It looks bad," she whispered to Nancy. "We'll never get past them."

"You're not bottling out, are you?"

"Certainly not," Rufa said briskly. "We'll have to resort to Plan B, that's all."

A slender, elegant man with thick gray hair stood aside, to let them stroll back to Roshan. Rufa gave him a gracious, slightly unfocused smile, and took Nancy's arm. "Keep looking casual."

"In this outfit? You must be joking. My skirt's so tight round the knees, I'm hobbling like the Widow Twanky." Nancy stifled a nervous giggle. "Let's just pretend we belong."

"I do belong," Rufa said. "I'm as good as anyone here. This is exactly the sort of world I want. And you should want it too. Think of The Zed, and remember you're a Hasty."

"I'm a Hasty. A Norman-blooded Hasty, with no seaside sweetshop in my coat of arms. Though the College of Heralds or whatever ought to design us a new one, with a Flake and ten Embassy couchant in one quarter. Or should it be rampant?" Nancy wrestled down another burst of giggling. The man with the gray hair was still looking at them. She lowered her voice. "Sorry. I'm babbling. Terror makes me facetious."

Roshan ran to them, and pulled them away from the legitimate guests. "This is a nightmare. Max says they've laid on extra security because Princess Michael of Kent is coming, and they obviously can't give anyone a chance to blow the wretched woman up."

Rufa frowned. "There must be another entrance. You could sneak round and let us in."

"There's another rozzer out in the mews at the back." He shook his head sorrowfully. "It looks hopeless. What on earth are we going to do?"

"Well, maybe a window—"

"Oh, for God's sake." Nancy took a firm hold of Rufa's hand. "Don't you two know anything about gate-crashing? Roshan—you go in and find that photographer of yours."

"What are you going to do?"

"We'll meet you in there. Go on!"

Roshan passed through the pillars, giving them a miserable look over his shoulder, as if they had pushed him into the last lifeboat on the *Titanic*.

Rufa asked, "What are you up to?"

"Shh, don't spoil it." Clutching Rufa's hand, Nancy fell into step behind a party of ten or so people. Behind the table where the invitations were being checked, the hall was crowded. In the far wall, a pair of double doors stood open, giving a tantalizing glimpse of rows of gilt chairs, set out for

81

the recital. Outside another pair of double doors stood a waiter, with a tray of glasses. They were close enough now to hear a solid hum of well-bred chatter.

Nancy waited until the watchful gray-haired man had taken a glass and disappeared into the crowded room, and the large party were swamping the table. Then she dragged Rufa through the glass doors, fixed her gaze somewhere in the middle distance, waved enthusiastically, and shouted, "Daddy! Daddy!"

There were a couple of indulgent smiles, but nobody took much notice of the two girls finding their father. They had passed the table. They were inside.

Rufa was breathless with surprise, and full of admiration. "Nancy, you're brilliant—I've never seen such utterly barefaced cheek."

Nancy felt the knot of hair at her neck. "That's as brilliant as I get, darling. You'll have to work out what the fuck we do next."

Rufa glanced around. New arrivals were making their way to a door on the left of the hall, shrugging off coats and wraps. They followed three middle-aged women along a passage hung with old engravings, to a small sitting room that had been turned into a cloakroom. Two smiling Filipino women in black dresses helped them out of their coats.

Rufa smoothed down her velvet skirts, rapturously inhaling the scented atmosphere—beeswax, potpourri, French perfume on incredibly clean flesh. A wrinkled lady with white hair, wearing dark blue chiffon, smiled at them kindly.

"What lovely frocks!"

Rufa said, "Thank you," with a plummeting heart. This was the moment she knew their dresses were all wrong. Everybody else here seemed to be old, and rather dowdy. Clare's superb gowns looked theatrical, showy, artificial. Still, it was too late to turn back now. And she was not going to worry Nancy. She shook back her hair, wishing Roshan had let her wear it in a seemly plait, and held her head a little higher.

They returned to the hall, and sauntered into the room where everyone was gathering before the concert. This turned out to be a library. Just inside the door, a small table held a heap of glossy programs. They each took one, and Nancy took a glass of champagne from the tray.

Rufa murmured, "Didn't we agree not to drink?"

"You and Roshie did. I agreed to no such thing. I'm not turning down free champagne."

"All right. Just don't get plastered." Rufa glanced around the room, searching for Roshan and the photographer sent by his newspaper. The library was large, with two windows looking out across the square at the park. Two walls were lined with books. These appeared ponderous and scholarly, but were mostly old bound volumes of the *Illustrated London News*. The other walls were hung with oil paintings of the earl's ancestors. Rufa thought wistfully of the mouse-ravaged drawing room at Melismate, where only five Hasty ancestors remained—those that had proved too ugly or too badly painted to sell. The Zed had called them the Old Lags. It was impossible not to make comparisons. When gentility decayed, she thought, it went off with an awful smell.

"There he is," Nancy said. "Come on."

She had spotted Roshan making faces at them from the shadow of an icy white marble fireplace. A large, red-faced man with a camera stood beside him, staring round with a mixture of resentment and contempt. Two other photographers were moving discreetly among the bony, dowdy, beak-nosed dowagers—it was easy to see why Roshan's editor did not want these people all over his glamorous and somewhat vulgar Style pages, even if they were authentic toffs.

"You got in!" Roshan whispered, almost skipping with glee. "Isn't this fabulous?"

"This? It's a collection of dull old farts," Nancy said. "I feel like organizing a game of musical bumps, to get the party going."

"You're in, and you're being seen. That, surely, is the point."

Rufa, taking care not to stare, glanced round the room. The slender man, with the neat gray hair, was still gazing at them thoughtfully. She turned her back on him. "Where's the earl?"

"Not here yet," Roshan said. "He's probably shut away inside some inner sanctum—there are always hierarchies within hierarchies. I daresay the truly elect are hobnobbing with the princess behind closed doors. This is Pete, by the way."

The photographer ran a finger round the inside of his collar. "Hi, gels. Where d'you want 'em, Rosh?"

Roshan nodded toward the door. "Here's the earl—see if you can get a couple of him with the princess."

Pete let out a slow chuckle. "Princess Pushy. I like her." Unhurried, he ambled off through the crowd. Rufa rather envied his confidence.

"He's not the snapper I would have chosen," Roshan told Nancy, "but let's be thankful for small mercies—at least he owns a dinner jacket."

Rufa was looking at Earl Sheringham. Her heart jumped nervously, but she felt nothing—except awe, at the huge gulf between breaking into this man's house, and persuading him to marry her. He was paler and smaller than his pictures; elegant in a brittle way, like a precious, faded piece of tapestry. When he turned toward the princess, his smile was gentle and charming. When he turned away to survey everyone else, his face became blank and cold. His gaze met Rufa's for a second, without changing its expression. Rufa felt less than the dust, and prickled all over with anger and embarrassment. She remembered what The Zed had always said about people who looked down their noses—"When William Rufus gave the demesne of Melismate to your ancestors, that guy's forebears were still pulling up turnips."

Pete shuffled back to the fireplace, changing his roll of film. "Let's get the gels by the mantelpiece, then I can bugger off."

"Good idea," Roshan said. "Chat to each other, you two. Try to look as if you're having a whale of a time—I'm going to paint you as hedonistic young Sloanes."

"Let's sing the Internationale," Nancy muttered. "I'm feeling distinctly downtrodden."

Rufa smiled at her. "You don't look it. You actually look rather amazing."

"You're too kind, darling, but I can't wait to get back to my own planet. When you're married to that man, for God's sake don't let him give any more parties like this."

Pete danced and ducked around them, firing the camera rapidly, without any apparent effort or artistry. "That's nice—put your hair back, love— yeah, that's great. Rosh, d'you want one with Pushy and Lord Snooty in the background?"

"Yes," Roshan said. "And remember, nobody must look posed. These are meant to be party shots." He took each girl by the wrist, and moved them into their new positions. Pete fired more shots. The whole operation had taken less than ten minutes, but they were already attracting curious glances.

"Wonderful," Roshan declared. "Just get me a couple of Radu Lupu, and you can call it a night."

"Who?"

"Dark hair, talking to Pushy."

"Oh, right." Unhurried as ever, Pete strode through the crowds.

"Next time," Rufa said, "I'm coming as a photographer. Nobody's gawping at him."

"No, and nobody will remember him afterward," Nancy said shrewdly. "It's his camera they're all sucking up to."

Rufa was covertly watching the earl, wondering how on earth to begin the mysterious process of making him fall in love with her. Should she faint at his feet? Display her adoration of music? Find some slim pretext to engage him in earnest conversation? If she could only get past that frigid air of superiority—

The earl moved away from the princess and the pianist. His eyes made one more chilly circuit of the room. Once again, his gaze snagged against Rufa's. Her spine turned cold. This time, there was a definite hint of opprobrium in his bad-smell expression. Roshan's friend Hermione—pretty and vacuous, and obviously harassed—approached him. She was with one of the forbidding men, from the table out in the hall. The earl turned his back on Rufa to talk to them. She shivered with relief.

The relief did not last long. The man from the hall table looked over the earl's shoulder, directly at Rufa. His expression changed to one of unmistakable annoyance, mixed with scorn. Rufa's ears rang. Oh God, she thought, remove me from this place. She knew what people meant when they said they wished the ground would swallow them. She had imagined she could handle something like this, and the mortification was absolutely piercing. She nudged Nancy.

"What? What is it?"

Wordlessly, Rufa nodded in the direction of the man, now walking purposefully toward them.

Nancy said, "Whoops."

The man came close to them, and addressed Roshan. The quietness of his voice gave it a disagreeable intimacy. "I don't believe these ladies, or you, are on our guest list."

Feebly, Roshan said, "I have a press pass—"

"We've only invited selected music critics," the man said. "We certainly did not give you permission to do a photo shoot. I think you and your—your models had better leave immediately. Don't you?"

"Drat," murmured Nancy, "we haven't done the topless shots yet."

Rufa, severely weakened by embarrassment, gave a great snort of terrified laughter. She caught Roshan's eye, and they both began shaking helplessly.

The man's annoyance deepened. He put a hand on Nancy's bare elbow, as if arresting her, and marched her toward the door. Rufa and Roshan stumbled after them, yelping with suppressed giggles. Rufa—while weeping with laughter—felt she was living through five minutes that would haunt her until the day she died. The horror of it was so huge, it was funny.

And then, near the door, one of her shoes came off. She stumbled, and halted to pick it up. The arresting man looked balefully over his shoulder. Rufa froze, not knowing whether he wanted her to follow with her satin shoe, or leave it marooned on Earl Sheringham's carpet. Heads turned all over the room; you could almost hear them.

A cool hand touched her sleeve. The elegant man with thick gray hair, who had been watching her every time she looked at him, was holding out her shoe.

"There you are, Cinderella," he said quietly, smiling.

"Thank you." Rufa took it, and limped over to the door, with burning cheeks and eyes wet with laughing.

The arresting man did not throw them out through the front door. He shooed them down the narrow passage leading to the cloakroom, and tried to push them past it.

Nancy whipped away her arm. "Excuse me, we have to collect our coats." Without waiting for permission, she swept into the cloakroom. The Filipino women were sitting in armchairs, with cups of tea. One of them leaped up guiltily, and scrabbled for their taffeta coats in the racks of glossy, scented furs. She did not need to ask which coats were theirs. They stood out a mile.

Rufa remembered that she had put a pound for a cloakroom tip into her evening purse. She advanced into the room long enough to take her coat, and place the pound in an empty saucer. Both the Filipino women grinned at her uncertainly.

"Will you come now, please?" The man was testy. "You can leave through the kitchen."

At the end of the passage was a door, which opened suddenly into the steely glitter of a large kitchen. Out there, the light was soft and golden. In here, it was hard and silver. A woman in an apron and two waiters gawped at them, as the man hustled them toward the back door, with very little ceremony.

He jerked it open. There was a rush of cold air, which made them all cringe. "I hardly need to add," he said, "that you will not be permitted to use any of those photographs."

It was over. The three of them were shivering on the other side of the back door, in the outer darkness of the mews behind Sheringham House.

❉ ❉ ❉

"That," Rufa said, "was the most utterly wince-making experience of my entire life."

Wendy was bristling with indignation. "Honestly, they might have let you stay. You looked perfectly lovely, and you weren't doing any harm."

An hour and a half after being bounced, they were all crowded round Wendy's kitchen table, sharing greasy packets of fish and chips. Roshan had removed his dinner jacket, bow tie, and stiff collar. He sat in his shirt-sleeves and red braces, delicately dipping chips into a plate of mayonnaise. Nancy and Rufa were in their dressing gowns. Max, summoned by Roshan's mobile phone, had driven round to the mews to collect the strayed revelers. It had been his idea to pick up a take-away on the way home. Roshan had got out of the car to buy the food, and his elegant appearance had caused a small stir at Captain Nemo's Fish Bar in the Kentish Town Road.

Max's hand accidentally brushed against Nancy's, as they both reached for the last piece of battered haddock. "I don't think we should write the evening off as a complete waste of time," he said. "We should think of it as a learning experience. A dress rehearsal."

"It was our bad luck to choose a party where they were so strict about gate-crashers," Nancy said, with her mouth full. "The great question is, have we messed up with the earl? I mean, should we carry on chasing him, or cross him off the list?"

Rufa frowned. "You can marry him if you like. I'm having nothing more to do with him. Nobody has ever dared to look at me like that." She was pale with outrage.

"Absolutely," Roshan declared. He could not bear Rufa to be slighted.

"I'll choose myself another target, from our list of also-rans. In the meantime, Max is quite right—we must at least have learned something."

"I'm surprised it hasn't put you off altogether," Wendy said.

"Just the opposite. I'm more determined than ever. While I'm selecting my new target, we must concentrate all our efforts on Tiger Durward."

Nancy sighed. "But if Lord Snooty wouldn't give you the time of day, what chance will I have with the big lummox?"

"You'll knock his socks off." Rufa smiled warmly at her sister. "If I've learned anything tonight, it's that you are our major asset—you were magnificent."

"Hear hear!" cried Roshan. "I thought I'd do myself an injury when you made that topless crack."

The reminder made them all laugh yet again. They had been in paroxysms since telling Max, who had laughed so much he had to stop near Oxford Circus for a pee. Rufa did not know why it struck them all as hilarious. Perhaps, she thought, because it put things in proportion, and helped them to feel they had kept a little dignity.

"It's a damned shame you won't be able to use the pictures," Max said. "I bet they're gorgeous."

Roshan became businesslike. "I'm afraid we went over the top with those frocks. We have to strike the perfect balance between being nicely noticeable, and positively sticking out."

Rufa stood up to make them second cups of tea. "We need to move downmarket. Whatever The Zed said about our wonderful ancestry, it obviously isn't visible to the naked eye. Next time, we need legitimate entry to an event where class doesn't matter so much. A place where photographers are welcome, and simple faith means more than Norman blood."

"Simple faith, or bosoms," Nancy said.

Roshan beamed, delighted that the Game was still up and running. "Leave it to me."

Chapter Nine

The official invitation to the Cumbernauld Foundation Ball said White Tie. Rufa was alarmed by this, but Roshan said not to worry—it was a ludicrous piece of affectation, since most of the guests would be aspirational suburbanites who had not yet twigged that the 1980s were over. "All it really means is permission to wear more glitter—half the women will use it as an excuse to give their big puffy wedding dresses another outing. If you two wear your Clares, you'll make everyone else look like trash."

Rufa, after last time, was anxious to know as much as possible in advance. "What if someone recognizes us from Sheringham House?"

He snorted. "Highly unlikely. None of those toffee-noses would be seen dead at a do like this. You must understand, it couldn't be more of a contrast. They want to make lots of money, they'll sell the tickets to absolutely anyone, and they adore the press. It's perfect for a spot of Tiger hunting."

Lady Helen Durward, mother of the more famous Tiger, was a patroness of the charity. Tiger (who had recently split up with his soap-star girlfriend) was to be at her table, along with Anthea Turner, who had agreed to draw the raffle, and Alan Titchmarsh, who was to conduct the auction.

"So it's not quite top-drawer?" Nancy asked.

Roshan said, "It's not even in the bureau. This time, we are entering at the highest level—I have a delightful acquaintance on the organizing committee." This was Anita Lupovnik, wife of the well-known Bond Street jeweler. Lupovnik's had generously donated a pair of diamond earrings for the auction. Anita had said she would be only too happy to let Pete take as many photographs as he liked.

"Fear not, we won't be getting the bum's rush again," Roshan said complacently. "Even if we strip naked and lick champagne out of each other's navels."

Egged on by Nancy, he hired himself white tie and tails. On the evening of the ball, he strutted down Wendy's staircase, singing.

Nancy, Rufa, and Max, assembled in the hall, burst into a round of applause. Unexpectedly, Roshan was ravishing. The tailcoat, and the expanse of boiled shirtfront, set off the grace of his slight figure.

Rufa kissed him. "You look like Fred Astaire. I wish Wendy could see you." (Wendy was in Kidderminster, staying with an unfortunate friend who had taken an overdose of Saint-John's-wort.)

Nancy gave Roshan a friendly slap on the bottom. "You look prettier than we do—where did you get it all?"

"He mugged a concert pianist," Max said.

Roshan shot out his white cuffs, to display his gold cuff links. "I went to an excellent hire shop near Savile Row. Everyone else will have gone to Moss Bros.—a white-tie affair brings on a positively biblical renting of garments. I wanted something a little more recherché."

Max tweaked one of his tails. "Must have set you back a bit."

"I'm putting it on expenses, you poor fool. Unlike BBC Radio, my boss can afford it. Now—" Roshan turned briskly to the girls. "Stand under that woefully inadequate light, and let's have a look at you."

That afternoon he had called Rufa from work, to tell her that he had been struck by a lightning bolt of inspiration—they must swap dresses. Rufa and Nancy had been thrilled by this idea. Though Nancy was two inches shorter than Rufa, and differently distributed, they were the same dress size. It was intriguing to see how the characters of the two gowns were transformed. The yellow crepe fishtail hung loosely upon Rufa's elongated frame, giving her the brittle elegance of a 1930s film star. Her thick auburn hair was wound into a ballet-dancer's chignon, exposing her back and shoulder blades. Nancy's curves gave a tactile sexiness to the sober bronze velvet, and her loose red hair was a magnificent riot.

"I'm a genius," Roshan announced. "And you two are simply divine. You'll break hearts right and left—they'll have to form an orderly queue."

The ballroom was a gigantic, flower-decked hangar on Park Lane, thronged with people. Instead of a genteel hum, the conversation was a roar, seasoned with brays and shrieks. There was a large and noisy band. From the top of the stairs that swept down to the dance floor, Rufa and Nancy gazed across a seething mass of black tailcoats and pastel tulle. As Roshan had predicted, several of the younger women sported low-cut meringues that were obviously expensive wedding dresses.

Nancy murmured, "This is more like it. We might even have a good time."

Pete the photographer, instructed by Roshan, had snapped them sipping champagne in several careless, hedonistic poses. He had now joined a battery of other photographers, to snap Anthea Turner beside the tombola stall.

"I'm glad we get dinner," Nancy said. "My stomach's growling like Vesuvius."

Round tables ringed the dance floor, bathed in silver flecks shed by the revolving disco lights overhead. There was an insistent, inviting undersmell of food.

"Come on," Rufa said, starting down the staircase. "Let's have a look at the seating plan, so we know where to find Tiger."

Nancy put a hand on her arm. "Wait a minute, I need another drink."

"Nance, please—we're here on business."

"I haven't forgotten. I'm more attractive with a drink inside me. And it'll take away the bad taste left by that old bum of an earl."

She knew this would persuade Rufa, who had been infuriated by the expression on Sheringham's face when he looked at her. The fury covered deep hurt. She had remembered The Zed quoting the classic definition of a gentleman: someone who never gives offense accidentally. Evidently, types like Sheringham were masters at giving offense on purpose.

"All right," she said. "We might as well get as sloshed as everyone else."

"Let me do the honors," Roshan said. "You need to save your money for gloves and stockings." There was a bar set into the wall nearby. He went to join the other tailcoats, leaving Nancy and Rufa to mop up admiring glances at the top of the stairs. Rufa was glad to note that Nancy was getting plenty of these—how could Tiger Durward, or any other available, minted male, resist her?

Roshan returned with more champagne. Rufa sipped her cautiously—her second glass—and found it delicious. Her spirits lifted. This time, everything seemed to be going beautifully. She went down the great staircase, feeling festive and elegant. This was exactly the sort of scene she had imagined when she first dreamed of the Marrying Game, under the dripping roof of Melismate.

At the foot of the stairs was a large board, displaying a list of the people at each table. Rufa quickly found their quarry among the Ds. "Here he is— Mr. Timothy Durward, Table Twelve."

"And here we are, right next door at number eleven," Roshan said. "I told you dear old Anita would do us proud."

Nancy pressed against him, to read over his shoulder. "Oh, God—I don't believe it!" She began to laugh softly. "I don't bloody well believe it. Ru, who's the last person you want to see tonight?"

"Edward," Rufa said promptly. "Please don't tell me he's here."

"Not quite as bad, but pretty nearly. It's the Abominable Dr. Phibes."

"You're joking!"

Nancy tapped the plan with a vermilion fingernail. "Sir Gerald Bute— there can't be two of them."

Roshan asked, "Who on earth are you talking about?"

"He's the master of our local hunt," Rufa said coldly. "He didn't exactly see eye to eye with The Zed."

"Could that be awkward?"

"I don't see why. He's at Table Forty-two; he ought to be easy enough to avoid."

A worrying thought occurred to Nancy. "Suppose he sees our names, and tells Edward? We'd have a lot of explaining to do."

Rufa was pale and haughty. "Edward wouldn't give that man the time of day. And I can't think why you're fretting about Dr. Phibes, when you're about to display yourself all over a national newspaper. Let's find our table." She swept away from them through the ranks of numbered tables.

Roshan whispered to Nancy, "God, I love her when she's like this!"

"She means it, darling—it's not put on," Nancy said, shaking her head. "Somehow, our parents managed to raise a perfect highborn lady. That's why I'm determined to bag Tiger. I can handle the vulgarity of marrying for money, but she can't. It would kill her. Deep down, she's an utter romantic still hoping to fall madly in love."

"She might."

"Yes, but we can't afford to wait for it. I'll win this game because I'm more of a realist."

Roshan laughed. "You? Rubbish. You're addicted to falling in love—I've heard your history in some detail, don't forget. Rufa will make a great match, and you'll elope with the window-cleaner."

Nancy tried to be indignant, but could not help laughing. "Horrid little man. Just don't let me weaken and elope with Max."

The band stopped playing. There was scattered applause, and a general surge toward the tables. After the mortification of Sheringham House, it was very pleasant to find place cards bearing their names. At the center of each plate, on top of a folded napkin, was a program with a gold tassel.

Rufa laid her napkin across her lap, and opened the program with polite interest. "Welcome to the Thirty-seventh Cumbernauld Ball, dedicated to raising funds for the Cumbernauld Foundation. Each year, the Foundation sponsors vital research into the diseases of old age. Money raised tonight will also help with the day-to-day running of five Cumbernauld Homes."

Nancy was less interested in the good cause. She was studying the menu. "Yum—smoked salmon terrine, lamb chops, and raspberry mousse. And here's a list of the stuff they're auctioning." Besides the Lupovnik diamonds, this included dinner for two at Thwaite Manor near Guildford, a week at a villa in Greece, and someone's signed knickers.

"I'd pay a considerable amount not to be lumbered with those," Roshan said. He was suddenly still and alert, staring at the next table. Without shifting his gaze, he laid his hand on top of Nancy's, and quietly said, "There."

A tall, broad man, in black tie and a loud brocade waistcoat, was taking his place. Nancy and Rufa beheld Tiger Durward, in the considerable flesh. He had the physique of a rugger player, poised to bloat and soften as soon as the rugger ceased. His ruddy, blunt features permanently hovered on or around an inane, face-splitting grin. His laugh honked, his voice made the glassware rattle.

Uncertainly, Nancy murmured, "Is he good-looking?"

"No," Rufa said.

Roshan said, "Yes, in a way. That sort of energy can be very compelling. And you must admit, his body's excellent."

"Nance—" Rufa leaned across Roshan. "You don't have to go through with it."

Nancy was looking thoughtfully at Tiger, trying to fit him into mental pictures of romance and marriage. "If I lose my courage at this stage, what the hell are we doing here? And I really think he has distinct possibilities."

"Are you sure?" Rufa could not imagine many things more ghastly than being yoked to Tiger Durward.

"You know me. I actively prefer the simple ones. They're usually kind-hearted."

Roshan filled their glasses with white wine from one of the bottles on the table. "Yes, in an animalistic sort of way—like a big dog that slobbers all over your shoes."

Their hostess, Anita Lupovnik, arrived at the table, dressed in blue lace with a blazing diamond collar. She greeted Nancy and Rufa with an easy kindness and lack of condescension that made Nancy privately determined never to hang out in the top drawer again, if she could possibly avoid it—the slightly lower drawers seemed to attract a far better class of person.

Dinner passed pleasantly, though it was impossible to forget they were here on business, with Tiger's loud laugh honking out every few minutes. By the time the raspberry mousses arrived, he was barking drunk behind a forest of bottles.

Coffee (tepid and sour) appeared, and the band started up again.

Roshan signaled to Pete, who was smoking and looking bored on the other side of the table. "We'll want some pictures of the girls dancing—with Tiger, if he can still stand up."

The younger, noisier guests were running onto the dance floor. At the next table, Tiger stood, and gaped around him, swaying slightly.

Nancy tipped a saucer of foil-wrapped mints into her bag, to send to Linnet. She rose. "I think this is my cue to introduce the notion of dancing into that solitary brain cell, before it shuts down."

Pete grinned, taking the cover off his camera. "If he gropes you, I'll deck him for you." Upper-class women were an aggravating mystery to him, but he had decided he liked Nancy.

"Thanks," she said. "It's nice to know there's someone to defend my honor."

Rufa watched, fascinated and fearful, as Nancy shimmered across the few yards of carpet to Tiger's side. All she had to do was brush against him, and murmur, "Sorry—"

Tiger made a series of dazed, effortful faces, drawing her into focus. Nancy walked in slow motion, waiting for the thought to form.

He put out his hand. "Hi. Want to dance, or something?"

And it really was as simple as that. Nancy introduced herself. Tiger, not listening, took her elbow, and steered her out onto the floor. Roshan and Pete sprang up, to bag the star shots of the evening. The band was playing "Red Red Wine." Tiger, as if someone had pressed a button inside him saying Dance, instantly began thrashing and leaping. Nancy caught Rufa's eye. She was laughing, ducking Tiger's windmill arms. Rufa was glad she found it amusing. It had been easy, back at home, to theorize about putting up with unattractive men. The reality of it was another matter entirely.

A little anxious about Nancy, but generally satisfied that the evening was going according to plan, Rufa rose, and made her way back up the staircase toward the ladies' cloakroom. There was not much for her to do now, except pose for another photograph. How long they would have to stay here depended upon Tiger, and how much he liked Nancy. This was difficult to judge—Rufa only hoped his romantic technique was better than his dancing.

The ladies' cloakroom was large, and as brightly lit as was consistent with flattery. There was a long row of pink cubicle doors, facing a row of gleaming sinks and mirrors. Half a dozen women stood in front of these, repairing elaborate makeup and unfamiliar hairstyles. The carpets were thick, there was a strong, powdery smell of mingled scents and air freshener. Here, the noise of the ball was reduced to a muffled thrum.

Rufa emerged from her cubicle, and faced one of the mirrors. Her hair was still fine, but her lipstick needed attention—Roshan had insisted on a stronger, redder shade than she normally liked. Frowning slightly, she leaned forward to apply the overpriced stick to her lips.

A cubicle door banged, and a lanky, middle-aged lady with neat gray hair took the sink beside Rufa. In the mirror, their eyes met. Rufa froze.

Lady Bute, wife of the Abominable Dr. Phibes, gaped at her for a moment. Her expression of shock hardened into one of righteous outrage. She hissed, "You!"

"Hello—" Rufa did not know what else to say.

"Well. Rufa Hasty. I must say I'm surprised to see you here." Lady Bute unscrewed a lipstick, in a vicious shade of pink. "It's not where I'd expect to see the daughter of someone apparently too poor to pay a debt."

Rufa stiffened furiously. How dared she bring this up? The Zed had always maintained that the Butes were essentially vulgar. "We are poor, Lady Bute. Thank you for reminding me."

"Your father owed us the cost of an expensive saddle, not to mention a pair of jodhpurs, after that disgraceful incident at that Boxing Day meet. He refused to pay—with an astonishing lack of civility."

"My father is dead," Rufa said.

"Yes, and that's the only reason my husband didn't pursue the matter. He heard you were selling up, and decided there was no point. But if you have enough money to swan around at a ball, in an obviously expensive dress—well, that puts a different complexion on the matter, doesn't it?"

Rufa's voice was tight with anger. She needed the anger, to boil away the threat of tears. "I didn't realize there had been a demand for money. Tell Sir Gerald to put it in writing. We'll add him to the list of creditors."

"Will there be enough to pay the creditors?"

"No."

"You're as rude as he was," Lady Bute snapped. "He was a very rude man, and I don't see why we should all pretend to forget it, simply because he's dead. He had nothing but contempt for his neighbors. That antihunting pose of his—"

"It wasn't a pose."

"Rubbish. It was calculated to annoy, and to cause trouble."

The door of a cubicle opened behind them. Anita Lupovnik emerged, rummaging in her sequined evening bag for a lipstick. Rufa and Lady Bute fell into shaking, incandescent silence.

Anita was plump, with vivid, humorous dark eyes. "I couldn't help hearing, and now I have to know—what was the disgraceful incident?"

Lady Bute bridled, and pointedly said nothing.

Rufa said, "My father put superglue on her husband's saddle."

Anita stared for a moment, then let out a shriek of delighted laughter. She leaned against the sink, and laughed until her mascara began to bleed.

White with rage, Lady Bute swept out of the cloakroom.

Rufa found that her back and shoulders were knotted with tension. When Lady Bute had gone, she relaxed, and some of her fury fizzled away. Enough was left, however, to give her a feeling of lightness and power. If it hadn't been for Anita, she might have melted into tears—she felt like kissing the woman. Instead, she smiled. "Her husband's the master of our local hunt. My father didn't approve of hunting. He said glueing up Sir Gerald's ass might stop him talking through it."

Anita's howls built to another crescendo, then subsided into giggles. "Oh, God, my makeup—I'm as pissed as a lemon." There was a frilled box of tissues in front of the mirror. She pulled one out, and began dabbing carefully at her eyes. "You look so bloody refined. I didn't imagine you knew words like *ass*. It's made my evening."

Rufa laughed. "I'm glad, since you paid for our dinner. I was going to thank you later, but I might as well do it now—it's awfully nice of you. We're having a wonderful time."

"Don't mention it. You'll find more coffee and a brandy back at the table. I'll join you when I've repaired the damage."

Rufa sailed out of the cloakroom like Boadicea, warmed with the knowledge that The Zed would have been proud of her.

At the top of the grand staircase, she met Roshan. He was breathless and agitated. "I've lost them."

"What?"

"Nancy and Tiger—they went off together. I've scoured that dance floor like a fucking Brillo pad, and I can't find them anywhere."

"Oh." Rufa considered this. "Well, that's good, isn't it? I mean, they must be getting on well."

Roshan did not stop glancing round anxiously. "I don't like losing sight of them. To tell the truth, Nancy didn't look all that keen—she was making faces at me—"

"She wanted to be rescued! Oh, Roshan, why didn't you just run up and grab her?"

"I tried, but they just vanished!"

Rufa gathered up her skirts determinedly. Nancy did not make rescuing signals lightly. "Show me where you last saw them."

He led her down the stairs. Rufa, eyes narrowed, searched the writhing figures on the floor, and the people waiting for the auction at the tables.

She asked, "Exactly where?"

"Exactly here. Next minute, they were gone."

"What's behind the stairs?"

"Just one of the service entrances, or something—oh, Rufa, don't be silly—" Roshan sprang to follow Rufa into the obscure shadowland under the stairs. "He's hardly going to take her here!"

There was a pair of swing doors, covered with dark red vinyl. Taking no notice of Roshan, Rufa swept through them. They opened into a carpeted passage, meanly lit, with three doors on one side. (She guessed they were offices of some sort—yet again, she had ended up below stairs.)

"No, for the last bloody time, I won't—I will not give you 'a snog,' you great slavering—let me go!"

It was Nancy's voice, rising from irritation to anger. Rufa pushed open the nearest door. Nancy, pressed uncomfortably against a bare desk, was furiously dodging Tiger Durward's fleshy sink plunger of a mouth.

"Look, I don't want to knee you in the nuts, but if you don't let me go—"

Rufa's simmering anger flashed out like white lightning. Yelling "You bastard, you take your hands off my sister!" she flew at Tiger's back and dug her fingers hard into his eyes. He roared. Both his hands flew to his face, and Nancy wriggled free.

She hugged Rufa. "I never was so pleased to see you in my life—where the hell did you learn that?"

"Edward, of course," Rufa said crisply. "He taught me basic self-defense when one of my dinner party men got fresh."

Tiger, his fists still balled in his eyes, let out another bellow and blundered blindly across the room. Both sisters regarded him with disgust.

"I couldn't stop him," Nancy said, smoothing her hair. "It happened so fast. He's as strong as a bloody ox. He just dragged me in here, and now I suppose my lipstick's ruined."

"Nancy, if you marry this hideous baboon, I will personally stand up in church and contest the banns."

"Thank you, darling," Nancy said. "That won't be necessary. Let's just make sure my next target isn't a lecherous piss-artist."

Tiger groaned loudly. He shouted, "Bitch. That really fucking hurts!"

Roshan had been standing in the doorway, gaping. This insult snapped him into his senses. "It was meant to hurt!" he hissed. "Dear God, you're not fit to kiss the hems of their dresses! Girls, go upstairs and tell security—I'll stay here with him. And you'd better call the police."

Nancy took his arm affectionately. "Darling, you're far too weedy and delicate to subdue this monster. And we don't need to involve the emergency services. I'm fine, and he's incapable. Let's just go home."

Tiger pulled his hands from his face. The first person his bloodshot eyes fixed upon was Roshan. He became still, and an eerie calm settled around him. There was a long moment of silence.

In a low voice that was neither barking nor slurred, Tiger said, "I've been looking for you all my life."

His eyes rolled back into his head, and he passed out.

Once again, the four of them were gathered round Wendy's kitchen table for a postmortem. This time, however, Max was not laughing. He looked at Rufa with a new respect.

"If you hadn't come in at that moment—well, you're not going out to anything else without an armed escort, that's all. I'd have killed him."

"I didn't need an armed escort, I had Ru," Nancy pointed out, leaning over to squeeze her hand. " 'For there is no friend like a sister / In calm or stormy weather, / To cheer one on the tedious way, / To fetch one if one goes astray—' "

"Don't!" Roshan pleaded, his large brown eyes swimming with tears. "If you quote any more of that, I'm finished."

Rufa and Nancy, who had been drifting dangerously toward solemnity, started laughing. Nancy said, "I wish we'd had Pete with us, though. I don't mean to protect us—I mean, wouldn't it be great to have a picture?"

Roshan blew his nose, and gave her a watery smile. "The sight of him, sprawled on the floor—we didn't know whether to leave him, or give him the kiss of life."

Max asked, "What did you do with the shitbag, in the end?"

"Before we could decide, he woke up and started sobbing."

"He followed us out of there like a lamb," Rufa said. "We left him in a chair under the stairs. He was sobbing so hard, we didn't have the heart to make a fuss."

"All the same," Max said, "he owes Nancy one hell of an apology."

To everyone's surprise, the apology arrived next morning. Rufa opened the front door to find a man holding two large hand-tied bouquets of tiger lilies, for Miss Rufa and Miss Nancy Hasty. Rather charmed, in spite of herself, Rufa thanked the man, and was about to close the door when he announced that he had one more delivery. He went back to his van and returned with an immense basket of blood-red roses, decorated with great slippery bows of scarlet silk ribbon. Rufa had to push some of the stems back to get it through the front door. Tied to the basket's handle was a white envelope, addressed to Mr. Roshan Lal.

She and Nancy laughed at this, but Roshan was shaken. "Anita must have given him my name and address—" He pulled the card from the envelope. It said, in clear round handwriting: "I meant it. We have to meet again."

The three of them, crammed into Wendy's hall beside the monstrous tower of roses, looked at each other with awe.

Roshan whispered, "He meant it!"

"If you'll excuse my French," Nancy said, "fuck this for a Game of Marrying."

Rufa would not admit defeat. Their first two outings had been dismal failures, but she insisted that they had to regroup to try again. "We'll just work our way down the list, until we find someone who doesn't either despise us, or fall madly in love with Roshan."

Wendy, back from Kidderminster, was highly impressed by the basket of roses. "I suppose, if Tiger is secretly gay, that would explain his terrible record with women. He's in denial."

"Thank you, Dr. Freud," Roshan said. "Not anymore. He's started ringing me at work—he wants me to have dinner with him. As if I would." The last sentence was very faintly tinged with wistfulness. He added bracingly, "Beast."

The Sunday after the ball, his Style section had printed the hedonistic photographs of Nancy and Rufa. Spread across the page in glorious color, the two of them looked—as Max said—good enough to eat. Rufa thought this must help. Rose had been absolutely dazzled, to the extent of ringing them on the off chance that they had some spare cash.

The sober truth, however, was that their funds were dwindling horribly fast. Rufa was wondering how she could find people to cook for. Nancy was, once again, threatening to get herself a job behind a bar. Rufa was even more against this after the publication of the pictures. The weather was cold and wet. Tufnell Park was dark and perpetually dripping.

"This Game is like snakes and ladders," Nancy observed, one dispiriting morning, gazing dully out of the bedroom window at the traffic swishing past. "The minute we get our feet on a ladder, we slide down a huge snake, straight back to square one. We've got to insinuate ourselves into some more parties, while we can still afford the bus fares."

Roshan, who felt rather guilty about rousing a target's latent tendencies, kept them supplied with magazines. Rufa, feeling horribly poor and unconnected, was dutifully poring over *Harpers & Queen* on her bed.

Nancy said, "First, the target has to see us. Then he has to ask one of us out. Then he has to decide that he's ready to get married, and be deeply enough in love to pay The Zed's debts. It might take months."

"Oh, God!" Rufa gasped suddenly.

"Well, we have to face it, darling. Rome wasn't built in a day."

"Look! Look at this!" Rufa, her face alight, leaped off her bed, and slapped "Jennifer's Diary" down in front of Nancy.

Nancy stared at the page. "It's Berry!"

"Yes, it's Berry—his father's a lord, and just look at his house!" She started to laugh. "Ran didn't bother to mention it, of course, or he could have saved us a lot of trouble." She was reading the captions of the photographs over Nancy's shoulder. "Shit, he's engaged—I forgot about that. Just our luck."

Lord and Lady Bridgmore were pictured in their splendid drawing room, before a Robert Adam chimneypiece and a large painting by Gainsborough, which looked sumptuous enough to buy up the whole of Melismate, debts and all. The occasion was a ball to celebrate their thirty-fifth wedding anniversary and the engagement of their son, the Honorable Hector Berowne. His fiancée—about whom he had been so reticent on Christmas Eve—worked at a famous Bond Street gallery, Soames and Pellew.

"Well, well, well," Nancy said softly. "The bluebird of happiness was right in our backyard all along. I vote we move Berry straight to the top of our list."

Rufa was uncertain. "He's engaged, though. It looks as if we've missed him."

"I don't care," Nancy said, frowning. "This is a chance from heaven, and I'm going to go for it."

"But Nance, he's engaged!"

"Tell me he didn't fancy me."

"He fancied you like mad," Rufa admitted, "but obviously not enough to change his mind about that girl."

"Just watch me," Nancy said. "You're looking at the future Lady Bridgmore."

Chapter Ten

The future Lady Bridgmore, known for the time being as Polly Muir, sat at her Hepplewhite desk in her Bond Street gallery. She was a slight, neat young woman, whose pretty features might have been rather non-descript, if her presentation had not been excellent. This morning she wore a short black skirt—her legs were admirable—and a plain white silk shirt. Her long, straight blond hair was tied back in a black velvet clip at the nape of her neck.

Understated, and then some, she always thought. When in doubt, take it off. The pursuit of understated excellence was her life's mission. Nobody appreciated the sheer hard labor involved. Soames and Pellew mainly paid her to be pretty and posh, and she could easily combine this with her real work, which was going through her immense data bank of mental lists.

Firstly, the list of those to be invited to her wedding. Polly had combed and manipulated her family history so that it could pass muster anywhere—but the fact remained that she was horribly short of suitable relations. Her great-aunt, widow of a Scottish baronet, could be flown in from Australia. The rest of that crew were hopeless, however: all twanging accents and per-matans. She must somehow fill her side of the church with well-born friends. And, somehow, she would have to persuade her father not to use his usual Christian name. Nobody was called Leslie. His middle name was Alistair, and that would sit far better with the kilt.

In Polly's life, everything had to be checked and double-checked for rightness. She spoke the language well, but not with total fluency. Was it absolutely right, for instance, to have one's wedding list at Peter Jones? Was it right to include the amusing china dog bowl, when neither she nor Berry possessed a dog? Come to that, was it absolutely right to have a wedding list at all? Polly did not mind appearing to be grasping. People born into the English upper class were the most grasping she had ever met. It was simply that one had to be careful to grasp in the right way.

When the two russet-haired goddesses walked into the gallery, Polly was resting her mind warmly upon the cozy figure of Berry. Darling old Berry, she could not wait to be married to him, and living in the sweet Chelsea house his parents were bestowing as a wedding gift. They were darlings too. Lady Bridgmore's dachshunds were darlings. The only nondarling in the glorious picture was Berry's ghastly sister, Annabel; and who cared about her? In the aristocracy, sisters did not count for much.

The redheads were examining the Victorian watercolors on the paneled walls. Polly rose behind her desk, and trained her radar on them. They wore excellent clothes—Polly owned the pale blue version of the taupe jacket. Their shoes and handbags were unmistakable Prada. As an afterthought, walking toward them across the mossy, muffling carpet, she noticed that they were both, in a purely physical sense, beautiful.

"Hello." Polly did not, of course, say "May I help you?," which smacked of the shopkeeper. She was part hostess here, and part angel-with-flaming-sword.

The girl with the redder hair (fitted taupe jacket) smiled. "Hello, I hope you don't mind us having a look. We just love smudgy pictures of flowers—and you never know when I might be making my wedding list."

Her tall, pale sister (black suit) looked alarmed, and murmured, "Nancy!"

"And anyway," Nancy went on, "we couldn't walk past when we saw the name in the window. Berry told us you worked here, and we've both been longing to meet you."

Polly's smile did not waver. Her light blue eyes were wary. "I'm sorry—I don't believe we've—"

Nancy held out her hand. "Nancy Hasty. This is my sister, Rufa."

Polly's mental computer processed the name. These were the people who had taken care of Berry when he had that idiotic adventure on Christmas

Eve. These were the well-born and romantically impoverished Hastys, who owned a tumbledown manor with a family motto over its crumbling door. She had rather hoped Berry would introduce her to the Hastys, and here they were. Dear old Berry—how like him to miss the glaring fact that the Hasty girls were stunning.

She shook their hands. Her smile stopped being conditional and became warm, making her neat, fair face very pretty. "Of course. How lovely to meet you at last. Now I can thank you properly for being so sweet to Berry."

Rufa said, "It was a pleasure. He sent our mother some gorgeous flowers."

"I know," Polly said. "That was my idea."

"I hope your Christmas improved after that."

"It was heavenly, thanks. Both of us desperately needed a rest, and your part of the country is so peaceful. Are you in London for long?"

"Well—" Rufa seemed confused.

"Just for a week or two," Nancy put in smoothly. "Until our money runs out. I expect Berry told you how poor we are."

Berry had mentioned their poverty, in a way that Polly had found rather worrying. Now she had seen for herself that theirs was a Prada-shod poverty, her last doubt died.

"I know he'd love to see you again," she said. "Look, this is wretchedly short notice—but why don't you pop along to our opening, tomorrow night?"

Polly's mind was working rapidly. Her employer, Jimmy Pellew, was always on at her to cheer up openings with ornamental people. Rufa and Nancy, merely by being beautiful, would lend the party glamour, and bring the smudgy watercolors out in a rash of red dots. "Six thirty—the usual champagne and canapés."

"What fun," Nancy said. "We'd love to."

Back on the other side of the glass door, in the sharp February wind, Rufa laughed shakily. "I don't believe it. Our first proper invitation."

Nancy took a Twix from her immaculate new handbag. "Now perhaps you'll stop going on about money, and buy those little chairs—go on!" She had seen two tiny wooden rocking chairs in the window of a toy shop, and was working on Rufa to buy them for Linnet.

"We mustn't be silly," Rufa said uncertainly.

"Go on, Ru—you know you're dying to. They're the perfect size for the Ressany Brothers. Imagine her face, when she opens the parcel."

"Oh, all right. All right," she began irritably, then started laughing. "Are you going to get the bears to order them from a bears' catalog, like you did with the tea set?"

"No, I thought I'd add a dash more drama this time," Nancy said. "The night before the post comes, I'll phone Linnet, and do the Ressanies complaining that there's nowhere nice to sit, and they're wearing away the fur on their bums."

"And then she'll get the parcel," Rufa said, relishing the thought. "Perhaps I could make a couple of little cushions. But do let's be careful—we mustn't get carried away, just because you're meeting someone who fancies you. I don't quite see what you're hoping to achieve just by seeing Berry again."

Nancy's lotus-eating lips bit into the Twix. "My wedding, darling. Call me a traditionalist, but I've always fancied myself as a June bride. We could have one of those stripy tents in the garden."

"I still think it's a waste of time," Rufa said. "Berry's engaged to that girl in the gallery. He'll never dump her for you."

"Why not, pray? What the hell's wrong with me?"

"It's nothing to do with you. He's not the type to go back on his word."

"Bum," Nancy said airily. "All men are the type."

Berry had not been looking forward to the evening. Left to himself, he would have gone home to the Fulham flat he shared with Polly, and eaten something comfortable in front of mindless television. Instead, he was doomed to hours of holding in his stomach, smiling until his face hurt, and trying not to guzzle too many tiny sausages. Thank God Polly was giving up her job when they married, and he would never have to stand through another private view.

"Victorian watercolors," Adrian mused, from the other side of the enormous Daimler. "They always make me think of table mats. But Naomi took her divorce settlement in paintings, and my sweet young decorator insists I need something uncontroversial for my walls."

"This is really good of you, Adrian," Berry said.

He had been amazed when the formidable director of his merchant bank had agreed to come to the opening. Adrian Mecklenberg was ludicrously rich, and a famous collector of beautiful objects. Polly said he was bound to buy something, since it was well known that his third wife had taken enough paintings off him to fill the Hermitage. She said that if Mecklenberg bought significantly, Jimmy Pellew would give her the Edward Lear parrot she had coveted for ages, as a wedding present. Being Polly, she already knew where she would hang it, in the Chelsea house she did not yet own.

The car slowed outside the gallery, and Berry stole a quick glance down at his shoes. How had they collected those splodges of coffee, when he had polished them like a maniac? Somehow, everything about him turned dingy and grubby when he was near Adrian. His ties unraveled, his collars wilted, his stomach popped through his shirt buttons.

Adrian sucked all available elegance from the atmosphere. He appeared taller than he was because his lean figure was perfectly proportioned. His clothes sat upon him without creasing, as if his flesh were made of something hard and chilly. The crotch of his trousers never got concertina folds at the end of the day, as Berry's did. His thick gray hair lay as sleek as a sheet of steel. Berry's brown hair was standing up like the crest of a cockatoo, despite being plastered down with a ton of fragrant gunk from Jermyn Street. He resisted an impulse to fiddle with his tie.

Polly was waiting, fresh and dustless in her green cocktail dress. She swept aside one girl holding a pile of glossy catalogs, and another bearing a tray of champagne. She kissed Berry. She kissed Adrian. She provided them both with drinks, and whisked Adrian away toward Jimmy Pellew, who was standing casually beside the most expensive paintings.

Berry's stomach leaped, with a terrible pleasure that was almost pain. Silhouetted against a faded pastoral landscape, he saw Nancy Hasty. Instantly, the whole world took on a new intensity.

Oh, God. Nancy.

What on earth was she doing here? This was delicious, and it was also dangerous. Since Christmas Eve he had flogged himself guiltily into never thinking of Nancy when he could possibly help it. Now, two months later, he had almost trained himself not to dream about her. And all that hard work was undone in a second. She was wearing a jacket that did not show her nipples. A tidal blush swept from his groin to his hairline.

"Berry—hello."

A soft voice cut across the upheaval. He turned, and was glad to see Rufa, whose beauty was of the distant, untouchable sort. She kissed his flushed cheek.

"Didn't Polly tell you we were coming?"

"No—she must have—she gets into the most tremendous state before an opening." Rufa was blessedly easy to talk to, and Berry found himself relaxing a little. "How are you all? How's my friend Linnet?"

Rufa smiled. "In fighting form, when I spoke to her last night. Nancy and I have to phone her every evening. Nance has to do a voice for Trotsky."

"Trotsky?"

"The guinea pig Ran gave her. He's rather witless and obese, but she hasn't noticed yet. How are you?"

"Oh—witless and obese as ever, thanks," Berry said cheerfully. "Do give them all my love, won't you?"

"Of course. Mummy loved the flowers, by the way."

Berry laughed. "I wanted to send something she could eat or smoke, but I couldn't make Polly understand."

"You gave us quite enough to eat. That hamper saved our lives."

"I take it things are—I mean, you both look—" Berry was struggling to be delicate.

Rufa helped him. "We've come into a little bit of money since then."

"Marvelous. So you moved to London."

"Yes. We're staying with an old friend."

In Berry's world there were always bits of money, and useful old friends. He was sincerely delighted to hear that the Hastys were, apparently, still hovering above the vortex. "Business or pleasure?"

"Mainly pleasure," Rufa said, "but I wouldn't mind finding some work. I've done a lot of cooking for dinner parties—I don't suppose you know anyone who needs an occasional caterer?"

"I'm sure I do. Polly certainly does." Berry manfully ignored a second wave of blushing. "Give me your number, and I'll ask her."

"Well, look who it is," Nancy said, stepping between them.

Berry squeaked, "Hello."

Nancy appeared not to notice the sudden falsetto. "Is Ru soliciting for work again? Don't listen to her. She does far too much as it is. She can't stop cleaning things."

"Do excuse me—" Polly appeared, apparently from nowhere. She took Berry's elbow, and pulled him away from the Hasty sisters. He experienced one split second of pure terror (Had she noticed? Could she tell?), then saw that her mind was firmly on business.

He managed to say, "What's up?"

"It's Adrian. He's ignoring the paintings. All he wants to do is stare at Rufa Hasty."

"At—Rufa?"

"Yes, you twit. Everyone but you can see she looks like a supermodel. You have to introduce them."

"Of course."

"Now! Do it now!" Polly glided away, to direct her determined sparkle at a gaggle of jeweled dowagers.

Berry snatched two prawn pastries from a passing tray, and returned to the Hastys. His guilty conscience made him brisk. "Rufa, do come and meet the big cheese from my bank. He's the most tremendous thrower of dinner parties." Not trusting himself to look at Nancy again, he steered Rufa through the press of people. "His name's Adrian Mecklenberg," he whispered into her ear. "And he's the richest person here. Think of my home life—beg him to buy something."

Rufa asked lightly, "How rich is he?"

"Rolling in it. He usually buys Picassos. And when his ex-wives make off with them, he buys more Picassos."

"Is he married at the moment?"

"No," Berry said. "He's just got shot of Number Three."

Adrian's pale gray eyes were studying Rufa, with the avidity of the expert collector. During Berry's introduction he held her hand a little longer than necessary, as if checking its weight and texture.

He said, "Hello, Cinderella."

Her polite smile disappeared. Her ears burned red. "You—you're the man who rescued my shoe. Oh, God." The watchful man, who had seen her being thrown out of Sheringham House. Would that mortifying experience never cease to haunt her?

"I thought it was you," he said. Her confusion and embarrassment appeared to please him. "I'm not at all surprised to learn your name. I thought I recognized you, at that tiresome concert. You could only be the daughter of poor old Rufus."

Forgetting her embarrassment, Rufa broke into a smile like the sun rising. "Oh, did you know him?"

"I certainly did. I'm so sorry I couldn't come to the funeral. I hadn't seen him for years—I was his fag, at school."

She laughed tremulously. "You're the boy who refused to make toast."

"The same. Though actually, I admired Rufus enormously. I think I rebelled purely to impress him—not that it worked. I can't get over how much you look like him. You're his feminine counterpart. You make me remember him with alarming exactitude."

Berry had never seen Adrian so animated. The man had a reputation for charm, which he had assumed was simply the kind of all-purpose compliment paid to the very rich. This was the charm at work, however. And it was working on Rufa.

Berry glanced round furtively at Polly, to check that this was part of the plan. Across the room, she smiled at him, and mouthed a kiss. Good.

Adrian was placing his red dot. As far as he was concerned, Rufa was sold.

❋ ❋ ❋

Adrian saw them into the taxi. The moment it had swung round the corner, Rufa murmured, "My God, I've scored a lunch!"

"Not with him?" Nancy, in the flashes of light from the streetlamps overhead, looked alarmed. "Oh Ru, you've got to be kidding. He's ancient."

"You're just jealous because I've got the first real date. With a properly available man."

"Jealous? You're welcome to him—"

Over his shoulder, the taxi driver called, "Where to, love?"

"Sorry, Tufnell Park Road, please," Rufa said. To Nancy, she added, "I couldn't say the address in front of Adrian. Was that very dishonest of me?"

"No, just incredibly snobbish—this marrying lark doesn't bring out your noblest side, old girl."

Rufa, used to the highest moral ground, stiffened defensively. "What's wrong with being asked out to lunch, and accepting? I like him. He knew The Zed."

"He gives me the creeps," Nancy said.

"He's rather nice. I think I'm looking forward to it. And I can't help feeling he's a much better bet than Berry."

"Rubbish. Berry's worth ten of him. He doesn't sleep in a coffin or avoid mirrors, for a start."

"Oh, ha ha. Adrian's charming," Rufa said crossly. "Yards better than the sort of man we imagined when we started."

"I'd just like to know what the first three wives died of."

"Well, you don't have to worry about him. I think he'll be perfect," Rufa declared. "For one thing, he's obviously a man of taste. I won't have to explain why Melismate is so important."

Nancy groaned softly. "You can't marry a man like that. You'll be miserable."

"That's entirely my business."

"Being miserable wasn't part of the deal. You know your trouble, Ru? You don't know anything about love."

"The Marrying Game isn't about love," Rufa said stubbornly.

"Oh, I know it's not about romance, or wild passion," Nancy said. "But when we started, I assumed we'd be looking for men we could be—I don't know—fond of."

"I was always afraid you wouldn't have the stamina," Rufa said. "You'd better leave it to me."

Nancy frowned. "Rufa, what's happened to you?"

"I don't know what you mean."

"You never used to be this weird." Nancy eased off her new shoes, and rummaged in her bag for her tube of Polos—her Prada handbag was already a chaos of sweet wrappers, tissues, bent combs, and hairy lipsticks. Her voice softened. "I know we've all been bonkers as conkers since The Zed died—but in your sweet, quiet way, you're the most demented by miles."

"Why did you come with me, then?" Rufa snapped. "Why did you sign up for the Game in the first place, if it's so demented? I've found a perfectly decent target—"

"No you haven't. I've got Berry, and I'm sure he'll make me deliriously happy. You can forget all about that creepy Adrian."

"I shan't do any such thing."

"OK," Nancy said. She sighed heavily, and threw three Polos into her mouth. "The battle lines have been drawn. I don't want you to marry Adrian. You don't want me to marry Berry—well, do you?"

Rufa was silent for a long moment. "This is silly," she said eventually. "We're arguing, and we both want exactly the same thing."

"If I bag Berry," Nancy said, "I'll be the winner of this Game. And my prize will be you ditching Adrian."

Another spell of silence. In the yellow glare of the streetlights, Rufa's face was white and tired. "If you bag him," she said. "If."

Chapter Eleven

The first lunch took place three days later, at the Connaught. Rufa wore the taupe jacket, over an ivory silk shirt.

Adrian gently suggested that he should order for her. "I know this menu extremely well, and I like to think I've worked out tastes and textures to blend with every sort of day. You must try my lunch for a wet day in February."

Rufa thought this was a neat way of getting round the tense ritual of studying the menu. She did wonder, however, how Adrian would have reacted if she had refused.

They ate English oysters and Dover sole. With each course, a delicate white wine appeared. Rufa sipped sparingly, just enough to hold each flavor on her tongue. It was essential not to get sloshed, and she sensed that Adrian would be repelled by gusto. He was watching her intently.

"I thought the Connaught would be a good backdrop for you," he said. "It's a timeless classic, and so are you. You're absolutely clear—like a piece of crystal, or a high, true note. You should wear more yellows and greens. Leave the autumnal tints to your sister. The jacket looked better on her."

Rufa smiled. "I wondered if you'd notice."

"When I notice a woman," Adrian said, "I always notice her clothes. You make me think of spring—you're Botticelli's *Primavera* made flesh, as I'm sure you've been told before."

He seemed to want a reply. The thing not to do, Rufa guessed, was protest. Adrian Mecklenberg would not care for a woman who flinched at a barrage of heavy compliments.

"Yes," she said. "The Zed used to say it."

Adrian said, "Botticelli would have loved the pure line of your nose, and those unspoiled lips."

There was no possible reply to this. Rufa watched his long, pale fingers caressing the stem of his glass. His movements were deft and precise, and curiously passionless.

"I own a Botticelli drawing," he said. "It's my favorite possession. Not even a wife has managed to chisel it out of me."

He smiled, to show he had not brought the subject up by mistake.

Rufa said, "Berry told me you're a famous collector."

"Rather denuded, at present. The last Mrs. Mecklenberg wouldn't budge without half my paintings."

"You must miss them."

"Yes and no," he said. "There was too much of her in them. I don't mean she chose them. The whole collection was a response to her. And she to it."

"I see." Rufa, still smiling, was wary. Where was this leading?

"All my wives adore art," Adrian said. "Two of them studied at the Courtauld. I'm obviously drawn to women who are profoundly affected by art. As I think you are."

Rufa changed her smile slightly, to accommodate the sudden intimacy. This, she thought, was like being interviewed for a job. Her qualifications—breeding and beauty—had got her past the first stage. Now, she was being examined more closely, to check that she would fit the corporate image.

"In any case—" Adrian began again abruptly, after a short silence. "I'm looking forward to beginning again. A new collection for a new era. Perhaps I'll only collect paintings of redheads."

It was difficult to smile graciously while eating fish. Adrian's compliments were cool and casual: statements of observation. It was a very deliberate form of wooing, and also a kind of test, to see if she could take admiration without squirming. Her role was to listen, to accept. Protests, even modest ones, would count as resistance. Rufa already knew that any form of resistance or argument would be simply incomprehensible to him.

"I cannot understand," Adrian said, "how Berry managed to keep you a secret."

"My brother-in-law was at school with him, but we only met last Christmas." Rufa told the story of the pond and the lost keys, and felt she was making progress when Adrian chuckled. She liked him more because he evidently liked Berry.

"A thoroughly decent sort," he pronounced. "A good egg of the traditional kind. It's virtually impossible to dislike a man with a talent for slapstick." Berry was dismissed, with a pat and a biscuit.

Rufa said, "Polly seems nice."

"Ah, Polly. Radiant with love for the title and the house, and the peerless collection of eighteenth-century paintings. She's not in love with Berry himself, of course—not in the accepted sense. That sort of woman doesn't fall in love in the ordinary way. She's programmed to hold out for the whole package. My first wife was one of those."

This was uncomfortable territory. "Surely Berry wouldn't want to marry her, if she's like that!" protested Rufa.

Adrian was watching her narrowly. "You're missing the point. A marriage is a contract, after all. It exists because each party has something the other needs. What Polly provides for Berry, in return for the title, is probably entirely satisfactory. Sex, affection, companionship. Effective management."

Rufa did not like the way the conversation was going. Was Adrian telling her she had been rumbled as a gold digger? Or was it a veiled assurance that her emotions were irrelevant to the final deal? She felt herself being appraised and considered and held up to the light. It was humbling, and she was hardly in a position to blame him for it.

Something in the defensive set of her shoulders pleased Adrian. He smiled, and, for the first time, it reached his eyes.

"I've shocked you," he said softly. "What a delightful experience. I forgot I was talking to a romantic Hasty. If ever I wanted you to marry me, I'd have to make you fall in love with me first."

Afterward, he saw her into a taxi, and put twenty pounds into the hand of the driver. He spoke of their next meeting. It was to be another lunch, but it would involve a drive out to a little place he knew in the country. Without a single kiss or caress, Adrian was assuming a courtship.

Staring sightlessly out of the rain-spattered window, Rufa assessed the situation. She had done amazingly well, with almost no effort. Adrian was beginning a process, at the end of which Rufa would be in love with him. Over coffee, she had told him something about the affair with Jonathan, leaving out the subsequent death of her libido.

Adrian guessed, however, and appeared to like the idea of waking the Sleeping Beauty. She wondered if he had the power to make her fall in love with him, and tried hard to imagine it. She wished (hoped) it would happen. He was charming, and very good-looking, if rather ancient. She had nerved herself to put up with much worse, for the sake of the Marrying Game. As far as she could be, she was attracted, and intrigued. Up to now this was all he had seemed to want from her. Perhaps this was a man who could lead her back to love, stage by stage?

It could never approach the ecstatic, all-consuming love she had felt for Jonathan—but she did not want to go through that again. Sex with Adrian, when she had eaten her lunches and dinners—like a barrister at the Inns of Court—was bound to be refined and highly bearable.

Rufa felt a little careworn when she let herself into Wendy's house, but she congratulated herself on a job well done. It was thundering now, and there were great flashes of lightning. A curtain of rain made the air livid yellow and black. She went to the bedroom and removed her expensive new clothes. She hung them carefully in the wardrobe, pulling on her jeans and guernsey with huge relief.

The others would be dying to know how it went. On her way downstairs, Rufa tried to decide how much to reveal. She felt oddly protective of the whole experience, and wished she did not have to talk about it. She was, she realized, on the defensive and slightly ashamed. Describing it would feel like a confession, though—God knew—she had done nothing wrong. Fortunately, Wendy was busy in the basement, prodding the feet of a client, and Nancy was still out, on some mysterious mission involving the wearing of a Wonderbra and a searing new lipstick. She had declared, before lunch, that she intended to make another move on Berry.

But she'll never see it through, Rufa told herself; the second Max makes a serious pass at her, she'll collapse like a house of cards.

She was glad to have the bedroom to herself. In the empty kitchen, under the ticking strip of fluorescent light, Rufa made herself a mug of tea, then went back upstairs with the early Anita Brookner she had found in Wendy's airing cupboard. She had earned a rest.

An hour later, the doorbell rang. Rufa ignored it, thinking it must be someone for Wendy. She was deep in the novel, wondering what on earth Anita Brookner would make of Nancy, when Roshan's sleek head appeared round the door.

"It's for you."

"Mmm?"

"Yes, there's a Captain Birdseye to see you. He's very wet and strict, and he insists that you know him."

Rufa shut the book, and leaped off the bed. Her heart galloped. "Oh, God. I know him, all right."

"Are you okay?"

She tried to laugh. It came out as a nervous whinny. "I told you about my godfather, didn't I?

Roshan mimed a shriek of glee. "The brooch man? I thought he'd be older—but he's certainly scary enough. What's he doing here?"

"He never comes to London," Rufa said. "I have a ghastly feeling I've been found out."

"Don't panic. Treat it as a social call—what a lovely surprise, and all that. Give nothing away."

"Edward never makes social calls."

Roshan whispered, "Shall I stay with you?"

"No, no." Rufa was whipping round the room, emptying Nancy's ashtray and hiding Nancy's packets of condoms. "I'd better bring him up here, out of everyone's way."

Edward waited rigidly in the narrow hall. His iron gray hair was black from the rain. Rivulets ran off his waxed coat.

"Edward, what a surprise!" Rufa ran down the stairs, and kissed his bristled cheek. "Why didn't you tell me you were coming?" She could not say it was a pleasure to see him. He was plainly furious.

"I need to talk to you." He rolled a baleful eye toward Roshan. "Alone."

Perfectly on cue, there was a deafening clap of thunder. *Dies Irae.*

"Of course," Rufa said. "We'll go up to my room. This is Roshan Lal, by the way. Roshan—Edward Reculver."

Behind Edward's back, Roshan mouthed, "Good luck!"

She led him into the bedroom, and closed the door. She knew she was about to get the dressing-down of all time. She dreaded it, but it was also a relief. Deceiving him had been horrible.

He asked, "Where's Nancy?"

"Oh—she's gone out." Rufa was glad about this. Nancy, in her idea of full campaigning rig, would annoy him mightily. "Won't you take your coat off and sit down? Can I get you a tea or coffee, or something?"

He loomed. The room suddenly seemed absurdly small. "No," he said. "Thank you."

"Let me know if you change your mind."

Edward folded his arms. "I will not change my mind. Since I've driven from Gloucestershire in a thunderstorm, and spent the past forty minutes trying to find a parking space, I think we had better get on with it."

Rufa sat down on her bed, on the other side of the room.

He said, "I daresay you know why I'm here."

"Just tell me, Edward. Please don't make a song and dance about it."

"All right. I was in Cirencester this morning, and I ran into Mike Bosworth."

"Oh." Bosworth's were the firm of auctioneers who had valued Melismate.

"I asked him what was happening about the sale," Edward said. "And I was absolutely staggered to discover that it had been postponed. Mike said your mother still hadn't given him the go-ahead."

There was a long silence.

Rufa looked down at her knees. "We wanted a little more time."

"The time ran out long ago." Edward shrugged off his wet coat, and draped it over the back of the single chair in the room. "The debts are piling up, the house is ready to collapse—I expected craziness from Rose. But never from you."

"Did you speak to Mum?"

"I drove straight round to Melismate to find out what was going on. And out it all came. How halting the sale was all your idea. How you were going to London, with the avowed intention of marrying a man rich enough to sort out the whole bloody mess."

Rufa hung her head. Her throat felt hot. Put like this, it sounded crude and stupid. She wished Rose had not blabbed, but could not blame her for it. When Edward sank his teeth into something, there was no point in not telling him the truth. Rose freely admitted she was scared of his moral dressings-down. And she had never quite grasped how essential his approval was to Rufa.

"I didn't bother to ask what you and Nancy were doing for money," Edward went on. "I naturally worked that one out for myself. It appears that I have bankrolled the entire operation. With the money that I gave you, on the understanding that you would spend it on some kind of further education. I know exactly how you spent it, because Rose showed me a photograph of you, in a very questionable Sunday newspaper. She appeared to think this settled everything."

"Edward, I'm sorry," Rufa said. She made herself raise her head, to look at him. She *was* sorry. "I had to tell you all those lies. If you'd known the truth, you would have taken back the brooch."

"The brooch was a bloody present," Edward snapped.

"With definite strings attached."

His dark gray eyes and hair looked black under the feeble overhead light. "You sound exactly like your father—which you will, doubtless, take as a compliment. And I really thought you were the one person in your family with some sense. Well, we needn't go into it any further. Get your things together—if you want to argue, you can do it in the car."

Rufa's guilt boiled over into anger. "We can argue right here, because I am not going home with you. And there's nothing crazy about my idea. It's perfectly possible for a girl like me to marry a lot of money. I know I can find someone rich enough to save Melismate—so why shouldn't I?"

"Do you honestly need me to spell it out?" Edward was quiet and still with compacted fury. "Because of the sheer immorality of it. Of course it's possible for you to find a rich husband—you're a beautiful girl. But to sell yourself for money—"

"Look, Edward, you have no right to storm in here giving me orders. If that brooch was a gift, I can do what the hell I like with the money. And I'm using it to save my home. Obviously, I'm not going to marry a man I can't admire and respect—"

"You think that will make you happy?"

"Yes!" she shouted—she had never shouted at Edward. "I'll be incredibly, deliriously happy with any man who gives me back my house!"

He was rattled. He had not expected to be argued with, once he had let Rufa see his wrath. "I didn't realize how deeply you cared about money," he said stiffly.

"You've never wanted to understand how much Melismate means to all of us. Just because you disapprove of inheritances and things, you won't see that it means more to us than money—that it's worth a sacrifice. You were just the same with The Zed."

Edward said, "I never saw him making any sacrifices."

This was true, and it made Rufa angrier. "You couldn't control him—that's why you were always carping at him, criticizing everything he did—"

White with anger, he took a step closer to her. "Is that what you think I was doing?"

He seemed to loom over her, overwhelming her. Rufa, her defenses weakened by the awfulness of arguing with Edward when she knew he was right and she was wrong, was suddenly stiflingly aware of his body. She smelled rain and wood smoke on his coat, and the Wright's Coal Tar soap he used on his hands, overlaying a musky tang of sweat.

For the first time, she was overwhelmed by a sense of him as a sexual being; someone who could lean six inches closer and kiss her. A picture came into her mind, of Edward's angry energy channeled into desire. The air suddenly tasted of sex. Rufa flushed, and backed away from him.

"You tried to manage him," she said. "We didn't give you permission to manage us."

His voice was very quiet. "I didn't think I needed permission, God help me."

"You have no right to charge down here and spoil everything."

"I'm trying to help," he said. "I—I do it because I care for you."

She could not accept this, without suffering agonies of guilt. "No you don't—part of you was jealous of The Zed, and now you're thrilled to see his show-offy family being forced to be ordinary! You think it serves us right! Oh, God—"

Rufa was appalled by this piece of horror that had bubbled out of her subconscious like pond scum. She pressed her palms into her burning cheeks. She knew at once that she had dealt him a serious blow. He was astonished that she had such weapons.

"I didn't understand," he said. "You're as much a fantasist as he was. I thought you had a grain of sense—and all the time you were clinging to this ludicrous notion that the world owes you a living—merely because you've

118

loafed around on the same bit of land for a few centuries. Does this make you a special case? There's nothing clever or admirable about getting yourself born into an old family!"

Rufa was trying not to cry. "You know it's more than that. Melismate is part of us, and what we are. Without it, we're nothings and nobodies."

Edward frowned. "Rubbish. You could do anything. Listen to me, Rufa. I'm only trying to stop you ruining your entire life for the sake of a heap of stones. What would it take, for God's sake?"

"You'd have to find a few million quid," Rufa said, "and give it to me— without telling me how to spend it."

"I see."

"You don't!" She found his obstinacy infuriating. "You never will! Oh, God, this isn't—Edward, I'm not—" She was trying to claw back some self-control. "I know you mean to be kind. But please don't interfere. Please. I want this more than I've ever wanted anything!"

They both stared down at the swirly carpet, arms rigid at their sides, casting around for some way to part as friends. There was a long, hardening silence.

"Well, I tried," Edward said abruptly. "I offered to help clear up this mess, and you turned me down. I won't interfere again."

Rufa moved to the bedroom door, making a wide circle around him, and jerked it open.

"Good-bye, then."

Chapter Twelve

After breakfast, on the morning of Rufa's first lunch with Adrian, Nancy had made a secret phone call to Rose. "She can't marry this man, Mum. Please take my word for it—he makes my blood run cold."

Miles across the rain-spattered country, Rose had chuckled. "She rang me last night, when you were in the bath. She said I had to talk you out of chasing young Berry."

"She thinks he's too good for me," Nancy had said indignantly. "Of all the sauce. Well, I'll show her. I've got at least two more assets than she has."

Rose had said, "I might have known the pair of you would start bickering. Do calm down. It's only a lunch."

"Only? He's taking her to the bloody Connaught!"

"Ah," Rose had sighed. "Did I ever tell you—"

"About The Zed washing dishes there when he was a student? Yes, millions of times. He dropped a tab of acid, and thought the *sous*-chef was an octopus—perhaps Ru will mention it, if she runs out of small talk."

"I'm sorry you've inherited my sarcasm gene," Rose had said, mildly but firmly. "Don't get into one of your states, darling. Rufa won't do anything silly."

Nancy was not so sure. The Marrying Game had seemed terrifically amusing when the rich men only existed in theory. The cold actuality of a man like Adrian Mecklenberg, and Rufa's willingness to sacrifice herself to him, had come as a severe shock.

Nobody, Nancy thought, could describe me as a prude—but there's something indecent about Ru trying to sell herself to that frosty old geezer.

What had got into her? Suddenly, the Marrying Game had the potential to turn rather nasty. Unless Nancy did something about it.

In the bedroom, Rufa had been dressing for her lunch. She was pale and overwrought, but looked wonderful—she was very convincing as a highborn virgin. Nancy knew that if she wanted to beat her vestal sister to the altar, she would have to ignore her advice about delicacy and refinement, and tackle things in her own style.

She had said, "Don't mind me," and pulled off her tight black sweater, treating a rainy segment of Tufnell Park Road to the sight of her bare white breasts. She put on her Wonderbra—that boon to the titless, which molded the naturally well endowed into queens. She put the sweater back on, applied fiery crimson lipstick, and added one of the creamy, supple, classic raincoats Roshan had made them buy at Margaret Howell.

Rufa had asked, "Where are you going?"

"The Square Mile, darling," Nancy had said, neatly swiping the best umbrella. "I'm doing a little research."

Nancy was impressed by the City. She looked, with great interest, at the shining slabs of buildings, and the majestic columns of Saint Paul's and the Bank of England. She noted, with increasing optimism, the huge flocks of personable young men, in identical charcoal suits. The whole warren of packed streets reeked of maleness. This was the Land of the Male: a hard, rapid, bustling place, where business ruled and sex was tucked firmly into corners. The few women bobbing through the endlessly surging crowds looked either cheerfully secretarial, or soberly dressed and harassed.

The offices of Berry's bank were in Cheapside, near Threadneedle Street. Nancy stood on the opposite side of the road, watching the building with open curiosity. Its sheer glass walls towered above a sea of moving corporate golf umbrellas, like huge mushrooms with logos. Berry emerged, struggling with his own umbrella. He was deep in conversation with another man, and did not see Nancy when she slipped into the crowd, a few umbrellas behind him.

They turned into a narrow side street. Nancy's interest quickened. Berry and his companion were furling their umbrellas at the low doorway of a place called Forbes & Gunning—which, though it claimed to be a wine merchant to the gentry since the year dot, was essentially a wine bar.

Nancy, folding herself into the tide of charcoal suits, went down a cramped wooden staircase and found herself in an enormous vaulted cellar, reverberating with male noise. The long bar was hidden behind a solid wall of charcoal backs. Some men were standing, with glasses of wine or beer and old-fashioned doorstep sandwiches. Through a glass door, more men were eating what appeared to be very posh school dinners, at crisp white tables. Berry and his friend fought through to the bar, emerged with a bottle of red wine, and sat down at a round table in a relatively quiet corner.

Nancy was just deciding she was too conspicuous here, and had better leave, when a beautiful opportunity presented itself—like the hand of destiny, as she said afterward. A young man, in a long apron like a Toulouse-Lautrec waiter, touched her arm.

"Hi—sorry to keep you waiting. You've come about the job, right?"

She did not get back to Wendy's until past midnight. Two bottles of Forbes & Gunning's house champagne distended the pockets of her Margaret Howell raincoat. The young man, whose name was Simon, had hired her on the spot. He had taken her into an airless underground office, given her a cappuccino, and formally telephoned the landlord of the Hasty Arms for a reference.

Nancy had explained that she could pull pints and do a perfect shamrock on the head of a Guinness, but that she knew nothing about cocktails, wines, or espresso machines. Simon said none of this mattered, and offered her an hourly rate which seemed like an absolute fortune. She went straight on to the evening shift, and was further dazzled by the amount she made in tips. The men had been surprisingly unbothersome. They had all flicked glances at her during their conversations, but none of them assumed that a tip gave them a right to heavy flirtation, or even a kind word. Often, they simply thrust a banknote into her hand with a brief smile. She could not believe how easy this was. She had forgotten how much she relished the raucous bustle of a busy bar.

"Well, madam," Simon said, when they had locked the doors after the last, lingering suits, and sat at a table drinking champagne, "I knew you'd be a fast learner." He thought Nancy, with her posh voice and village pub reference, a great novelty.

"None faster," Nancy said. "You run ever such a nice place, Simon. The streets of London really are paved with gold."

Singing to herself, she put her bottles on Wendy's kitchen table, and switched the kettle on. She had spent the tube journey home dreaming of the treats she would heap upon Linnet with her newfound wealth. The television murmured in the sitting room next door.

Wendy's high voice quavered, "Is that you, Nancy?"

"Yes," Nancy called back. "I'm making tea."

The noise from the next room abruptly ceased. Wendy came in, blinking (she liked to watch television in the dark). "Where on earth have you been?" She saw the champagne, and her eyes widened. "What have you been up to?"

"I've landed myself the most divine job—the job of my dreams. Where's Ru? How was her lunch with Count Mecklenberg?"

Wendy was solemn. "She's upstairs." Briefly and breathlessly, she outlined the visitation from Edward. "I didn't see him—I just heard the door slamming when he walked out."

"Oh, God," Nancy groaned. "The miserable old git—I suppose he accused her of being less pure than the driven snow. You know how she minds about things like that. I hope you told her not to take any notice."

"I couldn't tell her anything," Wendy said. "She won't come down. She won't even let me in."

Nancy was angry. She pulled another mug down from the shelf, and stuffed in a tea bag aggressively. "How could he? He knows perfectly well what Ru's like—she acts all cool and collected, but she's about as tough as a marshmallow. And she's the only one of us who gives a damn about Edward's good opinion."

"I'm rather glad I missed him," Wendy confessed. "When I lived at Melismate, I was always terrified of him."

"He doesn't terrify me." Nancy picked up the two mugs of tea. "We'll be down in a minute. Put the champagne in the freezer, there's a love."

She carried the tea upstairs, and went into the bedroom.

As soon as she turned the handle, a muffled voice cried, "Go away!"

"Darling, it's only me. I sleep here too—unless you'd like to exile me to Max's room."

Rufa lay sprawled across her single bed. It was obvious to Nancy that she had cried herself half blind. Her face was raw and bloated with tears. Nancy felt a spasm of pure rage against Edward, but managed to pin on a cheerful smile.

"I've brought you a cup of tea."

Nancy very rarely made tea for anyone. Rufa sobbed, "Th-thanks—" and struggled blearily into a sitting position.

"Well, I heard," Nancy said, dropping down on her own bed. "And I'm sorry I wasn't here to give him a handsome piece of my mind."

"He's found out about the Marrying Game. He thinks we're disgusting." Rufa shakily sipped her tea. "I said the most awful things to him—he'll never speak to me again, probably."

"Good," Nancy said. "I'm always telling you, don't listen to him. The Zed never took a blind bit of notice."

Rufa's lips quivered. "What's going to happen to us all without Edward?"

"We'll survive, that's what," Nancy declared. "Don't go nuts, but I've got myself a job—and not at the Duke of Clarence, before you say anything."

She reached into her Wonderbra, and pulled out a crumpled bunch of banknotes.

The corners of Rufa's mouth twitched into the beginnings of a smile. "Don't tell me you made all that pulling pints."

"Pints of champagne, my dear. I'm working at Berry's local—down a city alley with one of those tactless historical names, like Great Cripple Street, or Leper's Yard."

"What?"

Nancy laughed. "It's wondrously posh. When it's closing time, you don't have to turn off the telly, or dip the lights—they just leave by themselves. And when I dropped a glass, nobody cheered."

"Yes, that's certainly very posh."

"Admit it," Nancy coaxed, "you're impressed."

Rufa smiled now—a watery sketch of a smile that went to Nancy's heart. "God, yes. I've been feeling so hopeless and scared about money. It was stupid of me to be snotty about you being a barmaid. I wish I could find some work myself."

"Didn't Berry say he'd ask around about your dinner parties? I'll remind him."

"Of course," Rufa murmured. "You'll be seeing him."

"Seeing him? I'll be having a wild affair with him, and then I'll be marrying him. So stop crying, honey. Come down and have a glass of my champagne. Forget about Edward. Honestly, darling, it's not worth getting this worked up over a man unless you're in love with him."

"I can't bear that he despises me," Rufa said. "I can't bear that he sees me in this sleazy way. It makes me hate myself."

"You're not sleazy. He'll see that when he gets the invitation to my huge society wedding."

There was a box of tissues on Rufa's bed. A snowdrift of used tissues lay on the faded Indian cotton counterpane beside her. She extracted another clean tissue, and blew her nose. She was making an effort to pull herself together, but her voice was desolate.

"I don't think you should count on marrying Berry."

Nancy laughed, and dropped a kiss on her sister's head. "I'm not going to argue about it."

Nancy was Berry's introduction to the phenomenon of stress. In the usual way of things, he bobbed serenely between work, fiancée, and family, never much disturbed by anything. Nancy's astonishing, overbalancing appearance behind the bar at Forbes & Gunning rapidly turned him into a restless, coffee-guzzling nervous wreck.

The worst of it was that other men noticed her—how could they help it? She was a redheaded Hebe, dispensing nectar with unhurried ease. She smiled, she parried lubricious remarks, she never gave the wrong change or forgot an order. In a matter of weeks, she had a cult following. They were coming from as far as Canary Wharf to get a look at her wicked blue eyes and gorgeous breasts.

Other men asked her out, with varying degrees of seriousness. Nancy always refused, hinting that she was "spoken for." Berry heard this once, and was seized by a pang of jealousy, frightening in its intensity. On hearing someone call her "the Russet Gusset," he could, for a second, have committed murder. She upset him dreadfully. He knew he should have avoided her, for the sake of his sanity and peace of mind, but could not stop himself haunting Forbes & Gunning like a miserable specter.

Several times a day, as the winter began to soften into spring, he told himself that he absolutely refused to do anything to hurt Polly—utterly, totally refused. He told himself how deeply he loved Polly. Never mind the expensive arrangements for their wedding. This was a matter of principle. Call him old-fashioned, but he believed in the sanctity of a gentleman's word.

Unfortunately, he kept encountering a part of himself that would never be a gentleman. He had always assumed that this part was well under control. His cataclysmic discovery of sexual obsession pulled his entire life out of shape.

Two factors made the whole situation more complicated. The fact that Nancy worked at Forbes & Gunning, where all his colleagues drank and gossiped, was difficult enough. Staying out of the wine bar did not mean he could avoid her, because both Adrian and Polly were so deeply involved with her sister. The enigmatic Adrian was, as far as Berry could tell, very serious about his pursuit of Rufa. And the more serious he became, the greater Polly's determination to cultivate the future Mrs. Mecklenberg.

Adrian moved methodically. In a matter of weeks, the lunchtime assignations progressed to concerts and dinners. And as the courtship developed, Polly grew more friendly with Rufa and more willing to tolerate Nancy. The culmination came one evening when Berry returned from the office, sadly congratulating himself for his strength of mind in not going to Forbes & Gunning—and found a red-haired Hasty in each corner of his Knole sofa. Polly had invited them both to supper.

"I hope you don't mind," Polly said to him privately, in the kitchen. "I couldn't very well invite Rufa on her own."

She did not like Nancy, and assumed Berry agreed with her.

He said, hoping to heaven he sounded casual, "Oh, I don't mind Nancy."

Polly plucked the briefcase from his hand, and gave him the corkscrew. "I'm relying on you to talk to her, while I go over my contacts with Rufa. You know how Nancy hijacks the conversation."

Berry watched her arranging asparagus spears in balsamic puddles, and thought how exhausting and thankless it was to live perpetually on show. Even when they were alone together, Polly never entirely stopped playing to impress an invisible audience. As if, he thought, she had a satellite trained on her. She could let the Hasty girls think they lived like this all the time because they bloody well did.

"It's not that I don't like her," Polly said. She was now shaving Parmesan at the counter, with her back to him. "But let's face it, she'll never have Rufa's sheer quality. Well, can you imagine Adrian taking someone like Nancy to a chamber concert? I'm afraid there's something rather provincial about her. If not borderline vulgar."

To Berry's dismay, he was seized by a pang of active dislike for Polly. It had never happened before, and it shocked him into facing the truth.

This had turned into more than overheated infatuation. This was the real deal, the whole nine yards. He had fallen in love with Nancy. She brought the sun into a room with her, and it sank into chilly gloom when she left. Her charm, her laughter, and her high spirits charged the atmosphere with magic. Her unexpected flashes of pure kindness all but unmanned him. He was madly in love with Nancy, as he had never been in love before. And he was unavoidably engaged to marry Polly. He could jilt her, and despise himself forever. Or he could ignore Nancy and die of a broken heart. Either way, he was condemned to a lifetime of misery and a permanent erection.

He tried to exhaust his treacherous body into submission. Instead of drifting into the wine bar at lunchtime, Berry went to the gym (Polly had bought him a year's membership as a birthday present). Instead of eating a chocolate pretzel and three sultana muffins before work, he went to the gym. He went to the bar after work, as usual, but spent the whole time nursing a glass of mineral water and pining for Nancy's attention.

He lost interest in food. As the spring days lengthened, his paunch melted. All his suits were taken in three times, then discarded. His jaw was lean, and there were poignant hollows underneath his cheekbones. Berry stared at his new reflection when he shaved—disconcertingly huge brown eyes in a bony, boyish face—and thought himself a pathetic figure. Other people, however, kept telling him how marvelous he looked. Even his sister, who could usually read his mind, congratulated him for deciding not to turn into a blimp.

Polly was delighted. Why, Berry wondered, didn't she notice? How could she want to marry a man who was burning with love for someone else? He allowed himself the small treat of being annoyed with Polly for her complacency, but that was as far as it went. He was still determined to marry her. Let it be written on his tombstone that he was a man of his word.

In the middle of March, Nancy reported to Rufa that she was progressing extremely well. "He won't hold out for long. As soon as the weather gets warmer I'll leave off some underwear. He's just trembling on the brink of asking me for a date."

"It's a large and commodious brink," Rufa said. "He doesn't seem in any hurry to topple off it."

She was very pale, with bright, feverish eyes. This evening she had a dinner engagement with Adrian. Its significance was not visible to the naked eye, but there had been hints that it would mark an important stage in their courtship. Each meeting with Adrian was wrapped around a small test, and she had passed each one triumphantly. Her responses to art, music, and food had been spot on.

Now he was drawing aside another veil, by taking her to dinner with his sister, in Holland Park. The revelation that he had a sister at all had been, in itself, shockingly intimate. Her name was Clarissa Watts-Wainwright, and, as far as Rufa could gather, she was at the center of Adrian's private circle. She suspected this was the final inspection, before the runways were cleared for sexual contact. So far, Adrian had kissed her cheek on meeting and parting—with almost imperceptibly increasing warmth. Rufa (though she had said nothing to Nancy, who would never understand) was anxious to know how she would react, in the unimaginable event of Adrian making a pass.

She liked him. She was attracted by his cool cleanliness, and his self-containment—she could not have endured a man who pawed her about. Deep down (and she would never have admitted this to Nancy in a million years) she was very anxious to know if her urge-free body would submit happily to sex with him.

The affair was black tie. Rufa had cooked her first two professional dinners (for a charming, scatty acquaintance of Polly's, bristling with titles) and had invested her earnings in a long sheath of midnight blue chiffon. This way, she did not feel so guilty about Edward's diminishing money. Thinking about Edward at all made her sore all over. She bitterly regretted their quarrel. Roshan, who was acting as her lady's maid, pinned her long hair into a loose knot at the nape of her neck. "Remember, darling—if things are proceeding too slowly, pull out the top pin, and the whole lot will fall down, to ravishing effect."

Wendy sighed. "You're exquisite. I wish The Zed could see you."

"He'd sell the dress right off your back," Nancy said sourly. She hated seeing Rufa decked for the sacrifice.

Two or three lunches into the relationship, Rufa had told Adrian something about the real situation at Melismate. He knew enough now to send his car round to Tufnell Park. He never came himself. Nancy was disgusted by his snobbery. Rufa saw it differently, and appreciated his tact.

Arriving at the huge, stuccoed house, she felt she had shed Tufnell Park entirely. Adrian—sharp and clean as a polished blade—came into the hall, to kiss her cheek and peel away the ruinously expensive pashmina Roshan had made her buy.

He murmured, "You're beautiful." She entered the drawing room on his arm.

Adrian's sister was a female version of Adrian: less obviously good-looking, but formidably immaculate, and with the same very clean shade of gray hair. Rufa noticed, as she was introduced around the room, that everyone else knew each other. She was the youngest here by at least twenty years. One of the other women raised her eyebrows meaningfully when she offered her hand. This told Rufa, more plainly than the plainest words, that she was being presented, officially, as Adrian's next consort. Clarissa Watts-Wainwright reinforced this, by continually scooping her into the conversation during dinner.

Nancy would have hated the tedium of such compulsory refinement—"buttock-clenching," as she called it. Nancy was useless at any sort of clenching. Rufa felt she was good at it. She had never been afraid of hard work.

At the coffee stage, there was a movement back to the drawing room. Adrian appeared, with the pashmina. He draped it around Rufa's shoulders, and led her outside, on the pretext of admiring the communal gardens.

Holding his arm, shivering slightly in the raw spring evening, Rufa looked out across rolling lawns and shrubberies, ringed by banks of glowing, golden windows.

"You're cold," Adrian observed. He uncurled her passive hand, and put his arm around her. "I shouldn't expose a creature like you to the elements. You belong behind glass."

She was not going to argue with this, but couldn't help thinking how Nancy would have laughed to hear it.

"You shocked me," Adrian said, "when you told me you had never been to Paris. It's an appalling gap in your education."

"I'm afraid it's full of gaping holes."

"Don't apologize for your ignorance. I rather like it. It means you're unspoiled. Thanks to your astoundingly peculiar upbringing, you have a rare form of innocence. I now find I can't endure the idea of your seeing Paris without me."

His voice, in the huge, still garden, was very quiet. He spoke close to her ear. Rufa found she was holding her breath. "Do you have any plans for the weekend after next?"

A weekend meant sex. Rufa was suddenly frightened. If she could not handle it, she would be trapped. "You know I never have plans."

In the darkness, she heard the smile in his voice. "I thought you might be doing one of your dinner parties." He was amused by her genteel little "jobs."

"I don't have anything lined up," Rufa said. "Except the dinner for Berry and Polly. Which you'll be eating."

"Yes, and I admit, I'm curious. I don't often meet women who can cook. But my weekend in Paris doesn't depend on your performance. Will you come?"

"I—I'd love to."

"Good. Though there's nothing in Paris—or out of it, for that matter—to compare to you. I haven't said it often enough. I dislike stating the obvious."

His face was moving toward hers. Time slowed. She was aware of the sharp definition of his features. His lips were cool. Rufa was very still, willing herself to relax. After the initial shock of contact, she found that she could bear this easily. It was even pleasant.

For one mad second, she wanted to giggle. Beyond the act of sex, which she now knew she was unlikely to fail, lay the wild relief of saving Melismate.

"Don't do it, darling—please don't do it! He'll lock you away in a glass case, and you'll never see daylight again!"

Nancy, in a storm of shocking pink toweling and hot red hair, flung herself across Rufa's bed.

"Get off my dress," Rufa snapped. "What's the matter with you? This weekend in Paris is everything we've been working for. I'm positive Adrian's planning to propose."

"You're not in love with him!"

"Nancy, I am not having this conversation again. I like him, and that's enough. You're not in love with Berry."

"Berry's different," Nancy said. "And so am I. Please, Ru—listen to me—see some sense, before it's too late! You'll never be able to handle it."

Rufa snatched her chiffon dress from under Nancy's body. "I know what I'm doing. I might not be insanely in love with Adrian. But I'm not the type for wild passion."

Nancy sighed heavily. "Yes you are. You're exactly the type. The second you meet someone you really fancy, you'll go berserk."

"I'm far too sensible to do anything of the kind," Rufa said. "Some of us have a measure of control over our emotions. I know I lost it with Jonathan, but that was years ago, and it was nothing more than delayed adolescence.

Adrian understands me. He shares my tastes. He can give me the kind of security I've always wanted—and he's already hinted he knows I come in a package with Melismate. He'll turn it into the most gorgeous house in the world. This won't be any kind of sacrifice."

"Bollocks," Nancy snapped. "You're just trying to talk yourself into it. You're determined to come out of this smelling of roses."

Rufa worked the pins out of her hair. As Roshan had predicted, the heavy skein of auburn fell picturesquely over her pearly shoulders. "I'm not riding roughshod over his feelings, if that's what you mean."

Nancy snorted crossly. "I don't give a shit about his feelings."

"No—you don't give a shit about anyone. When I marry Adrian, you can stop trying to overturn poor Berry's entire life."

"He'll thank me for it. You're just getting squeamish because you've decided to like that bitch Polly."

"She's not a bitch, actually."

"Not to you. She looks at me as if she'd brought me in on the bottom of her fucking shoe."

Rufa was not going to be drawn into an argument about Polly. "Look, what is this? The Game's nearly over—I thought you'd be pleased."

"Adrian's as old as the hills, and the original toffee-nosed git. You know perfectly well he'll make you miserable."

"I can take care of myself." Rufa sat down in front of the badly lit mirror to smooth away her mascara with oil and cotton wool.

Nancy leaped off the bed. "Ru, listen to me. Forget your usual argument about Berry being a perfect gent. Suppose I got a proposal out of him, and he agreed to take care of Melismate, and all that jazz—would you still go after Adrian? Would it make a difference?"

"Obviously. But Berry will never propose, so why are we arguing?"

"That's all I wanted to know."

Chapter Thirteen

"You two were having a bit of a spat last night," Max said. "Is the famous Marrying Game running into difficulties?"

He was leaning against the counter in Wendy's kitchen, nursing a mug of tea and staring, with naked admiration, at Nancy's denim-clad bottom as she bent over the washing machine.

She slammed the door and stood up, brushing back her long hair. "The only difficulty is that it's going too well. If I can't do something, damn fast, Ru's going to make a really dreadful marriage."

"You shouldn't try to stop her," Max said. "Let her make her own mistakes. She can always divorce him, when she's spent all his money."

Nancy smiled. "That's what you'd do, is it?"

"Of course."

"I don't think getting divorced is exactly a barrel of laughs, darling. And just imagine how badly Rufa would handle it."

"True. Heaven save us all from serious types." Max's bright, pagan dark eyes raked over her slowly. "How come the two of you are so different?"

He could say anything to her, and, these days, it all meant the same thing. Every remark, however innocuous, was a gate standing open. Nancy felt the sex blasting off him in waves, and was amazed by her own strength of mind in resisting him. She fancied him desperately. Sometimes, lying late at night upon her chaste single bed, she raged against Rufa and her blasted Marrying Game for standing in her way. But so far she had always managed to deflect Max, without absolutely putting him off.

She smiled, dropping her gaze as she did so. "We're more alike than we seem."

This was meant to mean: I'm more of a prude than I look, and less easy to get into the sack than appearances suggest.

Such a waste, Nancy thought regretfully, watching Max covertly as he weighed up the likelihood of seducing her, and decided to go back to his work upstairs. For the first time in her life she had to hold love at bay, and waste no more languorous afternoons in a lover's arms.

Briefly, she fantasized about following Max to his room and blurting out that she adored him. He did not have to adore her back. In Nancy's moral scheme, declaring love for a man before you fell upon his hot, naked flesh was the essential, legal difference between high-flown passion and mere shagging. Nancy did not approve of mere shagging. Sex had to spring from love—sex without love was indecent.

This was at the heart of her objection to Adrian. When she agreed to the Marrying Game, she had assumed that love would come to meet them halfway, as soon as the ground was right. Perhaps she had been naive, but she was deeply disturbed by the utter absence of love between Adrian and her sister. And it frightened her to think of Rufa at the mercy of this chilly man.

Ru's so stubborn, Nancy thought; she insists that she can live without all that love stuff when she's absolutely screaming to be loved.

The doorbell rang. Nancy went to answer it. There was a man waiting on the doorstep: tall and lean, probably in his early forties. His hair was thick and dark gray, his face unlined and clean-shaven. His navy suit was several degrees too elegant for Tufnell Park Road on a weekday afternoon. And he was blindingly handsome.

He said, "Hello, Nancy."

The shock woke her like a hard slap. She met the cool eyes of the handsome stranger, and gasped, "Oh, my God!"

It was Edward Reculver.

Edward, without the beard and the darned clothes from Millets. Edward, with a proper haircut, instead of the usual convict's trim. He was speckless and razor-sharp, with at least ten years stripped from him, like the bark of an old tree. It was staggering. Nancy was both amused and impressed that she had been tricked into finding him sexy—old Edward, of all people.

"Yes, it's really me," he said. He smiled his usual, lopsided smile, unshadowed by the beard. He had worn that beard since he left the army. Before that, he had worn a heavy mustache. This was the first time Nancy had seen his face undressed.

She gasped, "What's happened to you?"

"I've learned humility, seen sense, and shaved," he said. "In that order. Do you approve?"

"Definitely," Nancy said, laughing softly as she stared at him. "You look about a million years younger. You look as if you've been privatized and expensively redesigned."

Edward laughed outright at this. "Ghastly child—that's exactly what your father would have said. Is Rufa here?"

Nancy remembered that she was supposed to be angry with him—the novelty of the transformation had blown everything else from her mind. "No. So if you're here to have another go at her, bad luck."

He winced touchily, but his voice was mild. "Before you say anything else, I'm really sorry about last time. That's why I'm here."

"You're kidding," Nancy said. "You never apologize."

"Well, perhaps I've changed," he snapped. Then he sighed heavily, and scowled down at his feet. "What Rufa said to me was unbelievable. But what I said to her was—bloody unforgivable." He glanced up at her sharply. "Am I making sense?"

"Perfect sense," Nancy said, thinking there was something very nice about Edward when he spoke in this quiet, direct way. Since The Zed's death, she realized, he had only shown them his lecturing, hectoring side. But this might have been as much a sign of grieving as Rufa's obsession with saving Melismate—or her own hunger for romance, or Lydia's hunger for Ran, or Selena's self-immolation behind a wall of books. Edward was reacting to grief as much as any of them. It was extraordinary, Nancy thought, how they had all forgotten how to behave normally. "You don't have to worry that I'll give you another earful," she assured him. "I'd be lying if I said Ru wasn't upset. But that's only because you hit a few bull's-eyes."

He was touched. "Am I crazy, to be worried sick about her?"

"No. I am too, rather." Nancy opened the door wider. She could not let him go yet. "Come on in. Have some tea."

"Thanks, I'd love to." He seemed relieved. Nancy wondered what sort of reception he had expected.

He followed her down the passage to the kitchen. Nancy was aware of his glancing round, taking in the general dilapidation but making a genuine effort not to pass judgment. Incredibly, he appeared to have listened to the terrible things (Nancy had not been told the details) that Rufa had said during their quarrel.

"Sit down," she said. "Do you fancy something to eat?"

"No thanks." Watching her curiously, as if he did not know what to make of her away from Melismate, he sat down.

"In that case, you'll have to excuse me while I stuff myself with toasted cheese." Nancy said. "I'm off to work in a minute."

"You've got a job?"

"Didn't Mum tell you?"

Edward said, "To tell the truth, I haven't been near Melismate since Rufa and I—since the last time I was here."

"Oh." Nancy grated cheese, not knowing what to say. Edward was a fixture at Melismate. Rose complained about his interference, but it would never have occurred to her to wish him away. She relied on him far too much. They all did. "Ru really got to you, didn't she?"

"I certainly didn't come here to accuse her," he said, bristling again. "If she 'got to me,' as you put it, I deserved it."

Nancy knew what The Zed would have said, and found herself saying it. "Look, Edward—sackcloth suits you, but don't get carried away. I haven't time to stand here disagreeing while you heap blame on yourself. It'll put me off my tea."

She saw his second of recognition, remembrance, and grief, before he relaxed back into a laugh. "All right. Tell me about this job of yours."

"Well, as I said to Rufa, there's always gainful employment for an experienced barmaid." Seeing Edward was genuinely interested and prepared to be amused, Nancy told him about Forbes & Gunning. She could not help embellishing the story, as The Zed would have done, and throwing in a superb impersonation of her boss. Edward rewarded her by laughing again—he had always loved to hear The Zed's stories. Nancy saw that he needed The Zed's way of turning life into a mad soap opera every bit as much as Linnet (and Rufa) needed the saga of the Ressanys. She ached for The Zed, and the gap he had left like an open wound.

Once Nancy was settled at the table, with a cup of tea and a plate of oozing toasted cheese, Edward said, with an effort, "I really upset Ru, didn't I?"

"She was devastated. I found her crying her eyes out. You know how she always wants the grown-ups to approve of her."

"Hmm. Do you think she'd let me see her, so I can show her how sorry I am?"

"Of course she'll see you," Nancy said. "She forgave you ages ago."

"Will she be back soon? I mean, will I be a nuisance, if I wait for her?"

Nancy thought his new sensitivity deserved a reward—and she was dying to hear Rufa's reaction to the transformation. "She's over at Berry's. His girlfriend's having a dinner party, and Ru's doing the cooking: eight-b Pemberton Villas, off the Fulham Road."

"Will she mind my just turning up there?"

Rufa would mind, Nancy realized. Adrian was to be present at Polly's dinner party, and the momentous trip to Paris was scheduled for the following weekend. Rufa would not care to have Edward turning up at this critical stage. But sod that, Nancy thought suddenly—it might be the saving of her earnest, hurtable sister.

"I don't care if she minds. See if you can stop her marrying Adrian."

This was the first time Edward had heard the name of Rufa's target. His eyes narrowed warily. "Who?"

The time had come, Nancy decided, to let him have the whole truth, served without one speck of Hasty bullshit. "He's called Adrian Mecklenberg. He's filthy rich, and cold as an icicle. She can't marry him, Edward. She's not remotely in love with him—though she's trying to kid herself that she is. Well, you know her. You know what a talent she has for making herself miserable."

He nodded thoughtfully. "Yes, I suppose so. And you're sure she's not—she doesn't care for this man?"

Only afterward did Nancy realize there was something odd about the deliberate way he put this question. "Positive. She's not fooling me—she's only doing all this because she just assumes she'll never be happy again. She thinks staying at Melismate is the best she has to hope for."

"You're worried about her too, aren't you?"

"What d'you think I'm doing here?" Nancy demanded. "I couldn't let her come to London alone, could I? She's the type to die of a broken heart—

sometimes I wonder if that's actually what she's doing. I can't watch her marrying that man, and killing herself by inches." She was pouring this out like a confession. She had turned Queen's evidence, and grassed Rufa up to the authorities, and it was a huge relief. "Someone's got to stop her throwing her life away, and she might just listen to you. If you can make her admit this Marrying Game is a load of crap, you'll be doing us all a favor."

Edward said, "I'll do my best."

Rufa thought it appropriate that Polly had a "galley" kitchen—she certainly worked her employees like galley slaves. All we need, she thought, is a surly man in a vest banging a drum, to keep us all in rhythm. The Colombian cleaning lady and a stout Spanish waitress were being lashed round the flat by Polly's high-pitched commands. Mindful that Rufa was the next Mrs. Mecklenberg, Polly was more gracious to her, and disguised her orders as sweet requests. Could she slice the smoked goose more thinly? Could she wash the rocket leaves in Evian, not tap water? Weren't the filo parcels too small? Would she mind wiping her fingerprints off the stainless-steel fridge? Rufa had met some hysterical hostesses in her time, but was amazed that any human being could make this much song and dance about a dinner party. She wanted to like Polly, because she liked Berry, but it was an uphill struggle.

She sliced and stirred, and fielded Polly's intrusions, tense and clumsy with anxiety. The anxiety bit a little deeper with every passing day. She could not make Nancy see how desperate things were getting at Melismate. The nightly conversations with Rose were catalogs of doom. They had had final warnings from the telephone and water companies. The ceiling had fallen down in the only leak-proof spare bedroom. Marrying Adrian, as quickly as possible, was Rufa's—everyone's—only hope.

Her family seemed to be disintegrating along with the house. Selena had dropped out of school. She refused to take her exams, and hung about all day, sulking and rereading Sidney's *Arcadia*. Rufa was in despair. Why, when she read all those turgid books for fun, wouldn't she do it at a university? And why couldn't Rose summon the energy to lay down the law, and bloody well make Selena go back to Saint Hildegard's? Rufa, Nancy, and Lydia had attended this excellent girl's public day school on the remnants of an impregnable family trust The Zed had never been able to rob. Selena had been awarded a scholarship, like a gift from heaven, after the trust ran out. If Rufa had been at Melismate, she would not have given her ungrateful little sister a minute's peace. She would have driven her to school, bound and gagged if necessary, and hauled her into classes by her hair.

Rose was preoccupied with Lydia, the daughter who most resembled her physically, and baffled her mentally. Ran was still alone at Semple Farm, and foolish Lydia was spinning away into realms of pointless hope. Both Rufa and Rose were afraid Ran would succumb to those great, lovesick blue eyes and sleep with Lydia—and then where would they be, when he inevitably took up with someone else?

Rose had said, "She must be an imbecile. Even Linnet knows he's only single because he's already been through every available woman for miles around."

Rufa longed to be at home, to massage some sense into her besotted sister. Lydia lived at a dreamy adagio, and had to be treated very gently. Rose was too impatient with her, and too insulting about Ran. In the meantime, if she sent them some of the money she was making from her dinner parties, would they use it to pay the bills, or would they fritter it away on gin? In the past, she had always been able to rely on Edward—she would never have left for London if she had not known he was nearby, permanently ready to avert catastrophe. Since their last meeting, however, Edward had not been near Melismate. Nobody had seen him, and nobody knew where he was. Rufa felt wretched about this. She desperately missed his comforting presence, and hated herself for scaring off the family safety net. Rose flatly refused to approach Edward for help—"I'll eat a turd on toast first." It all hung on the Marrying Game now. If Adrian did not marry her, what was to become of them all?

❄ ❄ ❄

At half past five Polly burst back into the kitchen, just as Rufa had perched on a stool with a cup of tea.

"There's a man begging to see you—and frankly, I wish it was me he was begging for, because he's quite a major dish. He says he's your godfather."

"Edward?" Rufa clumsily slopped tea onto the slate counter. "Oh, sorry—" She dived at the spilt tea with a J-cloth. "Do you mind if I—?"

She had not registered the part about Edward being a "dish." All she could think was that he had buried the hatchet because of some particularly dreadful disaster at Melismate. She pushed past Polly into the drawing room.

"Hello," Edward said. He came over to her and solemnly planted a light kiss on her forehead.

"Oh, God—you've gone as pale as a ghost. I'm not bringing bad news, all right?"

The transformation was extraordinary. Rufa was speechless, and suddenly shy. For a fraction of a second she had not recognized the handsome, dark-suited stranger. She could hardly go on about it in front of Polly, but did not feel she could treat this man in the usual Edward way—so how was she to treat him? She glanced uneasily at Polly, who was miraculously calmed and smiling.

Edward put his hand on Rufa's shoulder. "Polly, can I take her away for half an hour? We need to talk."

"Oh, I'm afraid I still have to—" Rufa began.

Polly continued to smile. "Don't be silly, there's ages."

"We'll only be in the coffee place across the road," Edward said. "Come and yell at me if I'm keeping her too long."

"Nonsense, I shan't do anything of the sort. You must come back soon, when Berry's here—I know he'd love to see you again." With a giggle, Polly tugged the J-cloth out of Rufa's hand. "Rufa, do take off your apron—the neighbors will think I'm a slave driver!"

Rufa had not admitted to herself how desolate she had felt without Edward. The relief of seeing him again almost canceled out her astonishment that he could be so embarrassingly good-looking. It was very pleasant and restful to let him lead her across the road, into the coffee shop. The long counter at the window was crowded, but Edward managed to find a small, marble-topped table in a corner. They sat down, and stared at each other gravely.

Edward suddenly laughed. "Go on, say it."

"You look terrific without your beard," Rufa said, smiling. "I almost didn't know you."

"Hmm. Is that a good or a bad thing?"

"I said 'almost.' You're not that easy to disguise." She could not stop staring at his shorn face, trying to work out his age. He could not be a day over forty-five, she realized. The trappings of relicdom had only been superficial. The eternally youthful Zed had been quite a few years older than his best friend. "Do you miss it? Does your face feel naked without it?"

"It feels a little cold," he said. "But it was time to get rid of it. I only grew it to see if it all joined up."

A waitress came to the table. Edward ordered them both large cups of tea and blueberry muffins.

"Sorry," he said. "I should have asked you first. But I know you're hungry, even if you don't know it yourself. You look bloody exhausted. What on earth have you been doing?"

He was right, Rufa was exhausted. Despite being up to her elbows in food all day, she had not eaten since breakfast. "This is my third dinner party in four days," she said. "Polly's been so kind about recommending me to her friends. She has millions of them, and they all seem to live at a perpetual dinner party."

The muffins arrived, smelling deliciously of vanilla. Rufa admired hers, and tried to work up the energy to eat it. She liked to be looked after by Edward.

He said, "Nancy's got her work cut out, if she's making a play for Berry. Miss Polly Muir strikes me as an absolute expert at your Marrying Game."

"That's what I keep telling her." Rufa was relieved—and surprised—to hear the casual way he slipped in the controversial Marrying Game. "Polly would never give him up."

"Like a German on the beach," Edward said. "She draped her towel over him at dawn."

Rufa laughed. "Nance hasn't quite grasped the amount of work involved in a marriage."

"Well, it's not all beer and skittles," he said gently. "But marriage isn't all hard work either. There is quite a bit of job satisfaction—if you do it properly."

She drank her tea. Edward was frowning; not angry, but deeply cautious, picking out his words with tweezers. He said, "Rufa, I have to apologize for the way I stormed out last time."

"Please—" Rufa felt she could not bear any replay of that argument, even in the form of an apology.

"It's all right, I'm not here to bully you." His gray eyes were very serious. Rufa could feel the weight of the matter, whatever it was. "I just want you to know what an effect it had on me." He smiled grimly. "I drove home in a fury. I didn't sleep for the rest of that night. But by the time I switched on the *Today* program at six, I'd more or less worked it out."

"What?"

"Eat your muffin. You'll have to be patient with me. There's a lot of ground to cover. I think I'll start with Alice."

Alice, his wife. Rufa had not troubled to draw her soft edges into focus for years. She felt guilty, observing the pain in Edward's eyes. She had not seen this expression since the terrible day of The Zed's death.

"I had to make my peace with the past," he said. "I had to force myself to admit that time has moved on. I saw how trapped I had become." He cleared his throat, and looked down at the table. "I think you know—maybe you remember—how devastated I was when she died."

"Of course I do," Rufa said. She did remember. It had been an accepted thing, at Melismate, that Edward was a man with a broken heart.

"I felt I'd let her down, in some way—that was what I couldn't get over. I thought I was being tremendously brave, but I was actually trying to stop time. To lessen the distance between us. Which I daresay you can understand."

"You couldn't allow any changes," Rufa said, "because they would take you farther away from her. Changes would have been like a betrayal."

Edward reached across the table, to squeeze her hand. "I should have understood, and I was too dense. That was what the Marrying Game was all in aid of, wasn't it?"

"In a way."

"And I wouldn't admit that I'd been doing exactly the same. We've both been humoring the dead."

She did not understand, and was alarmed by the undertow of pain in his voice. He would not look at her. He bent over the table, absently placing brown sugar lumps in a circle.

He said, "Alice and I were first cousins. She was the child of my father's older brother. We grew up together. We fell in love and got married." He glanced up at her. "Does that strike you as odd?"

It did, slightly. "No," Rufa said.

"There wasn't any particular moment of falling in love. We used to say we fell in love the moment we met, when her mother brought her to the farm." He laughed briefly. "She was three, by the way, and I was four. Before she died, she told me she used to wish to marry me every year, when we stirred the Christmas pudding."

"You were soul mates," Rufa suggested gently.

He was grateful that she was trying to understand. "Oh, yes. Different in lots of ways, but somehow locking together, in a way that made each of us complete. A good marriage works because it suits both partners equally. We needed each other, and needed to be needed. Do you see?"

"Of course."

"There was a tremendous fuss about us getting married. My mother loved Alice like a daughter—and that was just the trouble, she said. She thought we'd have defective babies. Though in the event, we didn't have any babies at all."

His face was a mask. The pain could not be expressed, only distantly described.

"She wanted a child," he said, "more than anything else in the world. And there was your mother down the road, dropping babies right and left. That was hard for her."

His hands became still. He studied the surface of the table, as if reading the past. Rufa waited for him to speak again.

He raised his head. "Anyway. That's not what I—the only thing you have to know about is the money."

"Sorry?" Rufa was lost again. He had taken another unexpected turning.

"A brief sketch of my dysfunctional family," Edward said. "Alice's father—my uncle—had two children. Besides Alice, there was Prudence, her half sister. He never married her mother. Alice and my aunt Katherine took refuge with us, essentially because they couldn't live with my uncle. My aunt must have loved him; she never entirely left him. The two of them were back and forth—" He cleared his throat, before hurrying on. "I won't go into details. One of these days, I might tell you the whole story, but it's not something I want to dwell on now. All you have to know is that he was a wicked man"—he brought the word out forcefully—"and they couldn't stay with him. He was also very rich."

He looked briefly up at Rufa.

She said, "Oh."

"He disinherited Alice. But she was married to me. So I, as his nephew, got most of the money."

"What—you?" Rufa was fascinated. Edward's rigorous parsimony was as much a part of him as the facial hair had been. "A lot of money?"

"Yes."

"What happened to it?"

Edward said, "Nothing." He was rigid with embarrassment. "Alice was still alive then, and there was a condition that made the whole thing ridiculous—we even laughed at it because it was all so Victorian. Put simply, I was only to get that bloody money if I divorced Alice and married someone else."

Rufa was amazed. She had never suspected the prosaic Edward of having such a piece of gothic romance in his background.

Edward gazed down into the palms of his hands. "Then, of course, Alice died. We were still living in Germany when it all started. She went to the doctor because she thought she might be pregnant, and we found out when he gave her a blood test."

"How awful. I didn't know."

He glanced up, trying to smile. "Don't let me go off into a blow-by-blow account. That's not the point. The point is, I wanted to die too. And the business with the money seemed like a perfect excuse not to even think about marrying again. I felt I owed it to her." He paused. "It drove my poor mother demented. She pointed out that Alice was dead and I was still young, and I had a positive duty to marry again. But I couldn't bear even the idea. I couldn't risk going through all that again."

He was silent and motionless for several minutes, head bowed over the table. Then he straightened, and said briskly, "I've told you about Alice, and the money. Now I have to say something about you."

"Me?" Rufa was puzzled.

He frowned, choosing his words cautiously. "I was insensitive last time. I didn't understand how deeply you felt about Melismate. I was tarring you with the same brush as your father. But I can see now, in your case, the purely romantic isn't necessarily bad. It took that obscene Marrying Game of yours to show me what Melismate really means to you. And—and—" He drew a deep breath. "And what you mean to me."

Heat surged into Rufa's face. His contrition made her ashamed.

Very gently, slightly formally, Edward held her hand. "I can't let you do it, Ru. It would break my heart. I've had a special love for you since I left the army and came home to find you'd grown up. If possible, I've loved you more since you lost your father. I can't tell you how I've admired the way you tried to hold your family together." He smiled. "Truth to tell, I even rather admired your determination to sell yourself. But there's no way on earth I'm going to stand by and watch you marrying a man you don't remotely love."

"How do you—?" Rufa began, with an unconvincing show of indignation.

"Please." Edward squeezed her fingers. The pressure made Rufa shiver. "I haven't finished. I now realize what I was meant to do with all that money. You must marry me."

The shock drove the breath from Rufa's body. She was light-headed with it, casting round for some sign that she had slipped into a crazy dream.

Edward's wary eyes left her face again. "I don't, of course, mean you *must* marry me—I put that extremely badly. I mean that I would be—I would love it if you did. You're not in love with me, in the usual sense. But I think you're fond of me. I think you'd be an awful lot happier with me than with your Mr. Mecklenberg." He risked looking up at her again. "For one thing, you'd be sure of getting Melismate sorted out—my God, I know exactly where you should start too. The next big storm will take the roof off."

After the astonishment, Rufa braced herself for an embarrassing declaration of passion. When it did not come she was relieved; though the relief was curiously tinged with disappointment. She wondered, before pushing the thought away, what she would do if he jumped on her. Was Edward the man destined to unfreeze her? She found that she was checking his features, one by one, for anything unattractive. To her bewilderment, there was nothing. Edward was not unattractive at all. There was bound to be a catch sooner or later, but, for the moment, he looked scarily impossible to object to.

He released her hand, and looked directly into her eyes. "Before you say anything, I don't want you to think I'm doing this to—the purpose of the offer is not to take advantage of you. That's the last thing I want to do. It doesn't depend on your having sex with me. Or not."

This was incredibly embarrassing. Rufa's face burned. She could not reply. Their gazes met, and immediately dropped. The idea of Edward as a sexual being—that perfect self-control surrendered to passion—was impossible.

Edward seemed to feel he had got through the worst part of his proposal. He sighed. His shoulders relaxed a little, and his tone became brisk. It was the sort of tone he might have used in the army, tapping a map with a pointer and saying, "Pay attention, men."

"Let's get this out of the way at once. This can't be about sex, Rufa. Not because you're not beautiful—which I think is obvious—but because I refuse to play your Marrying Game. I want to help you to save Melismate, but I can't do it as part of a sordid exchange for sex. Everyone else will think I'm buying you, but you have to know this is the exact opposite. We would have to treat it as a business arrangement—only that sounds too cold. You were right. I can't let Melismate die with your father. This is partly about him. Before he died, he asked me to take care of you all. This is the way it has to be done."

He spoke with the quiet, immovable assurance Rufa had missed so much. Since The Zed's death, she had relied on Edward to know how things had to be done. He was always absolutely certain, and never wrong. They were silent. Rufa was dazed, trying to work out the turmoil of her feelings. She tried to imagine being married to Edward. This was totally different from imagining being married to Adrian.

Adrian was unknown, and she had known Edward most of her life. She trusted Edward implicitly. She liked him. She liked the ordered sobriety of his life. And, in a way, she loved him. This had nothing to do with romance. He encapsulated all her love for the safe, the sheltered, the familiar. Gradually, Edward's staggering proposal began to dawn on her as a godsend. For the first time in years—most certainly, for the first time since the death of The Zed—she would be able to drift off to sleep without worrying about her family. Oh, the blissful peace and happiness of knowing, on a stormy night, that the roof of Melismate, and the beloved people beneath it, were utterly secure.

Edward said, very quietly, "Say yes, and you can stop all this nonsense about the Marrying Game, once and for all. You're very tired, Ru, and you're obviously miserable. You've been like this since your father died, and I can't bear it anymore. Tell Miss Muir where to stuff her dinner party, and let me take you straight home."

She closed her eyes. Home, with Edward. No more slaving in other people's kitchens. No more editing her personality to suit the pitiless standards of Adrian. She did not love Adrian, and she never would. He knew this as well as she did. And he also knew that he was buying her. If she married Edward, she would never have to see him again.

It was as if the iron band around her heart that had chilled her and trapped her since the day of The Zed's death had suddenly melted into air. If she drew a deep, unconstrained breath, she would soar away into the sky.

She was crying, weak and giddy with the relief of it. "Yes," she whispered. "Yes, please." She started to sob. The sobs had been battling to get out for months, and would not be pushed back.

Edward, in the unhurried and deliberate way he did everything, stood up and came round to Rufa's side of the table. She felt him pulling her out of her chair, and firmly propelling her out of the café into a dark corridor with a public telephone.

"Sorry—sorry—"

Rufa was mortified that she could not stop crying—Edward hated scenes. Instead of urging her to pull herself together, however, he wrapped his arms around her and drew her head down on his shoulder, as he had done on the terrible day of The Zed's death.

"It's all right," he murmured. "It's all over now."

Time reeled back to that day. It was unfinished business between them. Rufa had wept gallons for The Zed in private, but she had only lost control once—in the middle of apologizing to Edward, for not being able to clean the room where she had found her father. Her howls of anguish had taken them both by surprise. Edward, with barely a word, had held and soothed and stroked her, for the best part of an hour. That outburst and this one now seemed connected, as if she had not stopped crying since.

Eventually, she was able to take her wet face off his shoulder. He put a clean handkerchief into her hand.

She blotted her streaming eyes, and blew her nose. "Oh God, I'm so sorry—"

Edward said, "Stop apologizing."

"It's just that I couldn't help thinking of—"

"Yes, I know."

"What's the time? Hell, I should get back."

He smiled. "I think you'd better have some more tea first."

They returned to their table, and Edward ordered the tea. Rufa felt hollowed out and scraped clean. She had sensed the strength and depth of his love for her, and for her family. Melismate was saved. Cautiously, she tested her newfound serenity, to check that it held. The nightmare was over.

"You were right," she said. "I am tired. And I was miserable."

Edward had now regained all his briskness and composure. "Rufa, you don't need to tie yourself in knots anymore. I know what you were miserable about—and I promise to be kind to the idle bastards, for your sake."

Shakily, she laughed. "Have you seen them?"

"No, I haven't been near Melismate for ages. How are they all? I can't believe how much I've missed them."

Rufa could not help launching into her anxieties about Selena, the mountain of unpaid bills, and the crumbling state of the house. Edward listened impassively, as he always had. She was not asking for help, simply enjoying the novelty of pouring her worries into a sensible and sympathetic pair of ears.

It was nearly seven when she dashed back to Polly's flat. She had stepped through the looking glass, and the world was now entirely, enchantingly different. She felt fond of everyone, even Polly.

"I know I'm disgustingly late, but it got complicated."

Polly had just received an enormous bunch of astonishing bright orange and shocking pink roses, and was beaming. "Do tell me more about your impossibly young and tasty godfather. Is he spoken for?"

To her slight annoyance, Rufa felt her face turning hot again.

She said, "Yes."

"Adrian will be here soon. You'd better get changed."

Too late. She had got herself changed already. Now, she faced the unsaying of what had never really been said, to let Adrian know he had lost her. The Marrying Game was over.

Chapter Fourteen

Nancy morosely spooned the last bit of froth from her cappuccino.
How handy, she thought, that Berry lived directly opposite a trendy
coffee shop. It meant that she could watch his front door and recover
from the row with Rufa at the same time. She had flounced out of Wendy's
in a screaming fury, and sobbed her way through a whole packet of tissues
on the tube. God, that had been embarrassing—everyone had stared, and a
black man in a dog collar had started asking her about the Bible. But she had
been too far gone to care. Talk about out of the frying pan and into the
fire—she would never have opened out to Edward, if she had dreamed that
he would stop the Marrying Game by marrying Rufa himself.

She had told Edward about her sister's aching vulnerability, and he had
used it to take advantage of her. It was sick. It was disgusting. At the height
of the row, Nancy had screamed that it was practically incest. He had married his first cousin, after all—"So he's obviously not above screwing his
relations."

Her eyes smarted again. She sniffed angrily, sorry that she had spoiled her
own argument by overreacting. All right, incest had been a bit strong. But
Edward was one of the grown-ups, and she had expected him to give Rufa
nothing more controversial than a telling-off. The silly cow now thought

she was happy, when anyone could see she had forgotten the meaning of the word. She only wanted to marry Edward, as far as Nancy could see, because he was not Adrian, and better the devil you knew. He may have been too youthful and good-looking to cast as a dirty old man, but it was still gross. And The Zed would have counted it as a betrayal.

The nagging guilt made it all worse. Nancy avoided introspection if she possibly could, but now she was forced to look back at her own behavior. Since the death of The Zed, what had she done? She had congratulated herself for handling it all rather well, for not being as cockeyed as poor Ru about the house, and the "blood" The Zed had gone on about like a vampire. But she had dived for cover, by losing her heart to poor Tim Dent, and could not even remember now why she had fallen in love with him—except that the act of falling in love had been like sheathing every emotion in plastic wrap. She had simply refused to look into the future. She had left all that to Rufa, because Rufa was better at worrying. And here was the result. Her favorite sister, who was worth all the rest of them put together, was about to fling herself into a marriage that could only be grotesque.

There was just one way to save her. Nancy had come here for the express purpose of screwing a proposal out of Berry. Before she had started howling, when she was still being swept along on the tide of fury, she had remembered Rufa saying that Polly was due at the hairdresser's this morning. That had carried her straight to the tube, absolutely determined to seize the day. Rufa would have tried to stop her, but she knew nothing about it. She was driving to Melismate with Edward, supposedly in triumph.

Nancy sighed impatiently. Forty-five minutes she had been sitting here, waiting for Polly to emerge from the smug blue front door across the road. Surely Polly the Perfect, with those complicated highlights, could not afford to cancel her hair appointment?

At last the door opened. The brisk, assisted-blond figure of Polly appeared on the front steps and paused for a moment, to eye the smiling blue sky with approval. She dug in her Fendi handbag for her car keys, climbed into her dainty silver jeep, and neatly removed herself.

Action stations. Nancy wiped her lips with her napkin to remove all traces of cappuccino, hoping her eyes were not too puffy. She left the coffee shop, walked across the road, and pressed Berry's buzzer. Her heart was beating hard. She was nervous, which was unfamiliar and rather exciting.

His voice crackled out of the Entryphone. "Hello?"

"Hi, it's Nancy Hasty. Can I come up?"

"Nancy?" Berry's voice leaped up to a quavering falsetto. He cleared his throat. "Er—Polly's not here, I'm afraid."

"Oh, drat," Nancy said. "What a disappointment. Still, you're here. I'll pop in anyway."

There was a short but significant silence. The door buzzed, and Nancy pushed it open. The communal hallway of the house was extremely tidy, with a fat beige carpet and a polished cupboard for letters. Nancy smiled at her own wicked reflection, in a large gilded mirror. She wore her tight jeans, and an embroidered silk cardigan that practically lit her nipples in neon. If she said it herself, she looked fantastic.

Berry was waiting for her upstairs, at the door of his first-floor flat. He was barefoot, in black jeans and an old blue sweater. She realized that apart from Christmas Eve, she had only ever seen him in his City overalls—dark suit, tie, cuff links, hard collar. Without these, and with his tousled hair falling over startled deer's eyes, he looked absurdly young and extraordinarily sexy. Nancy's spirits rose.

"Hi." He was tense and anxious.

She firmly kissed his cheek, and pushed past him into the flat. A *cafetière* of coffee stood on the low table in the drawing room, beside Saturday's *Financial Times* and a handsome plate of croissants. Nancy looked at these affectionately, hoping there would be time to eat a couple later.

"Polly's out," Berry said, too loudly. "At the hairdresser's."

Nancy sank into the embrace of the sofa cushions. "Highlights, is it? Poor thing, she'll be gone for ages. How very tiring, to have roots that need so much attention."

He hovered, visibly trying to control a rising agitation. "Would you—er—like some coffee?"

"Not yet." Nancy slipped off her shoes. Her toenails were painted magenta. "Do sit down. It's actually you I came to see."

"Me?"

"It's a delicate matter—not the kind of business I can settle with Polly around. Now, sit down—you're making me nervous."

"Sorry." Berry lowered himself cautiously onto the sofa, staring at Nancy with helpless fascination. "Business?"

"You'll never guess," Nancy said. "So let's cut to the chase. I popped round to fuck the daylights out of you."

Berry whispered, "Oh, God—"

She leaned across the sofa, unhooked his glasses, and kissed him on the mouth. He submitted as if in a trance. His arms went round her. He sighed tremulously into her lips, and pulled her against him. They kissed rapturously.

Gently, he pushed her away. Nancy lay back against the cushions and began to unbutton her cardigan.

"No," Berry said breathlessly.

"Mmm—want me to keep it on?"

"Yes. I mean, yes. I do." His voice gathered force. Painfully, he scrambled for his glasses, and stood up. "We mustn't—I can't." He sounded as if he were trying to convince himself. "Nancy, I can't do this."

"What?" Nancy was astounded.

"I'm awfully sorry—" He looked grief-stricken, but determined. "It's just not possible. It's out of the question."

"Are you saying you don't want sex with me?" Nobody had ever not wanted sex with Nancy. "Don't be silly." She sat upright, her voice sharpening. "Of course you do."

Distractedly, he raked his hair into Stan Laurel peaks. "Nancy, for God's sake, please don't make it harder for me."

"What's the problem?"

"Stop it. You know perfectly well. I'm not saying that if I'd met you sooner, or in another life—God, I'm babbling." He was gathering dignity with every word. He stood straighter, and squared his shoulders. "Because I'm going to marry Polly."

Nancy stared at him. "But you don't love her nearly as much as me!"

"I do love her."

"You're lying!"

"No I am not!" Berry said fiercely. "I love Polly far too much to cheat on her. I can't even think of it. I couldn't live with myself afterward."

He meant it. The world darkened around Nancy, as the truth sank in.

Rufa had been right. Here was a rare man who valued other things besides sex. He refused to break his word to Polly. He could not be seduced, and would never be persuaded to marry Nancy, which meant that Rufa would certainly ruin her life by marrying Edward. She drew in a breath, and exhaled it in a loud sob. This time she wept not with anger, but with despair. She covered her face with her hands, and wailed to feel the fissure in her heart.

"Nancy—oh, my God—" Berry sounded appalled. She felt his tentative hand on her arm.

"It's not you," she gasped. "It's everything—everything bad that's happened to us—if he hadn't done it, we'd all be fine, and it would all be the same—"

"Hadn't done it? Oh, God, you mean your father."

The cushions beside her sagged under his weight. He put his arm around her, and she found herself sobbing into his shoulder. She wept and wept, for what seemed ages. He did not move or speak, but stroked her back gently, in a way that was deeply comforting. Eventually, she pulled herself blearily away from him.

"Sorry. I'm a stupid cow. Don't worry, I'll go now."

She risked a look at him, and almost dissolved again when she saw how kindly he looked back at her.

"Don't go yet," he said. "I'll make some tea, or something."

Nancy tried to laugh. "Some of that coffee will be fine."

"It's freezing. I'll get some more." He unwound his arm, and stood up. "How do you like it?"

"Black, three sugars, strong enough to blow a safe."

"Righto." He dug in his pocket for a handkerchief. "Have this. It's clean."

He went to the kitchen. Nancy curled on the sofa, mopping her wrecked face, feeling an utter fool. When he came back with the coffee, she had rallied a little.

"Berry, you are nice. I'm so sorry for ruining your Saturday morning."

"You haven't. Honestly."

"I'm having one of those days when everything looks bloody, that's all. Usually, I have an incredible capacity to ignore it." She sipped her coffee. "Did Ru tell you?"

"About her engagement, you mean? Yes, she did. It was rather a shock, because we assumed that she and Adrian—"

"This is far worse," Nancy said. "This is a catastrophe."

Berry handed her the plate of croissants. "Have one of these. Why is it a catastrophe?"

"Oh, come on. Edward Reculver, of all people. Don't you think it's disgusting?" Nancy bit angrily into a croissant.

"No," Berry said. "I like Edward. Rather more than Adrian, actually. And not just because Adrian is my boss. To see Rufa's face, when she came back with him—well, Polly said it was too obvious for words. She said she was a bit cross with Rufa, for stringing everyone along. But even Adrian could see she was radiantly happy. She looked as if she'd swallowed a lightbulb."

"She's not happy," Nancy said, through a mouthful of croissant. "She only thinks she is."

Berry smiled. "Well, isn't that enough?"

"You don't understand her. Nobody does, because she looks so capable. She's been totally bonkers since The Zed died."

"She never talks about it. Did she take it harder than the rest of you?"

"Yes." As she said it, Nancy saw that this was true. "She found him—that must have made it worse. And she was alone in the house with him. I'd changed my shift at the pub so I could go out with Tim—my boyfriend—in the evening. If I hadn't done that, I would have been there too. I should have been there."

"But what could you have done?" Berry asked gently.

Nancy shrugged. "I don't know. Just been there with her. She didn't know what to do."

"My God, I'm not surprised. What did she do, in the end?"

"She couldn't think whether to ring the police, or an ambulance—so she rang Edward. He was there, thank goodness, when everyone else—anyway, he did the rest." Nancy frowned, holding back the tears. "He's awfully good at managing things. I suppose it comes from the army. Of course, he reacted by giving orders. He ordered Ru to go and sit outside until he came. Not to touch anything, or make any more calls. He did all that."

"Kind of him," Berry said.

"Yes. He was very kind. He did his best to take care of us, when we were all quite barmy. Death makes you barmy, you know—you don't even cry, and then you think you must be fine. But you're not. None of us were. Particularly Rufa."

Berry said, "You love Rufa a lot, don't you?"

"Ru's my right arm. I can't bear that he's taking her away." Nancy willed herself not to start crying again. "I can't believe I've blabbed all this out to you. I've never really said it aloud to anyone. If you want the ghastly truth, I came here with the dotty idea of making you marry me, so Ru wouldn't have to go through with it."

Alarm flashed across Berry's face for a moment, then he smiled. "And you were going to stick me with the bills for mending your house?"

"I'm afraid so, darling. And the debts. You've had a lucky escape."

"So have you," he said, laughing softly. "I couldn't have afforded you."

"What?" Nancy was startled. "Don't be daft—I've seen pictures of your house!"

"I thought you, of all people, would know what big, posh houses cost to run. Most of my father's money goes straight back into the estate. It won't be my problem until I inherit—and, thank God, my father is exceptionally hale and hearty. We fully expect him to last another thirty years. He's giving me a house, when I get married. Otherwise, I have to work, like everyone else. And I'm not the sort of City person who earns enough to save Melismate."

"But—but—" Nancy was bewildered, and rather indignant. "The way you live—this flat—"

"This? It's Polly's."

"Oh."

"So there you are," Berry said, manfully keeping the wistfulness out of his voice. "Marrying me wouldn't exactly be love in a cottage. But the only roof my family can afford to worry about is our own. We haven't any millions to spare."

"Oh," Nancy said again. She started laughing. He laughed too. They both reached for the last croissant, and laughed until they almost wept.

Berry solemnly tore the croissant in half, and went to the kitchen to make another pot of coffee. Nancy lay back against the soft cushions of his—Polly's—sofa, and listened to him singing to himself as he banged the cupboard doors. Berry's voice was sweet and buoyant, and nearly made her cry again. She wondered what on earth had got into her.

"You've been an angel," she said, when he returned.

He grinned shyly. "Rubbish."

"You have—I can practically see your wings. Old Waltzing Matilda is a lucky girl, and I hope she knows it." She sighed gustily, and reached for her half of the croissant. "I'm glad you're not as filthy rich as we thought—it makes you less likely to end up with a gold-digging bitch like me."

"You're not a bitch, Nancy," Berry said, reddening. "You were doing it to help Rufa—but I doubt it would have worked, anyway. Even if I had been able to save Melismate. You'd never have talked her out of marrying Edward."

"How right you are." Nancy was gloomy. "Once she's made her mind up, nothing on earth can budge her. I think that's what scared me—seeing that she was totally set on him."

"I still don't see why you're so against Edward," Berry said, in a firmer voice. "I think he's terrific. That night he rescued my car keys, he told me how much he loved you all."

"Did he?"

"I got the distinct impression that he'd pulverize anyone who tried to hurt you—any of you. He said he owed it to your father."

Nancy's sore eyes filled with yet more tears—the tears she had not shed for The Zed because she had been so busy being cheerful. "I wish he'd just married someone else, got his hands on the money, and given it to us when we needed it."

"Perhaps he didn't think your father would take it."

She blew her nose briskly. "Oh, you must be kidding. The Zed was like a very lazy version of Dick Turpin. He'd take money off absolutely anyone, without a second thought."

"Perhaps Edward's sorry, and marrying Rufa is one way of making it up to you all. I bet he'd have given every penny of it, and married absolutely anyone, to save your father. That's the kind of man he is. It's obvious, really."

There was a silence. Nancy said, "You think I'm too hard on him."

"Yes. I think he loves your sister very much."

Another silence.

Nancy said, "Oh, God. Oh, hell. You've been so kind, and I've behaved like a total cow. I screeched at Ru this morning. I threatened to have her sectioned under the Mental Health Act. And now she's gone home thinking I hate her."

"Rubbish. She'd never think that."

She blew her nose again with finality, like a full stop. "I'd better start mending a few fences."

Chapter Fifteen

Spring had come to the soft countryside around Melismate, scattering bluebells and pale primroses in pockets of woodland, and tufts of green across the raw brown fields. The broom was out, and there were banks of waxen yellow daffodils. The air that rushed through the open window of Edward's Land Rover smelled of damp soil and young grass.

Rufa, now officially and publicly his fiancée, was in the passenger seat beside him. The change in the weather was appropriate, she thought, for the first day in this new era of her life. She wanted the world to look different, so that she could see the happy ending with her own eyes. She was still angry enough with Nancy to want continuous proof that she had been in the right.

Nancy had been out until the small hours, working at her bar and then carousing at a Soho club with Roshan. Rufa had broken the news of the engagement this morning. She had been genuinely unprepared for Nancy's outrage, taking it for granted that her sister would be pleased, or at least relieved. Nancy's disgusting accusations had made Rufa furious. Apart from anything else, the sheer ingratitude took her breath away. Didn't she realize what Edward was doing for them? Where did Nancy think they would all be without him? He had baled them out of one mess after another, never expecting thanks—and not often getting them.

But she would not sustain her indignation. The truth was that she was desperate for Nancy's approval. Nancy was her favorite sister, and as necessary to her as salt. Her absence took the gloss off Rufa's triumphant homecoming. She would have to come round, however, when she saw the relief and happiness of their mother. Rufa was sure Rose would be delighted. She tried to focus on the joy of engineering a real, oceangoing happy ending. Nancy was bound to come round in the end.

Edward glanced aside at her, trying to puzzle out her mood.

Somehow, before reaching Melismate, the two of them had to step into their new roles as lovers. Edward could not see how they were to do this. Rufa had not guessed—he had been unable to tell her—how passionately she was loved. It was still surprising to Edward. After their quarrel, when he had stayed up all night wrestling to the bottom of his anger, this was the great discovery he had made. For the past six years, since his return to the farm, he had been living out the private drama of being in love with Rufa. It had fed all his relations with the family, like an underground stream.

She had been a child in his mind, until he had met her again as a young woman of twenty-one—tall, grave, and disturbingly beautiful. And the idol of her father's heart. Edward recalled speeches The Zed had made, when plastered, about how he dreaded "surrendering" Rufa to any other man.

The Zed had confided in Edward because he had not considered him a rival. Edward had not considered himself a rival. Any feeling he had for Rufa—any pang he might have felt at her loveliness—had been strangled and buried immediately. There had been no question of declaring his love to her. He had assumed that she would never think of falling in with him. He had pushed his feelings deeper underground when she had fallen in love with the ghastly writer who had rented his cottage.

Marrying Rufa would mean the unburying of all that imprisoned desire. He had meant every word of the speech he had made to her, about sex not being part of the deal. But of course Edward wanted sex with her. He wanted it desperately, and suddenly having permission to think about it was driving him crazy. Their situation was ridiculous, he thought. They were engaged, but if they were ever to be real lovers, he now had to begin the process of courting and winning her. And God alone knew how he was to do that, when he had such a terror of seeming to force her.

He had, he realized, lost the language of sexual courtship. Sex belonged to the side of his life Rufa knew nothing about. He did not think he could ever explain to her why he had kept part of himself sealed off from Melismate. Hopefully, he would be able to tidy it all up without Rufa finding out. Edward looked aside at Rufa, and could not imagine how to break through the smiling silence that surrounded her.

I'm calcified by loneliness, he thought; it's turned me into a statue. I don't know how to set about showing this girl I'd die for her.

He cleared his throat. "Are you all right?"

Rufa, turned to him, still smiling. "Fine." When they spoke, normality reasserted itself.

"You're not fine," he said. "And I wish to God I knew what to do about it. Is it me?"

"No, of course not."

"Is it Nancy?"

Her silence told him he was right.

"I was under the impression," he said, "that I would be driving Miss Nancy today. Am I to take her absence personally?"

Rufa had her meditative, inward look, which he recognized as anger. "She's in one of her tempers. We had a massive row."

"About me, I suppose. About you marrying a superannuated old fart."

"Well, yes. But she'll calm down." Rufa said this forcefully, willing it to be true. "She usually does in the end."

Edward gripped the steering wheel aggressively, swallowing his intense annoyance. Nancy had all The Zed's faults, he decided, and precious little of his charm. Rufa's feelings, however, were his chief consideration. He had been alarmed by the chasm of pain that had opened up in her yesterday, when he proposed. She was not as self-possessed as people thought. Thinking of this reassured him. He was doing the right thing; he was not taking advantage. She needed him.

He said, "I don't suppose your Mr. Mecklenberg was too thrilled, either."

Rufa sighed. She had not yet told him about telling Adrian. "No, he wasn't, though he wouldn't let me explain. He just gave me a dreadful look that left me covered with ice."

"Rather awkward, I should think."

"I deserved it," Rufa said. "It was the least I deserved. Proper behavior is what matters most to Adrian. In front of the others, he was very nice. He made everyone drink a toast to me, and said you were a lucky man. I felt about an inch tall."

"Well, you've done it now."

"Yes." She was drifting back into silence.

Edward asked, "Do you mind if we stop off at the farm on the way?"

"I'd love to."

He kept his stern eyes on the road. "You might think about what needs to be done there. The outside's in good nick, but the inside hasn't been touched in twenty years." He added, "Since the last bride came home, in fact."

"Don't let me change anything," Rufa said. "I couldn't stand the responsibility."

"It's not a shrine." Edward was firm. "It's got to be your home. Our home." He dropped this in carefully. They had not mentioned it before—that Rufa, in order to save the house she loved, must live in exile. They must live under the same roof, or where was the point of getting married? He felt brutal for pointing it out, and half expected her to protest.

She was still smiling. "Okay, but nothing fancy. I like the farm as it is. It reminds me of your mother."

"She'd be terrifically pleased about this," Edward said, touched that Rufa had invoked that benign, hectoring presence.

"Only if I make you happy."

"You will."

"I hope so—I mean, I hope there's something in it for you. I'd hate it if marrying me was just another example of your doing something kind."

Here was his cue to assure her that there was everything in it for him, because he adored her. And all he could manage was, "I don't go and marry people in the way that I fix drains."

He turned the car off the road, down the narrow track that led to the farm. They halted in front of the plain, square, trim house that had not changed since Rufa's childhood. It was scrupulously clean, and achingly bare. The big Georgian windows had a chilly glint where the sun caught them.

Rufa got out of the car, and stood gazing at her new home. Edward was surprised to see how happy she seemed: eager and determined to be pleased. The sunlight on her hair almost disabled him with a sudden, blinding awareness of her beauty. He wanted to fill her arms with great bales of spring flowers.

He unlocked his front door. There was a pile of mail on the mat. He stooped to pick it up, and went across the broad, tiled hall to the drawing room. Rufa followed obediently, like a visitor.

In his army days the house had been let to a series of tenants, while he and Alice had mostly lived abroad. It still had an impersonal feel. There were no traces of Alice except for two photographs in silver frames on the chimneypiece. One was of Alice, squinting against the sun, outside their army house in Germany. In the other, she was holding her baby nephew, son of her half sister. Rufa looked at these, then looked away. Light-headed with the longing to touch her, Edward wrapped his arms around her.

For the smallest fraction of a second, Rufa tensed defensively. A quarter second later, she smiled again, and relaxed against him in the old friendly way, but it was enough. He released her gently. She was not ready. It horrified him that she might think of sex with him as a duty. Too many ghosts. He saw Alice, faded to sepia, quietly leaving and closing the door behind her. He pushed away a disturbing memory of standing beside the font in the village church, with the weight of a baby in his arms. It was too soon. They both needed more time.

He said, "Do you want some tea?"

She was grateful, which was awful. "I'll make it."

"Thanks. There's a carton of long-life milk in the larder."

Rufa went to the kitchen. Edward heard her opening doors, humming to herself. He sat down on the sofa to open his letters.

She brought the tea things in on a dented tin tray, decorated with a worn picture of a Scottie dog, which she had coveted as a small child. The cups were clean and chipless, but of different patterns. The teapot was a thick brown clod, with a rubber tip over the broken spout.

"You need a new teapot," she said. "Nobody uses these little condom things anymore."

Edward laughed, suddenly feeling more cheerful. He loved it when she gave him orders. "Don't they?"

"No. It just looks mean, in a weird way."

"Hmmm, they are getting rather hard to buy, now that you mention it. Condoms are a hell of a lot easier."

Rufa set the tray down on the hearthrug and knelt, like a geisha, to pour it. She had found a jug for the milk. "Don't worry, I'll drag you into the right century." She handed him his tea, and settled contentedly against his leg— the unthinking physical contact moved him deeply, and increased the distance between them.

"Isn't this lovely?" she demanded. "It feels like we've been married for ages."

"Well, here's to the latest Russian play," Rose said, holding her fourth glass of champagne up to the bleary light. "The one where Rufa Rufusova marries the elderly neighbor to save the orchard."

"He's not elderly, but you can say anything you like now," Rufa said calmly. She was moving between the range and the kitchen table, assembling a lavish supper. She had made Edward take a detour to the supermarket in Cirencester on the way, knowing there would be nothing at Melismate. "I don't care—as long as you're civil to him when he's here."

"Come on—wasn't I the very pink of politeness? Weren't we all?"

Rufa said, "You know what I mean." There was steel beneath her serenity. She was alone with her mother for the first time since her triumphal return. Edward had wisely lubricated the homecoming with a dozen bottles of supermarket champagne. Even so, Rufa had sensed that her mother and sisters did not protest only because they were too limp with amazement. She had been acutely aware of Rose's anxiety and skepticism. It had been a relief when Edward went home, leaving her here. Now they could talk about him openly, and have a screaming row if necessary.

Rose, slouched in her drinking chair beside the range, watched Rufa narrowly.

"Daughters are the most puzzling creatures," she said gloomily. "How can you possibly be happy?"

"Mum, for the last time, please believe me." Rufa turned to face her, so that Rose could see she meant it. "I'm happier than I've been in ages. I feel as if a great weight has been lifted off my shoulders."

"Darling, that wasn't for you to carry. You weren't designed for weights."

Rufa's lips twitched. She was so light and giddy from the sudden removal of the pain, she was finding their objections to Edward rather comical. Rose, Lydia, and Selena had wanted to be cold and disapproving, but they had not been able to resist the free alcohol. The savages of Melismate would have sold each other for a drop of the white man's firewater.

"You shouldn't drink champagne," she said. "It makes you lugubrious."

Rose let out a yelp of laughter. This was not what she had expected from her earnest, Victorian daughter. "Oh God, does it?"

"I love Edward very much, and I'm radiantly happy." This absolutely had to be true, and therefore was. Rufa did love Edward, in the sense of being deeply fond of him, dependent on him, anxious to have his good opinion. At the farm, seeing the changed Edward in the familiar setting, she had found herself thinking how easy it would be to fall in love with him if they had only just met. She was sorry she had not been prepared when he put his arm around her. Edward had backed off too quickly, she thought. It was difficult, when both of you felt you were play-acting at being in love.

If he had ignored her surprise and ravished her, would she have enjoyed it? Or would she have despised him for behaving as if he had bought her? Any reaching out to Edward would carry embarrassing implications of buying and selling. These were complicated questions, only beginning to form in Rufa's mind. She did not want Rose to put them into brutal words. Her mother's role in all this was simply being overjoyed, nothing more.

She asked, "Why can't you accept it, and start looking forward to the future?"

"I've lost the art," Rose said sadly. "The future always looks shitty to me."

"It's going to be heavenly. I'm so excited." Rufa squeezed lemon over plates of smoked salmon. "Edward says he'll bring over a friend of his who's a structural engineer, to decide what major work needs to be done—the foundations, the roof, the west wall—"

Rose groaned, and leaned forward to dribble the last champagne in the bottle into her glass. "Spare me."

"I'm sorry if it bores you," Rufa said, with the first hint of lemon-sharpness. "But it's not as if he's asking you to actually do anything. All you have to do is live with the workmen, and try not to subvert them."

There was a sour twist to Rose's smile. "You even sound like him."

"Perhaps I am like him."

"It's not the plans for the house I mind," Rose said. "The Zed would have been thrilled."

Rufa ground black pepper over the salmon. "I keep thinking about him. I wish we'd been able to save the house before, when he was alive. It might have changed everything." She had tried to make her voice sound casual, but it cracked.

Rose said, "It wasn't really because of the house."

"Because of everything it stood for, then."

"No, there was more." Rose was finding it easier to talk about The Zed with resignation, if not detachment. "Lost looks, lost years. Hitting fifty was dreadful for him. He couldn't roll back time."

"All the same, I wish time did roll back." Rufa's voice cracked again.

Rose swallowed a twinge of anger with The Zed. Though she had barely admitted it to herself, she read selfishness and aggression into his suicide, and despised him for it. Couldn't he have seen what it would do to his girls? Especially Rufa, his best beloved. He must have known there was a good chance that Rufa would be the one to find his body. She had been a basket case ever since. In the end, it had been very hard to feel he gave a damn about any of them.

She levered herself out of her chair. "You're right, champagne obviously does make me lugubrious—bloody nice engagement party this is. If you're really happy, I suppose I am too. All right?" She filled the battered kettle at the stained butler's sink in the pantry, and banged it down on the hot plate. "It's you I'm worried about, darling. If Edward truly is the man you want, I'll welcome the tiresome old fart with open arms."

Rufa's face brightened. "He is. Don't you think he's handsome, without the beard?"

"God, yes, there's no dispute about that. I must say, the pair of you look fabulous together—you'll be the best-looking couple this parish has seen in years." Rose poured water and made tea. She took her cup back to the drinking chair. "But I just can't stretch my imagination into picturing you sleeping with him. And that does worry me. Sex is a lot more important than you seem to think. Being able to live without it is not the same as living with someone and not doing it."

Rufa took a deep breath. "I do assure you, sex with Edward is—is very nice indeed."

"What—you mean you've done it?"

Rufa bent over the table, keeping her face hidden. "Yes. What's so odd about that?"

Rose gasped, "Oh, God—you've done it with Edward!" She went off into a fit of nervous laughter. "You've seen his bum! I'll never be able to look him in the eye again!"

"Stop it." Rufa was smiling.

Rose played up to her audience, as she had not done since the death of The Zed. "Tell me the truth, dear—remember, you can say anything to Marmee—are his pubes gray?"

"I'm not telling you. Ask him yourself."

"Roger's are. I used to pull them out with tweezers, but it got too much. His scrotum started to look like a plucked duck." Rose let out a great sigh, full of relief. "Sit down. Stop doing things."

"If I don't, who will? Oh, all right." Rufa sat down at the table, taking her cup of tea. Rose had forgotten to take out the tea bag and it was brick-red, but it was home tea. There was no other tea like it in the world. She did not care that she had lied about sleeping with Edward. The lie had put her mother's mind at rest.

"I'm glad your Marrying Game turned out so well," Rose said. "I've never seen Edward so angry as the day he found out about it—God, you'd think I'd sold you into slavery. It was like the bit in *David Copperfield* where Mr. Peggotty finds out about Little Em'ly."

"You'll have to cheer up your literary allusions now, Mum. We're not being scripted by Chekhov. Or Dostoevsky, or Dickens—or Stephen King. This is more like the last chapter of a novel by Jane Austen. A happy ending, with all the ends tying up neatly."

"I hope so," Rose said. "Because if you're honestly happy, I can start enjoying the un-pain. It feels blissful. No more agonizing over the debts. A mended roof over my Linnet's little head. Unlimited gin."

At last, at last, Rufa thought. This was the reward she had been working for all along: to see the strain and sadness lifting off her mother's face.

"I wish Nancy felt the same," she said.

"That horrid girl." Rose drained her glass. "I had her on the phone this morning, screeching like a fishwife."

"She's like you," Rufa said. "She refuses to believe I can possibly be happy. Me saying so isn't enough. God knows how I'm supposed to prove it. Couldn't you talk to her?"

"I could try. She won't listen, though. Leave her to come down in her own time—she's mostly hot air. God, she's like The Zed sometimes."

The door to the stairs opened. The small, airy figure of Linnet ran in, strangely bulky because the Ressany Brothers were stuffed into the front of her darned yellow jersey.

"Granny, are you too drunk to give me a bath?"

"Drunk? Me?" Rose stood up, gulping her tea. Rufa had noticed before that however much she had put away, Rose was always brisk and collected with Linnet. "Certainly not. But don't you want Ru to do the bath?"

"No," Linnet said imperiously. "She's going to tell me a story afterward. A new one."

"Am I?" Rufa laughed. "Okay."

"It has to be about the Ressanys. I wish Nancy was here to do the voices." Wistfully, she checked the faces of Rose and Rufa. "Is she coming soon?" Like her late grandfather, Linnet needed to have all her people around her.

"Very soon," Rose said firmly, with a smile at Rufa. "As soon as she's got all the hot air out of her system."

Linnet was interested. "I didn't know Nancy had hot air. Is it in her bosoms?"

Rose and Rufa, weakened by champagne, howled with laughter.

"Well. I must say." Linnet scowled, and tried to fold her arms across her stuffed jersey. "I asked a perfectly reasonable question. It's appalling to laugh at children just because they don't know."

"Sorry, darling," Rufa said.

"And yet you're still doing it," Linnet said coldly.

At this difficult moment, the front door slammed. Out in the empty, echoing Great Hall, a high voice shrilled, "Trotsky! Put on your saddle, we're going for a ride!"

A guttural, accented voice replied, "Yes, Mr. Ressany—"

"Nancy!" Linnet shrieked, the light flooding back into her disapproving face. The door between the Hall and the kitchen opened, and there was Nancy.

She knelt to embrace Linnet, and to cover her face with smacking kisses. "Oh, my peach blossom! My silk princess! I've missed you so much, and I've such naughty stories to tell about the Ressanys!" She kissed the bears, through Linnet's jersey. "What are they doing here?"

"They're not born yet," Linnet said. "They're going to come out as tiny new babies, and I'll have to get up in the middle of the night to feed them. But"—she added quickly—"they can still talk. And sit in their rocking chairs."

Rose crossed the room to kiss Nancy. "My darling, how lovely to see you."

Over her mother's shoulder, Nancy looked imploringly at Rufa, and mouthed, "Sorry."

Rufa smiled at her delightedly. "I'm so glad you changed your mind, Nance."

"Oh, I couldn't have stayed at Wendy's. It's like a funeral parlor, stuffed with great triffidlike flowers for Roshan, from that bloody Tiger Durward."

"You're just in time for my story," Linnet said.

Nancy turned her attention back to the little girl. "All right. Give me a few minutes to have a cup of tea, and I'll tell you about the Ressanys' school trip to London."

"Oh yes! But they don't go to big school. It was a nursery trip."

"Sorry I got arrested," Nancy said, in a deep, growling voice. "I won't take a bomb with me next time."

Linnet giggled, showing a row of tiny, perfect teeth. "Did he go to prison?"

"Where's Mummy?" Rose asked.

"Upstairs."

"Ask her to do your bath, darling. I want to talk to Nancy."

Linnet considered this suspiciously, then nodded. "All right. If Nancy comes up straight afterward. And brings up Trotsky's cage. And if Ru sings me a song and switches the light off."

"Yes, yes—God, you drive a hard bargain," Rose said. "If only your poor parents could be more like you."

The moment Linnet had scampered away upstairs, Nancy blurted out, "Ru, I'm so sorry. I was an utter bitch, and I didn't mean a word of it."

Rufa put the red-hot kettle back on the range. She was radiant. Nothing felt right when she was at odds with Nancy. "I'm sorry too. Let's just forget it. You're just in time for a superb supper."

"Is Edward here?"

"No, he had to go back to the farm. He's coming back for supper, though—you'd better get used to it."

"Ru, darling—I actively want to see him. I want to apologize."

"That'll be worth watching," Rufa said, laughing. Nancy being home made this seem like a happy ending.

Rose was wrestling with the foil of a champagne bottle. "This is just like the bit in *Little Women* where Jo and Amy bury the hatchet, after Amy nearly drowns—"

"Shut up, you doting old crone," Nancy said. "Get me a drink. And a large cup of strong tea. I've had a very stressful day."

The champagne was opened, with a festive pop. Rose handed Nancy a generous glassful. Rufa made more tea. The three of them settled at the kitchen table. Rufa and Rose were in a state of vast contentment.

"So," Rose said, "you've decided not to have your sister sectioned. You've decided to give her your blessing."

"I was crazy this morning," Nancy said, pensively sipping champagne. "It seems ages ago now."

"Where did you storm off to?" Rufa asked. "I made Edward wait half an hour, to see if you'd come slinking back."

Nancy's eyelids were swollen. She looked tired, but she was smiling. "I was too far gone to slink. In fact, I was so bonkers, I went straight round to Berry's and asked him to marry me."

"You didn't! What on earth did he say?"

Nancy's smile wavered a fraction. "I had a go at seducing him. It didn't work. He turned me down, actually. You were right, Ru—he obviously doesn't fancy me as much as I thought. He's determined to marry the Digger." She sighed, and made a visible effort to brace her smiling muscles. "And this is the really good bit—he's not rich enough for us, anyway. I was aiming myself at the wrong target all along." Her smile finally gave up, and faded away. "He was absolutely lovely, though. He made me coffee, and let me rant at him, and pointed out what a good egg Edward is. And then he drove me back to Wendy's. So I rang the bar to bunk off work, got on the train—waited at Swindon for half a lifetime, and took the world's most expensive taxi from Stroud. And here I am."

Rose and Rufa shot curious glances at each other. It was a long time since they had seen Nancy so subdued.

Rufa touched her hand gently. "And you're not cross anymore?"

"No," Nancy said, "I'm not cross. I suppose I should be pleased, because you marrying Edward means I can let my foolish heart out of its chains." She raised her glass. "Here's to wild, imprudent romance!"

Edward came into the kitchen before supper and found only Nancy, smoking a joint over a pan of the lamb sausages he had bought in Cirencester. When she saw him, she crushed out the joint, pushed the pan off the heat, and faced him like a mayoress opening a bazaar.

"Before you say one word, I'm sorry. I behaved disgustingly this morning."

He smiled, watching her shrewdly. "You were shocked."

"That's no excuse."

Edward took off his waxed jacket, and reached over to empty a brimming ashtray into the bin. "Apology accepted. No need to go on about it."

"Thanks. I've been apologizing all day." Nancy turned away from him, back to the sausages. "Ru swears she forgives me, but she's still a bit pained."

"Well, she can be rather prissy sometimes," Edward said, briskly and surprisingly. "How she manages it, after twenty-seven years living with your father, is utterly beyond me. Don't take any notice. She's thrilled that you made it up."

"So am I. I hate it when we fight."

"Ru doesn't mind so much what the others think. But, for some reason, she values the good opinion of the local barmaid above all others. The Zed always said you two were the Colonel's Lady and Judy O'Grady."

Nancy turned back to face him. "You're laughing."

Edward said, "You're crying."

The lamp on the edge of the dresser caught the tracks of tears on Nancy's face. She rubbed them away with the back of one hand. "It's been that sort of day."

There was a silence. When he spoke again, Edward's voice was gentle. "I know you think I'm taking advantage of her. Maybe I am. But Nancy, please don't think I'm doing it just to get her into bed. You know as well as I do, someone has to take care of her. God knows what she thinks is going to happen, once this house is restored."

"She hasn't accepted reality," Nancy said. "She still thinks something will change."

"The point is, she needs someone, and it might as well be me. Because I love her."

"Oh, I know," Nancy said. "I was thinking about it on the train, and it hit me that you've been in love with her for years."

"Was it obvious?"

"Far from it—and a good thing too. The Zed would have killed you."

There was another spell of silence. Edward asked, "Do you think I'm betraying him?"

"No," Nancy said. "At least, I did a bit, at first. But he hated any man who fancied Rufa." She sniffed, and began to turn over the sausages. "You're not a bad old stick, and it's fantastic that we're keeping the house. You're right, she does need looking after. I wasn't crying because of you."

"Thanks. I need your approval too," Edward said. He smiled. "Have some more champagne."

"I'm legless already."

"Go on. It's been that sort of day." He bent down to the cardboard box on the floor. "Only three gone? You girls are losing your touch."

"Okay." Nancy held out her glass. "You've talked me into it."

He opened a bottle of champagne, as efficiently as a professional sommelier. "Why were you crying just now?"

"Nothing," Nancy said. "A completely silly reason." Her eyes brimmed again. "I was just feeling rather wistful about weddings."

Chapter Sixteen

Rufa rose to meet her future in a state of joy that was almost dreamlike. Everyone else, however, found living happily ever after rather hard work. Edward quickly made it clear that there was to be no more muddling, botching, or making do. Melismate was under new management, and the days of moldy damp blotches and howling pipes were officially over.

On the Monday after his engagement, Edward sat Rose down at her own kitchen table and bombarded her with details of builders and scaffolders, foundations and drains. There was no point in hanging about, he said. The structural work should begin as soon as possible.

Rose did her best to keep up, but it was too much to take in all at once. Bewildered, she sipped the strangely excellent coffee Rufa had made, in a gleaming new *cafetière*. She nibbled at the posh chocolate biscuits Rufa had laid out on a plate (on a plate!). She looked at Rufa herself, as serenely radiant as the mild spring weather, so certain that Edward's fearsome plans were filling them all with rapture.

Had they really slept together? There was a formality about Edward's courtship (there was no other word for it) that puzzled Rose. At this stage of her own courtship, she and The Zed had spent entire days in bed, beyond the reach of the world. Edward and Rufa were strangely visible, Rose thought. In front of other people, they exchanged decorous kisses, like heads of state. You might assume nothing had changed between them, except that Edward had taken to arriving at Melismate with bunches of spring flowers, beaded with dew, from his garden. He had given Rufa a fabulous ring, an old-fashioned hoop of whopping great diamonds, that had belonged to his mother. This had delighted her—and her delight had delighted him. It did not, however, seem to raise the temperature between them. Rose guessed a little about the life Edward had kept separate from Melismate, and wondered what he had told Rufa. Presumably, being Edward, he had sorted everything out before making his proposal. But, for the moment, romance appeared to be the last thing on his mind. He and Rufa seemed to think about nothing except restoring Melismate.

Edward said that he would oversee the building work, while Rufa dealt with the interior. They had obviously spent hours discussing this, when normal couples would have been thrashing about under a duvet with the phone off the hook. Rufa would be responsible for (Edward produced yet another long list from his clipboard) painting, plastering, curtains, bathrooms, kitchen, and furniture. She would also arrange for the cleaning and restoration of the remaining family portraits.

"The what?" Rose asked vaguely.

Edward translated. "The Old Lags."

"Oh," Rose said, brightening. "I'm glad they're getting a lick of varnish out of all this, poor, hideous old souls."

Edward, as if she had not spoken, launched into a complicated lecture about the wiring.

"Do you know," Rose interrupted cheerfully, "that would be just the job for Roger's friend Spike—shall I give him a call?"

Rufa looked embarrassed. Edward was elaborately patient. "Is Spike the character who covered your main fuse box with Sellotape?"

"That's right."

"Hmm, I think I'll stick with whoever the Bickerstaffs send, if you don't mind."

The Bickerstaffs were identical twins who had been at Stowe with Edward, and now did most of the important building work in the county.

"Goodness, I don't mind," Rose said. "I'm rather honored they'll take us on. I expect it's because Davy Bickerstaff still has a crush on Nancy. He always asks after her with a sort of leer, and tries to do it without his wife hearing. Not that he stands a chance—he's as old as the hills." She became aware of Edward, Rufa, and Roger round the table, all staring at her with varying degrees of impatience.

"Mum," Rufa murmured, "do let him get on."

"What? What?" Rose asked irritably. "I'm not stopping him."

Edward, his brow darkening ominously, resumed his lecture. Rose sipped her excellent coffee and tried very hard to take in the details. It was all extraordinarily dull. Her attention strayed to one of the posh biscuits, which had a little picture of something engraved in the chocolate. She took off her glasses to examine it more closely.

"Mummy—" Rufa was plucking gently at her sleeve.

"Oh, it's an elephant," Rose said happily. "I thought its hat was an udder."

"Wake up, old thing," Roger said, with his mouth full. "He's asked you three times now."

Rose put on her glasses. "Asked me what?"

The muscles of Edward's jaw were tense. "I want to know if you can be ready to move out in ten days."

Rose shrieked, "What? Move out? But you promised we wouldn't have to leave!"

"Just for a few weeks," Rufa assured her, "while the work's being done. It's going to be a huge upheaval."

Rose was outraged. "Where the hell are we supposed to go?"

"My mother's old cottage is empty at the moment," Edward said. "And pretty well ready to move into. The furniture's a bit shabby, but I'm assuming you won't mind that."

"Well, you can assume again, because I'm not bloody going," Rose said hotly.

"Mum, don't be silly," Rufa begged. "You don't want to live on a building site!"

"Why does it have to be such a hassle? All we need is a spot of paint, and a bit of cement."

Edward slammed down his pencil. "Rose, have you listened to a single word? This house is going to fall down—quite literally—unless we take it apart brick by brick, and reassemble it from scratch."

"What are you talking about? I won't let you destroy my house!"

"Destroy it? I'm doing the exact bloody opposite!"

"You're trying to tear the heart out!"

Edward snapped, "I'm actually trying to tear the dirt out. But if you prefer, I'll leave it to biodegrade naturally—then you can sell it for compost, and build yourselves a bungalow."

"This is The Zed's home," Rose said stubbornly. "I'm letting you change it because you're marrying my daughter. But I refuse to move out."

Roger laid a hand on Edward's rigid forearm. "Count to ten, Ed," he advised softly.

"No I will not count to bloody ten!" Edward barked. "You can camp on the lawn if you like, but you're having this house repaired properly—not by some local half-wit with a roll of Sellotape!" He caught Rufa's reproachful eye, and groaned. "Oh, God. I've shouted at them already."

"Please don't make trouble, Mum," Rufa said, trying to rein back her impatience. "You know it has to be done. Taking over Edward's cottage was my idea—I thought you'd be pleased."

"Oh no, you didn't. You thought I'd be compliant. But I won't be rail-roaded, Rufa—I won't be managed."

Edward angrily slopped more coffee into his chipped cup. "Look at me, swilling caffeine," he said to Rufa, "I'll get an ulcer at this rate."

Rufa tried a gentler approach. "Think how lovely it would be to have Melismate looking beautiful for the wedding."

"Why?" Rose asked, puzzled. "Who's going to see it? You'll only be having a quiet ceremony, presumably."

"Quiet?" Edward was very still. His eyes were black with fury. "As in *furtive*, do you mean?"

"You know. What with you being so much older, and knowing her from a baby, and waiting till The Zed was dead before you made a move—"

"Whoops," muttered Roger, shaking his head. "Whoops-a-daisy."

Edward's temper broke like a sudden clap of thunder. "For your informa-tion, Rose," he yelled, "Rufa and I are planning an enormous and hugely noisy wedding, to which we will invite absolutely everyone in the neighbor-hood—despite the fact that the bride is a baby, and the groom is a toothless old git on a walking frame!"

The back door opened, and Linnet walked in. Ran had picked her up from school and dropped her at the gate. She was wearing the multicolored jersey Rufa had made, and the furry Pikachu rucksack Nancy had bought her in London. She looked severely round at their frozen faces. Edward and Rose, both breathing heavily, subsided into glaring silence.

"I heard shouting," Linnet said.

"Sorry, darling," Rufa said, looking reproachfully at her mother. "We've finished now."

Linnet dug a dirty hand into the pocket of her jeans. Very solemn, she walked round to Edward. "Daddy gave me fifty pence to stop being cross. I think you'd better have it."

For a long moment, Edward stared down at the coin she had put in the palm of his hand. Then, as suddenly as he had lost his temper, he started laughing. Rufa remembered that The Zed had always managed Edward by making him laugh, even when he had goaded him to gnashing fury. For once, Linnet did not seem to mind being laughed at. Satisfied with the transaction, she stood on tiptoe to reach the plate of biscuits.

Edward, still chuckling, handed back the fifty pence. "Thanks very much, Linnet, but just this once, I'll stop being cross for nothing. Sorry, Rose. I was being high-handed, wasn't I?"

"I can't get over you apologizing all the time," Rose said irritably. "Why bother, if it's not going to change your mind about throwing me out of my house?"

Rufa sighed. "Mum, he's not throwing you out!"

"If you want to stop Rose being cross, it'll cost more than fifty pence," Roger said.

This made Edward laugh again. He pushed the plate of biscuits closer to Linnet. "We were talking about all the repairs this house needs," he told her. "A lot of workmen have to come, and make enormous holes everywhere—"

"You're wasting your time!" Rose interrupted. "Linnet won't see why we need repairs—you think this house is fine as it is, don't you, duck?"

Linnet was frowning up at Edward. "What will they make holes in?"

"You need an entire new roof," Edward said. "Those old attics will be open to the sky. Then you need to knock down the wall behind where Granny's sitting, to build a new one that doesn't sag. It's going to be a terrible mess for a while—though it'll be lovely when it's finished. In the meantime, I thought everyone here could come to stay at my cottage. But Granny doesn't want to."

"I don't either," Linnet said promptly. "This is where we live."

"Told you," Rose muttered.

Edward ignored her. "You could think of it as a holiday," he suggested. "It's a very nice house, you know. It's right next to Chloe's field." Chloe was Edward's stately, rather elderly horse.

"And you wouldn't have such a long drive to school," Rufa put in.

Linnet went straight over to the enemy. "Can I give Chloe an apple every morning? Can I have a ride on her? Will she let me comb her mane and tail?"

"She'll be only too happy," Edward said, with a teasing glance at Rose. "She needs a new friend. And she's a quiet old thing. She won't mind giving her friends riding lessons." To Rufa, he added, "It's high time Linnet started riding. Might as well do it properly."

It was settled, though Rose was still chafing rebelliously, and muttering under her breath. While Rufa cooked pasta shells for Linnet's tea, they began to discuss arrangements for the move. The cottage had three small bedrooms. Rose and Roger were to have one, Lydia and Linnet another, and Selena could have the triangular room under the eaves.

"But what about Ru, what about Nancy?" mourned Rose.

"Nancy will be going back to London," Rufa said, "and I'll be staying with Edward—I suppose."

She smiled at him, to cover her doubt. It was impossible to imagine living with Edward: sleeping beside him, watching him shave. When she tried, she found the prospect mildly thrilling, but also confusing. If she lived with Edward, would that change their agreement about sex? In a way, she was desperate to sleep with him, in order to feel truly safe—without sex, what could hold him?

Edward said, "Actually, I was assuming you'd be going back to London too. I'm rather relying on you as the shopping end of the business."

Rufa felt relief, with a curious, panicky undertow of dissatisfaction. "You're right, there's loads to do. I'll get on far better down there."

"And you'll want to stay here for a couple of days in the meantime," he suggested.

She did, of course. Now that she knew they did not have to leave, Melismate felt like home again. "Yes, I'd like to rest here, at least until the end of the week."

He tucked his fearful clipboard under one arm. "Good idea. You're tired."

"Me?" Suddenly elated, feeling she could make time stop and swing into reverse, Rufa laughed. "Mum's just complained about my terrible energy."

"No I didn't," Rose protested.

"Yes you did. You said it was like living with Donald Duck."

"I complained that you can't stop doing things. It's driving me crazy."

The atmosphere in the house was tense, with quarrels seething under bright-eyed celebrations. Rose and Rufa, in particular, veered between adoring each other and finding each other infuriating.

"I wish I knew why she's being so troublesome," Rufa said later, while she and Edward were walking through the meadows toward the park fence.

Edward said, "She'll come round. They all will."

"I hate the way they treat you—as if you're the one who ought to be grateful."

"Well, so I ought," Edward said quietly. "I have you."

She turned quickly, hoping to see the tenderness of his voice reflected in his face. But he strode on steadily, eyes fixed to the horizon.

"I'm glad I got you on your own," he said. "I wanted to speak to you. I have to go away for a few days."

He made the announcement sound momentous. Rufa—surprised that he felt in any way accountable to her—murmured, "Oh."

"To Paris," he said.

"How nice."

"Hmm. I rather doubt that." He glanced aside at her. "I'm seeing Prudence. Alice's sister."

"Oh." Rufa remembered the immaculate, air-brushed blonde she had seen at his side in the magazine picture.

"I have to tell her about us getting married. It's something that has to be done in person." He halted, and turned around to face her. "The money aspect makes it a bit of an issue for her."

Rufa was, distantly, alarmed. Any threat to Edward's money was a threat to Melismate.

"Why?"

In the brief silence that followed, she understood two things—first, that she had asked a difficult question, and second, that he had prepared an answer to it.

"If I died unmarried—she had every reason to think I might—her son would have inherited everything I've been planning to spend on your house."

"But that's totally unreasonable," Rufa said, "surely."

"Not totally. I was in the army, and I could have died several times. That bullet in Bosnia, for instance. Six inches to the right, and I'd have come home in a bag."

"Don't." Rufa could not bear to think of corpses. The Zed had left Melismate in a bag. The memory had to be buried immediately, before she was sucked back into that nightmare.

"Sorry." He had noticed her pain. He hurried on. "It's not just the money. Pru's loaded with money. The fact is, she and I have a bit of a history."

"You mean you had an affair with her." There was no reason why this fact should chill her blood. Rufa fought down her paranoia. "Well, I knew there had to be someone." There were a million things she wanted to ask—starting with "Did you love her?"—but she did not feel she had the right. "You've heard my history, after all."

"It happened the year after Alice died," Edward said sternly. "We both missed her. And since Prudence had just got divorced, it seemed natural. Maybe it was all too easy. I began to think I might be falling in love with her—but then it finished."

"Oh," Rufa said. Her voice was pregnant with unspoken questions.

"She fell in love with someone else. It wouldn't have worked out, in the long term. If you knew her, you'd know there was no way Pru could handle being the wife of either a soldier or a farmer. She wasn't Alice, that was the thing." He sighed, relieved to have got the hard part over. "But it does mean I have to tell her properly about you. I owe her that much. Do you understand?"

"Of course I do."

"I knew you would. While I'm in Paris you can start choosing wallpaper, and so forth. I think," Edward said carefully, "that we could both do with a few weeks' grace." He did not want to talk about Prudence. Rufa sensed his annoyance when she asked questions. He made her feel that her curiosity was indecent. She was uncomfortably aware of Edward experiencing passion behind closed doors. She tried not to worry that the unknown woman had already taken the best of him.

Selena took her head out of her book long enough to announce that she refused to live in Edward's cottage. "What am I supposed to do there? Why can't I go to London, and stay with Wendy?"

"I thought you'd be going back to school," Rufa said.

"Bum to school. If you make me go back, I'll burn the fucking place down."

"But Mrs. Cutting said you were her star pupil," Rufa begged. "She said you could take your pick of universities—"

"Watch my mouth," Selena said, stubbornly shooting out her studded lower lip. "I am not going to university."

Rose said she was not letting Selena loose in London. "You're seventeen years old, and you've never seen a town bigger than Stroud—you must think I'm crazy."

"Ru and Nancy could keep an eye on me," Selena said. "They'd make sure I don't get knocked up, or start selling heroin."

Nancy pointed out that she would be working five evenings a week. Rufa slightly wondered what made her so impatient to get back behind the bar at Forbes & Gunning, but was too anxious about the Selena question to probe any deeper. She had been so sure that her youngest sister would stop being difficult now that they knew Melismate had been saved.

Rufa had expected Edward to support her, but he was on Selena's side. "Why shouldn't she see something of London? Ru will be there, and you know what a fusspot she is."

"I am not!"

Reluctantly, Rose laughed. "You're right, she's far worse than I am. With Ru around, it'll be just like a convent. And I must say, it'll be nice to have a holiday from Selena. She only raises her head from that bloody book long enough to sneer at us."

Rufa was the soul of familial duty, and agreed to return to London with both Nancy and Selena. In her heart of hearts, she did not relish the prospect. She felt she had lost the plot with Selena when she had changed from an amusing child to a sullen adolescent. She had been ten times worse since The Zed died—if you asked her a simple question, you practically had to hold a séance to get a reply. At school, she had gone out of her way to annoy her patient and well-intentioned teachers. She had withdrawn from the other girls in her form, and was seen hanging out at the bus station with various charmless specimens of local youth.

Edward had a way of being right about things, Rufa reflected. Perhaps Selena did need the experience of London, to blast her back into the land of the living. She was ashamed of her reluctance. It was not fair to blame Selena for making her feel uneasy, when she knew the real cause of her unease was Edward himself.

If he had changed overnight, Rufa would have been alarmed. But there was surely something equally alarming about his stubborn sameness. When they were alone together, he spoke to her so lovingly (intervals of tenderness, in the unending saga of practicalities) that she felt herself becoming frighteningly dependent on him.

Yet he demanded no kisses or embraces. He was, she decided, too punctilious to let her feel sex as an obligation. He could not bear anyone to think there had been an exchange of sex for money. And perversely, as he kept his distance, Rufa began to be disturbed by how handsome he was. She found herself mesmerized by the watchful glitter of his eyes, under his black brows. She was increasingly aware of great gaps in his history, which he never offered to fill in.

He had said nothing more about his relationship with Prudence. Rufa tried not to worry about it too much. She wondered why she was so worried. It would hardly have been realistic to expect a man like Edward to live without sex for all those years. Perhaps, she thought, hearing about Prudence had highlighted the fact that she knew so little about him. He had devoted himself to the family at Melismate as if he had no other life. But he had another life beyond it: an unmapped continent. And since the death of The Zed, she had been fighting a terrible, griping fear of the unknown.

Suppose Edward really had offered her marriage out of some quixotic sense of loyalty to The Zed? He was quite capable of doing such a thing. Perhaps chivalry came easily to him because he did not fancy her. In that case, what on earth could she give him, in exchange for all this? To put it at its lowest, if he did not fancy her, what was in it for him?

During her week at Melismate, Edward took her out to dinner, at charming old manor houses. He took her on very grown-up dates, to concerts and plays in Cheltenham and Bath, as if they had been a couple for twenty years. Rufa saw other women looking at him, and tried not to be tormented by knowing so little about him.

She returned to London, her victory a little curdled by the doubts. Shameful as it was, sex with Edward would have made her triumph more secure. Jonathan had been her only lover. She had no idea how to take physical possession. Somewhere at the core of herself, she was still paralyzed, or frozen.

On her second morning at Wendy's, a special messenger arrived with a large cardboard box. It was lined with damp cotton wool, and densely packed with bluebells from the little wood behind Edward's house. They filled the kitchen with the sappy oozings from their pale stems.

There was a soggy card with them. "I Love You. E."

Rufa saved this carefully, wishing she could wring the love out of it to warm away the fear.

Wendy was delighted to clear her remaining bedroom for Selena. As far as she was concerned, the youngest Hasty was the family baby for all time. If that baby had not been a lanky six-footer covered in sharp studs, Wendy would have sat her on her knee. Having Selena in the house brought out the dormant nanny in Wendy. She worried that the child was too thin, and filled her cupboards with treats she had enjoyed as a little girl. Selena, wrapped in the eternal book, silently chomped her way through packets of Jammy Dodgers and Wagon Wheels. Occasionally she stowed the current book in her rucksack, and disappeared for hours.

She never said where she was going, and Rufa worried endlessly.

Nancy said, "Stop fussing, Ru. You've already decided she's a total dropout and no-hoper, just because she wouldn't go to college. She's probably met someone—and I say good luck to her."

Rufa said, "Anything might happen to her. She acts tough and streetwise, but she's only seventeen."

In fact, Selena was leading a blameless life. Between bouts of reading and eating, she was steadily indulging her passionate and un-Hastyish craving for culture. She would not have dreamed of telling her love-fixated sisters what she was up to. They would never have understood. As far as Selena was concerned, Rufa was tiresomely obsessed with Edward and Melismate, and spent her days in a welter of paint books and swatches of fabric. Nancy was so obsessed with her job, you'd think she was painting the Sistine Chapel instead of pulling pints behind a bar. Neither of them, Selena decided, deserved to be told. London was wasted on them. Shuttling around the city in the warm, sooty tube, Selena worked down her list of essential places to see.

She went to Dr. Johnson's house, Keats's house, and the British Museum. She wandered around the Inns of Court and the alleys of Clerkenwell. She ate packed lunches of Wagon Wheels, and spent the money Rufa gave her in the secondhand bookshops of Charing Cross Road. She examined the Wallace Collection and the V & A. She attended a series of baroque concerts at Saint John's Smith Square. It was more than blissful. Everything mattered so intensely, she felt she needed three more lifetimes to absorb it all. Her head swam with phrases and colors, scraps of poetry, ideas impatient to be formed.

Selena had always been addicted to books. After the death of The Zed, the magical, bodyless realm of the mind had been her only refuge. The physical world was dark, and horribly fragile. Literature was eternity. Selena could not make Rufa see that schoolwork—or any kind of interference with her thoughts—was a monstrous intrusion. She wished they would all get off her case.

To Rufa's slight surprise, however, Selena was markedly less surly with Roshan. He had read English at Cambridge, and dared to interrogate her about her reading. Once she realized he was not—as she poetically put it—"taking the piss," Selena had the intoxicating experience of trying out her opinions. Rufa, listening to their involved discussions, blessed Roshan for coaxing Selena out of her spiky shell. She prayed he would sell her the idea of university. He managed, before Selena had been in London a week, to remove the studs and dreadlocks, which he despised on the grounds that they were "provincial."

Without the facial armor, and with her dark blond hair shorn close to her skull, Selena was suddenly as graceful as a swan, and looked ridiculously young. Rufa heaped her with new clothes, taking her transformation as a sign that her shattered family was finally pulling itself together. Roshan assured her that Selena was "seriously clever," and she allowed herself to dream of her little sister cycling along the Backs at Cambridge.

Unfortunately for Rufa's dreams, however, Selena found herself a career. On one of her wanderings around the National Gallery, she was caught by a "spotter" from a model agency. Her long, skinny body proved to be a perfect hanger for clothes; her brittle, thin-boned face photographed like a dream. In a shockingly short space of time, she was pulled into a vortex of studios and magazine offices, photographed for *Vogue*, and dazzled by the promise of future riches.

Nancy thought it was brilliant, and proudly pinned one of Selena's contact sheets behind the bar at Forbes & Gunning. Rufa was, very secretly, annoyed. Ten years before, as she could not help remembering, she had been "spotted" herself. The Zed had detested the bare idea of modeling, but there was no Zed now to stop Selena doing anything. It was impossible not to be a little jealous.

"It's a short career," she told Nancy, rather sourly. "She'll be over the hill by the time she's my age."

"So what? She might have made an absolute pile of money by then," Nancy said. "God, the irony. There we were, working round the clock to marry money—and there it was all along, right in our own backyard. We could have sent Selena out to work and stayed at home."

Rufa murmured, "I'm so glad I didn't have to marry for money, in the end."

Privately, Nancy was beginning to find Rufa's premarital bliss a little smug. "Would you take Edward without it?"

"Of course I would!" Rufa snapped back. The snapping was automatic; Nancy was constantly picking holes. Only after she had said it did Rufa realize she was telling the truth. If Edward suddenly lost all his money she would be devastated, but she would never be able to let him go. In some way she did not quite understand, she was bound to him.

They were suddenly face to face, on the narrow strip of pavement outside the Coffee Stores in Old Compton Street.

"My God, Rufa," he said. "Rufa Hasty."

He seemed smaller and shabbier, and altogether diminished. Rufa, breathless with the shock of finding herself in the middle of a fantasy she had outgrown, stared at his untidy brown hair, slightly downturned brown eyes, and thin, intense features.

"Jonathan," she said. "How are you?"

There had never been a moment of falling out of love with Jonathan. When he left so suddenly, leaving unwashed cups in the sink and a terse note on the back door, Rufa had frozen right at the summit of besottedness. It had never occurred to her then that there would be a day when she could look at him like this, and know that she was cured. When had it happened? The back of his neck, the shape of his earlobes, his sensitive and oddly expressive nostrils—she had branded all these details on her soul. Now, she felt nothing more than the memory of pain. There was only scar tissue left. She realized all this with a surge of triumph, and almost felt fond of him.

Jonathan was far more shaken. "My God," he said again. He cleared his throat. "What on earth are you doing in London? I've never been able to picture you out of your pastoral setting."

Rufa wanted to laugh. It was so extraordinary that she did not care. What had she ever seen in those ludicrous, quivering nostrils? "Actually, I've just been to a fitting, for my wedding dress."

He winced, as his own scar tissue throbbed. "You're getting married? That's great. Well done—I mean, congratulations."

"Thanks."

"When's the Big Day, in inverted commas?"

"June, of course," Rufa said. "We're doing it all in a tearing hurry, so I can be a traditional June Bride—without the inverted commas."

He relaxed into a laugh. "What's his name?"

"You know him," Rufa said. "It's Edward Reculver."

She thought his reaction strange—first, a flicker of alarm at the sound of Edward's name, then half-amused resignation. "Of course. I should have guessed."

Rufa wanted to know why he should have guessed. Jonathan was the first person who had not been surprised by her engagement.

He was smiling. In a way, he seemed relieved. "My darling. You're as fearfully beautiful as ever. And I made such a mess of it."

"I forgave you ages ago," Rufa said.

"You've had other things to think about." He laid his hand on her arm. "I heard about your father—we were staying in Cirencester, and I read about the inquest in the local paper. I'm so sorry."

"I had to give evidence," Rufa said, "in a sort of court."

"I wanted to write to you. I thought I'd better not."

"That's all right."

They stood together in silence, paying their respects to the drama of the past.

His hand still rested on her arm. "We're blocking the pavement. Come and have lunch with me. Then we can treat ourselves to explanations and recriminations, and tie all the ends up neatly."

Rufa smiled. "Like a novel."

"I beg your pardon, not like one of mine. I'd sell far better, if I didn't have this uncommercial itch to reflect real life."

Jonathan's novels, she thought, were quite a lot like real life, in that they were repetitive and often somewhat dull. It had taken her ages to realize that he was not a genius. Because she was so curious about her own feelings, she agreed to lunch, and they walked round the corner to L'Escargot. It was still early. The covetable table beside the window was free.

Jonathan murmured, "Do you mind if we don't sit here? Harriet works in Soho Square, and I daren't risk her walking past."

Harriet was Jonathan's wife, hardworking bankroller of his novel habit, and mother of his two children. Rufa had never met her, but Jonathan's guilt at betraying her had made her a constant third presence in their relationship. She had walked at his side like a reproachful phantom, and every encounter with him had begun with some kind of sacrifice to the angry goddess—tears, perhaps, or a rant against the narrowness of sexual convention. He had lived in terror of Harriet finding out.

They were shown to a discreet and intimate corner table upstairs. Jonathan ordered a bottle of white wine.

"Do you realize, we've never been in a restaurant together?" He rested his elbows on the table, and folded his hands under his chin. "I couldn't have done it when we were—when I was in love with you. I was afraid you'd perish in the outside world, like the Lady of Shalott."

"And you were paranoid about being spotted," Rufa said.

"That as well, obviously." He had the grace to look slightly ashamed. "I really was in love with you, Rufa. Madly in love."

"I know. I read the novel." She could not resist gently rubbing it in. "It was awfully good."

"Oh, God. I mean, thanks."

"The end was a bit of a downer, though—why did I have to die?"

"Sorry about that," Jonathan said. "It was a touch of what your father would have called 'symbollocks.' Seriously, were you furious?"

"Of course not. I was flattered."

He frowned down at the tablecloth. "I'm sorry. I know you must think of me as a complete bastard, and you're right. I'm not cut out for adultery— you were the only one."

"Did you ever tell Harriet about me?"

"Well, yes," he said. He looked pained. "She would have worked it out when she read the book—but I had to do the full confession well before I'd finished it. Harriet couldn't understand why I'd come back to London, when I was working so well in the country. Then she got it into her head that she wanted to rent Edward's cottage long term, and move there with the children. So I absolutely had to tell her."

"Poor you," Rufa said. "Was she angry?"

"She certainly was."

"But you made it up, didn't you?"

"Yes, in the usual way." Jonathan reached into his breast pocket for his wallet, and flipped it open to show a snapshot of smiling children.

He had never shown her his children. Once, not long ago, the picture would have caused her agonies of shame and sorrow. Now, it meant nothing. She said, "You've had another one."

"That's right. The big ones are Crispin and Clio, and the baby's Oliver, the olive branch—the price of Harriet's forgiveness. One of the mysterious and slightly depressing things about marriage is that you can always buy a woman off with another baby."

"I think you got off lightly," Rufa said. "He's gorgeous."

"Thanks, he is rather."

Their first courses, two buttery molds of potted shrimps, arrived at the table. Jonathan stowed his wallet away protectively. They had done the foothills. It was now time to scale the main peak.

Rufa fortified herself with a sip of wine. "Jonathan, do you mind if I ask you something? I'd really like to know what made you leave so suddenly. It was The Zed, wasn't it? Something he said or did—I know he didn't like us being together."

"Your father?" Jonathan was taken aback. "No, it had nothing to do with him. He extracted a high price for his daughter, in the shape of free drinks at the Hasty Arms. But he wasn't the one who ran me out of town. That was Edward."

"What?" She frowned. "You left because of Edward?"

"Didn't you know? He was fine when I first moved in," Jonathan said. "I explained that I was a writer, and needed to be left alone, and he never bothered me. That all changed when we—when I started seeing you. He started appearing in the cottage doorway, with a shotgun broken over one arm. One fine day, he came to tell me that I was a shit."

"That's serious," Rufa said, feeling the blood rushing into her cheeks. "Lots of people are sods and swine, but he saves *shit* for types like Colonel Qaddafi. Was it because of me?"

Jonathan was watching her oddly. "Well, of course. He said I was using you, leading you on, ruining your life. He said I richly deserved to be horse-whipped, and if I didn't leave his cottage immediately, he'd tell my wife what I was up to." He paused, and smiled sheepishly. "I had no idea what a horse-whip is, or what damage it can do to the tender hide of a novelist. But I wasn't going to hang around to find out."

"So you left me—just like that—because Edward told you to?"

There was disbelief in her voice, and a dash of scorn. Jonathan said, a little testily, "I'm afraid so. Us novelists are a lot of namby-pamby cowards, aren't we?"

"Didn't you think you might be overreacting?"

"I'd like to say he made me choose between you and Harriet—but he didn't actually give me much of a choice." Jonathan laughed to himself, shaking his head. "He said I had twenty-four hours to fuck off out of his house, after which time he would personally tell Harriet and break both my legs."

"*Edward* said all that?" This was fantastic. Rufa had no idea how much of it to believe.

"And plenty more, though he's not a man of many words. He said he refused to stand by and watch while I broke your heart."

She stared down at her plate, trying to adjust her internal picture of her great, doomed love. It was dead and buried, but her pride still hurt. "I was blissfully happy. How did Edward know you were going to break my heart?"

Jonathan sighed. "Do we have to go over all this?"

"Yes," she snapped. "You promised to tie up all the ends."

"All right, all right." He laid down his fork, which had a pathetic shrimp impaled upon one prong. "Before we got to horsewhips and leg-breaking, Edward asked me about my intentions."

"You mean, if they were honorable?"

"More or less. He asked me if I intended to leave Harriet and the kids, and marry you."

There was a silence. "And you said no."

"Rufa, please try to understand—quite apart from the children, I couldn't bear to turn my back on Harriet. I just couldn't do it."

"So you always meant to leave me," Rufa said coldly. "It was just a question of when."

"Look, I'm sorry. I suffered too."

"Why didn't you put that in your novel, instead of getting rid of the heroine by killing her? It would have made your noble, anguished hero far more like an ordinary sort of man."

Jonathan frowned. Once, she had thought his frown full of strength. Now it seemed more like a pout. "I'm sorry," he muttered crossly. "Sorry, sorry, sorry. All right?"

Rufa took another sip of wine. Recriminations were ridiculous, but they had dragged out the past, and it disturbed her that it could not be put back into its old box. "I'm sorry too. I didn't mean to start accusing you—it's all ancient history now. And I suppose I'm relieved, in a way. I didn't enjoy blaming The Zed." Her eyes smarted. She willed them not to fill with tears.

Jonathan took a few deep breaths. His voice, when it emerged, was deliberately friendly and bracing. "I hope I haven't made you blame Edward instead. I don't. It was obvious where he was coming from."

"We're sort of his adopted family," Rufa said. "He's always looked after us."

Jonathan smiled. "Yes, and if I'd had my wits about me, I've have noticed sooner."

"Sorry—noticed what?"

"Well, that he had the major hots for you."

Rufa whispered, "What? No—you're quite wrong—" And as soon as she said it, she knew he was not wrong.

He tipped more wine into her glass. "That's quite good, isn't it? Major Reculver, with the major hots. Frankly, if I'd realized, I might have thought twice about falling for you myself. He certainly looked as if he knew what to do with that gun."

She was bewildered. She had persuaded herself that Edward had offered his hand and fortune as a matter of high principle. Now, she suddenly saw why the Marrying Game had made him so furious. And she understood the nature of his struggle after their row about it.

Her face was hot. She was shocked to hear about this unfamiliar version of Edward. He did desire her, and that underground desire had escaped in a flash of searing sexual jealousy. Rufa was ashamed to be excited by this. For a moment, she was weakened by a longing to make him lose control again.

Jonathan lit a cigarette—Rufa remembered, with wonderment, the time when she had found his incessant smoking interesting. "I'm glad we got all that out," he said. His shoulders relaxed, and he smiled at her.

"So am I. Now we can just enjoy our lunch. You can tell me what you're working on at the moment."

They talked of his work, his children, his slightly larger new house in Dulwich. Rufa smiled and prompted, encouraging Jonathan to take over the conversation. She did not want him to guess how much he had revealed, and needed to be alone to think through the implications. She ought to have been angry, because he had made her doubt The Zed. But her main emotion was a restless, fearful excitement.

Chapter Seventeen

Sunlight shifted and gleamed on the surface of the moat, newly cleaned in honor of Rufa's wedding.

It was nine o'clock. Gnats and dragonflies were assembling above the glassy water, like the first guests. Rufa wandered out of the front door onto the terrace. She was in her dressing gown, holding a cup of tea. Smiling, she breathed the golden, hay-scented air. A perfect June morning. This was her last chance to savor its loveliness, and the miracle of Melismate Regained, before the bustle indoors escalated into pandemonium.

Lydia was leaning against the lichened stone balustrade, gazing out across the gardens. She smiled as Rufa joined her. They stood in companionable silence, listening to the peckings and splashings of the two swans in the moat. These graceful but evil-tempered creatures were a wedding gift from the Bickerstaff twins, who had also kindly cleared away evidence of the ongoing building work for the great day. One wing of the house was swathed in scaffolding and tarpaulin. Rose had insisted on moving back the moment the water and electricity had been restored. The Great Hall, drawing room, and kitchen were finished. One room upstairs had been cleaned for the putting-on of bridal finery. The family were camping in the attics under the good part of the roof.

Lydia softly asked, "Well, are you nervous, then?"

"Yes. Is that normal?"

"I was incredibly nervous," Lydia said.

"You were incredibly young."

"It all seemed so momentous and emotional. Ran was even worse—don't you remember how he kept dashing into the hedges to pee? But I remember it as wonderful. Magical." She turned mournful blue eyes toward her sister. "I hate it when people say marriage is just a worthless bit of paper. It's so much more."

On her own wedding day, Rufa found Lydia's failed marriage wrenchingly sad. She wondered if all failed marriages carried this air of unfinished business. Was a marriage ever truly over, when one partner refused to admit it?

"You give a part of yourself when you get married," Lydia said. "And it never grows back."

"Oh, Liddy," Rufa said gently, "I'm so sorry, but I think walking away from Ran was the best thing you ever did."

"I didn't want to."

"You were miserable!"

The stubborn blue eyes turned back to the sunlit landscape. "I hung on as long as I could. In the end, Ran made me leave."

"That's not the version we all heard. Are you saying he threw you out?"

"Oh, no. But you know Ran. He always has to be the innocent party. So he pretended I wasn't there. Until I actually wasn't." She smiled painfully. "I thought I'd better take the hint, before I disappeared."

Rufa watched one of the swans, patrolling the moat below in a menacing manner. "I do wish you'd get over Ran."

"So does he, but it's no good. I can't. None of you understand. He's the only man I've ever loved."

The historic coming together of Lydia and Ran was part of family legend. Lydia had lost her heart and her virginity to Ran at the age of fourteen, when he returned from India to live at Semple Farm. Rufa had a clear memory of Lydia that summer, drifting home in the warm dusk with her hair full of dried grass. She was happy with a barefoot existence; she had never been materialistic. Just as Ran did, she lived contentedly in the bubble of the present, with only the sketchiest notion that there was such a thing as a future.

On her own wedding morning, another clear memory came to Rufa, of Lydia as a bride. Her sheer loveliness had transcended the silliness of the event. They had all trooped off to the registry office first, and The Zed had kept them in agonies of giggles—he had always mocked everything to do with officialdom.

At the main part of the ceremony, however, when Ran and Lydia had exchanged their homemade vows in the meadow, The Zed had been inconsolable. Lydia had stood barefoot in the long grass, wildflowers winding through her hair, as ethereally beautiful as an Edwardian dream-child. The Zed's loud sobs had nearly drowned her hesitant voice, as she promised to love Ran until the stars turned cold.

Lydia had certainly kept her side of the bargain. She had never looked at another man. She had been convinced that marriage would fix Ran permanently, and was still astonished that it had not. She clung to the belief that he would come back, and nothing her mother or sisters said made any difference.

Very secretly, Rufa envied Lydia for embarking on marriage in such a state of certainty. She wished she could be as sure that she was truly loved. The idea of Edward's love was no longer blush-making. She longed for a sign that he truly loved her. Since his return from Paris, all those weeks ago, Edward had been distant and preoccupied, preparing for the wedding with a kind of grim resignation that did not fit Jonathan's intriguing description of a man in the grip of wild passion. All he would say about Prudence was that their meeting had been "difficult." He had looked thunderous, and Rufa did not dare to press him for the details she longed for. The headline was that Prudence and her son—Edward's only family—were not coming to the wedding.

It might have been a sign of disapproval. And it might have been because Prudence could not bear to see a stranger in her dead sister's place. Rufa tried to imagine how she would feel if she were Prudence—for instance, if Lydia had died, and Ran had married someone else. She wanted to give the woman the benefit of the doubt, and to find nonsexual reasons for Edward's black-browed silences.

He had explained that he was anxious about some business connected with his time in the army. Upon his return from Paris, he had immediately disappeared to London. Once again, though his face and voice had expressed pain and fury, he had refused to go into detail. Edward was bad at explaining. He had only made his business sound more mysterious. Rufa sensed something heavy on his mind, and worried that it was the prospect of marrying her. She wished Edward trusted her enough to confide in her. He had saved her home, but this was not enough. She was oppressed by the enormous leap of faith that was needed, when you put your whole heart into the hands of a virtual stranger.

Rufa, feeling it was only proper, had asked Clare Seal to design and make her wedding dress. Left to herself, she would have chosen something more conventional, perhaps from Liberty's. She had to admit, however, that Clare had been inspired. Seeing the elegance Rufa had given to the yellow crepe, she had made another slender column, cut on the bias with a nod to the 1930s, in heavy white silk. It left Rufa's arms and shoulders bare, and was of a ruthless simplicity. The veil was of stiff, filmy white silk, which lay around her in crests and billows. It was held in place by old Mrs. Reculver's diamond tiara, which Edward had unexpectedly disinterred from a bank vault.

Rufa stood rigidly in the gleaming Melismate kitchen, displaying her bridal finery. Her mother and sisters stared at her, almost afraid of her white perfection. Rose was trying not to cry.

Linnet said, "You look just like a princess."

"What's that round your mouth?" Rose made a dive at Linnet and grabbed her chin. "You've been at the chocolate! For the love of heaven, don't eat anything else till it's over, do you hear?"

Linnet was offended. "What if I'm starving?"

"I'll put you on a drip."

Until twenty minutes ago, Linnet had been wearing pajamas crusted with Weetabix. She was now as exquisite as a china fairy in a Kate Greenaway dress of pale yellow silk and white kid slippers. To her deep, serious joy, Linnet was Rufa's only bridesmaid. Edward, a stickler for tradition, had given her the heart-shaped gold locket round her neck. He had also (advised by Rufa) given her two toy cradles, of a size to fit the Ressany Brothers. Even without the presents, however, Linnet approved of Edward. In her eyes, he was the man who had brought order into her home, and she liked order. She had enjoyed staying in the clean cottage beside Chloe's field. Though she still slept in Lydia's bed, she was pestering the Bickerstaffs to finish her new, pink-painted boudoir.

Rufa touched the chaplet of yellow rosebuds on the small dark head. "You look like a princess yourself. Doesn't she?"

"Better," Nancy said. "Real princesses would be jealous. I'm quite jealous myself."

Nancy wore a clinging but essentially sober dress of dark gold silk, and a black cartwheel of a hat. Selena—down for two days between photo shoots—had appeared in a short skirt and skimpy silk cardigan of pale blue. Her cropped hair was now silver-white, and Rose could not get over her elegant otherness. Selena revealed very little about her mysterious new life, but it appeared to suit her. She had sat through a whole dinner the previous night without once opening a book. She had a new coolness and detachment, and regarded them all with distant amiability, as if through the wrong end of a telescope.

Lydia was a hedge-creature who cared not what raiment she put on. Rufa had bought her a trailing purple dress from Ghost. It made her look absurdly juvenile. She refused a hat, and wore her long curls loose. Rose was unrecognizable, and surprisingly pretty, in a dress and broad-brimmed hat of spotted navy silk. For the first time in years, she had put on makeup.

"Okay, girls. Time to scramble." Roger, in a hired gray morning suit, appeared at the door. "The cars are here, and I swore to Edward we wouldn't be late." He was to give Rufa away. To honor the occasion, he had cut off his ponytail.

The hour was at hand. Rose and her daughters stared at each other, trying to take in the reality of the transformation. They were new women, in new lives and a new setting. The kitchen had only been finished three days before, and they were still coming to terms with the amazing lack of squalor. The sagging, nicotined walls had been freshly plastered and painted white. The rotten wooden cupboards had been replaced. The range, a museum piece, had been lovingly cleaned and restored. A regiment of wine bottles was drawn up on the kitchen table, and there were huge sprays of roses and lilies exploding out of unexpected places. In the Great Hall, the caterers were setting four long, flower-decked tables.

"It's incredible," Nancy said. "You did it. You said you'd marry money, and you did it."

Rufa smiled uncertainly. "Not in the way I thought. It was silly of me to think I could go through all this with any old rich man. Thank God it's Edward."

"I don't know," Rose said. "I quite fancied having Tiger Durward as a son-in-law."

This relaxed them all into brittle, edgy laughter. Tiger Durward had become the new family joke. After weeks of bombarding Roshan with flowers, he had booked himself into the Priory. He had emerged clean and sober, to carry on the pursuit with renewed intensity. After checking with Nancy that she did not mind, Roshan had twice been out to dinner with the reformed rake, and was bringing him to the wedding as a semiofficial partner. It was only a matter of time before Tiger burst out of the closet like a June morning and gave the tabloids a field day.

They were all grateful to him, because they needed a family joke. The anniversary loomed—The Zed had died on a still, warm, sunny day, very like this one. The last time they had all gathered in the village church, with its memorials to past Hastys and Reculvers, The Zed's coffin had lain in the aisle. The last time the table had been covered with bottles of wine, they had all been in a state of shock bordering on insanity. They were all praying, though nobody had said anything, that this wedding signified the end of mourning.

"Rose, Nancy, Liddy, and Selena in the first car," Roger said. "Ru, Linnet, and I will follow exactly ten minutes later. Get a move on—Edward's timing me with a stopwatch."

Rose stared again at Rufa, then leaned forward to give her a delicate kiss. Finding her daughter did not feel as changed as she looked, Rose followed it with a fierce hug. "You look stunning. The Zed would have been so proud of you."

Rufa asked, "Would this have pleased him?"

"Yes, when he'd had time to think about it," Rose said. "He loved Edward. He wouldn't have let anyone else catch you."

Forgive me, Rufus, Edward thought. Forgive me for loving her so much that I dared to marry her.

She was here, at the other end of the aisle, smiling at him, when he had been half expecting her to call the whole thing off at the last minute. He had not even allowed himself to dream of Rufa in her bridal gown, and here she was: lovely enough to break her father's heart.

But I'll take care of her, Edward promised the shade of The Zed.

He had hardly slept the night before, keeping a last vigil with the shade of Alice. It was lucky, he thought, that he had not married her in this church. They had run off to a registry office in London, to escape old Mrs. Reculver's lingering disapproval. At the time, Rufus had reproached him—why hadn't he been best man, and his pretty little daughters bridesmaids? Well, thank God it hadn't happened, or this would have been far too strange.

This time, Edward's best man was an old friend from Sandhurst, now a colonel in a Scottish regiment. His wife and two teenage daughters stood on Edward's side of the church, among the soldiers and farmers who made up his circle. He could see, from the expressions on their faces, that they could hardly believe Edward had won such a woman. He hardly believed it himself. He could not go through with it unless he banished all ghosts, dead and living.

❋ ❋ ❋

"Come down, O love divine," Berry sang. "Seek thou this soul of mine—"

People often had this one at weddings. In just under three weeks, everyone would be singing it at his own wedding. The reality had not hit him, until he saw the transformation of Rufa. What power a wedding dress gave to a woman, he thought. It was the oddest mixture of the sacrificial and the triumphant. He hoped he would look as splendid as Edward, but did not think he would cut such a commanding figure in morning dress. Edward stood, with squared shoulders and a ramrod back, his eyes burning into Rufa. But he was controlled enough to flash a grin at Linnet.

Berry thought Linnet looked scrumptious. He surprised himself by thinking how extraordinary and wonderful it would be, if he ever had a little girl of his own. No wonder Ran driveled on about fatherhood—it was the only thing he had ever done properly.

Ran was an usher, along with the plump, sandy-haired Bickerstaff twins. The twins wore full, correct morning dress. Their gray top hats lay like two buckets on the table beside the door. Ran wore a peculiar blue suit with a jacket like a frock coat, buttoned to the neck. He had greeted Berry with a smacking kiss, and Polly's eyebrows had shot up toward her hairline.

Polly turned to smile at him. Berry felt fond of her, and very proud that he had had the strength of mind to resist Nancy. This wedding was a test for him, to see if he could look at Nancy without wanting to throw himself at her feet. It was tough, when she was so divine, so seductive, in that big hat. Some women could really carry off a big hat. He did not think Polly was one of them, bless her. The pale blue thing she was wearing put Berry in mind of the lampshades over the billiard table at home. Its absurdity made him fonder of her. He squeezed her hand, with its Boodle and Dunthorne diamond engagement ring, in an affectionate and husbandly manner.

Polly had high standards for weddings. This one had already won her approval. The dusty village church, so cozily nested in rich Cotswolds countryside, delighted her. Rufa and Edward made a breathtaking couple. She

193

had chosen to be amused when Ran kissed Berry. And she had been intrigued to recognize Tiger Durward, on the opposite side of the aisle (Berry and Polly had been put on Edward's side, since the bride's was overflowing with a mixture of local gentry for whom she had cooked, and colorful rural bohemians who had known The Zed).

Polly had whispered, "What on earth is that Durward man doing here? Could he be going out with Nancy?"

Berry had gamely risen above his pang of jealousy, and said he did not believe so. He was not worried about Tiger, nor the pretty Indian who was obviously Nancy's gay best friend. He was far more suspicious of the other man in their pew: tall, dark, and devilishly handsome, in a style even sensible women could not see through. This must be the other lodger. If Berry had not been entirely happy to be marrying Polly, he would have detested the man.

Yes, he was looking forward to the peace and certainty of being married to Polly. This was surely what marriage was all about—escape from the debilitating furor of romance. They would have a magnificent wedding and a superb honeymoon in Kenya, and Polly would set the rest of his life running on oiled casters to the grave. Certainty was a blessing. Everything else was an illusion.

For Rufa, the rest of the day was a series of snapshots from a dream. She spoke her vows, and signed the book in the vestry. Edward was her husband. She posed for photographs outside the church, clinging to his arm. Hundreds of people, including the vicar and Tiger Durward, kissed her.

Wendy, incoherent with happiness, threw biodegradable confetti. She wore a purple velvet hat, like a squashed pancake, and darted about taking photographs with a very small camera, getting in everyone's way. The new gravel on the weeded Melismate drive was scrunched by the wheels of dozens of cars.

Rufa and Edward took their places at the door for the receiving line. They were wearing their public faces, and could not look at each other. The guests trooped past them; figures from their old lives.

Roshan formally introduced Tiger, last seen sozzled and sobbing after Rufa had nearly clawed his eyes out at the ball. He was paler and thinner now, and offered congratulations and apologies in a shadow of his old, braying voice. Rufa decided she liked him—he obviously adored Roshan, and love made angels of the most unlikely people.

There was champagne, of course, chosen and paid for by Edward. There was a wedding breakfast, which was a proper lunch (poached salmon and strawberries, both of them wild and wildly expensive), because Edward said scarcity of food at weddings made people quarrelsome. There were speeches, to which Rufa listened carefully and instantly forgot. Edward's best man told lumbering anecdotes about the army, and proposed a rousing toast to Linnet. Edward himself spoke very briefly, mainly to thank everyone for coming.

Everyone around the long tables took the depth of his feelings for granted. It was known far and wide that Edward had saved the whole family, in the nick of time. The locals studied the improvements to Melismate, and measured them against the beauty of the bride. Nobody was at all surprised that Rufa had married so well. She had always been the sensible one. And after the food and the speeches, there was a general spillage onto the sunny terrace for more champagne. The guests fell back into their cliques, to tell each other that the Hastys had an inborn talent for landing on their feet.

Nancy had taken off her hat and let down her hair. She and Berry had greeted each other with strained jollity, and a brief kiss that left them both blushing. They had seen each other in the wine bar since Nancy crashed into his flat, but she had avoided serving him if she could. Occasionally she found herself sweeping his credit card through the machine. This was the nearest they came to intimacy.

Polly the Perfect had not registered the blushes. She's counting the hours till her own wedding, Nancy thought dully. She had never seen the Digger looking so pretty. Polly wore a mimsy linen suit and her hat was just plain stupid; but, somehow, she shone. There was a dewy freshness to her skin. She had been very gracious to Nancy, partly because she was entranced by the golden stones and briar roses of Melismate. She had not, of course, seen it in the days of glorious filth.

Nancy supposed she wished the woman joy. Berry, of all people, deserved joy. She dared to glance at him, and caught him at the exact moment when he was sneaking a glance at her. They both reddened again, and turned their backs. The aura of failed sex around their last encounter was a permanent embarrassment. Nancy ran down the terrace steps, across the moat, and out over the sweep of turf. She was totally unused to carrying a heart that was at all heavy. It was bewildering, and perversely delicious.

"Nancy—"

Max was a few yards behind her, hurrying to catch her up. She slowed down, thinking how sexy some men could look in morning dress. Together they strolled toward the huge acacia tree near the park fence. Beyond the fence lay the meadows, lushly overgrown and quivering with butterflies.

"This place is fabulous," Max said. "I think I begin to understand your Marrying Game now. I never imagined you came from a place like this."

Nancy laughed—she had been hearing versions of this all day. "The point is, I didn't come from a place like this. Before Ru liberated Edward's money, it was a dump."

"I'm sure it was always beautiful," Max said. "As beautiful as you are."

"Oh, get along with you."

"I mean it. Why did you take off the hat?"

"It was in the way," Nancy said. "I couldn't kiss anyone."

Max followed her into the ragged circle of shadow under the acacia. "Talking of which, why haven't I kissed you yet?"

"Because you haven't been asked." Nancy fancied Max, of course she did; but it was an increasingly academic fancying. Her insides no longer turned somersaults when he raked her body with his wicked eyes.

"Why haven't I been asked?" He was laughing, but the question was serious. "We had something brewing at one time, you and I."

"Yes, but other things kept getting in the way."

"You were chasing your Lord Whatsit. But you don't have to do that anymore." Max leaned against the trunk of the tree. "Now that your sister has effectively won the Marrying Game, you can relax. Go back to playing for love."

"I wish it was that simple," Nancy said. She had caught, and resented, his opinion of Rufa's marriage.

His voice softened. "What's happened to you, Nancy? The Game's over. You're free—so why aren't you up for being seduced and ravished?"

"Goodness, where did you get the idea that I liked that sort of thing?"

He laughed and retreated, but he was ready to leap in again when she gave him the chance. "So, what are you going to do with yourself now? Come home to the ancestral pile?"

"Don't be silly, I only took two days off work. I have to be back behind the bar on Monday."

Max was thoughtful. He settled his back more comfortably against the tree. "Is it such a great job?"

"Best I ever had."

"And the only place you get to see him."

Nancy groaned. "God, am I that obvious?"

"Glaring. It seems that Cupid's little arrow has at last found a chink in your tough hide. You've gone and fallen in love with your target."

"Yes," Nancy said, "I think that's what this must be. I think this is what being really in love is like, as opposed to being nearly in love. It's the difference between *Romeo and Juliet* and a musical comedy." She sighed. "Max, have you ever been in love?"

"Do you want gallant or truthful?"

"Truthful."

"Okay, I have been in love," Max said. "Passionately—by which I mean sexually. That stage of burning infatuation. But it never seems to last long. I'm gutted when it ends, and it's probably my fault that it does. I don't know why."

Nancy liked Max when he knocked off the flirting, and spoke honestly. It made him yards more attractive; perhaps he was aware of this. "That exactly describes my own romantic career," she said, "until I met Berry. You'd better be warned."

He smiled at her, evidently not devastated by the rejection. "What's it like, then?"

"Rather shitty, darling," Nancy said. "Especially when he's about to marry someone else."

"I wouldn't totally bet on it. He hasn't taken his eyes off you for a second. You should send him a rope ladder as a wedding present."

"Not a hope," Nancy said sadly. "You haven't met Polly. She's had him electronically tagged. No power on earth will loosen her grip."

Polly now knew what she had sometimes suspected. She had never been properly in love before. At some point during the service, between the Wagner and the Mendelssohn, she had slipped into another dimension. At last she understood what people went on about, and wrote poetry about—as for the poems, she suddenly saw the point of half the world's literature.

His name was Randolph Verrall. He wore a foolish suit and his hair was far too long. He was being shadowed by a droopy ex-wife and her beady child. None of this was relevant—this charming country property was simply in need of a little renovation. Polly had been swimming in Ran's black velvet eyes since Berry had introduced them. In this perfect setting of moats and swans and historic gentility, she had found a jewel—quite literally, she thought with wonder, the man of her dreams; the ideal receptacle for the fantasies and aspirations of a lifetime.

"Careful," Ran said.

They were walking round the moat, away from the noise of the reception, and the haunting presence of the droopy ex-wife. Polly's pale blue heels were black with mud and, amazingly, she did not give a damn—Polly the fastidious, who found Glyndebourne almost unbearably stressful because of grass stains and rogue blobs of mayonnaise. Ran took her hand, to steady her. She felt the contact hit her heart, like a rush of electricity.

She murmured, "This is the most disturbingly beautiful place I've ever seen."

"Ridiculously romantic," Ran said. "There ought to be a law against it."

They halted, still hand in hand. The two swans paddled past majestically, their long necks arching and twining. A weeping willow, newly pollarded, sheltered a keening choir of gnats.

"So this is where Rufa grew up," Polly said. She was fascinated by Rufa. "Mariana in the moated grange."

"The moat was two inches deep and choked with weeds, until about a month ago," Ran said. "In hot weather, it stank like the shit pit at the Glastonbury Festival. They had to keep all the windows shut."

The uncouth words *shit* and *Glastonbury* would normally have made Polly shudder. All she thought was that he had the mouth of an angel. "Of course," she said, "you know them all terribly well. You were married to one of them."

Ran said, "How could I help it? I was the boy next door."

Polly shivered a little, because Ran's warm fingers still held her hand. "Did you fall in love with them all?"

She was bantering, in a fie-fie, fan-tapping style that seemed to come out of nowhere.

Ran, however, considered the question seriously. "I fancied the older ones, but that all stopped when I got it together with Liddy. Women change when you marry their sisters. They turn into harpies." His great eyes were tragic. "You won't believe this, but Nancy chucked a dustbin at me once."

Polly asked, "Why? What had you done?"

"I fell in love."

"Oh."

"That's the only crime I ever commit."

Breathlessly, Polly stated, "Falling in love can never be counted as a crime."

"Do you think so? I wish Liddy would see it." Ran heaved a sigh. "We turned into a habit. Spiritual development between us was at a standstill. The bond is eternal, but there's no more music."

"Music?" Polly was mesmerized.

"The music two people hear when they fall in love." His voice was low. "Listen!"

They were silent for a long moment.

"Violins," whispered Polly.

"A fanfare," Ran said, his mouth moving toward hers. Their lips met.

Polly caught the bouquet, and Lydia began to leak tears. Berry might not have noticed anything, but she had seen the hormonal storm clouds gathering round the angelic form of her ex-husband. He was falling in love again. She knew the signs.

Rose knew them too. She was faced with the ghost of her former self, wincing over the romantic follies of The Zed. With a sigh of resignation, she collapsed into the chair beside the range, and eased off her new shoes.

"Have a cup of tea," Roger suggested, looking down at her tenderly. "You're knackered."

They were alone, in the chaos of bleary glasses and empty bottles. The caterers were clearing away in the Great Hall. Nancy and Selena had dragged Lydia up to the old nursery, for red wine, consolation, and bracing advice. Linnet was in a sticky sleep, clutching the Ressany Brothers, on the new sofa in the drawing room.

"It went all right, didn't it?" Rose asked.

She expected to be reassured, and Roger was reassuring. "Brilliantly. Edward even thanked me. Nothing to worry about."

"And Ru's okay, isn't she?"

"I'd say so." He handed Rose a mug of tea. "Wouldn't you?"

"I don't know," Rose said. "She swears she's happy. I have to take her word for it. But I don't believe she's ever slept with Edward—she was lying, to get me off her back. Or maybe it's just the champagne, making me lugubrious."

"You're thinking of the old 'un," Roger said gently.

"Well, look what that bugger of a Zed has done to my girls." Rose had never before said this aloud. She would not have said it to anyone but Roger. "Here's Liddy, still obsessed with the Village Idiot, Nancy moping like Madame Butterfly, Selena—"

"Selena's great," Roger interrupted.

"She's left us. She came back for the wedding as if she was visiting another planet. But she doesn't worry me like Rufa. I can't make Ru talk about the future, beyond finishing this bloody house. As if she were taking orders from beyond the grave."

"You'd better change," he said, hearing the dryness of his own voice and cursing himself for it. "The traffic won't be too bad, but we ought to leave plenty of time." Owing to what Edward described as "a slight balls-up on the booking front," they were driving straight to the airport, to catch their flight to Italy. He thought it was probably just as well. His blood raged to make love to Rufa, but while they were in his house, or anywhere near Melismate, there was too much awkwardness to work through first.

He had chosen the villa in Tuscany because it was the most obviously romantic backdrop he could imagine. Somehow, in the space of a few hours, he had to shake off the image of faithful family friend, and transform himself into a lover. The act of marrying Rufa, and submitting to the carnival of an enormous family wedding, had not been enough. The oddity of their situation paralyzed him. He kept hearing Prudence: "Of course she married you for your money—do you honestly imagine a girl like that would sleep with you for nothing?"

But Prudence—so woundingly and amazingly determined to make trouble—had no idea what kind of girl she was talking about. All she knew about Rufa was that she was young and beautiful. She would never understand the detailed delicacy, the fine filigree of scruple, that made up Rufa's moral landscape. Edward knew that any feeling of owing her husband sex would make Rufa wretched. He was alarmed by the distance that must be traveled, before they could reach the right level of intimacy. How was he to reach her?

He took an envelope from his breast pocket. "I nearly forgot. Nancy told me to give you this."

Rufa took it from him. The envelope said: "Mrs. Rufa Reculver. Don't open this until you are at home."

Inside was a Polaroid photograph of a row of bare bums. Nancy, Lydia, and Selena—their best wedding clothes bundled untidily round their waists—were doing low Japanese bows away from the camera. Underneath was written: "Full moon tonight!"

Rufa laughed till she cried. Then she did cry. Tears spilled from her eyes. She buried her face in Edward's shoulder, suddenly shaking with sobs. He put his arms around her, and felt the love she had for him, trying to beat its way through the barrier of the bargain they had made. He felt strong, and strangely peaceful. The shadows darkened around them while he held her.

"It's all right," he whispered.

"I'm so sorry. I'm sorry about everything."

"There's nothing to be sorry for."

Rufa said, "The thing is, I do love you. I haven't told you properly."

"You don't have to."

"I do," she insisted. "You have to know." She drew apart from him, trying to scoop away the tears with the backs of her hands. There were two streaks of dark eye makeup on her cheeks.

"Edward, I'm so ashamed."

"Ashamed?"

"I must have been mad. I was mad."

"Here." He dug in his pocket, pulled out a handkerchief and put it into her wet hand.

She laughed dismally. "You're always having to find me hankies."

"Well, I'll find you as many as you want."

She mopped at her eyes. "You have to know. It wasn't just about the money."

"Are we talking, by any chance, about your infamous Marrying Game?" Edward was smiling, a little grimly.

"Yes."

"Hmm. The general consensus seems to be that you could play it for the national Olympic team."

"Please don't joke about it. Until you asked me, I hadn't really admitted how wrong it was. I sort of knew deep down, but there didn't seem to be any other way out. And now I don't know—I can't find a way—" Rufa was struggling for words. "I probably would have married Adrian, but I knew it would make me miserable. And then you came along, and saved me."

Edward did not like the avuncular, Father Christmas image of himself as family savior, but he could not help being touched by her faith in him. She was still so certain that she had been saved. He circled her waist with his arm, manfully ordering his erection to subdue itself until they were several hundred miles outside Gloucestershire, and led her to the window. The night was clear, hung with stars. There were bars of moonlight across the lawn.

"Perhaps you saved me too," he said gently. "If you hadn't dreamed up your Marrying Game, I'd have been trapped in my old life, rapidly turning into a gray-bearded, barmy old git. I can't let you think the favors are all on my side."

"You might have married someone else."

"I didn't, though, did I? Because I happened to be in love with you."

She whispered, "Were you—did you love me before we had that row?"

He could tell this question was crucially important to her. He was cautious. One word out of place now, and he would lose her. Mentally he shuffled the pack of truth cards, to find a configuration that would not alarm her. "It's not as simple as that. My life came to a standstill when I left the army. Without that to hold me together, I found I was still grieving for Alice. I wasn't in a position to fall in love with anyone. Your Marrying Game forced me to take action, when I thought nothing on earth could. I'd never have married you—or anyone—without it."

She had stopped crying. "Honestly?"

"Honestly—so, for the love of God, stop being grateful. You can't build a marriage on gratitude. Whether I admitted it to myself or not, I realized I've loved you for years."

"Why didn't you tell me?"

"Would you have looked at me?"

"That's not a fair question—you didn't want to be looked at."

His voice was as gentle as he could make it. "The Zed would have made me feel I was messing about with his little girl—he never could accept the fact that you were grown up. Neither could I, when I came back here after the army—it seemed to me that I'd been taking you all to the pantomime incredibly recently. But even I couldn't help noticing that you'd turned into a woman. An astonishingly beautiful one."

"Did you? I mean, had I?"

"Oh, God." Edward was laughing softly to himself. "I don't believe it.

I've never actually spelled it out to you." He held her face between his palms. "Rufa, you're the most beautiful woman I've ever seen. Even with makeup running down your face." Smiling, he wiped the smudges under her eyes with his thumb. "All the times I've watched you—whether you've been happy, or sad, or angry—I've never seen one mood of yours that made you anything but beautiful. Your soul shows in your face. And that's beautiful too."

He was deeply moved to see how eagerly Rufa drank in his tribute.

She said, "Then I don't need to worry that you're sorry you married me."

"Absolutely not." Sorry? He wished to God he had the words to tell her that his happiness was almost too great to comprehend. "I wish I knew how to stop you being so anxious, Ru. What are you afraid of?"

"I don't really know." She looked at him in silence for a minute, searching for an answer. "Of not being good enough for you. I still think you deserve something better."

He smiled down at her. "Then it's up to us to build something better. The real Marrying Game is only just beginning."

Part
Two

Chapter One

"Her name's Polly," Linnet said. "I call her Smelly."

Rufa tipped fat beads of Arborio rice into her new kitchen scales, doing her best to swallow an unholy snort of laughter. "She's not that bad."

"Yes she is. She's as smelly as a fart. She keeps whispering with Daddy."

Linnet was severe, but dismissive. Though she never approved of Ran's girlfriends, she seldom lost much sleep over them—they came and went too frequently. Rufa was glad she had not yet noticed that this affair seemed to be far more serious. She reached over to caress the dark head. Touching Linnet gave her a blessed sense of control, when she felt power slipping away.

"Look on the bright side," she said, "Polly might persuade Daddy to buy a television."

Ran thought television was the new opium of the people, used by the government for mass brainwashing; but Rufa could not see Polly surviving a child in the house without one. Television was certainly the opium of the Linnet.

"Might she?" Linnet's face was inscrutable as she considered this. Then she became brisk. "Can I watch some now?"

"All right. As long as you don't make a fuss when it's time to go home."

"I won't." Linnet jumped from her chair and scampered along the stone passage to the drawing room, completely and unquestionably at home in Edward's house because Rufa lived there. Rufa only wished she could accept change as easily. Her own head was swimming with the strangeness of everything.

Ran had dropped his daughter off at the farm. He had stuck his head out of the car window long enough to shout, "Hi, Ru—hope you had a nice honeymoon—can't stop—I expect you've heard about Polly."

Rufa had heard. She and Edward had returned from Italy at eleven the previous night. In the middle of carrying his bride over the threshold, Edward had found a Post-it note from Rose stuck to the front door. "Guess What!!! Ring me. Mum."

"Typical," Edward said. "Not a word about you and your honeymoon. Just the headlines about the latest drama."

But he had encouraged Rufa to ring Rose as soon as the cases had been set down in the hall. He was curious too. This morning, Rufa had found the whole countryside seething with the news—in a small community, as Edward was always saying, everyone was ten feet tall and bathed in a permanent spotlight. There was no such thing as privacy. In the village post office and store, while buying bin bags and furniture polish, Rufa had heard it all again from Sandra Poulter, whose husband was managing Edward's farm. Then the landlord of the Hasty Arms had mentioned it—indeed, had come out of the pub specially to tell her, though he pretended to be asking after Nancy. It was the sensation of the hour.

Ran had a new girlfriend: a posh blonde who had made rather a fool of herself at the shop asking for balsamic vinegar. This blonde had left a fiancé standing at the altar, chucked in her job, and moved stacks and stacks of luggage into Semple Farm.

If Rufa had not spoken to Rose first, she would not have believed it. She had seen Ran and Polly together at her wedding, but had no idea their heated glances could have boiled over into this, in just three and a half weeks. Polly Muir, of all the unlikely people. Had she lost her neat and tidy mind? This was a woman who lay awake worrying about place settings, and Semple Farm was a dump. Edward, who considered Ran anything but a catch, laughed every time he thought of her among the floor cushions and joss sticks.

Now, with Linnet safely immersed in *Sabrina the Teenage Witch*, Rufa examined her own feelings again. Her concern for Lydia and Linnet added to her sense of things slipping out of her grasp, beyond understanding or control. Nothing was predictable. Nothing was simple. Even Polly Muir valued passion above good sense. She had won herself a splendid prize in the Marrying Game, and thrown it all away on the very eve of her triumph. What cared she for her goose-feather bed?

Rufa wished she could relearn the mysteries of passion. It must be something I'm doing wrong, she decided. With Jonathan, her only other lover, passion had been instinctive—but she now saw that she had only responded to him, without first having to win him. The Tuscan honeymoon had been paradise seen through a sheet of glass.

She had been enchanted by the hard blue skies, the hot nights ringing with crickets, the beauty that dripped from every medieval gable. They had arrived, euphoric with lack of sleep and the sense of escape, in the afternoon of the day after the wedding. On the journey, Edward had become more relaxed, more attentive, and generally more fun than he had been for weeks. When they sat on the terrace of the villa, he had been tender with her; gentle and loving. It had seemed natural to Rufa to go ahead of him up to their shuttered bedroom. Her throat dry with anticipation, she had slipped off her dress and stretched naked under the lavender-scented linen sheet.

But Edward had not come. She had fallen asleep, and by the time she woke up, everything had changed. She had found Edward tight-lipped and abstracted. There were patches of sweat on his shirt—he said he had been out walking, as if still on his bracing Gloucestershire farm. His manner to her had been as considerate and courteous as ever, but something had upset him.

Later—in no detail at all—he had told her. Prudence had called him, and although the conversation had not been easy, they were, essentially, reconciled. What did this mean? If the news was good, why did Edward seem so angry and anguished? And how had Prudence found the number of their honeymoon retreat? Edward had forbidden her to give it to Rose or Nancy, on the grounds that they needed a holiday from the everlasting demands of her family—but had he given it to Prudence? Rufa did not want to consider why the woman thought she had a right to intrude. At the time, she had been too confused and fearful to ask him.

The official delayed wedding night had been a washout. Not knowing what else to do, Rufa had once again gone upstairs first, and once again lain in naked anticipation under the single sheet. And Edward had bewildered her by reacting with anger. He had told her no performance was necessary;

he could not make love to her until he had lost the sense that he was collecting a purchase.

Rufa, numb with humiliation, had spent the night clinging to the extreme edge of the bed, muffling her sobs in the hard pillow, while Edward—forbiddingly clad in pajamas—had slept beside her.

The following morning he had apologized very sweetly. They had spent a magical day together, strolling round a local market and eating lunch under a vine. Edward had honored her by confiding in her. He explained that he had more than Prudence on his mind—he was engaged in a long and painful correspondence with the War Crimes Commission in The Hague, concerning his experiences in Bosnia. For the first time, he talked to her about the disillusion with soldiering that had made him leave the army. Almost in passing, he had added that Prudence kept the power to hurt him because she was almost his only family, and Rufa (who knew only too well how tiresome families could be) was not to worry.

He had been fascinating, charming. Rufa had wrapped herself in his undivided attention, always so difficult to win at home. And at the end of this golden day, they had gone up to bed together, and still not made love. Rufa, sizzling with embarrassment over her failed "performance," had covered her nakedness with a T-shirt. The tone of the honeymoon was set.

Not making love had become a routine. Night after night, Rufa had lain awake beside her husband, listening to his steady breathing. Incredibly, he slept. He had been trained to fall asleep in tanks and trenches, and other places even more uncomfortable than a double bed with an unfucked wife in it. Rufa would have worried that there was something wrong with him, or with her, if not for that one time.

The memory made her breathless and clumsy. She returned to it obsessively and a little shamefully, as if clinging to the memory of a dream.

"It's a sort of local version of brandy, I'm told," Edward said. He poured two measures of pale golden liquid, and handed one to Rufa. The scent, like the concentrated essence of a million grapes, mingled giddily with the scents of lavender and pine, and the thick hedge of rosemary that grew under the terrace. Silvia, the elderly housekeeper whose services had been hired with the villa, had cleared away the remains of a long, lazy lunch. They were both languid with heat and repletion.

Rufa knew she was not good at drinking, and usually limited herself to one glass of rich red wine. But the brandy was different. Each mouthful spread lassitude and dumb contentment through her body.

They sat in the shade of a big green umbrella, on fat calico cushions that smelled of baked dust. Whitewashed tubs brimmed with scarlet geraniums. The walls of the villa were splashed magenta, where bougainvillea climbed around the shuttered windows.

"This is heaven," Rufa said. "Total heaven. I never want to leave."

Edward said, "Have some more," and refilled their glasses.

They had been talking, as they often did, about the work still going on at Melismate. Edward was making Rufa laugh with some of Rose's dottier suggestions for improvements. She was drowsily aware of his fondness for them all, and the feeling of ultimate safety this gave her. The brandy flooded her senses with sweetness. She held out her glass again.

Edward, relaxed and affectionate, was laughing at her. "Don't be silly, you're completely pickled already."

"Why not? I never get pickled. I didn't realize it felt so lovely. I think I'm discovering alcohol—I never knew what all the fuss was about, until now."

"It makes you wonderfully mellow," Edward said. "At last you've stopped looking round for the next thing to do."

"I wish Mum could see me. She'd know how good you are for me."

Rufa sipped more brandy. She lay back against the cushions, gazing out across the patchwork of ochre and umber fields, and her whole self was miraculously free from any kind of pain. Profound peace swirled around her—though when she moved her head, the world rocked alarmingly. It was better if she shut her heavy eyes, but she did not feel she wanted to sleep. Her body ached with tenderness. Every cell felt alive. She was dreamily conscious of her nipples brushing the inside of her silk dress, and the swollen warmth between her legs.

Edward's arms were around her. His voice was soft and teasing against her ear. "Look at you—drunk and incapable. You'd better lie down."

She sighed. "I can't move."

"You don't have to." The world rocked again as he lifted her out of her chair and carried her across the terrace. They were both laughing. Rufa did not know what was so funny, except that life suddenly felt brilliant. Her consciousness flickered between stupid, fuzzy happiness and intense awareness of Edward's body. She rested her swimming head on his shoulder.

The soft mattress of the big double bed was underneath her. Very distantly, she felt Edward pulling off her sandals.

He murmured, "Do you want me to take your dress off?"

"Mmmmm. Yes." She could not have done it herself, if her life depended on it.

She felt his fingers, warm and firm, unfastening the buttons down her front. She felt him peel away the silk, exposing her flesh. She felt his lips on her breasts, and heard—as if from a great distance—her own shuddering sigh of longing.

And suddenly, jumping ahead several frames, he was on top of her, still fully clothed, moving inside her. Another jump ahead, and her legs were around his waist, gripping him against her. Nothing existed, beyond the delicious urgency of being fucked by him. She came, tightening around him, and he came too, rocking the bed beneath them.

Afterward, Rufa lay watching Edward in the shadows of the shuttered room, swiftly and silently tearing off his clothes. She felt as if he had shattered her, and reassembled her into a new person. At the back of her addled, crazed mind, she marveled at the old Rufa, who had considered poor Jonathan a good lover. Edward was in another league entirely. His body was hard and lean, with two dark triangles of hair on his chest and groin. Mesmerized, she stared at his erection, wondering how he had got such a thing inside her; faint with the desire to have him inside her again.

He made love to her slowly this time, gazing down into her face, keeping iron control until he came with a long groan of release. The room dissolved around Rufa. She lay against his chest, and slipped into a sleep of dizzy, mindless happiness.

Sighing, she pushed the memory away—but too late to avoid recalling the next day. She had woken in the early morning with a ferocious headache, and spent the entire day throwing up and swearing never to touch alcohol again. Edward had been marvelously considerate. That evening, when she had recovered enough to drink chamomile tea under the moon, he had quietly apologized. When she begged him to believe that no apology was necessary, he had ignored her. She could hardly blame him—the face she met in the mirror was pasty, with black semicircles under her red eyes. She looked like death warmed up. A couple of times she caught Edward watching her with a kind of horrified concern, as if he had killed something by mistake. They had not made love again.

Rufa longed for Edward to make love to her, and had several times humiliated herself by dropping delicate hints—which he had ignored. It had been like dropping hints to a brick wall. She did not dare risk rejection by asking him outright. His spells of depression, when he would raise a black wall around himself, intimidated her too much. Just occasionally, she had even been a little afraid of him. Though the moods had never been directed at her, they had turned him into a stranger.

He was more like himself now that they had come home. The two of them had not made love the night before, but they had been very cheerful in bed together—Edward's pungent comments about Ran had made her laugh hugely. Today, Rufa's spirits had risen to something like their premarriage level. This was the same old world, after all. Being married had not pulled it so dreadfully out of shape.

She poured boiling water over dried porcini mushrooms, blissfully inhaling their mossy forest scent. It was lovely to be cooking privately, without having to consider the cost of the ingredients. She had overcome her last shreds of reserve about spending Edward's money, and begun to indulge her passion for excellence. At the delicatessen in Cirencester she had bought a big lump of Parmesan, hard and chalky. She had bought a great bag of fresh, fat, purple figs, and slices of Parma ham and air-cured beef, thin as whispers. From Italy she had brought bottles of Marsala, jars of powerful black olives in oil, and gaudy pottery bowls. From Edward's garden she had gathered a large basin of scarlet tomatoes, and aromatic handfuls of oregano and rosemary. She was in a quiet, sunny kitchen, creating a beautiful dinner. If this was not happiness, it was surely very like it.

They had invited Rose and Roger to dinner this evening. Rufa was designing an Italian banquet. She decided to make a zabaglione for pudding, with the Marsala. She had only made zabaglione once before, for a dinner party in London, and had been too anxious about following the recipe to enjoy the experience. She was looking forward to whipping up a cloud of warm, spiced foam, in the copper pan she had found in Florence.

The Italian theme was all the more appropriate because the countryside was basking in a heat wave. The heat lay like golden syrup, making the bees sleepy. One blundered stupidly through the open window, and lay placidly in Rufa's hand when she turned it outside. This heat, both heavier and softer than the heat of Italy, made her overwhelmingly aware of her own body. She wanted to work hard, to find as much as possible to distract her from the permanent ache of desire. She had not been alive like this since the height of her affair with Jonathan. It was uncomfortable, like the feeling returning to a limb that has gone to sleep.

A door clicked across the passage. Edward came in, massaging his eyes. He had found a large pile of letters waiting for him, including one about Bosnia, which had taken most of the afternoon to answer. Rufa assumed this was the reason he looked so tired.

"Darling," he said. He was not a great man for endearments, and when he used them, they had a special resonance.

Rufa was wary. "What's the matter?"

"My darling, I'm so sorry. You're going to have put off Rose and Roger."

"Oh." She was disappointed, but determined to be positive. "Oh, well. It's not the end of the world."

"I wish to heaven I didn't have to throw this at you, but it's too late to do anything about it now. I'm afraid Prudence is about to land on us."

"What?" Rufa could not help sounding dismayed.

He sighed. "She'll be here in about an hour, and she intends to stay. I know it's impossibly short notice. She didn't tell me she'd invited herself until she was on the motorway. I suppose she knew I'd say no."

"Why didn't you?"

"There's been a fire at her London flat, apparently."

"What's wrong with her Paris flat?" Rufa snapped. She was surprised by her own waspishness.

"She lent it to someone. But she won't be staying here for more than a couple of days—I can promise you that." The look of vexation melted from his face. He smiled wryly at Rufa. "Think of it as the first big test of your married life—putting up with Prudence and her troublemaking."

"Has she come to make trouble?"

"Probably." Though he was still smiling, Rufa sensed his anger.

"But you said she'd forgiven you for marrying me."

"Not exactly. I said she said she'd forgiven me. Oh, God. What a grisly homecoming." He wrapped his arms around Rufa. "I really am sorry about this." He kissed her neck. Rufa sighed, leaning against his chest. He stroked her hair with the backs of his fingers. "She'll be incandescent when she sees how beautiful you are."

"Did you tell her I was plain?"

"Tristan will be impressed with my pulling power. He thinks I couldn't pull a muscle."

Rufa had started to laugh. "So we're expecting the boy as well. I'd better make up the beds."

"It's nice of you not to be furious," Edward said.

"I know."

"Thank you. I'll make it up to you—and I'll confess to Rose that it's all my fault."

"Don't worry, Mum won't mind. They can always come another time."

"There's bound to be a bit of subdued aggro about the money." Edward released her, with another affectionate kiss. "But Tristan won't hold it against us—he's a nice kid. And Pru's far too well behaved to make scenes."

Warm from his embrace, Rufa said: "Thank God someone is. Everyone else seems to have spent the last few weeks making absolutely operatic scenes. Why do changes have to happen all at once?"

Polly tipped the contents of the cutlery drawer out on the scarred kitchen table. It was nasty stuff, stained and bent. She would add it all to the teetering pile of rubbish outside the back door. There was a terrifying amount of throwing away to be done before she could unpack her own immaculate kitchenware. Now that Ran had removed his daughter, she was free to tear through his cupboards.

It would all have to go. One expected a certain amount of dilapidation in a farmhouse kitchen, but it only suited things that had been good in the first place. Everything here was shoddy, dented, buckled, and grimed. If necessary, they could stay in a hotel while Semple Farm was being gutted. Polly was not so gaga with love that she had not registered the sweet little hotel in the nearest market town.

And a temporary relocation might have the welcome side effect of keeping the child out of the way, until Polly had worked out how to treat her. Children were such a mystery. What did one do with them all day, if one did not have a nanny? Possibly, if the little girl was to be here often, a housekeeper might be in order. Linnet had spent the whole time clinging to Ran like a limpet, and looking utter daggers at Polly. They had not had a second to themselves.

Polly had not discussed this state of affairs with Ran. There was never time. They could not be alone together without falling ravenously on each other's bodies. Polly sighed, and stretched luxuriously. The heat made their passion more intense. Night after night they lay naked under a single sheet, moist and musky with sweat. Polly, who had never admitted the existence of something as ungenteel as sweat, loved to lick the salty sheen on Ran's smooth skin. Ran parted her legs in the moonlit darkness. The springs in his lumpy, world-weary mattress creaked when he rolled on top of her. They became one flesh, rocking urgently toward climaxes that seemed to last for hours.

Rufa's wedding had been on a Saturday. On the following Monday Polly had brazenly told Berry that she was driving to Petersfield, to see her parents. Poor Berry had assumed it was business to do with their own wedding, and had kissed her good-bye with grateful affection.

Polly had driven straight to Semple Farm, not caring who saw her. Ran had been waiting, as they had arranged in a hot exchange of whispers. Minutes later they had been making love, on a twanging sofa that smelled of dog. It had been a rebirth. Polly had only dimly noticed the surrounding squalor. She had been too drunk with the wonder of Ran's extraordinary beauty. At a great distance, she was aware of his awful clothes and nutty opinions, but these did not matter. He was an innocent, an angel. The clothes could be changed, and the opinions were adorable. Polly had been light with the joy of shedding her old skin.

Later they had walked hand in hand down the rough track to where she had left her car. They ended up making love again on the grass, under the huge, orange, blue-veined moon. Ran's loud groans of pleasure had mingled with the cries of foxes and owls. Afterward, he had dropped juicy tears on her collarbone, and begged her to stay forever. She was the woman he had been searching for all his life. There was no life without her. On her second illicit visit, Polly had known, beyond all doubt, that she could never leave him again.

The jilting of Berry had been ghastly, but she had made up her mind to manage it as efficiently as she managed everything else. She had made sure it was a Friday, so Berry did not have to go to work next day with a broken heart. Before he came home, Polly had rung a very good firm of packers, and booked them in for Monday morning. She had already taken Jimmy Pellew out to lunch, to thrill him with her story and resign from the gallery.

By the time she heard Berry whistling outside the door, Polly had fired the cleaner, called an estate agent about putting the flat on the market, and arranged for Harrods to store her bulkier furnishings. Berry did not realize it, but his home had gone before he turned his key.

Remembering the scene gave Polly pain. Obviously, it had been frightful.

She had sat poor Berry down on the sofa, and given him a glass of brandy. She had explained—looking bravely into his shocked, vulnerable brown eyes—that her sudden rebirth was no reflection on him. She was dreadfully sorry, but this passion was bigger than both of them.

Berry had, of course, been severely upset, but (this was something Polly refused to dwell on) in a way that was somehow not quite satisfactory. He had not cried, or begged her to stay. Mostly, he had tried hard—too hard?—to be helpful. This was typical of his sweetness and consideration, but still. During an interval in her confession, Polly had gone to make tea. Berry had telephoned his sister to ask if he could crash out in the spare room of her flat in Clapham. And she had seen him holding the receiver away from his ear, because bloody Annabel was singing "Zippedee-Do-Dah" loud enough to wake the dead. Thank God that bit was over.

Polly had gone home to Petersfield that weekend, to give Berry time to move out his belongings, and to break the news to her parents. Her mother had been devastated, and inclined to be bitter about the money spent on engraved invitations, royal florists, and vintage champagne. Every time she thought of the wedding presents that would have to be returned, she had gone upstairs to lie down.

Her father had seemed relieved, on the whole, mentioning more than once how glad he was that he had not shelled out for a new sporran—he had never been enthusiastic about wearing his kilt. That unpleasantness too was now history. Polly had spent all her time since then at Semple Farm, falling deeper and deeper into fathomless love.

Love had not affected her capability. Ran had to see his child, and pootle about at what he described as "work"—for instance, taking the late plums to the Farmers' Market, and digging sporadically in his onion patch. Love certainly did not blind Polly to the fact that he was a useless farmer, but his renovation would come later. Polly spent the hours without him making plans for the future.

The house was Georgian, and rather a gem. It could be made gorgeous—once Polly had provided Ran with more children, and the two smelly dogs were dead. This was a long-term project. Polly loved a challenge. She sang to herself as she dumped a pile of his plates on the rubbish with an almighty smash, and moved to open her box of third-best crockery.

It took her a few moments to notice the slight figure in the open doorway. She looked up, and after an awkward stretch of silence said, "Oh. Hello."

Lydia, smaller and more girlish than ever in a flowered cotton dress and sandals, put one trembling hand to her mouth. The two women studied one another. Polly decided that Lydia's disturbing prettiness was more or less canceled out by her appalling presentation.

She carefully set down a stack of soup bowls. "I'm afraid you've missed Linnet. Ran took her over to Rufa's."

"I came to see you," Lydia said. Her voice was soft and hesitant.

"I see," Polly said cautiously. The wise thing was to be as gracious as possible, she thought. "Well, here I am."

"Why—why did you break the yellow plates?"

It was an odd question, and Polly did not like to think she had been observed singing and smashing. "They were chipped."

"They came from Ran's mother," Lydia said tragically. Everything she said sounded tragic.

Polly said, "Really? The writing on the bottom said Hotel Dinnerware Ltd. I didn't think they could be heirlooms."

"She bought them when we got married."

"Oh." What on earth was she meant to say to this? Did Lydia expect sympathy because she had failed to win custody of the Hotel Dinnerware?

"If you're throwing them away, could I have them?"

"I suppose so. I mean, of course." Polly was nonplussed. "I haven't asked Ran, but I have no intention of keeping any of that china—I rather loathe the pattern, to be honest. I'll find a box for you."

It was not yet clear how Lydia intended to treat her. Polly waited to see if she was hostile, or disposed to give her a hippyish welcome of peace and love. You never knew with that family.

Lydia asked, "Do you have to give the presents back, when you don't get married after all?"

Polly smiled, but was furious. This woman was smarter than she looked, or she would not have touched the sorest place so quickly. "I'll send some back, naturally." (The gravy boat from the Royal person, the canteen of cutlery from Berry's aunt and uncle.) "But I'll be writing to some people, to explain the new situation. They might want me to keep them."

Lydia stared, digesting the part about the "new situation." "It's not your fault," she said. "I don't want to blame you. You couldn't help falling in love with Ran. But don't go thinking he loves you back."

Polly now knew exactly how to handle this. Her tone was pitying and patient. "Sit down, Lydia. I'm afraid Ran warned me something like this might happen. He said you'd had difficulty accepting the divorce."

218

Lydia clenched her fists. "There was no divorce."

"That's just silly, isn't it? Of course there was a divorce."

"There was a bit of paper, that's all. It didn't stop me being married to Ran. I think you should go back to London, before he breaks your heart too."

"Don't be ridiculous," Polly snapped. "Nobody is going to break my heart. I'm afraid you're hysterical."

"I am not!"

"I'm extremely sorry for you, Lydia. I think it's all a symptom of underlying depression, and you should see someone for it. You obviously need help. But the fact is, Ran has fallen in love with me. He's told me he can't face life without me." Polly's voice rang with confidence. "He says he'd die for me."

"That's what he says to everyone."

"Nonsense. You know this is different, or you wouldn't be here. I suppose I should be flattered."

"The garden path might be longer," Lydia said, "but you're being led up it, all the same."

Polly had had enough of this madwoman and her gnomic utterances. "No, this time it truly is different, and you'd better get used to it." She pointed to a blue plastic bulge, hanging on one of the cupboard doors. "See that? It's my wedding dress. It's my wedding dress. I brought it with me because Ran and I are getting married."

Lydia flinched, as if Polly had slapped her. "Did he—has he asked you?"

"Yes."

"You're lying!"

Polly was lying. She was outraged that she had been forced to lie. What the hell did it matter whether Ran had actually asked her? He had seen the wedding dress. Why else would she be keeping it?

"I've done my best to be civil to you," she said, "since you're the mother of Ran's child. But I think you'd better leave now. This isn't your house anymore."

"No, and it's not yours either!" Lydia's deep blue eyes swam with tears, but her voice was high and firm. "Not now, not ever! *You are not marrying Ran!*"

Chapter Two

Rufa closed the kitchen door behind her, and punched Wendy's number into the phone. It was answered almost immediately by Nancy, who had a sixth sense for Rufa's calls.

"Nance, hi. It's me."

"Darling, I was hoping you'd ring. How's it going?"

"Fine. Really. I just wanted to talk to someone normal, who doesn't put every word I say under a microscope."

Nancy laughed softly. "Are you safe?"

"More or less. I'm making her some coffee." Rufa, the receiver tucked into her shoulder, was deftly assembling old Mrs. Reculver's white-and-gold coffee set. Her strivings for perfection grew more relentless every day. "Give me a fix of ordinary, unrefined life, for pity's sake."

"The headlines haven't changed since yesterday," Nancy said. "Except that Tiger is begging Roshan to move in with him."

"And he won't? Why? He's in love with the big lummox, isn't he?"

"It's the coming-out aspect," Nancy said. "He's getting cold feet about being spread all over the papers. Tiger's just as much of an exhibitionist when he's sober."

Rufa spooned coffee into the pot. "Tell Roshan to ring me. Preferably in the early morning, but anytime's fine, as long as he doesn't mind edited answers."

Nancy said, "He has to edit what he says too, if Tiger's hovering. Or the big lummox gets jealous and starts to cry."

"Oh dear. We can't both talk in code. Tell him I'll ring when Prudence has gone." She opened a box of posh chocolate biscuits—mostly for the look of the thing, since Prudence seldom ate anything except steamed spinach—and arranged them neatly on a china plate.

Nancy asked, "When's she going?"

Rufa lowered her voice, though a corridor and two closed doors separated her from the drawing room. "Not till Tuesday."

"Why do you have to put up with her? She's Edward's responsibility."

"He's doing his best, but he's so busy." Rufa did not add that Edward was also short-tempered and secretive; or that the queenly presence of Prudence drove him into his office for hours at a time. There were all kinds of involved reasons why she could not tell Nancy about this. "She's not all that bad, and Tristan's lovely. But she makes me realize how much I miss Wendy's. Do give them all my love."

Nancy asked, "Are you really okay?"

"I told you, I'm fine. How about you? Have you seen Berry lately? Is he visibly heartbroken?"

A heavy sigh gusted down the phone. "He's gone to Frankfurt. He's taken a posting there, and he won't be back for months."

"You should follow him." Rufa was firmer, now that she had managed to nudge Nancy onto her favorite subject. "Get a job in a *Bierkeller*."

"Don't encourage to me to make an idiot of myself," Nancy said disconsolately. "I have to face the fact that I blew it. The first decent man ever to cross my path, and I scared him off. I'm a poor, tragic casualty of the Marrying Game."

"Rubbish," Rufa said bracingly. "You wait, he'll be back. Oh, God, the kettle—I must go. Speak tomorrow?"

"Ru, wait! What's up? I know something's the matter."

All sorts of things were the matter. Glances, hints, veiled anger. Rufa could not explain it to Nancy. She could not describe something as insubstantial as an Atmosphere.

"I'm fine," she said. "Bye." She hung up.

The silence of the house washed over her again. She gazed out of the window at the rolling quilt of fields and hedges, shimmering in the heat. Outwardly, everything was cordial and charming; so much so that Rufa would have felt foolish trying to put her uneasiness into words. It was all buried beneath a hard veneer of civilization.

Edward had retreated into himself, as he did when he had something on his mind. He could not sleep. He lay motionless beside Rufa, with the tension crackling round him like electricity. Last night she had felt him getting out of bed. She had waited for him for twenty minutes. Something made her want to know where he was. She got up, and found him down in the kitchen, listening to the World Service. He had whipped round almost angrily when he heard her, then he had apologized, said he was anxious.

Rufa had not been satisfied. When Edward said he was anxious, he meant he was worrying about the War Crimes business, and she had already agreed not to expect him to talk about that. But there was something else, she was sure. She felt the weight of history between Edward and Prudence without understanding it, as if she had arrived halfway through a film.

She carried the tray of coffee to the drawing room, and was annoyed when she caught herself wondering if she should knock. This was her own house—why was she behaving like an upper servant?

Probably, she thought suddenly, because I'm being treated like one.

Prudence, in a white linen shirt and gray linen trousers, was on the sofa, leafing through a copy of *Vogue*. She was discreetly but perfectly made up, and looked completely at ease. The face of Selena, glowing against a dark background in frosted mauve lipstick, was on the front of the magazine. The camera gave her bony, elfin features a mesmerizing, otherworldly beauty. The sight of her printed eyes, half hidden by Prudence's thigh, added to Rufa's sense of reality suspended by a thread.

For some reason, Prudence was annoyed that Rufa's sister was on the cover of *Vogue*. The edition had been lying in the drawing room for two days, and she had become disagreeably personal whenever it was mentioned. Several times, when the atmosphere had thickened unbearably, Rufa had mentioned it on purpose. She did not know why there was a war, or why it involved her, but she was getting an instinct for her weapons.

Prudence was in her late forties, but her age was irrelevant. She was beautiful, and the beauty had been perfectly maintained for at least thirty years. She was taut and tanned and gleaming, and could still carry off a certain pertness; though only in the company of men. She had recently divorced her fourth very rich husband. Edward had explained that Pru's upbringing had been very different from Alice's. Their father had seduced his housekeeper, and though he never married the woman, he had lavished money and attention on their child, Prudence. If his intention was to divide the half sisters, however, he failed. The two households, both miserable, had huddled together for warmth. They had protected each other during the frequent switches of affection, joining forces so that no one would be in complete outer darkness. Money had shuttled between them. The sisters had spent holidays together. It had been an eccentric and painful situation, and Edward still found it distasteful to talk about. He had only sketched it for Rufa so she would understand why Prudence and Alice were so different.

Alice had been quiet and retiring, devoted to Edward both for himself, and as a symbol of the place where she had been happiest in her childhood. Prudence, who had no scruples about her father's money—or anyone else's—had chosen the exotic international lifestyle of the very wealthy. Rufa did not see why the woman had to stay here while her London flat was being cleaned up after the fire (a very small fire anyway, as far as she could make out), when she had perfectly good flats in Paris and New York.

"How lovely," Prudence exclaimed. "You're so sweet. I'm afraid I'm being the most frightful nuisance."

"Not at all." Rufa set down the tray on the low table, and knelt on the floor to pour the coffee. She was not up to taking the other end of the sofa.

"Sylvia's coffee set. I haven't seen this for years. Is that cream? Yes, I will have a little, please."

Sylvia was old Mrs. Reculver. Rufa gave Prudence a cup of coffee.

Prudence said, "Mmm, you do everything so exquisitely. You're a paragon. No wonder Edward fell madly in love with you. The way to a man's heart, and all that."

Rufa smiled. "He just eats what's put in front of him. I don't think he particularly cares."

"Oh, all men care. And life with you seems to suit him—have I mentioned, he's looking tremendously well?"

"Yes."

Prudence had mentioned it, at least twice a day. She went on, "You deserve a medal for making him shave off that beard."

"It wasn't anything to do with me."

"Come on. Of course it was. He wanted to impress a beautiful young woman. And he's at the age when men start to panic about their lost youth."

"Edward's not old, though." Rufa was self-conscious about the gap of eighteen years between them, which Prudence always managed to turn into a yawning gulf.

"Oh God, no," Prudence said, with a short laugh. "If he's old, what the hell does that make me? But a man as frankly handsome as him is bound to want to make up for lost time."

Rufa said, "Do have a biscuit."

"No thanks. I had to more or less give up eating twenty years ago. I can't tell you how huge I was after I had Triss. Have you seen him this morning, by the way?"

"He went for a walk, I think," Rufa said.

Prudence smiled. "Good. He's rediscovering energy, after spending about five years in a darkened room. Do I have to remind Edward about lunch?"

"No, he won't forget." Rufa knew he had not forgotten. He had complained about it that morning, before Prudence was up, and said that if she dropped one more hint about the money, he would "scrag" her. Rufa had enjoyed this.

"He does seem distracted at the moment, doesn't he?" Prudence mused. "Not like my idea of a man newly returned from his honeymoon. I do hope he's all right."

"He's fine," Rufa said lamely.

"You know," Prudence went on, with one of her pretty, catlike smiles, "I might get him to talk to me when we're alone. I was always rather good at getting him to open out."

Rufa struggled for a polite and casual way to assure her that Edward told her absolutely everything. "He tends to clam up when there are other people in the house."

Prudence was having none of it. "Yes, it must be odd for him, having you here when he's been alone for so long. The poor man hates expressing his feelings. It all reminds me—you probably don't remember what he was like after Alice died."

"Not really."

She scrutinized Rufa, narrowing her tight eyes. "Well, you were a child."

"I was eleven."

"It must be odd for you, living in the shadow of your predecessor. Especially when it was such a famously happy marriage."

"Edward doesn't talk about her much."

"The trouble with that marriage," Prudence said, "is that it spoiled Edward for life."

"Sorry?" Rufa had not expected this.

"I think Alice took the best of him with her. He lost the ability to fall in love. Something got burned away. Don't you find him a little unresponsive sometimes?"

She seemed to expect an answer. Rufa bent her head to fiddle with the crockery on the tray. Prudence took her silence as affirmation. "I suppose he's told you about his thing with me? Yes, of course—he's such a stickler for being truthful, and all that jazz. And I've always found you had to absolutely trample on his feelings to get any sort of reaction. It didn't work out because I needed more warmth. More passion, if you like. I assume he *was* passionate with Alice. Although she never confided in me—she was like him, the buttoned-up type." With a smile, she crossed her long legs and changed gear. "Mind you, both of them were much less buttoned with Tristan. He adored coming here when he was little, and he still worships Edward. When I was out of the country, I used to send Edward to his school sports day—frankly, I couldn't stand that kind of thing, and Edward's one of those people who can just naturally talk to housemasters and so on. I never had the knack."

She paused, to let the message sink in: Edward was a father to her son; the center of her family. Rufa heard it. She thought what a cow Prudence was, getting someone else to visit her child at boarding school.

"It's so funny seeing Tristan's sudden passion for the countryside. I sent him to school in the middle of nowhere, and he never stopped complaining about it. And now he's begging to stay here until term starts. Do you think Edward would mind?"

"No, of course not. He'll be really pleased." Rufa could say this with confidence. Edward was very fond of Tristan, now twenty and at Oxford. "But won't you miss him?"

"Not if he's in one of his sulks."

"I've never seen him sulking."

Prudence said, "There's a lot you haven't seen." She sipped coffee, leaving another pause for Rufa to read possible meanings into this. "He saves all the tantrums for me. You'll know what I'm talking about when you have a child yourself."

Rufa felt crushed. Was it possible that Prudence knew she and Edward had achieved sex only once?

"I'm assuming you'll start all that pretty soon," Prudence said. "It's obviously the reason Edward was in such a rush to get married. For your sake, I hope you're the maternal type."

Faintly, Rufa asked, "Why did you only have one child?" She had asked it innocently, but instantly realized she had scored another hit, by reminding Prudence of the disparity in their ages.

Prudence laughed merrily. "Tristan was quite enough, thank you. When you have two or three days to spare, I'll tell you all about my lurid relationship with his father." She sipped coffee, picked up a biscuit, looked at it, and put it back on the plate. "The first divorce is the worst. I'd never have survived it without Edward."

Her eyes were blue, of a precise almond shape, set in very tight skin. Perhaps, Rufa thought, it was the tightness that made them seem so hard. Mentally she begged Prudence not to confide in her.

But she was not to be put off. She was making various graceful movements, settling herself for a barrage under the white flag of confession. "He's been a rock to me, an absolute rock. Through all my ghastly life, all my stupid marriages. I freely admit, I took him rather for granted. I assumed he'd always be there for us. I should have bagged him while I had the chance."

Rufa's cheeks burned. Panic gripped her stomach. "When did he ask you?"

"He didn't," Prudence said. "I should have asked him. But you see, Rufa, I didn't think it was necessary." She continued to smile, but Rufa was left in no doubt of her furious anger. "Did he say anything about what happened in Paris?"

"Yes, he said you'd had a row. About me."

"Not about you personally," Prudence said. "I suppose about the fact that Edward thought he was single. And therefore free to marry anyone else at all."

This changed the world too much to be understood all at once. Did Prudence think she was his rightful wife? Surely this could not be possible.

Something in her reaction softened Prudence. The aggressive sweetness left her face. She looked tired. "It's one of the basic differences between men and women," she said. "When a woman says she's single, she means just that. But when a man says he's single, he only means the woman he's screwing isn't good enough."

"Edward's not like that," Rufa stated. She was not going to take Prudence's word for this.

"Oh, I know he's the soul of honor and chivalry—and God, he never lets you forget it." Prudence was bitter now. "This was why he had to ride in like the cavalry, to mend your roof and save your family. It was all tied up in his ridiculous loyalty to your father."

Rufa bowed her head. Her own silliness, coupled with the family poverty, had virtually forced Edward to do the decent thing and marry The Zed's eldest daughter. Prudence meant her to know that Edward had committed this romantic act without considering the feelings of the woman who loved him. And he would not make love to Rufa because he felt joined to this other woman. The cruelty of the situation Prudence was describing made Rufa think it must be the truth.

"Pru?" Edward's voice was in the corridor.

"In here!" A male voice galvanized Prudence, as if she had switched on an internal light.

Edward came into the room. "Oh, here you are." He looked at both of them.

Prudence smiled up at him. "Hello. Where have you been hiding all morning?"

"Sorry, I had work to do."

"Rufa's been taking wonderful care of me."

Edward frowned. He often frowned when with Prudence. "Good. I think we ought to leave, if we're having this lunch. Please don't make me wear a tie."

"In this heat? I'm not such a sadist." Prudence jumped up to kiss Edward's cheek. Her fingers brushed an imaginary speck off his shoulder. "And in any case, you look gorgeous in that shirt."

He frowned, but Rufa saw, for the first time, exactly why it made her so uncomfortable to observe Edward and Prudence together. There was no physical reserve between them. In the private language of women, as inaudible to men as a dog whistle, Prudence was telling her what had happened in Paris. She and Edward had still been lovers, and as far as Prudence was concerned, the affair was not yet over.

❄ ❄ ❄

After that, everything was different. Prudence could not have made it clearer if she had shouted it through a megaphone—she and Edward had a

227

far longer and more elaborate history than Rufa had been led to believe, and Prudence just wanted Rufa to know that the position of being a young, beautiful new bride was not as unassailable as it seemed.

Was this a warning that she was still dangerous? Rufa waved the two of them off to lunch, oppressed by the sheer peculiarity of her situation. Prudence would not have been dangerous at all if Edward had been getting sex anywhere else. He lay beside her through the hot nights, never touching her except by accident. Inches separated them, and miles. Had Prudence guessed? Was it obvious?

For a moment, standing in the empty drawing room gripping the tray, Rufa was giddy with fear. The old terror of the surrounding blackness that had tormented her since the death of The Zed came rushing back. Edward had slept with this woman when he went to Paris to end it all. Prudence had power where she had none. If Prudence wanted to smash the tender shell Rufa had just begun to build against the blackness, she could.

The fear receded as soon as Rufa thought of Edward, and took him properly into account. He was the world's most honorable man. He loved her. The least she could do for him, when he had done everything for her, was trust him. She did not need to look very deep inside herself to know that she trusted Edward with her life.

Sunlight lay upon the clean kitchen surfaces in pools of silver. Screwing up her eyes against the dazzle, Rufa set the tray down on the draining board. It disturbed her to be made conscious of Edward as a sexual being, when she craved sex with him so intensely. But if she could not trust him, what was left to believe in?

She picked up old Mrs. Reculver's white-and-gold coffeepot. It slipped through her fingers, smashing explosively on the stone floor. Rufa leaped with shock, and burst into tears. She was sick of performing and pretending. She was sick of skivvying for Prudence, who managed to convey hostility and dislike with every sweetly worded request. She wanted to be at home, where you could have an ordinary, unambiguous row.

"Rufa?"

She leaped again. Tristan stood in the doorway—she had forgotten she was not alone in the house. Mortified to be caught sobbing, Rufa snatched a strip of paper towel and pressed it to her face.

She gasped, "Hello, you made me jump—" with a ridiculous stab at sounding breezy.

Rufa and Tristan had been careful to maintain a distance. This was not because they disliked each other, but because they were both aware of the potential embarrassment of their situation. Rufa, as the wife of Tristan's uncle by marriage, had the same status as a grown-up. Tristan, as the son of Prudence, had the status of a child. But he was only seven years younger than Rufa, and this made them feel as if they were playing charades.

It was further complicated by the fact that Tristan was beautiful. Prudence and Edward spoke of him as a boy, when he was actually a young man, a few weeks past his twentieth birthday. He was tall and graceful, with golden brown hair that curled to his shoulders and eyes of a warm blue. "Sorry," Rufa said. "This is silly of me. It's nothing. Don't take any notice."

He was distressed to see her crying. He looked down at the shards and slivers of porcelain strewn across the floor. Bitter-smelling coffee grounds splattered the wooden cupboard doors. "Was it really valuable, or something?"

Rufa did her best to smile. "God, no—it was just the last straw."

Tristan stood in the kitchen doorway, absurdly Rupert Brookeish and Bridesheadish, gazing at the dirty floor like a juvenile lead who has bounced in through the wrong set of French windows.

"I know what this is about," he said gravely. "My mother's been having a go at you."

"Oh, no—" This was exactly the matter, and she could not make the denial sound anything but feeble.

"And you're exhausted, because you've been letting her treat you like a slave." He was indignant, which was comforting. They were not pretending anymore.

Rufa leaned wearily against the counter. "I can't not do things when she asks."

"Yes, you can," Tristan said energetically. "She should wear a sign round her neck: Don't Obey Me. Like the diabetic dog at the pub you mustn't feed."

Rufa laughed properly for the first time since the arrival of Prudence. "I do find it difficult not to run round after her."

"My mother has her moments," Tristan said, "but I'm not blind to the blemishes in her character. I've begged her to stop being a bitch to you, but she pretends not to know what I mean. I think I'm supposed to be too young to understand what you've done."

"Done? Me?"

Tristan was matter-of-fact. "Well, you married Edward, didn't you?"

"Was that wrong?"

"Terribly. He wasn't meant to marry anyone. Let alone someone like you, with a sister on the cover of *Vogue*."

"Why did she come here, then?"

"To get a good look at you," Tristan said. "To get a handle on you, so she can make snide remarks about you to Edward."

The relief of calling things by their right names was immense. Rufa, almost without realizing, had started to relax. "Do you think that's what she's doing now?"

"Probably."

"She's wasting her time. Edward doesn't understand hints." She blew her nose. "This is awful of me, to be talking like this. Criticizing your mother."

Tristan grinned. "Feel free to criticize. You have to learn to ignore her. Think of this small strop as a kind of backhanded compliment."

"I'll try."

"Sit down. I'll clear away the remains of the Golden Bowl."

"Oh no, I couldn't—"

"Please, Rufa. I haven't done a thing to help you. Let me show you I'm not totally useless." He came into the room, put a warm hand on her elbow, and steered her to a chair. "I presume the cleaning stuff's under the sink."

He knelt, in his grass-stained white jeans, in front of the cupboard. Rufa mopped at her face, watching as he swept the pieces of the coffeepot into the dustpan, and moved the grounds about with a J-cloth. He left fragments and smears everywhere. The kitchen looked worse when he thought he had finished.

"There you are." His face was flushed with the effort of banging ineffectually round her cupboards.

Rufa stood up. "Thanks, that's terrific. Did you come in search of lunch just now?"

"Well, yes. I'm sorry, but I'm ravenous."

"I'll make something."

"No, please—how can I let you cook for me now?"

They both laughed and stared at each other curiously, as if they had only just been introduced.

He asked, "The pub does lunches, doesn't it?"

Rufa said, "You seem to know quite a lot about the pub. I thought you were out taking long walks."

"It's too hot. I have to get away from Mother, so I sit in the pub with a book."

Now that the Chinese wall was down, Rufa could imagine herself in Tristan's place. "You've been having a dreary time. I'm so sorry."

"Not at all." He was serious, eager. "Honestly, it's wonderful here. I've done half my reading for next term." The color deepened in his face. He looked away from her. "Would you let me take you out for lunch?"

Rufa smiled. "You're very kind, but my sister used to work at that pub, and she told me what they put in the steak and kidney pies. The food's much better here."

"Okay, let's stay here. Only I'll make the lunch, and you can sit and watch." He looked into her eyes again. "On the understanding that comments are forbidden."

His attempt to be masterful was unexpectedly endearing. Rufa said, "Well, if you really insist, there's some very good ham in the fridge, and I picked—"

"Shut up, I'm in charge now." Tristan turned away from her to open the large and vulgar new refrigerator Edward had installed for his bride. "All you have to do is sit down and make polite conversation. Or better still, very rude conversation. I don't know about you, but I'm sick to death of politeness."

Rufa, beginning to enjoy herself, sat down and surrendered herself to the lazy pleasure of watching him. She did not care what she ate. It was lovely to feel delicate and cherished, after all Prudence's admiring remarks about her capacity for drudgery.

"It's not politeness," she said. "I'm sick of hiding what I really feel."

He looked over his shoulder. "What's that? Don't be afraid of telling me."

It was easy to talk to him. Somehow, he made Rufa aware that he was on her side. But he was the son of Prudence, and it was wise to be tactful. "I suppose I'm tired of pretending to be part of an old married couple, when I haven't even been married two months. I still feel rather like a visitor here. I get rather tense."

Tristan grabbed a bottle of champagne. "This should help."

"Oh, not for me, thanks."

"Why not? It's high summer, it's boiling hot, and neither of us have a thing to do." He opened the bottle and poured two glasses.

Rufa, taking hers, felt she ought to say, "I have to think about dinner."

"Let them eat salad."

"It wouldn't do any harm, would it?" She sipped her champagne. Its delicious coldness spiked her bloodstream. "Edward only ever seems interested in baked potatoes, and your mother barely eats at all."

"Now I feel guilty, because I eat you out of house and home."

"Nonsense. You're very rewarding to cook for." As she said it, Rufa recognized that this was true. She would have been far more demoralized if Tristan had not hoovered up the exquisite terrines and timbales his mother barely touched.

He was making sandwiches with huge slabs of crusty white bread, hard chips of cold butter, thick slices of farm-cured ham, and lumps of fresh tomato. His sandwiches were like Nancy's—vast and unwieldy, oozing good things. Rufa had never been able to match their hearty prodigality. She often thought it took an amateur to make a truly satisfying doorstep sandwich.

"Let's eat outside," Tristan said. He put the sandwiches on a large pottery plate Rufa had found in Siena, and took a colander of washed white grapes from the draining board. Rufa had bought these for Prudence, who liked to have the better class of food around, even if she did not eat it. Suddenly enchanted by the idea of a picnic, Rufa took the champagne, their glasses, and the remains of a very successful *tarte tatin*.

There was a large oak tree on the sloping ground behind the house. Tristan had been reading out here this morning. A rug was spread on the baked earth. A copy of John Clare's *Midsummer Cushion* lay facedown where he had flung it. Rufa picked up the book. "Is this your work?"

"Sort of." Tristan was shy. She sensed he would have liked to talk about it, but was cautious. "It suits the weather, and being out in the country. And—" He was unwilling to go on.

Rufa handed him his glass, and settled against the trunk of the tree. She could tilt her face upward and see the boughs arching and interlacing against the hot blue sky. They were in a tent of leaves. Daubs of sunlight shifted around them. One lay upon Tristan's forehead, heating his hair to gold. They ate his huge sandwiches in a haze of contentment, laughing softly when pieces of tomato dropped out into their laps.

Tristan refilled their glasses. The champagne was turning warm, its bubbles lazily deflating. Rufa, stuffed and sleepy, could not manage any of the *tarte tatin*. Tristan ate it, then tore off a handful of grapes. He lay sprawled on his side, propped on one elbow, gazing at Rufa. They were very still. The only sound, in the great stillness around them, was of distant hammering across the valley. A bee droned clumsily between them.

Rufa sighed luxuriously. "This is bliss."

"You should do this more often," Tristan said.

"I'm bad at doing nothing."

"This isn't nothing. You're having lunch with me." His voice dropped to a confessional murmur. "Talking to me. Letting me talk to you, without treating you as if you were as old as my mother."

"It makes me feel guilty," Rufa said. "I get twitchy if I'm not doing something practical that has a tangible result. I have to see that I've made a difference."

"That's only the outside. It's just as important to pay attention to the inside of yourself." He reddened, forcing the words out. "Don't tell me you don't like poetry, because I won't believe you. You couldn't look like that and—and not have a soul to match."

Rufa opened her drowsy eyes properly. Tristan stared, impressed by his own boldness, wary of her response. He was so lovely, she thought her heart would break. Tentatively, he reached across to touch her hand, which was lying in her lap. As his warm flesh met hers, Rufa felt a tautening at the pit of her stomach and languid heat between her legs.

She twitched her hand away smartly, wondering why she was not angry, or afraid.

Chapter Three

Two days after the departure of Prudence, Edward abruptly told Rufa he was leaving. For a splinter of a second, her undisciplined mind—which was veering off down all kinds of crazy paths these days—was gripped by terror, and various phantoms threatened to burst out of the door marked Denial.

Then she realized he was not talking about running off with his Camilla Parker-Bowles. He was only explaining that he had to go away for a few weeks, perhaps a month. He had been summoned to The Hague, to give evidence to the judges of the War Crimes Tribunal. This was the business that had been grating at him for most of the year, and Rufa felt vaguely guilty for not treating it more seriously.

"Sorry," he said. "It's a nuisance, but I'm sure you see I can't even try to get out of it."

"No, of course not."

They were driving over to Melismate. Edward liked to discuss difficult subjects in the car, where they could not be complicated by eye contact.

He was frowning at the road. "Ask me about it, then."

"You don't have to go into detail," Rufa said mildly. "You don't have to tell me anything." Before he sprang this on her she had been gazing out of the window at the cow parsley and late poppies, thinking about something quite different.

"It's ridiculous of me to be secretive," he said. "But the full story is very long and very complicated—and connected with all sorts of other stuff I don't like to dwell on."

"Other stuff?" Rufa echoed dutifully. She resigned herself to listening, when her whole being was in rebellion against the lurking unpleasantness beneath the surface of everything.

"My reasons for leaving the army. The questions I had to ask myself about the morality of what I was doing."

"Oh."

It was a limp response, but Edward was too intent on the effort of opening out to notice. "Basically, I'm to be a witness at the trial of a Serbian gangster with an unpronounceable name, who has finally been fingered for God knows how many murders. As many as they can pin on him, I suppose. It would certainly give me deep satisfaction to see the little shit behind bars."

Rufa asked, "How well did you know him?"

"I've never laid eyes on the man," Edward said, with a harsh laugh. "I've only seen his handiwork. Do you remember when I told you about serving with the UN force?" He did not expect an answer here. "Someone took me and five Dutch officers to a mass grave. We met two women who claimed to have witnessed the massacre." His voice was dry and dismissive: a sign of deep feeling.

She said, "Oh God," hoping he would not tell her too much, and uncover the things she could not bear to face. Lately, she was finding it hard to ignore them. The Four Horsemen of the Apocalypse had started galloping across her dreams. Edward knew she had been having nightmares—though she had fiercely resisted all his attempts to talk about them.

"They'd excavated the grave by the time we got there," he said, "like an archaeological find. The bodies lay at the bottom in a pathetic tangle."

Faintly, Rufa asked, "How many?"

"Forty-nine. We counted, of course. Forty-nine Croatian Muslims—so we were told—rounded up and shot in the name of ethnic cleansing. They looked just like the pictures you see in the papers. Bones, with enough rags of cloth and flesh to look personal." He slowed the car briefly, to let a tractor turn into a gate. "Unfortunately, the grave was destroyed during the NATO bombing, and nobody seems to know the whereabouts of the women who spoke to us—the chaos there is beyond belief. So that leaves the report we filed at the time."

"Did you—aren't there any photos?"

"One mass grave looks a lot like another," Edward said. "I think they're trying to make out that we photographed another one, somewhere else. There's no shortage of them, in that bloody country." He kept his eyes sternly on the road ahead. "The whole experience was one more reason why I couldn't take the army anymore. When you see what an army can do, in the name of God knows what—the men in that grave had their hands tied behind their backs. They'd all been shot in the head, at close range. Absolutely no doubt about that—the skulls all had great gaping holes in them. Though I daresay the defense will swear they all died of fright, and the holes were nibbled by field mice. These people are atrocious. They don't know the meaning of shame."

"Edward—"

"They don't deserve democracy. They deserve a totalitarian regime. We should have bombed the lot of them to hell."

"Edward—please—could you stop?"

"What?" He looked round at her sharply. Rufa's face was bloodless, with lips the color of lead and a sheen of sweat on her white forehead. Immediately he swerved off the road, braking the car on the narrow grass verge.

Rufa wrenched the door open, almost fell out of the car, and vomited over the grass. Her body was possessed and consumed with throwing up. She was being turned inside out, from the soles of her feet upward. Distantly, through the miasma of sickness, she was aware of Edward getting out of the car, putting his arm round her shoulders, and gently pulling her upright when the horror had been expelled. She managed to draw a proper breath, and felt better. She was even vaguely pleased that she had got rid of it all so quickly and efficiently. There seemed to be a loop in her brain, which carried the horror away before it could kill her.

"Ru, darling, I'm so sorry." He wrapped his arms around her. "I can't believe I said that—I'm a complete insensitive idiot—I wasn't thinking. I should have remembered."

Rufa was determined not to remember. With her accustomed briskness, she straightened her picture of the world. "Sorry about that. I don't know what got into me."

"Ru—"

"Do you think it might have been the smoked haddock?"

Edward said, "Smoked haddock my ass. I wish you'd see someone about these nightmares."

Rufa determinedly did not hear this. "Are you feeling all right? You ate more of it than I did."

He groaned softly. She felt his breath warm in her hair. "Tell me when you're feeling better, sweetheart, and I'll take you home."

Rufa ducked irritably away from his arm. "Rubbish, I'm fine now. Let's forget it." She was ordering him to forget it, and he went on staring at her with that terrible compassion—couldn't he see that going on about it would bring it back? There was nothing wrong with her. She moved back toward the car. "Let's go. I don't want to miss Linnet's bedtime."

"Wait—" He put his hand on her arm. "Don't rush away from it."

"From what?" she snapped. "I'm not rushing away from anything. I'm totally fine. Please let's go."

He sighed, disturbed but resigned, taking his hand away. "All right. Just get a breath of air first, eh?"

They stood in silence for a few minutes, both overwhelmingly aware of what could not be said.

In the most normal, conversational voice she could summon, Rufa asked, "When do you go to The Hague?"

"End of next week." There was another silence. "Terry Poulter says he can manage the farm. And Tristan's coming back tomorrow, so you won't be alone."

"There's no need for Tristan to stay. I'm fine on my own."

He smiled, with a warmth and kindness that were, for some reason, almost unbearable. "Darling, you've never been on your own in your life. You've always been surrounded by a cast of thousands. You've never heard real silence."

"I have." There was nothing more silent than the silence you heard when you called out to the dead.

He said, "I'm not talking about metaphorical silence. I mean the physical kind, when there's no other living human being for miles. That house can be incredibly lonely. And if I have to think of you being lonely, I'll go mad."

"Being alone for a few weeks never killed anyone," Rufa said.

"Hmmm." He was annoyingly skeptical. "I'd still rather know you have Tristan around, even if it's just to scare the burglars. I wish I could take you with me, but—"

"But Terry has to get in and out of the office, and you need someone to pass on messages. And we couldn't leave the place completely empty. I do wish you'd stop treating me like the walking wounded." She was challenging him, knowing that if he wanted to disagree, he would have to open the closed book. Knowing also that he could not bear to put her through that pain.

He did dare to say, "You're not as tough as you think. You've got to get rid of this idea that you have to be responsible for everyone and everything, and allow me to take care of you."

"Sorry," Rufa said. "It's lovely that you want to. I'm not used to it, that's all."

Edward stepped forward long enough to kiss her forehead, and got back into the car. Over his shoulder, he said, "I feel I've almost worked you to death since we got back. At least you won't be peeling grapes for Pru."

"I absolutely hated her," Rufa announced suddenly.

He laughed. "I gathered."

"Did she notice? I mean, did she say anything?"

"No. She's not like you. She doesn't lie awake worrying about what people think of her."

Letting him have her opinion of Prudence had given her a rush of exhilaration, even if his reaction had turned out to be rather an anticlimax. Rufa got into the car, and they were back on the road. They drove through a village.

Rufa, on an impulse, asked, "Did you sleep with her in Paris?"

He was startled—more startled than she had ever seen him—then wrathful. "No," he said shortly. "I did not."

"But you did sleep with her recently, didn't you?" The weeks of pining for his sexual attention had made her reckless. "Not just after Alice died, I mean."

Edward scowled blackly at the road. "I can't imagine what she's been telling you, but it's over. All right?"

"Where is she now? London?"

"Rufa, it's over. That's really all you need to know."

He was silent for a long time, until Rufa began to be afraid that she had offended him. The car slowed at the new gates of Melismate, decorated with the family motto, *Evite La Pesne*. Edward turned into the drive.

He said, in his calm but firm officer's voice, "The past doesn't matter. I won't say you're the only woman I've ever loved, but you're the woman I love now." He pulled the hand brake sharply, and turned to face her properly. "Pru may have kicked up a bit of a fuss, but you won. All right?"

They were at the door, and Linnet bounced out of it before he could say any more.

Rufa kept reminding herself that being loved by a man like Edward was a privilege. His declaration went some way toward driving out the poisonous snake Prudence had planted in her heart. She was ashamed of the way that her rediscovered yearning for sex made her ungrateful. It was not his fault that she was threatening the whole symmetry of the arrangement by desiring him. She longed to know exactly what had passed between Edward and Prudence. She even found herself trying to work out whether they would have any opportunity to have sex. The whole situation—the whole marriage—was hurtful, embarrassing, and ridiculous.

She waved him off to The Hague with as much serenity as she could muster. Only at the very last minute, when Edward was on the point of going through to his gate at the airport, did Rufa understand how desperately she would miss him. Her world, without his reassuring presence, looked unfamiliar and frightening. He put his arms around her, and she clung to him fiercely, burying her face in his shoulder, gripping his arms with her hands.

Hurriedly, and with an air of doing something illicit, Edward kissed her on the mouth with real and startling heat. Then he was gone, and Rufa was left to feel lonely and useless, and tormented by sexual longing for him. On the first night without him, she only fell asleep when the sun came up.

Tristan came back, and Rufa had to admit that Edward had been right— she was glad not to be alone. The presence of Tristan did not exactly add to her security, but it infused the place with quickness and youth. Though he was the easiest of guests, he diffused a kind of subdued clatter, as a child would. He had arrived for what he described as his "one-man reading party" with one box of books, one box of CDs, and a small rucksack, which appeared to contain two pairs of white jeans, two T-shirts, and a packet of disposable razors. Rufa gave him permission to use Edward's shaving soap.

Tristan spent his days reading, with music pouring into him through the headphones of his Walkman. In the evenings he ate supper in the kitchen with Rufa. These evenings quickly became the focus of her day. She tenderly cooked for him, and he entertained her with the stories of his life. Words gushed from him. He could not tell her enough.

He told her about his moneyed, unsettled childhood with Prudence and a succession of stepfathers. He told her about his boarding school, and about losing his virginity on the tennis court, with his housemaster's daughter.

Rufa said—as she had said to nobody else—"I lost mine in the bedroom of old Mrs. Reculver's cottage. It was enormously romantic."

Tristan's eyes were deep blue in his tanned face, and full of devotion. He said, "My experience was mainly drafty, and I felt stupid with my bare bum in the air. I wish I'd saved myself for someone more like you."

He told her about the college production of *The Tempest*, in which he had appeared naked, to great acclaim, the previous term. The moody, gifted young director of this production had fallen wildly in love with him, and had thrown himself into the river when he discovered Tristan only liked girls.

"It was fine, though," he assured her. "He just got wet, and he was that anyway. I didn't understand about love then. I didn't know what it could do to people."

All their conversations turned to love. Rufa knew perfectly well that Tristan was in love with her. He watched her constantly. He moved around her with exaggerated respect. He was in a constant state of wonderment at the strength and poetry of his own emotions. If her hand brushed his accidentally, a blush surged up to the roots of his hair. He stammered if she stood too close to him.

Rufa did not feel there was any harm in this, as long as nothing was said. She congratulated herself for maintaining a distance, knowing that the distance increased his worship. She found herself watching him, noticing the smaller details of his unsettling beauty: the shadows his long lashes made on the silken skin under his eyes; the blue veins on the insides of his elbows. She was piercingly aware of him, and acutely conscious that his eyes followed her everywhere. She was sure she could handle it, however. All that blushful worship only made her more conscious of the difference in their ages. His looks were dazzling, but his immaturity could be extremely irritating. He was only just twenty. Two years ago, he had been at school. Two years ago, Rufa had been trying to earn a living. Sometimes, she felt a thousand years older.

Edward seemed impossibly far away. When he telephoned, Rufa took great pains to sound interested in his accounts of wrestling with Eurocracy and waiting in windowless, air-conditioned corridors. None of it was real, because it was happening outside the enchanted circle. With the innocent egomania of youth, Tristan filled the house with his love—the very air tasted of it.

All the surplus love washing round the house made Rufa's longing for Edward more acute. Their nightly phone calls were deeply unsatisfactory. She tried not to remember Prudence saying he was "unresponsive." He was as remote as Australia. She wanted him, and he apparently wanted her—why, why, was the marriage going so badly? Whatever the reason, she was determined to make it work when he came home.

An outsider might not understand the oddity of the whole situation. Rufa was careful not to let her mother and sisters come sniffing round. They would see Tristan's infatuation in a moment; particularly Rose, who had a bloodhound's nose for romance thanks to the antics of The Zed. Rufa prevented their visits to the farm by driving herself over to Melismate, without Tristan. She described Tristan dismissively as a "boy," omitting to mention that he was twenty and taller than she was. She found all kinds of reasons not to introduce him.

Fortunately, most of Rose's attention was taken up by a new episode in the drama of Lydia. As if Rufa's marriage really had solved all the family's problems, Lydia was undergoing an awakening. In the face of the upheaval at Semple Farm, she was rediscovering her purpose and energy. She sent Linnet to her father with ironed and mended clothes. She helped Rose to hose away the filth that still accumulated on every surface of the restored house. She cooked, without being asked—rather well, and far better than Rose. And one morning she announced to Rufa that she had joined a choir, the Cotswold Chorus. It was a highly regarded and well-established choir, of which Edward was a patron. He had taken Rufa to a performance of Haydn's *Creation*, at Cirencester church, the week before their wedding. Rufa, who remembered a worthy evening watching a lot of middle-aged men and women with mouths pursed up like hens' bottoms, was surprised out of her dream of Tristan.

"You're kidding."

"You remember how much I loved the choir at school. It was practically the only thing I was good at," Lydia said. "So I plucked up my courage and wrote in for an audition."

"You had to do an audition? Singing by yourself?" Rufa could not imagine her subdued, lovelorn sister daring to do such a thing.

Lydia giggled. "I was incredibly nervous. But Phil Harding—he's the conductor—was really patient. I actually sight-read a line of music, for the first time in yonks. I'm going to the rehearsal this Friday. Phil swears it's very informal. They're just starting the Mozart *Requiem*."

This was the longest speech Rufa had heard from Lydia in ages, and certainly the longest that did not contain a single reference to Ran.

"Hooray for you," she said warmly. "Actually, I had forgotten how faithfully you turned up for choir practice at Saint Hildy's." She took a piece of shortbread from a plate in front of her on the table. "Didn't The Zed sing at one of their concerts?"

Lydia smiled. "The Bach B Minor—we were short of tenors. Don't you remember? He stood next to Nancy, and the two of them fooled about till we nearly died of laughing."

Both sisters sighed.

Rufa said, "This shortbread is fab."

"I made it with Linnet this morning."

Privately, Rufa was amazed to hear of Lydia doing something as normal and organized as making biscuits with her child. "How on earth did you stop her ruining them?"

"We made a tray each," Lydia said, laughing. "She took her grimy efforts over to Ran's."

Rufa leaned forward earnestly. "This isn't for Ran's benefit, is it? Please don't tell me you're trying to win him back by turning yourself into Nigella Lawson."

Lydia's Giocondo smile did not waver, but there was a lurking steeliness in her soft, pale eyes. "Don't be silly, I'm not doing anything for him. I've decided I have to start doing things for myself." She was hesitant, and very serious. "To find myself, if you like. You've all been lecturing me for years about wasting my life, and you were absolutely right. I can't hang about waiting for him. I owe it to Linnet to move myself on."

"I don't believe it—that I should live to see this day." Rufa was laughing softly. "Wait till I tell Nancy."

Lydia looked puzzled. "Tell her what? That I've joined a choir?"

"That you've finally given up on Ran, of course."

"Oh, no," Lydia said. "I'm never doing that—I'm as married to him as I ever was. But he's got to come to me. He's got to want me enough to win me back."

Rufa was gentle. "I can't really see him doing that. Polly's a very determined person, and I can't see her living in sin on a smallholding. She's bound to make him marry her."

"He'll never marry her," Lydia snapped.

"Liddy—" Rufa had not heard this timid sister of hers snap for years.

Lydia was fierce. "I know he thinks he's madly in love with her. But I know—I absolutely know—that in the end he'll see where he truly belongs, and come back to Linnet and me."

Rufa was silent, thinking. There was no point in arguing with Lydia about anything to do with her ex-husband. But the signs of waking up to the rest of the world were distinctly promising. She thought how excellent it would be if Lydia's choir practices turned up a decent man or two. She was so pretty—if only she would stop dressing in frayed, faded cotton sacks, and not tie her hair back with old tights.

"We should go shopping," she said impulsively.

"What?" Lydia was bewildered. Her mind did not change gear quickly.

"You're the only one of us who hasn't been made over—the only bit of Melismate that hasn't been restored. Let's go down to London and be ridiculously extravagant." The idea of extravagance was suddenly intoxicating.

"But I can't leave Linnet—"

"It's only one day, Mum and Roger can look after her. Or Ran."

Lydia shook her head, smiling with a certain grim pride. "She won't have anything to do with Smelly."

Rufa giggled. "Poor old Polly—it's not much fun being on the wrong side of Linnet. She'll be fine with Mum, though. We'll bribe her, if necessary." She was eager. "Come on, Liddy. It'll be brilliant. We can see Nancy, and Wendy—I haven't seen anyone since I came back from Italy."

"Are you sure? I mean, I haven't any money."

Reaching across the table, Rufa took Lydia's hand. "You don't need any. This is all on me. You're going to be waxed and dressed and groomed, and then Ran had better watch out, because you'll be the most gorgeous woman for miles."

Chapter Four

"And the first thing you should do when we get there is cut off your hair," Tristan said. "It's utterly lovely, but you could make a still lovelier impression with about seventy percent less of it."

Lydia began, "Oh, I don't think I could do anything that drastic—"

"You're a genius," Rufa told him. "It's a marvelous idea. I'll ask Roshan if he can recommend a hairdresser."

Tristan was at the wheel of Edward's Land Rover Discovery (Edward, with typical efficiency, had rearranged the insurance before he left). Tristan had insisted upon taking over the driving after they stopped at a service station. He had come on the shopping excursion without being asked, and was assisting at Lydia's transformation with touching eagerness. Rufa thought it very sweet of him, though she was a little anxious about introducing him to Nancy. Lydia was too dazed by the novelty of it all to pay close attention to Tristan, or to wonder why he was there, but Nancy was another matter entirely. Nancy could read Rufa like a menu—better, sometimes, than she could read herself.

Lydia was in the back of the car, because sitting in the front for long periods made her queasy. She had not been to London since before Linnet was born, and then only to visit the nursery and layette department at the

Oxford Street John Lewis. She was slightly awed by Rufa's casual familiarity with the seething, exotic Babylon.

Tristan glanced at her in the mirror. "Forgive me, Lydia. I know we only met this morning, but the dispassionate eye of a stranger can be useful."

"She should show more of her face," Rufa agreed. "You do hide behind all that hair, Liddy."

Her voice very faintly spiked with resistance, Lydia said, "The Zed loved our hair."

"Selena cut hers, and the sky didn't fall in," Rufa said briskly. "The point is, we should listen to Tristan. He knows what looks normal. Don't you want to look normal?"

"Well," Lydia said doubtfully. A part of her had begun to crave normality, but it was a big step. "I haven't asked Linnet's permission. She might hate it, and we'd all be blacklisted."

This was a good point, but Rufa knew her sister was also talking about Ran. "She might love it."

Tristan was laughing. "Who is this kid? Mussolini?"

Both sisters chorused "Yes!" and joined in the laughter.

"For God's sake," Rufa coaxed, "live a bit dangerously." The early morning was silver, promising more blazing heat. She felt reckless and young and lighthearted. "Do something for yourself, without consulting anyone else. If it makes you feel better, I'll cut my hair off too."

"No," Tristan said. He was suddenly serious—he could move from merry to serious like mercury, and inhabit both with his whole being. "Not you."

"I suppose," Rufa said carefully, after a brief, breathless silence, "that it would be rather a production. And anyway, this isn't my day, it's Liddy's." She had to keep reminding herself. It felt like her day.

They had all got up horribly early, to miss the traffic and give themselves plenty of time to raid the shops. Rufa was good at getting up, and she had promised to knock on Tristan's door. In the gray dawn of the summer morning, she had stood outside it with her hand rolled into a fist, and before she rapped on the door, she had listened. His breathing had just been audible: lapping, rhythmic sighs, like waves. When she knocked, he had groaned. A few minutes later, down in the kitchen, she had heard blundering movements above her. She had switched off the kettle to hear more completely. The lavatory flushed. From the boiler cupboard came the metallic hum that happened when someone had a shower in the guest bathroom. An amazingly short time later, Tristan had leaped into the kitchen with wet hair, blasting out energy. He had eaten four slices of toast, and a handsome omelette, lovingly made by Rufa, light as foam.

They arrived at Wendy's just before nine o'clock—to leave the car, and eat more toast. Nancy, dressed for the heat in a kind of elongated orange vest with apparently nothing underneath, made piles of seared white bread under the grill. She had taken Tristan on board with her usual easy warmth, but the raised eyebrow she cocked at Rufa behind his back was a little disturbing. Roshan (an effortless early riser, like Rufa) had prepared a plate of croissants and a jug of fresh orange juice. Selena had left a rather grumpy note, explaining that she could not join in the shopping because she was "on some stupid shoot."

"Doesn't she like being a model, then?" Lydia asked, opening wide her innocent eyes.

Roshan, crisply elegant in white linen, pounced on the coffeepot. "She'd rather die than admit it, but she'll never last the course. She's only doing it to score some obscure point against you lot. Rufa—will you make the coffee? You know Wendy and Nancy can't be trusted to do it properly, and I have to make a pot of herbal tea for Tiger."

"Tiger?" Rufa was taken aback. "Is he here?"

"Oh, yes. Fast asleep upstairs." Roshan was brisk and businesslike, but even he (Rufa was interested and alarmed to notice) could not hide the glaring fact that he was in love—utterly besotted and bewitched, his soul locked into someone else's. "I didn't wake him, because sex and natural sleep are just about the only pleasures he has left in life. He's given up booze, drugs, fatty food, and assaulting young women. Without the chemicals, he turns out to be quite anxious and unsure of himself. I have to keep encouraging him—well, he's doing it all for me, as he keeps saying."

"Love is a many-splendored thing," Nancy said. "Dear old Tiger's quite a fixture in Tufnell Park these days. I can't find it in my heart to condemn him. Even Max has admitted he grows on you."

"He hoovers the stairs," Wendy put in. "He learned in rehab."

Rufa smiled at Roshan. "So it's the real thing, at last?"

He was solemn. "Rufa, I never knew it could be like this. Tiger's a complete mess. He's so tiresomely jealous I can't even write a note to the milkman. The first time I saw him he was trying to force his slobbering attentions on my dearest friend. And yet I'm quite madly in love with him."

"We're frightfully grand these days, what with the Savesmart heir sharing our bathroom," Nancy said. "I bet you hardly recognize the old place."

Rufa looked affectionately around Wendy's cramped, crowded kitchen. It now seemed agreeably raffish and bohemian—how unhappy she must have been, she thought, when she had found it depressing and tacky. "I think it's looking better than ever. I've missed this house."

"It's funny how quickly things change," Wendy remarked happily. "Max sent his love, but he's staying with his new girlfriend, I think in Shepherd's Bush."

Lydia asked, "Isn't he the one who fancied Nancy?" She had not kept pace with the plot. Her own plot was too absorbing.

Tristan, his mouth full of toast and jam, said, "Excuse me, must have a pee," and left the room. His energy had a nervous edge today, and he needed to pee constantly. Rufa found this almost painfully endearing.

The second he had gone, Roshan turned on Rufa. "What's going on?"

"What do you mean?"

"I mean, Mrs. Reculver, who on earth is that divine boy?"

"I told you, he's Edward's first wife's—"

"Yes, yes, we've had the family tree, thank you." Roshan sat down at the table, in Tristan's vacated chair. "But I take it you've noticed he's a burnished young sex god?"

"Of course she hasn't," Nancy said. "Ru never notices a man's attributes without written permission."

"Don't be silly." Rufa's cheeks warmed. She attempted a laugh. "He refused to be left behind at the farm, and he's sharing the driving. He's—awfully nice, actually." She lowered her voice. "I didn't really want him to stay, but Edward seems to think I need someone male to look after me."

Nancy laughed. "You do, as a matter of fact. God, he knows you well. You've lived your entire life in the shadow of some supreme man or other."

"I have not!" Rufa was stung, because she realized this was true. First, there had been The Zed himself, briefly eclipsed by Jonathan. Then, after the disaster of The Zed's death, she had gratefully transferred her allegiance to Edward. It was annoying to see herself in this pathetic light.

"Well," Roshan said, "if it was any other woman but Rufa, we'd be deep in the third act of *Desire Under the Elms*. Because that young man is so gorgeous, it's a joke."

Nancy helped herself to coffee. "Leave her alone. Can't you see she has no idea what you're talking about?"

Rufa, who knew exactly what he was talking about, was relieved that Nancy had not read the signs. For the moment, she was off the hook. It had been too easy—the state of unrequited love was taking the edge off Nancy's natural suspiciousness. Here was someone else obviously changed by being in love. She was a shade thinner. Despite the peculiar orange dress, which Rufa considered terrible with her hair, Nancy looked disturbingly stunning. Her white shoulders were dusted with freckles. Her feet—always smaller and more delicate than Rufa's—were bare inside minimal sandals, the toenails painted gold. She wore a silver bracelet on one arm, just above the elbow. Though she was ashamed of it, Rufa felt a twinge of anxiety. What did Tristan think of Nancy? He had been very quiet since their arrival, but that might be because he was shy.

Then he came back into the room, and gave Rufa a smile of special intimacy. Warmth spread through her, like the sun rising inside her rib cage. It was followed by a piercing shaft of guilty yearning for Edward; an internal scream begging him to come home and rescue her. She could not risk letting any of this show, when Nancy and Roshan were watching.

Fortunately, there was no danger of Lydia drawing any awkward conclusions. Her senses, already overloaded with the unfamiliar, were too busy grappling with the awesome prospect of spending real money, in shops that were not run by charities or local rainbow-jersey friends of Ran. In any case, she seldom had attention to spare for men who were not her ex-husband. Rufa tried to deflect Roshan's beady gaze by asking for advice. It seemed to work. He fetched paper and pen, furnished them with a neatly written list of shops, and personally telephoned a hairstylist who owed him a favor. Wendy kindly called a minicab to take them down to the West End. Rufa began to think she had hauled the general attention away from anything awkward.

Nancy, however, managed to corner her in the hall before they left. She grabbed Rufa's wrist. "Are you all right?"

The oddity of the question, when she was so plainly and radiantly all right, made Rufa smile. "Of course. Edward said I should feel free to push the boat out for Liddy."

"That was nice of him." In the dim light of the passage, Nancy was watching her narrowly. "How's he doing?"

"Still waiting to give his evidence, poor man. He says the pointless hanging about is worse than the army." At the very back of her mind, Rufa was challenging Nancy to accuse her of something.

Nancy said, "You're awfully thin, Ru."

Rufa laughed. "I thought one couldn't be too rich or too thin. And look who's talking—if you lose any more, there'll be nothing left to snare Berry."

"Are you sure everything's okay?"

"Nance, what is this? Why shouldn't it be?"

"I don't know." Nancy was searching her sister's face. "It's just so long since I've seen you properly—not since your all-star wedding. You look different."

"Of course I do," Rufa said, more forcefully. "Think of me this time last year—making jam like a woman possessed, to pay the undertaker's bill before they took us to court. I don't even want to think what I looked like then. If I've changed, it's because things are so much better."

"Are they?" Nancy was doubtful. "I suppose so." She hugged Rufa quickly. "Keep ringing me. Promise you'll ring me. Tell me everything, just like you used to. It doesn't feel right that you're so far away."

Rufa glanced outside, through the open front door, to where Tristan stood beside the minicab. "Come home occasionally. Then you'll see for yourself that we're all absolutely fine."

By eleven o'clock Lydia was sitting in front of a mirror at John Frieda's salon in New Cavendish Street, gazing with mingled fascination and terror as the stylist sifted her masses of light brown hair through his fastidious fingers. Rufa and Tristan left her, to buy Linnet's bribe at Hamley's. They bought her a Spacehopper (Tristan's idea) and two dolls' jerseys for the Ressany Brothers. Rufa could not resist dragging Tristan into Gap Kids, to whisk three enchanting cotton frocks off the sale rail. She loved buying clothes for Linnet—she had arrived home from Italy with an extra suitcase packed full of them.

Back at John Frieda's, they found Lydia quivering with excitement, and deliciously transformed. Heaps of her hair were being swept off the floor. The stylist had reduced it to a short bob, which curled as sweetly and naturally as a lamb's back. It exactly suited the fragile prettiness of her heart-shaped face. She looked youthful and vibrant, and unexpectedly chic—every stitch she owned suddenly seemed wrong. Lydia had now awoken to the urgency of the situation, and was impatient to remake herself.

Tristan gently hinted that he was hungry. Rufa bought them all a hurried lunch at Dickins and Jones, then she and Lydia plunged into an orgy of shopping. They bought linen trousers and striped Breton jerseys at Margaret Howell, jerseys and jackets from Joseph, a suit, jeans, and a handbag from Emporio Armani. They bought stilettos with lethal pointed toes from Russell and Bromley, and silver Donna Karan trainers. They bought armfuls of underwear from Marks and Spencer (Lydia favored wholesome under-garments), and a dashing little coat for Linnet, which neither sister could resist.

They returned to earth outside John Smedley's shop in Brook Street, when Tristan plaintively said, "Rufa, hasn't your credit card suffered enough? I've been busting to pee for the past hour."

Lydia slumped forward to let her load of carrier bags rest on the pave-ment. "And if I don't sit down, I'll faint."

"You're both wimps," Rufa said, laughing. "I'm hardly started—this is exactly what I dreamed of doing, when I dreamed of having money. All right, we'll call it a day."

She was entirely satisfied, entirely happy. The three of them sat in the heavy, late afternoon heat, around a table in a coffee shop. Slippery cairns of carrier bags were heaped around them.

Lydia attacked a chocolate pretzel, with something approaching gusto. "Ru, I've had the most terrific day. Thanks so much—and please say thanks to Edward." She smiled at Tristan. "I should thank you, too. I know men don't like being dragged round shops. When it happens to my husband, he starts to cry."

He laughed. "I managed to fight back the tears. It wasn't too bad."

"No need to thank me," Rufa said. "I've had a sublime day. I'm sorry to say I love it when people let me boss them around."

Lydia wrapped a second chocolate pretzel in a napkin, for Linnet. "Will the traffic be dreadful if we go home now?" She was exhausted, suddenly smaller all over, realizing how far she was from home.

"Don't worry." Rufa squeezed her hand. "It won't take long."

Tristan leaned forward, smiling persuasively. "Lydia, why don't you take the train? We could take you to the station, someone could meet you at the other end. And then Rufa and I could drive down when it's quieter."

Rufa's heart lurched. The prospect of being alone with him in London was dazzling, and also terrifying. The delight and the sense of impending disaster were impossible to separate.

He stared into her eyes, as if they were the only two people in the world. "I had this mad idea that we might catch the *Dream* at Regent's Park. This is the perfect weather for it."

Rufa cried, "Oh, how lovely! But we'll never get in—"

"Prudence uses this upmarket ticket agency that gets her into everything. Let me phone them."

"I really don't mind going on the train," Lydia assured her, perking up hopefully. She liked trains. Cars made her feel hemmed-in and powerless, especially when there were traffic jams. Their several stops that morning, for Tristan to relieve himself, had increased her worries about breaking down or crashing. "Honestly. Then you wouldn't have to hurry."

It was settled seamlessly. Tristan arranged the tickets for the Open Air Theatre with his mother's breathtakingly pricey agency. They bundled Lydia and her shopping into a taxi, escorted her to Paddington Station, and put her on a train. With one more flourish of wicked extravagance, Rufa bought her a first-class ticket. She rang Melismate, and told the affable Roger when to meet Lydia at Stroud. Tristan ran off to get her a cup of tea.

Lydia kissed them both gratefully. "This has been wonderful. When I wake up tomorrow, I'll think I dreamed it."

The train pulled off toward the green fields of the west, and Rufa and Tristan were alone. Being alone with him on the crowded Paddington concourse somehow felt more intimate than being alone in Edward's house. He tucked Rufa's hand firmly into his arm, and dragged her through the streams of hurrying people to the taxi rank. He was taking care of her—not as if she were an invalid; which was sometimes Edward's way, but with a formal consideration that was almost reverent.

Nothing could be said aloud, but the guilty, dreadful, intoxicating fact shouted in both their minds. Tristan was more desperately in love than ever, and his love was chafing inside him, fighting to express itself.

Rufa had never been to the Open Air Theatre at Regent's Park. The place enchanted her. In the center of London, on this still and tropic night, they sat, leaning against each other's shoulders, inside a magic circle of trees. The sounds of traffic were distant and muted. On the stage below them, Shake-speare's lovers suffered and sighed while the fairies played football with their hearts. Above them, the sky slowly faded from blue to pearl.

After the interval—spent battling for plastic glasses of orange juice—the stage was a pool of light in a nest of gray shadows. It became dark, and points of light appeared in the trees. It was beautiful. They could not have found a more purely beautiful spectacle in the whole city. Rufa felt torn open and ravished with delight. As the moon rose, the conflicts of love were sweetly restored. Puck, perched upon a spotlit bough, offered them his goodwill—"Give me your hands, if we be friends, and Robin shall restore amends." The night fell softly around them, in deep peace spiked with erotic longing.

Rufa, like a child at the pantomime, could not bear the enchantment to end. Her head was filled with poetry and romance. Her heart felt absolutely raw; as sensitive to the smallest touch as a snail's horns.

Tristan kept his hand on her arm while the rest of the audience surged around them, spilling out of the theater onto the dark lawns of the park. Globes of lamplight from the road shone through the trees, turning the leaves emerald. They stood at the park gates, unwilling to return to reality.

"Shall we walk to the main road?" Tristan asked softly. "We need to get back to the car."

"Yes." Rufa let him take her hand. She walked beside him, through a dream, until they met a lighted taxi. Tristan did all the work of hailing it, and giving the address to the driver. They sat in silence, not looking at each other, their mouths dry. They were still holding hands when the taxi dropped them in Tufnell Park Road.

A light was visible behind the skimpy curtains of Wendy's sitting room.

"Let's not go in," Rufa murmured. "Let's go home."

"Okay. Give me the keys. I'll drive—you're too tired."

Edward's car was under a lamppost, reproaching her with its stoic familiarity. "Would you mind?" She was deathly tired; far too tired to think.

Tristan stood under the light, his hand on her shoulder, gazing down into her face. "You look exhausted. Oh, Rufa, there are shadows under your eyes, you've been up since dawn. I promised Edward I wouldn't let you wear yourself out."

Rufa smiled. "He makes far too much fuss. But I don't think I can quite handle driving."

He took the keys from her and opened the passenger door. In the car, he tilted her seat back a few inches. She clipped in her seat belt. Her eyes slid shut. Inside her head, she saw lighted trees, fairies in glinting spangles, bewildered lovers falling thankfully into each other's arms. The warm dream of a midsummer night.

❋ ❋ ❋

She woke up to a fuzzy awareness that the car had stopped, and that Tristan was gently shaking her shoulder.

"Rufa—"

"Mmm—what?" Blinking, Rufa registered that they were in a car park, outside a motorway service station. "Where are we? Oh God, I was asleep—"

"I'm so sorry to wake you, I'd love to have let you sleep all the way home, but—guess what—I have to pee again, and I can't leave you alone here."

Rufa unfastened her belt and opened the door. "Let's go in, then."

The place was glaring and brutal; stretches of concrete, cruelly lit. Her dream evaporated. She felt bruised and tender.

Tristan took her hand, leading her through the long lines of cars. They agreed to meet outside the restaurant in ten minutes. Rufa went into the ladies.' On the back of her cubicle door, someone had scrawled: "Romance suks, forplay is when he asks your name first!!" Reality mocked her. She studied herself in the long, unforgiving strip of mirror over the sinks. Her face looked pale and frowsty, she thought. There was a red patch on one cheek, where it had pressed on the seat while she slept. She splashed cold water, forcing herself to snap out of her light-headed state.

Tristan was waiting outside the restaurant. "I've just realized that I'm ferociously hungry. We forgot to have anything to eat."

"So we did." She looked at her watch, and laughed. "We really have been away with the fairies. It's nearly midnight."

"It was brilliant, though, wasn't it?"

"Haven't I said so?" Rufa was dazed. Since they left the theater, they had been communicating with such draining intensity that she had virtually passed out. But they had not, apparently, had a proper conversation. "It was gorgeous beyond words. I almost cried when it was over."

His face was close to hers. "You did cry. I saw a tear come out of your left eye, the eye nearest to me."

"All right, I did cry." Rufa smiled. "I'll get some sandwiches—the hot food in these places always seems rather sinister." She sensed that he had been about to say something else about her eyes, and this could not be allowed. The day was over. She now had a duty to return to the old boundaries. They seemed suddenly safe and comfortable, and she had a giddy moment of intensely missing Edward.

He was bewildered for a moment, as if thrown off course. Then he smiled back at her cheerfully. They bought damp cheese sandwiches and carried them back to the car, talking amiably and quite normally about the production.

"I'm completely awake now," Rufa said. "I'll take over the driving, if you like."

"No. You're far too tired—you'd crash, or something. And anyway, I positively enjoy driving this car. It makes me feel such a grown-up."

For the moment, the deflecting had worked. On the road, Rufa passed Tristan pieces of sandwich. Their conversation was bright and aimless. It faltered, and finally petered out altogether, after the car had turned off the motorway. They drove through the hot, sleeping lanes and black hedgerows. Rufa's heart was beating hard. She could hear the blood thrumming in her ears. The tension between them tightened as Tristan carefully maneuvered the car along the unmade road to the farmhouse.

She climbed out as quickly as possible, before the engine had stopped humming, and went to open the front door. It seemed years since they had left. The solid sameness of the house—yesterday's post still on the hall table, yesterday's vase of Michaelmas daisies still fresh—helped her to wrestle back some self-control.

Outside, the car door slammed, the electric lock cheeped. Rufa hurried along the passage to the kitchen, switching on all the lights. Her hands were shaking and clumsy. She filled the kettle and plugged it in, frantic to look casual and ordinary when Tristan came in.

He stood in the doorway, staring. She stared back, mesmerized. It was too late. He could not be stopped. Slowly, never taking his eyes from hers, he went across to her and took her in his arms. A great pang of longing shuddered through her. His warm lips gently met hers, and when their mouths locked together the delight was so intense, she almost came. Alarmed, she pulled away from him.

"I can't," she said.

His arms tightened round her waist. "My darling." He bent his head to kiss her again.

Rufa broke free, with some force. She retreated to the other side of the room. They stared at each other in shocked silence, both breathing heavily. Tristan covered his mouth with the back of his hand. His eyes were wide with astonishment.

"No. Sorry," Rufa said. She was trembling fiercely. "I'm very sorry. But you know I can't."

"Why not? What have I done?"

"For God's sake." Rufa was bewildered. "I was talking about Edward. I'm married—for God's sake—there's no question of my—"

"But what have we been doing all day?"

Rufa was angry. She refused to countenance any suggestion that she had already committed adultery. "Shopping with my sister, and going to the theater."

Tristan's own bewilderment was hardening into anger. She had never seen him angry. He looked bigger and stronger and harder—and also younger.

"You know it was more than that," he said. "You've been sending out the signals all day. That was the whole point of getting shot of Lydia and going to the theater. You were telling me it was going to happen."

"I didn't tell you anything of the kind," Rufa said. Being angry with Tristan made it easier to resist him, and to call up her love for Edward. Because she did love Edward—even though he did not seem to want her. Without him, the darkness would engulf her. "You've imagined the whole thing, without bothering to ask me how I feel. Don't you think I love my husband? This is his house, for God's sake. Do you really think I'm the type to cheat on him the minute his back's turned? Is that the kind of woman you think I am?" Her outrage was genuine. She was appalled by the kind of woman she had nearly become.

"No, of course not." Once more Tristan was bewildered, wondering if he could possibly have imagined the momentary strength of Rufa's kiss just now. "Rufa, I'm sorry—I'm really sorry if I was wrong. But this isn't just about sex." He bounded across the room to seize her hand. "Don't be angry with me, I can't stand it. I wouldn't have touched you if I thought you didn't know. God, Rufa, I'm so in love with you it hurts."

It was no use. She was powerless. The pain in his eyes melted her. She felt one more pang of hurt that she had never heard these words from Edward.

She said, "I did know."

"I didn't come here thinking I could sleep with Edward's wife. I came here thinking it would be good to see Edward—besides which, I had nowhere else to go that didn't cost money. I imagined Edward's wife would be some farming type in her forties." He reddened. The confession poured out of him. "I nearly keeled over when I saw you. I couldn't believe you were so beautiful. I wouldn't have dared to even dream about touching you. But you've been such an angel to me. You're so sweet, so wise—"

"Don't—"

He would not release her hand. "Hundreds of times I've wanted to fling myself on the ground and beg you to love me. I didn't know falling in love could ever hurt as much as this." His clear eyes were swimming with tears.

"Sometimes, I've felt I'd die for a smile from you. I'll go mad if you say you don't feel anything for me."

Two hot tears scalded Rufa's cheeks. She reached up to touch his hair. "There wouldn't be any point in lying about it. Of course I feel something for you. But it's totally against my will, and I have to fight it."

"You're going to say it's your duty, or something," he said sadly.

"I don't think you know what duty means. You think it has nothing to do with love. But it's actually all about love—that's the whole point. And when I say I love Edward, it doesn't sound nearly big enough for what I mean. It's not just a matter of liking him a lot. He's everything that holds me together. If I ever forget that—"

"But he's not here," Tristan murmured urgently. "If we made love, how would he know? He'd never find out, and you wouldn't have to tell him. Please, Rufa—" He pressed her hand into his groin, against his erection. "Please—please, or I'll die of wanting you—"

Rufa whipped her hand away. He was begging her for illicit sex, in the house of her husband. The picture veered round to another angle, and the romantic idyll suddenly appeared shameful and sordid. Tristan seemed to think that because she had lost her heart to him—quite against her will—she owed him something. If he was so madly in love with her, why could he not see the dreadful situation from her point of view?

"Tristan, I'm sorry," she said, with more firmness than she had found all day. "You picked the wrong woman to fall in love with."

He frowned. "You're just too cowardly to admit what's happened. This isn't a nothing event—this isn't just some little crush I'll get over. I'll never get over you."

"You will if we don't take it any further," Rufa said. "We'd better forget this."

"No!" It came out as a shout, and startled them both. Tristan was deeply wounded, and the pain made him furious. "You can't just tell me to forget it. I've given you power over my whole life. You refuse to see how important it is because you're so scared of screwing up your nice, comfy house, and all those sacks of money—"

"How bloody dare you talk to me about the money?" Rufa screamed. The mention of Edward's money dissolved reality, and lashed her into rage. "Oh, you bloody well worship me when you think everything's going your way—but the minute you don't get what you want, you accuse me of only wanting Edward's bloody money!"

256

"Well, are you telling me you didn't? Come on, Rufa. Stop playing games."

"This isn't a game. Why won't you believe me when I say I love him?"

Tristan shook with anger. The tears jumped and sizzled on his lashes like sparks. "If you really loved him, you'd sleep with him."

Rufa whispered, "Who—what the hell are you talking about?"

They were both very still. Tristan was almost afraid to look into her white, anguished face, but he was still angry enough to blurt out, "Prudence told me. She said she asked Edward what was wrong, because she knew something was on his mind, and he told her you don't have sex. And frankly, it's the only thing that's been keeping me sane—I mean, I like Edward, and all that. But if I'd had to think of you having sex with him, I'd have killed myself."

Rufa leaned against the kitchen table. She felt as if a great fist had punched into all the assumptions of her life, shattering it to fragments. Edward had betrayed her. He had discussed their deepest, darkest secret with—of all people—Prudence. The darkness swirled, inches from her front door. It would be easy to die now, if it meant not feeling this pain.

"She was lying. It's not true."

"No—you're the one who's telling lies. You're living in one. Your entire life is one, enormous lie." Tristan was crying and burning; battering her with his fury.

"It's not true. Please—you don't understand—"

"You know what the irony of this is?" he demanded. "I might have been able to protect myself from you, if I'd paid more attention to Edward. He more or less told me the truth, and I wouldn't listen."

"Truth? What—"

"Why do you think he asked me to stay here with you? Why do you think he insured me to drive the car, and all that shit? He doesn't think you're fit to take care of yourself. Until I came along, you were one step away from falling apart."

"Get out!" Rufa shrieked. She did not recognize her own demonic voice, dredged up from the soles of her feet. "Get out! Get out!"

"And why do you think they had that row in Paris? Did he tell you he's been Prudence's lover for fucking years and years? I mean, why d'you think she can't make her marriages last more than five minutes? I'd say she had a right to be burned up about you—if he'd married anyone, it should have been her!"

"Get out!"

Tristan dragged the sleeve of his shirt across his face. "Oh, I'm fucking going."

"Leave me alone!"

"You've destroyed my life. I hope you're satisfied, you frigid bitch." He pushed past her roughly. The front door slammed with such force that a pane of glass fell from the back door and shattered on the kitchen floor. Rufa heard Edward's car hurtling away down the track.

Then the sound was blotted out by the roar of the silence. She stood listening, absolutely still. The terrible anger had passed. She felt giddy, and slightly sick. Tristan had gone. She had lost him, and she loved him more than she loved anyone on earth. He loved her, and she had thrown his love away.

She had resisted for Edward's sake, and Edward thought she was a basket case. How could he, how could he discuss their marriage with Prudence? Why, when he could apparently chat about their nonexistent sex life over lunch with that beady old cow, could he never mention it to Rufa? Because Edward and Prudence were lovers, of course. Successful lovers, who went back years and years. For all she knew, he was carrying on those cozy chats in phone calls from The Hague—when he only phoned her to check that she was still holding together. He thought of his young wife as a liability, a mistake. Perhaps he had told Prudence about the nightmares. Why not? She had been stupid to imagine he would not confide in someone about the barrenness of their life together. Tristan was right, the two of them were living out a huge, outrageous lie.

Reality dimmed, as the pictures took over her mind—visions of Edward, of The Zed, of Tristan, always rushing away from her, leaving a world utterly bereft of love.

She sat down, buried her head in her arms, and cried until she lost consciousness.

Chapter Five

She woke, with a racing heart, to the shrilling of the phone. Snapping suddenly back to consciousness, she found herself lying with one cheek pillowed on the kitchen table, almost glued to it with dried snot and tears. Sunlight poured in at the window over the sink. Rufa jumped up, staggering slightly because one leg had gone to sleep. If this was Edward, she must do her best to sound normal.

"Hello?" It came out as a croak.

"Ru, it's Tristan. And before you say a word, I'm sorry about last night. I was a shit to you, and I'll never be able to make it up." His voice was rapid, pleading, and full of energy. "I should be dragged through the streets and publicly flogged. You have every right to slam the phone down and never speak another word to me ever again—I mean, obviously, it would utterly break my heart, but I'd deserve it. Hello? You are there, aren't you?"

Rufa felt she had been reborn in Technicolor, after months in miserable monochrome. The world clicked back into its right place, and she was suddenly aware of the morning's shimmering beauty. "Yes, I'm here—where are you?"

"Cirencester. It's a long story. Basically, I need a lift home and I need my credit card—it's on the dresser, in my wallet. Could you bring it?"

She laughed. "What on earth is going on? Why do you need a credit card?"

"Because—look, please don't be furious—I've had a bit of a problem with Edward's car, and I need to pay the guy who towed it to the garage."

"A bit of a—?"

"Come and fetch me, and I'll explain everything," Tristan said. "To know all is to forgive all. Are you really not cross?"

"How cross should I be?"

"Well, very cross indeed, if I'm honest."

Laughter bubbled up inside Rufa. She was suddenly ridiculously happy, in a way she had not been for God knew how long. She did not realize she had forgotten how to be happy like this, until she remembered it now. It was like a veil lifting, or a mist clearing. "You'd better tell me where you are," she said.

He was waiting on the forecourt of a garage near the public car park. The moment she saw him, Rufa's heart contracted with longing. His white jeans and shirt were streaked with grime, and one side of his long hair was matted and blackened. There was a square of gauze taped to his forehead. He looked beautiful. She saw all this as she braked her Renault beside the car wash.

Tristan ran over, she leaped out. They did not know how to greet each other, and stood awkwardly looking at the ground.

A young man in overalls, with a lumpy head shaved to stubble and an earring, ambled over to them. "This is her, is it?"

Tristan looked up. "Yes, this is Mrs. Reculver. It's actually her husband's car."

"Oh, right." The young man grinned at them significantly. "You'll have some explaining to do."

"This is Ken," Tristan said. "He very kindly towed me here and took my credit card on trust—did you bring it?"

"Tristan, what happened to your head? Are you all right?" Rufa lightly touched the bandage on his forehead.

"He's got stitches," Ken said. "I had to pick him up from casualty."

"Casualty? For God's sake, why can't you tell me what happened?" She was alarmed.

"You're going to do your nut when you see the car," Ken said, still grinning. He led them round the side of the main building into an oily, echoing

260

shed, with tufts of coarse grass poking through the cracks in the concrete floor. Rusting oil drums and thick coils of wire were stacked along one wall. Directly in front of them was a wrecked car, lacking a windscreen and one door. The bonnet had buckled like a concertina, and the airbag drooped limply off the steering wheel. Rufa suddenly realized she was looking at Edward's Land Rover Discovery. The world reeled.

Tristan quickly took her hand. "Sorry, I should have warned you."

"God almighty," she said. The color had drained from her face. "You—you could have been killed."

"He's the lucky sort, this one," Ken said, staring at Rufa. "He walked away from this mess with just a couple of stitches."

"Rufa, I'm so sorry," Tristan said. "But you should be able to collect on the insurance, because I wasn't pissed or anything."

"It's not the car I care about, you idiot." She was recovering. "It's you. I nearly lost you."

"Would you have minded?"

"Don't be stupid. It would have destroyed me."

"Oh, my darling—" He was radiant. It was settled, and there was no need to say any more. Tristan gently took Rufa in his arms. She wrapped her arms around his neck, holding him close to feel the beating of his heart. The dreadful nearness of death terrified her. A single second could have stilled all the glorious life that pulsed through him. She wanted to hold him forever.

Ken coughed elaborately. "Where's that credit card, then?"

Rufa and Tristan disengaged, and climbed down from the realm of the angels. Rufa produced Tristan's wallet. They went into a small office, full of heaped ashtrays and dented filing cabinets, and Tristan paid the bill.

Then they were free. They walked out of the garage hand in hand, happy for the moment just to be together and in love.

Tristan glanced at his watch. "Half past ten. Can we have a coffee somewhere?" He smiled into her face, his own face so close that her vision was swamped by his clean, glistening eyes. "I always seem to be saying this to you, but I'm absolutely starving."

"I'll buy you some breakfast," Rufa said. "Then you can tell me the whole sordid story—and we can dream up a version that will be acceptable to Edward." It was strange how theoretical Edward seemed at this moment. If her mind rested on him for too long, the pain was unbearable—the man who had married her because he thought her family deserved his money more than his long-term lover; who had, apparently, resisted having sex with her because he felt he was being unfaithful to Prudence. It was far safer, and far more pleasant, not to think about Edward at all.

They found an old-fashioned café, its paneled walls crammed with horse brasses and speckled engravings. Rufa sat down at the table in the window. Tristan went to wash the dried blood out of his hair.

"How's that?" he asked, when he returned to her. "Less like Rab C. Nesbitt, I hope?" Rufa thought he looked like a young cavalier, wearing the mud of Naseby or Edgehill.

She laughed. "You're dirty, but moderately respectable. That'll do. The Zed used to come in here barefoot."

They ordered tea, croissants, English muffins, and a toasted bacon sandwich. Tristan fell upon this savagely—he had not eaten, Rufa remembered, since she fed him cheese sandwiches on the motorway, the night before. Yesterday seemed another era.

"I was mad," Tristan said. "I hardly even knew I was driving. I kept thinking how you'd pushed me away. I was convinced you hated me. I hated myself for what I said to you—which I didn't mean."

Rufa looked down at the surface of her tea. "Some of it was quite accurate."

"No, it was all totally childish." He was forceful. "I should never have jumped on you like that. I had no right to assume anything."

"Where did you crash?"

"I went into a stone wall near Hardy Cross. It was on a bend, and I didn't see it in time." The color rose in Tristan's face. He took her hand across the table. "Actually, I didn't see it because I was crying."

She looked up quickly. "So was I. How ludicrous, to think of us both crying, when all I had to do was admit the truth."

"The truth that you love me?"

"Yes. I don't know why I got so scared." This was not true. Rufa did know. She was scared of losing her anchor; the person whose good opinion mattered most in the world.

Tristan said, "Because of Edward," as if Edward were a tiresome obligation.

She added quickly, "I'm not saying I'm scared of him."

"God, I am," Tristan said. "Particularly now that I've fallen in love with his wife and trashed his car. He'll probably get me in one of those SAS tackles, and garrotte me."

"Don't be silly." Rufa was sharp; annoyed to be put in the position of defending Edward, and slightly annoyed by Tristan's levity. At this stage, she did not need any more reminders of his glaring youthfulness.

She was silent for a moment. "You have to understand how much I love you," she said. "You have to see how it hurts me to betray Edward. But I've gone too far now. And if I can't love you, it'll kill me." She was starving to be loved. It made her light-headed with desire to be with a man who made passionate speeches and professed a readiness to die for her.

Tristan withdrew his hand. "You're always talking about dying, and being killed."

"Am I?"

"You're so intense, feelings are like knives to you. I knew that the first evening we spent together—when you cooked that fabulous Italian meal. You were impossibly beautiful, but I had a tremendous sense that you were unhappy. Sort of lost inside yourself. That's how you got to me." He reached blindly for the other half of his sandwich, took a wolfish bite, and hurried on with his mouth full. "I don't know how it happened, or whether I even like it. You haven't given me a choice. When I drove off last night, I thought the world had ended—I couldn't bear to live without you. The second before I crashed, I think I felt rather noble, because I was dying for you." He smiled radiantly—as far as he was concerned, everything was happily settled now. "Then I wasn't dead, and I just felt like a prat. The door was bent, or something, and I couldn't get out."

"Were you there for long?"

"Well, it seemed like ages. Apparently some old biddy in a bungalow heard the smash and didn't dare to come out and look because she thought I'd be a mangled cadaver."

Rufa winced. "Don't." He was extraordinarily cool about it, as if the crash had proved him immortal.

"She called out every service short of Mountain Rescue—I had the flower of Gloucestershire's manhood swarming all over me. The Fire Brigade got the door off, the police breathalyzed me, the ambulance took me to hospital."

"Did the police charge you with anything?"

Tristan, gulping tea, shook his head. "I wasn't drunk, and you can't book a guy for driving while sobbing uncontrollably, can you? As a matter of fact, they couldn't have been sweeter. They all said it was obvious you really loved me."

Rufa could not help laughing. "Oh God, how much did you tell them? I'll never be able to look a policeman in the eye again." Tristan had managed, while trapped in a wrecked car, to charm them. She was reminded of The Zed—always being arrested, and on terms of positive affection with half the law in the county. Dozens of policemen had turned out for his funeral.

"I didn't give any names," Tristan assured her.

"That's a comfort, anyway."

Behind her, there was a brisk tapping on the plate-glass window. Rufa turned, and saw the wild head of Rose, beaming and mouthing something incomprehensible above the strip of gingham curtain. The last person she wanted to see, when all her defenses had been torn away. She smiled and waved, doing her best to look delighted.

"My mother," she muttered to Tristan.

"Oh."

"She's coming in. Just agree with whatever I tell her."

They both stood up as Rose came crashing into the café, laden with clinking shopping bags. If Rufa had had her wits about her she would never have brought Tristan to this place. It was not at all discreet, but it had not occurred to her, until now, that she had anything to hide.

The middle-aged waitress behind the counter greeted Rose as an old friend. "Well, look who it is, we haven't seen you for ages. And we've got some of those long doughnuts you like."

"Oh, yes please—and a cup of coffee. No, tea. No, definitely coffee." Rose embraced her daughter. "Darling, how lovely to see you. I was just thinking, I must ring you to say what a duck Linnet looks in the yellow frock you bought her—she insisted on wearing it today." She beamed at Tristan. "And you're Tristan. Liddy's been singing your praises. She says she never knew a man could behave so well in shops. What on earth have you done to your head?"

Without waiting for a reply, Rose thumped down into a chair, and began rummaging in one of her bags. "I got some arnica cream at Boots, fab for bruises, would you like some?"

"No thanks. It's not serious." Tristan shot a questioning glance at Rufa.

Rufa, however, could see that Rose's sensors were switched off. Shopping did this to her—it was so long since she had had any money. Legitimate buying, with the small allowance Edward was giving her "to keep you out of my short hairs," was the great delight of her life.

"Liddy had a marvelous time yesterday," Rose said. "You sent her back looking absolutely adorable—when that man who runs the choir sees her, I daresay he'll propose. I'm positive he fancies her."

Tristan asked, "Did Linnet like the Spacehopper?"

Rose chuckled. "I would have brought her with me today, but that fucking Spacehopper is all she can think about. Rodge managed to blow it up with the foot-pump, and I left her bouncing madly all over the terrace. Hence the arnica, antiseptic wipes, and novelty plasters. She's already grazed one knee and bumped her head." She finally settled her bags to her satisfaction, and focused her attention properly upon Tristan. "I'm awfully glad to meet you. I can't think why Ru hasn't brought you over to Melismate."

"He's meant to be too busy studying," Rufa said.

"In this heat? Nonsense. Come over one evening, when Liddy's cooking. You'd better look to your laurels, Ru—she's turning into quite a rival."

"I'd love to see Melismate," Tristan said. Under the table, his knee brushed Rufa's. She did not dare to meet his eyes. They could not possibly go to Melismate. For once in her life, her feelings were totally out of control. She did not trust them not to betray her.

Fortunately, Rose's coffee and doughnut arrived at the table to distract her. Unfortunately, once the waitress had moved away, she said, "Well, how's Edward?"

"Fine." Rufa kept her eyes turned toward her plate. She had not spoken to Edward since the day before yesterday. It had not occurred to her to check the answering machine. She realized she should leave a reassuring message at his hotel, as soon as possible. She did not want to speak to him in person, and she did not want him to be worried. "He has to wait around a lot, while the court decides whether or not his evidence counts. He hasn't given any yet."

"Poor man," Rose said. "Barely married a month, and he has to hang about pointlessly, miles from home. Do give him my love, when you speak to him."

"I will."

"It must be maddening for him. I know Edward can't stand not being busy. He has to be running something. I've always thought a South American dictatorship would suit him."

Tristan laughed—Rufa could see he liked Rose, which was both gratifying and alarming. "It would be a highly efficient dictatorship—no more lounging in the sun under enormous hats."

"Well, you know him," Rose said. "Luckily, Ru's just the same. Forever making and mending, cutting and contriving."

He smiled at Rufa, in a way that made Rose's eyes quicken curiously. "Yes, Rufa's a living reproach to the idle. That's why I've got through so much work—my tutor will pass out with the shock."

He was teasing her, wrapping her in warmth. Rufa smiled, for it felt lovely. "Thanks a lot. You make me sound totally dreary."

"Nancy used to call her Tin-Drawers," Rose said cheerfully, watching Tristan. "She said every time you sat down for a rest, you heard them clanking at you."

They all laughed. The hands of Rufa and Tristan touched under the table, and Rufa ached to kiss him again. When they returned to the farm, they would make love. Her stomach lurched with anticipation.

Rufa took her purse from her bag. "We should go."

Tristan jumped up. "I'll pay for this." He went to the till at the counter.

Rose continued to watch him, her face thoughtful. "A young Apollo," she said.

"Sorry?" Rufa seemed not to have heard.

Rose's eyes turned toward her. "Don't forget to send love to Edward, will you?"

"I won't."

"Tell him to come home soon."

"There's no point in being impatient," Rufa said.

"Come over to see us, my love." Rose briefly stroked Rufa's forearm. "The old place misses you. So does my little Linnet. I don't like to think of you rattling about in that farmhouse."

"I'm not rattling. Tristan keeps me company."

Rose said, "Yes, well. Take care of yourself, anyway."

Chapter Six

The barber's was a deeply unprepossessing shop. There were tufts of hair on the dirty checked lino. Black-and-white photographs of common-looking men, sporting various antiquated hairstyles, leered around the yellowed walls. The barber stood behind one of the two vinyl chairs at the mirror, clipping the sparse locks of a balding pensioner. Heaven only knew why Ran had insisted upon coming to this place, when there was a perfectly adequate, if rather naff, hairdresser's round the corner.

The barber was not pleased to see Ran. He gave the pensioner's head a final polish, and whipped the nylon bib from his shoulders. "Yes?"

Polly firmly pulled Ran into the shop, shutting the door behind them. "I'm sorry, but there seems to have been a slight misunderstanding."

"Eh?"

"We wanted a haircut."

"But I just cut his hair!"

"I'm afraid you didn't do it properly."

The barber looked belligerent. He was a thin, sour individual. "What's wrong with it?"

"Well, it doesn't look any different—I can't see that he's had a haircut at all. He came out exactly the same as he went in." Polly picked up a lock of

Ran's glossy, shoulder-length hair. "I thought I explained what he wanted. And frankly, I think it's a bit much to charge him, when you haven't actually done anything."

The barber put his hands on his hips. "Look, I only did what he asked for, right? He said to only take a bit off. He said just tidy the ends. Tell her, mate."

He turned to Ran, who shrugged helplessly.

"There must have been a mistake," Polly snapped. "I thought I made it quite clear that he wants it short at the back and sides, with a long bit on top—well, I don't suppose the name Hugh Grant means much to you." She swept a contemptuous glance across the gallery of photographs, and singled out the least offensive. "Rather like that one, only without the gel. Tell him, darling."

"I don't want it that short," Ran muttered. "I'll look like a dick."

"No you won't. For the last time, your hair looks perfectly absurd like that. Only motorcycle messengers have ghastly long hair."

"But this is me," Ran said, with the beginnings of petulance. "This expresses who I am."

"Rubbish. You weren't born with it, for God's sake." Polly faced the barber. "Cut it again, please. Obviously we'll pay again." Satisfied that the matter was settled, she sat down on a small and wobbly plastic chair in one corner, flicking open her new copy of *Vogue*.

The barber looked doubtfully at Ran. "Well?"

Ran stood, his hands balled in the pockets of his new black linen trousers, miserable and defeated. "Yes, all right. I mean, thanks."

"Sit down, then." The barber gestured at the vacant chair. "I'll be with you in a second." He produced a large wooden brush, and whisked it around the shoulders of the pensioner, as if he would have swept all of them right out of the shop.

With a long, tremulous, poignant sigh (which did not have the smallest effect upon Polly), Ran sat down in front of the mirror.

The pensioner paid his bill and left. The barber picked up the scissors, and took up his station behind Ran. "Okay, let's start again. How much off?"

"Like she said," Ran muttered. He winced as the blades hovered over him.

"I'm not a bloody mind reader," the barber said. He was also muttering, mindful of the implacable blond head bent over *Vogue*. "Next time, you'd better bring a note from her."

"Next time? Oh, God."

"Well, hair grows, doesn't it?".

"I suppose so. Oh, God."

"Shut your eyes, mate. We'll do it quicker."

Ran scrunched his eyes shut. Deftly and neatly, but with no very good grace, the barber attacked his hair. He snipped close to the back of Ran's skull, and reached across for the electric clipper. When he switched it on, Ran bleated pitifully. The barber hesitated.

"Oh, for heaven's sake," Polly said.

The clipper whirred. Ran's hair was shorn around the back and sides, sleek and smooth as a seal's. One thick lock fell romantically across his forehead. Polly closed her magazine, to watch intently.

"All done," the barber said. "You can open them now."

Ran opened his eyes, met his new self in the mirror, and let out a long groan. "Shit!"

"Yes, that's excellent—and it didn't hurt a bit, did it?" Polly was on her feet, digging in her handbag. "Exactly what we wanted." She paid, adding a handsome tip, and led Ran out of the shop.

He said, "I look like an asshole."

"Darling, don't be silly. You look stupendous." Polly was jubilant. She could hardly believe how beautiful he was now: sensitive, with just a seductive hint of tousling. Dressed in the new linen trousers and white linen shirt she had bought him, he was utterly mouthwatering. She surveyed their reflections in the window. This was just how she wanted to appear before Justine and Hugo that evening. Justine had been at school with Polly, and she had telephoned to say they would be coming into darkest Gloucestershire to stay with Hugo's mother. Naturally, though she had fed Polly all the formalities about missing her, Justine was desperately curious to get a good look at Ran. She would rush back to London to report to the rest of Polly's circle, so proper presentation was essential. Semple Farm was not yet fit to show off. Polly had arranged to meet Justine and Hugo at a concert, and take them to dinner at a country house hotel afterward. She was now able to look forward to this, confident that Justine would be riven with envy.

If only Ran would cheer up. He shook Polly's hand off his arm, and mooched gloomily along beside her. Deliberately ignoring this, she took the latest list from her bag.

"I saw a rather fascinating little shop, with some adorable hand-painted cabinets. And some lovely tapestry cushions, which might take the newness off the sofa covers. I want a sort of organic, antiquated look."

He did not reply. Polly, however, was used to this. Bless him, he did not like changes, and tended to react by sulking—as if that bothered her. He was, at last, learning that she always got her own way in the end.

Just before they turned into the main street, Ran halted. From the back pocket of his trousers he pulled a knitted Peruvian hat, with earflaps and a tassel at the point. He put it on.

Polly snatched it off. "What the hell are you doing?"

"My head feels naked."

"Rubbish. It's boiling hot. And even if it wasn't, I refuse to be seen with anyone who goes around in a pointed hat, like some enormous elf."

"Come on, Poll!"

"And don't call me Poll. I'm not a parrot." They were near a waste bin. Polly threw in the hat, with a shudder of disgust.

"Hey!" Indignantly, Ran darted forward, sank one arm into the bin, and rescued his hat. It emerged with an ice-cream paper stuck to one flap. "You're not even trying to understand. This hat means a lot to me. Not just because it's my style—it was a gift from a real shaman. He'd seen the village where it was made." He pulled the hat back on.

Polly whipped it off again, and shut it inside her orderly handbag. "Let me make myself plain, Ran. I don't care who gave it to you, or where it comes from. You look perfectly stupid in it."

"Stupid?" He was wounded. "This is a piece of my past!"

"Perhaps you can frame it. Because it has nothing to do with your present."

She made an effort to hold on to her temper. Delicious as he was, Ran was becoming increasingly stroppy. His air of lost-boy wistfulness covered a worrying obstinacy. He kept taking back things she had thrown away. The attic at Semple Farm, which Polly had privately earmarked for a future nanny, was crammed with rubbish. Did the idiot not realize she was doing him a favor? More to the point, did he not realize how much money her plans were going to cost her?

But he had stopped fighting now, as he always did in the end. Yet again, Polly was melted by his beauty. She reached up to caress the back of his shorn head. "Please don't be cross, darling one. I'm trying to make the whole world see how divine you are."

Their eyes met. The current of mutual desire crackled between them. Polly slowly ran the tip of her tongue round her pink lips. This was their private code for oral sex—though she had not cared for this sort of thing with Berry, she could suck Ran by the hour. He smiled, his blood heated as predictably as a pan of milk on a stove. All resistance was at an end, for the time being. Polly slipped her hand into his. He squeezed her fingers lovingly. Securely wrapped in their unquenchable passion, the two of them sauntered into the main street.

"Look," Ran said, "it's Rufa."

She was on the other side of the road, almost running. Her car keys were in one hand. She carried a round wicker basket full of cut flowers and bottles of wine. Polly resolved to get herself an identical round basket, then realized this was not the key to Rufa's air of glamour.

"She looks wonderful," Polly said critically. She had not seen Rufa since the fateful day of her wedding. "What has she done to herself? Marriage suits her, obviously." This was a small hint for Ran, who was curiously reluctant to set a date.

"She's happy, that's all," Ran said, his dark eyes following her sadly. "You don't have to get married to be happy."

Tristan rolled onto his back, with a long sigh. "Sorry, that was quicker than I intended. If you want me to last, you shouldn't be so bloody beautiful."

"You're utterly depraved," Rufa said. "You'll get us both arrested."

They were lying in a patch of cowslips, at the edge of a flat field full of stubble. The Renault clung crazily to a sloping grass verge at the roadside.

He propped himself on one elbow, leaning over to kiss her nipples. "I can't help it. I want to fuck you all day and all night. I want to make you come till you cry. I want to worship you with my body."

Rufa's purple silk dress was bunched around her waist, and unbuttoned down to her navel, exposing her breasts to the warm sky. Her dishevelment was more wanton than nakedness. She felt replete and tender, unwilling to cover herself. Tristan had begged her to stop the car. He had threatened to have a loud and conspicuous orgasm in the middle of the concert if she did not. She loved the urgency of his demands. Since the day of the car crash, they had been making love continually. They had shut themselves away at the farm, resisting all callers, ignoring time. Tristan was a sublime lover, young enough to come again and again, and sleep like the dead in her arms afterward. He did not know that she watched him while he slept, dripping tears into his hair. The happiness was painful, because it was bought with the pain of others, and could not last. It was hard to convey this to Tristan. His emotional vocabulary simply did not contain the concept of betrayal.

She needed a lover who would understand her, and empathize with her pain. Tristan had not matured into this tower of strength. He had to be entertained and distracted, like a child. Anything too heavy made him fretful. There was no question of leaning on him.

"We ought to go," she murmured, not moving.

Tristan asked, "Did you catch Edward?"

Rufa tensed, and tried to push the memory away. Yes, she had caught Edward. For the first time, she had not been available for his daily call—she had allowed Tristan to lure her into making love standing up, in the shower. She had felt terrible when she found Edward's message on the machine. He had sounded particularly distant and disapproving when she called him back—though he might simply have been in a hurry. Their conversations were rarely intimate, in any case. Edward's telephone manner, though affectionate, was laconic in the extreme. He tended to confine their talk to farm business, and the work at Melismate. There was never an opening through which she could fling a confession, a plea to be rescued.

She said, "Yes, just briefly."

Aware that the subject upset her, Tristan made his voice mild and neutral. "Did he say anything?"

"He doesn't know when he's coming back, if that's what you mean."

"Good."

"Don't, Tristan—it makes me feel so evil."

"You're not evil. You're an angel." He sat up, fastening his trousers. "I'm not, and I can't feel as guilty about Edward as you do. He's across the sea. That means I have more time in paradise."

Rufa sighed. "I wish we could live like this forever—properly together, so we don't have to hide. I can't bear to think of you going away."

"Stop talking about it," Tristan said. "It hasn't happened yet."

"Term will be starting soon."

"Forget about it. Concentrate on the eternal now."

"I wasn't properly alive till I found you," Rufa said. "How can I go back to being half dead?" The colors of the real world were hard and painful. She knew that the place she inhabited with Tristan was only a pastel-shaded dream, and she did not care. For the first time, she began to understand why The Zed had committed adultery on such a scale. He had been chasing the same magic realm; the weightless land of newborn sexual passion. Reality had hurt him—just as it was hurting her now—and he had only been trying to escape. She could not bear to think from what.

This was a dangerous train of thought. She forced herself to smile at Tristan.

He bent down to kiss her forehead. "You're having one of your dreaded attacks of postcoital heaviness."

"Sorry. I'll lighten up, or the concert will be too turgid for words." I talk too much about myself and my dreary feelings, she thought. Tristan was not good with intensity. He thought that when people were depressed about romance they were only striking a pose, like people in a play. She sat up, to button her dress. They brushed crumbs of earth from each other, laughing as they checked for grass stains. This was the sealed bubble of now, and he was right not to fret about the future. Being together was all that mattered.

Rufa no longer cared about appearances. Lydia was singing the Mozart *Requiem* with the Cotswold Chorus tonight. She could not miss it, and she could not leave Tristan behind. She had brazenly ordered two tickets in Edward's name, at the special rate for CC life patrons. Many of the other life patrons had attended her wedding, and there would be a lot of tiresome and unconvincing explaining to do, but it was better than being without Tristan.

Fortunately, they would be part of a group—there was safety in numbers. In the large church at which the concert was being held, Rufa quickly found Rose, Roger, and Linnet among the milling crowd of people at the back.

Rose greeted Tristan with a resounding kiss. "Lovely to see you."

Linnet wrapped her arms around Rufa's legs. "I'm not letting go of you— you'll have to come home with me."

"I've stayed away for far too long, haven't I? But I'll come to see you tomorrow." Rufa stroked the dark head, despising herself for neglecting the little girl. "It's the last day before you go back to school, isn't it?"

"Yes, and I'm in a new class, and guess what, the two girls I hate are in Miss Shaw's."

"Oh, good."

"They can still chase me at playtime, but they can't sit at my table and say things to me in quiet, mean voices."

"Oh, I am glad," Rufa said. "Now you can just concentrate on the girls you like."

Linnet's attention had darted to the main door of the church. "Daddy! It's Daddy! HI, DADDY!"

Ran had come in, with Polly and two well-dressed, well-pressed strangers. His rather careworn face lit up. He rushed toward Linnet and swept her into his arms.

"Ye gods," Rose muttered, "what has she done to his hair? Eaten it?"

Oblivious to the expression of dismay on the face of Polly, Ran swung Linnet back down to the floor. She perched her dusty pink trainers on top of his new loafers, giggling as he danced her through the crowd. People stood back to make way for them, smiling indulgently at the exuberant young father and his gleeful little girl.

Rose kissed him warmly. "Fancy seeing you. I wouldn't have put you down as a friend of the Cotswold Chorus." She made it sound like a sexual perversion.

His face clouded. "I respond at a very deep level to all types of music, Rose. I thought you knew that. What are you lot doing here?"

"Mummy's singing in the choir," Linnet said, swinging on his hand. "This is her very first concert."

"What? What?" Ran was startled. "You're joking."

"You've got short hair," Linnet noticed, at last. "You look rather silly."

"I know. Sorry. When I come to fetch you from school, I'll wear one of my hats."

"I expect Smelly made you cut it."

"Yes, it was all Smelly's doing."

"Ran!" Rose protested. She was laughing. "Don't encourage her."

"You match Mummy now," Linnet said. "She's cut all her hair off too."

"What?"

Polly approached, with her friends, in time to see the pained indignation on Ran's face. "Liddy can't cut her hair!" he exclaimed. "It's her best feature! Who made her do it?"

Linnet tugged energetically at his back pocket, slightly ripping one seam. "Can I cut my hair too?"

He shuddered. "Heaven forbid."

Polly, with a blazing social smile, moved forward to embrace Rufa. It was the first time they had met since the wedding. "You look simply marvelous, I do hope you had a wonderful time in Italy." She giggled softly. "Oh God, people are staring at the Scarlet Woman."

Rufa flinched, then realized Polly meant herself. "You certainly surprised us all."

"We must have lunch, so I can tell you the whole, incredible story. My life—well, I've been living on an absolute roller coaster. This is Justine D'Alambert, and her husband, Hugo."

"How do you do." Rufa shook hands with Justine and Hugo.

"This is Rufa Reculver, indirectly responsible for my fit of madness. What a shame Edward can't be here." Polly took hold of Ran's sleeve. "Come along, darling, or all the good pews will be gone." With one more conspiratorial smile at Rufa, she marched her party away up the aisle.

"We ought to bag a place near the front," Rose said. "Liddy's so nervous, I don't want her to have to search for us."

Rufa hung back, so that she could take Tristan's hand without her mother seeing. She needed to touch him, to hold on to him. He was looking a little bored. She pulled his hand against her thigh. A tall, gray-haired woman jostled against them. Rufa turned, and met the outraged gaze of Lady Bute. Her cold eyes traveled from Rufa to Tristan, filling with contempt when they went back to Rufa.

"Excuse me." She moved away from them, exuding distaste.

The encounter, which lasted only a couple of seconds, left Rufa wanting to cry. The Abominable Lady Phibes had forced her to see herself as she must look from the outside—a new bride, openly nestling up to another man. Behaving like a foolish teenager. Behaving, in particular, like a true daughter of The Zed.

Tristan gently pulled his hand away, to stop the two of them blocking the aisle. He moved a step or two in front of her. Rufa stared at his back, suddenly frightened. She had loaded everything onto the shoulders of this boy—betrayed Edward, sacrificed her family. If he could not carry the load, she had nobody left in the world.

He turned, and smiled into her eyes with special intimacy. Rufa did not care that Rose's head was bobbing curiously behind him. She smiled back, and they both reconnected with the blissful memory of making love less than an hour before. She must not doubt their love now, or she would drive them both crazy. Tristan tended to distance himself if she wanted too many assurances of eternity. Unlike Edward, he could only live in the present. She sat down close to him, feeling the warmth striking off his body, smelling her own scent mingled with his.

The members of the orchestra had taken their places in the nave. There was applause, and a general settling down, as the choir filed into the chancel. The tenors and basses wore dinner jackets and black ties. The women wore long black skirts and white blouses. Lydia had managed to give this unpromising uniform a miraculous appeal. Her short curls were deep gold under the lights. She was wearing makeup, and looked altogether as elegant and finished as a china figurine. Clutching her score, she looked round anxiously, saw Linnet, and shot her a sudden, enchanting smile.

On the other side of the aisle, Polly felt a frisson of alarm. She had not taken in that Lydia was singing—if she had known, she would never have come to this blasted concert. She searched the ranks of white blouses for the droopy creature, trembling under a bushel of hair, who had dementedly screamed at her that she would never marry Ran. It was a considerable shock to find Lydia transformed into what she could only count as a rival. She felt Ran tensing beside her, evidently as surprised as she was. He was quite silly enough to be smitten by his ex-wife's unexpected loveliness, as if they had not spent years together making each other miserable. Proprietorially, she hooked her arm through his.

The applause rose to a crescendo, filling the church up to its fan-vaulted ceiling. The soloists entered, followed by the conductor. He was a tall, thin man, with a fresh face and a balding head. The coughs and rustles died away into silence. The first chords sounded.

Polly hissed, "Stop fidgeting!" and nudged Ran hard in the ribs.

❄ ❄ ❄

"He's utterly gorgeous," Justine said. "I'd leave Hugo for him like a shot. No wonder you lost your marbles and left poor old Berry at the altar. Is the sex divine?"

Polly laughed. "Utterly. I never imagined it could be this good."

"Well, you always were a lucky cow."

Justine would broadcast Ran's gorgeousness around every lunching place in London, and this was gratifying. On the whole, however, this evening was becoming increasingly vexing. It was the interval, and Ran had rushed away outside to smoke, though he knew it was a habit Polly abhorred. She had not bargained for the ex-wife, the daughter, or the huge contingent of Hastys. Couldn't Ran get it through his head that he didn't belong to that clan anymore?

The musicians were taking their places again, and only a few people remained at the back of the church, hurriedly draining their glasses of flat Perrier and warm white wine.

Hugo said, "I suppose we ought to—er—"

"Yes, we won't wait for Ran." Polly led the way back to their pew, pretending not to be furious that Ran had not rejoined them in time—what the hell was he playing at? How could he be so ill-mannered? How dared he leave her looking like a bloody lemon? She spent the second half of the *Requiem Mass* seething. Evidently a lot more work was needed before her new lover was fit for public display.

Afterward, she found him among the knot of Hastys, holding his sleeping daughter in his arms. He did not seem to think he owed any kind of apology. He did not even seem to notice her, until she touched his arm.

"Oh, hello," he said listlessly.

She hissed, "What happened to you? Where were you?"

"I was desperate for a pee, and the queue was a mile long. So I nipped out to the pub."

"For God's sake! You might have told me."

"Hmm. Sorry." Ran's heavenly black eyes were fixed on the people around Rose. Lydia, flushed and smiling, was introducing the conductor.

"Phil's been so kind," she was saying. "He refused to let me wriggle out of it, though I was petrified about squawking a duff note in the middle of the Sanctus."

"Phil" shifted his feet self-consciously. "She wanted to sell programs, but I told her we're not so rich in good sopranos that we can afford to let her off."

They shared a laugh, weighted with their private history. Polly watched the way he automatically sheltered Lydia from the people trying to push past. It was obvious to her that the man was deeply smitten—and what a wonderful solution he might be, to the eternal problem of the ex-wife and the child.

Ran had noticed too. His angel's face was nakedly, chillingly outraged.

Chapter Seven

"I s this all right?" Ran asked. "I mean, you don't mind me coming in here, do you?"

"Darling, of course not," Nancy said. "This is a bar. We actively encourage people to come in. And anyway, it's nice to see you."

"Thanks. You don't know how much that means to me."

Nancy's lips twitched. She longed to laugh, but did not have the heart when Ran was obviously in woebegone mode. Though Rose had told her about his renovation, the reality of it still came as a shock. Short-haired, and stripped of all visible silliness, he was almost ridiculously handsome—the other girl behind the bar at Forbes & Gunning could hardly take her eyes off him.

Sighing deeply, Ran climbed onto one of the tall stools. "Nancy, can I talk to you?"

"Feel free. Think of me as a confessional, or a well-sprung psychiatrist's couch. My Barmaid's Vows will protect your privacy."

The normal Ran would have found this funny. The renovated version only sighed again.

Nancy asked, "Well, what are you drinking? I'm afraid we don't do wheatgrass juice."

His great, poignant black eyes were reproachful. "I'll have anything with a lot of alcohol in it, please."

She leaned forward. "Don't be daft. You know you can't handle it."

"I have to practice," Ran said lugubriously. "It's the only mood-altering substance Polly allows."

Nancy poured him a glass of fresh orange juice, from the fat, dew-pearled jug in the fridge behind her. "How is dear old Polly?"

"Radiant, thanks." Ran's gloom intensified. "She says she never knew such happiness existed."

"Goodness, how wonderful."

"Yes."

There was a significant silence.

Nancy asked, "What are you doing in London?"

He shrugged listlessly. "Polly's meeting someone for lunch. And I've just been measured for a suit."

She could not help laughing now. "What—a proper, tailor-made suit? The Digger's determined to turn you into a gentleman. Wait till I tell Mum."

"Yes, tell Rose—why not?" His voice was hollow. "She already despises me."

"Come on, Ran, do lighten up. What's the matter?"

"Why should you care? I don't belong to you anymore."

Nancy briefly squeezed his hand. "I love you dearly, whoever you sleep with. You know that. Please don't get maudlin on me—our Maudlin Hour doesn't start till six."

"My life is running out of control," Ran said. He frowned at the surface of his drink, before knocking it back as if it had been single malt. "This is the fiercest passion I've ever experienced, and I don't know where it's taking me. Polly has colonized every cell of my body. And every second of every minute of every day. Which is fantastic, of course."

"Oh, of course." Under the bar, Nancy was spooning green olives into small bowls. She had heard many Ran speeches concerning passion.

"But Nance, I'm losing my sense of self. My identity. All the things that make up who I am."

"She's chucked out your caftans, has she?"

"And my temple bells, and my shrine to Lakshmi." He detected no satire. "I wouldn't care, if she left me a bit of personal autonomy. Nancy—I miss you all so much!"

279

Unexpectedly, she was touched. "But you're always welcome at Melismate."

"Polly seems to feel threatened by it," Ran said. "She won't come there with me, and she goes crazy if I try to drop in alone. She doesn't understand that you're the only family I have. Rose has been a mother to me, and you're all my surrogate sisters. I'm exiled from the people I love."

"Oh, Ran—you're Linnet's father. Nobody wants to exile you."

He was in full flow. "Do you know what I keep thinking about? That book Rose quotes all the time."

"Which book, darling? She's read more than one, you know." Nancy's sympathetic tone was wearing a little thin. She had always been the first of the girls to tire of his violin solos.

"We took Linnet to see the film. The one about four sisters."

"*Little Women*?"

"That's the one. And there's a boy who lives next door, who falls in love with the girls."

"Laurie," Nancy supplied.

"Yes. They teach Laurie the meaning of love, and sort of adopt him into their family. That's me. I'm exactly like Laurie."

"Steady on," Nancy said. "Laurie didn't seduce one of the girls when she was under age, then knock her up, then proceed to misbehave with every other female in Concord, Mass."

Ran's lips quivered. "I'm trying to tell you, I've changed. I'm starting to see, with horrible clarity, everything I've lost. I've realized I'm in this situation because I've been very selfish, and very stupid."

There was another short silence, during which Nancy pointedly did not disagree.

"Anyway," he muttered, "it's my own fault, and I have to deal with it alone. Totally alone."

Nancy felt her face change color. Berry was in the doorway, in his shirtsleeves, carrying his jacket over one arm. She had not seen him since Rufa's wedding. For the first time, he was meeting her as a single man. There were teenage flutterings in the pit of her stomach. For the millionth time, she cursed the dog's breakfast she had made of seducing him. If only she had known Polly was about to bolt, she could have waited and done it properly.

Ran yelped when he saw Berry. The two men stared at each other, horrified. The bar was empty. They could not possibly avoid each other. Berry was unsure how to react. He was beginning to be grateful to Ran for taking Polly off his hands, but it was surely rather bad form not to at least pretend to be angry. Out of the corner of his eye he could see Nancy trying not to laugh, and he longed to laugh with her.

Oh, God, how he loved her. It was eating him up and driving him mad. And this was his one little window of opportunity. He had flown in from Frankfurt that morning, and would fly back that afternoon. He had two precious hours to bask in her smiles, before returning to the cheerless flat provided by his bank.

He smiled at Nancy, and held out his hand to Ran. "Hello."

"Berry, darling," Nancy said, "I thought you were in the Land of the Lederhosen."

"I am—I'm only in London for the day, I'm afraid."

Ran jumped off the stool. He clasped Berry's hand between both of his. "You're amazing—aren't you angry? Aren't you going to challenge me to a fight, or something?"

Berry chuckled. "Don't be ridiculous."

"I thought you'd hate the sight of me. I stole Polly and ruined your life."

"Oh, I wouldn't put it quite like that." Gently, he disengaged his hand. "Polly does have a will of her own, after all."

"You can say that again," Ran agreed.

Berry heard a stifled snort of laughter from Nancy, and had to bite the insides of his cheeks for a moment. "She didn't want to marry me," he told Ran, "and I had to respect that. It's totally fine now. I can even say I hope you'll both be very happy."

"Oh God, that's beautiful!" Ran grabbed his hand again, before Berry could stop him. "That's so—so magnanimous, so generous—"

Rather more firmly, Berry reclaimed his hand—there was always a danger that Ran would kiss it. "Don't mention it." He turned to Nancy. "I've got some time to kill before my flight. I don't suppose you could make yourself free for lunch?"

He was gratified to see the delight in Nancy's heavenly blue eyes. It faded, however, when Simon, her boss, emerged from his office. The bar was filling. He frowned at Nancy. "This isn't the Rover's Return, Nancy. Less natter and more work, please."

"There's your answer," Nancy said disconsolately. "But you owe me a lunch now—a very good one."

He laughed. "The very best."

"And give me a bit more notice." She intercepted a glance from her boss, and rapidly moved away along the bar.

Berry sighed. Then he smiled at Ran. "Are you free for lunch?"

"What, now? Are you sure?"

"Absolutely. Just to prove there are no hard feelings." The angel had smiled at him; she had been glad to see him. It was one of those times when he felt fond of Ran. He felt fond of the whole world.

❋ ❋ ❋

The restaurant was packed with men in identical striped shirts, ties, and cuff-links. An identical dark gray jacket hung upon the back of every chair. Ran, in his modish black linen, stood out like a peacock among pigeons. Berry wished the tables were not set so close together. He thought how awkward it was to be seen with a man who was seriously beautiful, when neither of you were gay. He hung his jacket on the back of his chair.

"Tomato soup," Ran said, behind the dog-eared menu. "Steak and kidney pie with mashed potato and onion gravy. Chocolate custard pudding." He handed the menu across the table.

"In this heat?"

"Polly never lets us have food like this."

"No, not quite her style." Berry felt uncomfortable discussing Polly with Ran. He hoped Ran had the basic normality not to expect him to compare notes.

"She's a very good cook," Ran went on. "But she doesn't seem to do much ordinary stuff. I miss stuff like fried eggs and baked beans."

Berry beckoned over the waiter, to order food and bottled water. It was hot. He wished he could rip off his tie.

"This is very good of you," Ran said, once the waiter had gone.

"Don't mention it."

"Some guys would want to kill me."

Berry laughed. "You really can stop mentioning it. Let's just relax, and take it as read. It's too hot for drama."

"Okay." Ran tested his elbows on the table. "Can I ask you something?"

"Well, I suppose so."

"It's rather intrusive of me, but it's been bothering me for ages—how did you propose to Polly?"

Berry was startled. "Sorry?"

"You know. Going down on one knee, or over a romantic dinner. How did you do it?"

"I don't know. The same way everyone does. How did you propose to Lydia?"

"Oh, I'll never forget that," Ran said wistfully. "We were lying naked under a hedge."

"Hmm. How romantic. But if you're thinking of trying that with Polly, I don't hold out much hope." Berry gave up the struggle, and resigned himself to the ungentlemanly act of talking about his former fiancée.

"It would make her angry, wouldn't it?"

"Definitely."

"It's really awful when she's angry, isn't it?"

"I'll say." Berry could not tell a lie. By God, it was awful. She had a way of ripping off all your self-esteem, to leave you shivering and whimpering. Deflecting Polly's anger took years of study. He was moved to sympathy. "Look, I'll be honest. I don't actually remember the moment I proposed. There was never a point at which I uttered the words 'Will you marry me?' I knew I loved her, and wanted to be with her, and all that. I'd just got my first job after Oxford, and her parents had given her a flat for her twenty-first birthday—"

"So it was natural for you to move in with her," Ran suggested.

Berry nodded. "That's it—completely natural. And that's when Polly simply began talking about our wedding. Jokily, at first. It only gradually got serious."

Ran was listening with all his attention. "And when did you realize there was no going back?"

"Oh, that's easy. She mentioned our wedding in front of my mother. So I couldn't very well say I knew nothing about it. Though I was very pleased, of course. Delighted." Berry cleared his throat. "Anyway, the hints went on. If I wanted her to be happy, all I had to do was pay attention. She kept showing me pictures of rings, and leaving her rings lying about so I'd know the size. So I went to her favorite jewelers, and bought her a ring." He could not help adding, "A bloody expensive one, too."

"And that was it?"

"More or less. I took it home and gave it to her. And for some reason, she was incredibly surprised. She told all her friends I was very impetuous and impulsive."

"Were you?"

Berry sighed. "Come on, you know me. I'm the least impulsive man on earth."

"You're lucky." Ran was gloomy. "I'm always leaping into things headfirst. That's how it all ended up like this. She's going on about our wedding as if it was all arranged. That means I'm going to end up married to her, doesn't it?"

"I thought that's what you wanted."

"Everyone thinks that. Nobody bothers to ask me what I think." Ran's arched eyebrows, black as Indian ink against his parchment skin, drew together in a frown. "The walls are closing in on me. I nearly had hysterics at that fucking tailor's."

"Sorry?"

"She sent me to be measured for a suit," Ran said bitterly. "I had to stand still for ages, with some old queen feeling up my inside leg—and at the end of it, he let slip she'd ordered a morning suit. I felt as if I'd been measured for my coffin."

A waiter arrived, with Ran's soup and Berry's smoked salmon.

"It's difficult," Berry said. "Other people tend not to understand about Polly. My sister used to think I was pathetic for not speaking to her plainly— laying down the law, if you like. But the few times I tried it, Polly always managed to get the wrong end of the stick, and I ended up begging forgiveness for some awful thing I didn't know I'd done." He shook black pepper over his salmon. "I'll be frank with you, Ran. If you don't want to marry her, the suit doesn't bode well."

Ran stirred his soup, as if searching for something in its red depths. "I've let it go too far. I can't turn back." He laid the spoon down in the bowl. "What the hell am I going to do?"

"What do you want to do?"

"Would I be asking if I knew? God, I've made a mess of my life. I've alienated all the people who loved me, I've thrown away everything I hold dear—" His eyes flooded. Rich tears dripped from his lashes. "I wish I was dead sometimes."

Berry froze, with smoked salmon on his tongue. Please, not tears. Not here. If he kept still and said nothing, Ran might pull himself together.

"She's come between me and Linnet," Ran said. "She doesn't understand Linnet, she doesn't like talking to her. She doesn't like it when I pop round to Melismate to see her. Now my baby thinks I love Polly more than I love her. It's like a knife in my heart." A loud sob shook him.

Berry hissed, "Ran, for God's sake—" The men at the table on either side were flicking doubtful glances.

"Yesterday I went to fetch her from school, and she came running out to meet me. And when she saw I had Poll with me, she just stopped short, and all the light went out of her. I can't describe the expression on her face." He drew his linen sleeve angrily across his streaming eyes. "I've blown it. I've lost my daughter. She'll be living with that lecherous choir bloke."

"Choir bloke?" Berry echoed. The adjacent tables were now listening openly. One man had put down his fork, to watch.

"He runs this posh choir Liddy's joined, and you should have seen him, he was all over her. Normally, when men get amorous with her, she runs away. This time, she was smiling, and hanging on his every bloody word— 'yes Phil, no Phil, you're so fucking talented, Phil'—I couldn't bear it!"

"But you're not married to her anymore." Despite the glare of publicity, Berry felt he should point this out.

Ran was beyond reason. "She's having private rehearsals with that slavering old goat—for her line in 'Spem in Alium,' which is a very challenging forty-part motet. And it had better not be subtitled 'Sperm in Lydia'—or I'll kill myself!" He buried his face in his napkin.

Berry leaned across the table toward him. Very quietly, but very clearly, he said, "You're making a complete ass of yourself. Get a grip."

He sat bolt upright, and ate his smoked salmon.

Ran sniffed loudly, mopping at his face. He finished off by blowing his nose on the napkin. "Sorry. God, that was quite cathartic." He blew his nose again, and attacked his soup, almost cheerfully.

"Seriously," Berry said, "nobody can force you to get married. Do talk to Polly—she's not such a bad old stick."

"Polly's wonderful. It's disloyal of me to complain. But I'm looking back at things I did in the past. I don't think Liddy and I achieved closure." Ran slurped the last of his soup, wiped his mouth with the remains of his napkin, and sighed. "That family, eh? If you're doomed to fall in love with one of them, she'll be in your hair forever."

Chapter Eight

Linnet charged into the Melismate kitchen, clutching a battered piece of sugar paper. "H'lo, Granny." Rose bent down, trapping the little girl long enough to plant a kiss on her head. "One of your paintings? How lovely. This kitchen needs some good paintings."

"It's some apples and a banana. It's called a Still Life, because there aren't any things that move in it. Can I watch *The Worst Witch*?" Not waiting for a reply, Linnet shrugged off her Pikachu rucksack and her pink cardigan, dropped them on the floor, grabbed the Ressany Brothers from the dresser, and dashed out of the room. Over her shoulder, she called, "Juice please— not with bits in!"

Rose picked up the rucksack and cardigan, glancing round warily as Rufa came in. She knew her oldest daughter had strong views about videos straight after school. When Rufa lived at Melismate, she had worked hard to establish a proper routine for Linnet. Even when up to her eyes in jam-making, she had religiously observed bedtimes, mealtimes, basic good manners, and healthful food. But Rufa had not been here for weeks, and, Rose was the first to admit, things had got rather lax. She was fully prepared to defend herself, with a detailed speech about routines smashed by a summer of upheaval.

Rufa, however, did not appear to have noticed the video, nor the rudely dumped belongings. She hovered near the door, clutching her car keys in one hand. She was smiling—but miles away, Rose decided; bathed in the light of some other planet.

Rose moved to put the kettle on. "Thanks so much for fetching her, lovey."

"Oh, I don't mind." Finally, Rufa met her mother's eyes. "I love picking her up from school. She comes out so full of her own world."

"Well, it got us out of a hole, what with the car languishing at the garage, and Ran off at the races."

"Off where?"

"He's eating mini sausage rolls in a box at Cheltenham. Polly wanted him to meet some friends of hers. So, of course, that took precedent over picking his daughter up from school."

Rufa smiled. "She's not the sort of woman you disagree with. Where's Lydia, anyway? Isn't she here?"

Rose took a clean mug from the new dishwasher. "No, she's rehearsing with Phil Harding, and I wouldn't make her miss it for the world. Phil's choir has brought her back to life. She hasn't been this unzombified since she left Ran. Do sit down, darling."

"Oh, I'm not staying, thanks."

Rose turned to face her squarely, hands on hips. "Rubbish. We haven't seen you in ages. I absolutely forbid you to leave without having a cup of tea."

Rufa laughed. "All right. A quick one." She moved away from the door and sat down at the table, still clutching her keys.

Like a visitor, Rose thought. As if this house, and the people in it, no longer concerned her—and this was the girl who had offered herself as a sacrifice to preserve them all. She studied Rufa covertly while she made two mugs of tea-bag tea. There was definitely something different about her: something glassy-eyed and unconvincing in her air of serenity.

"Tell me how you are. Give me details of your every waking thought and act." Rose joined her at the table. "I've missed you. We all have."

"I've been busy," Rufa said. "There's such a lot to do."

"Such as what?"

"At the moment, I'm making tomato chutney."

"Oh, good—Roger adores your chutney. May we have a couple of jars?"

Rufa laughed. "You can have a caseful. I've made tons of the stuff. The jars are crowding me out of house and home. I thought I might sell a few dozen to that shop in Bourton."

"Darling, I thought you'd given up flogging your wares round the tourist traps. You don't have to slave over a hot stove anymore, so why on earth do you do it?"

"Just for fun," Rufa said. "We have a ridiculous glut of tomatoes, and I've run out of ways to use them up." She laughed suddenly—a lightning flash of animation. "Tristan picks the bloody things faster than I can bottle them."

Rose sighed. "Listen to us. A year ago, your cooking activities made a real difference. I'm ashamed to remember how I relied on your jam."

"You were extremely good at finding bargain sacks of fruit."

"Yes, but I thought you'd finished with all that. Edward will have a fit."

"No he won't." The light dulled. Rufa's face became tense and still, as she put the shutters up against the pain, or the guilt—or whatever else it was that made her, for a moment, visibly anguished. "He likes me to be enterprising."

Rose thought how transparent she was—you could always tell exactly what she was feeling because it was written in those great, serious, radiant eyes. Watching narrowly, she asked, "How is he, by the way? Any nearer getting home?"

"There's a good chance he'll be called next week. Once he's actually in the witness box, it shouldn't take long. He's not the only witness."

"Why the delay?"

"Oh, apparently the man on trial keeps claiming to have terrible illnesses."

"I never thought I'd hear myself saying it, but I miss Edward," Rose declared. "Apart from anything else, we had to call a plumber about the downstairs lav. Edward would have fixed it in a second."

"Yes, poor you." Rufa picked up her mug of tea, blowing on the surface to cool it.

"It was only the ball cock. The man gave it one little jiggle, and charged me about a million pounds. So I refuse to call anyone about the drain, till Edward's had a look." Rose waited for Rufa to protest that Edward was not the family's unpaid handyman. But Rufa had crossed back into the blessed safety of her secret realm, and only smiled.

Rose recognized her daughter's blank terror of facing the unfaceable. She remembered how Rufa had been in the weeks after The Zed's death—frantically building a shell of sensible coping, to hide her deep loopiness. Rose blamed herself, for not fighting through her own grief to reach her daughter. Edward seemed to understand, and she wished to God he would come home.

The front door banged.

"Anyway, here's Roger," Rose said. "Which must mean the car has lived to fight another day."

It was not Roger. The kitchen door opened. Selena, thin as a wishbone in baggy jeans and a cropped T-shirt, dragged in a bursting rucksack.

"Hi, Mum. Hi, Ru." She grinned at them shyly. "Can you give me a hand with my bags?"

❋ ❋ ❋

Selena had two large leather suitcases, both crammed with books. They were incredibly heavy. It took the combined muscle of Rose, Rufa, Selena, and the taxi driver to heft them into the house. Rufa, jolted back into her usual energy, put the kettle on the range.

Linnet scampered into the room, shrieking with joy, and she and Selena wrestled on the floor like puppies. Once she had got her breath, Selena dug in her rucksack to produce a battered plastic bag. It contained a pink velvet handbag, ornamented with a red sequined heart.

"Oh, THANKS, it's lovely, lovely—" Linnet examined it reverently. She found some chocolate buttons inside, which made her shriek again. She hugged Selena's legs. "Are you back forever and ever?"

"Not forever," Selena said. She glanced warily at Rose. "For the moment."

"But you promise not to get married, or get a job?"

Rose and Rufa were making significant faces at each other, and Selena ducked out of their eye line. "I promise."

"Good. Do you want to watch *The Worst Witch*?"

"No thanks. I'd like to talk to Granny."

"All right." Linnet ran off again, clutching the handbag to her bosom.

"She'd like to talk to me!" Rose murmured. "Did you hear that? She actually expressed a wish to talk to me!"

"Do shut up, Mum," Rufa said. "Selena, have a cup of tea, and don't take any notice."

"Relax, I knew she'd be sarky." Selena folded her long body into a chair. "I'm glad you're here. I was going to ring you."

Rose took the chair opposite. "I'm overjoyed to see you, darling—but what on earth is going on? Are you really moving back?"

"If you'll have me."

"Of course I'll have you, don't be dramatic, but what about your stupendous career?"

"I'm not doing that anymore," Selena said. "Modeling is a crap career." She smiled lopsidedly at Rufa. "I've decided to try for Cambridge."

"Seriously? Oh, God, that's fabulous!" The old Rufa was thoroughly back with them now. "I knew you couldn't be that brainy for nothing!"

"I've obviously died," Rose said. "And this is heaven. My problem teenager is giving me something to boast about, at long last." It was like turning back the clock, she thought fondly, to the days before dreadlocks and nose studs. For the first time in God knew how long, she was reminded of how Selena looked when she was happy. "So, what brought it all on?"

"Roshan's been nagging me for ages," Selena said. She reached blindly for a biscuit. "But it was Max, in the end. I was complaining about the people I have to work with—the photographers who think they're God, the whining anorexics, the creepy women who talk about you as if you're not there. And Max said I should just admit I didn't belong. He said he didn't know what point I was trying to make, but he doubted it was worth wasting my whole life for."

Rose asked, "What point?"

"I don't know." Selena was uncomfortable. "Maybe I had to prove I wasn't the plain one."

Rufa laughed softly. "You've certainly done that—we've all been dining out on your *Vogue* cover. Tristan says you're like an art deco statue."

"Who's Tristan?"

Rufa flushed painfully. "I forgot, you haven't met him. He's Alice's nephew. He's staying at the farm."

"Oh."

"The Zed always maintained you'd grow into a raving beauty," Rose said. "That's why he was so strict about putting those ghastly metal things on your teeth. He even paid the bill."

Selena gave her a rare, full smile, showing her perfect teeth. "I hated him at the time. But I'm obviously so grateful now."

Rufa said, "You and your teeth were probably the only good investment he ever made."

"So go on," Rose urged. "Get back on the road to Damascus. Did you decide there and then to jack it all in?"

"Nope," Selena said. "That was last night. I had my blinding flash this morning. I was wearing a mauve ballgown with a tulip skirt, and standing up to my knees in the Serpentine."

"Good God—why?"

"For a shoot, obviously," Rufa said, laughing. "Why else would she be wearing a ballgown in the Serpentine?"

"It was for *Harpers & Queen*," Selena said. "The agency's going to be furious with me—I haven't told them yet. But I suddenly wondered what the hell I was doing there. I couldn't see a single person I respected, or even liked. Everyone treated me as if I was made of plastic, anyway. And I knew the next job wouldn't be any better. So I thought, fuck it. I got out of the water, stripped off the dress, got back into my jeans, and went back to Wendy's. Max was working at home today—I bought him a drink at the Clarence before I left, to say thanks." She was animated and confident. "He sends his love, by the way."

Rufa caught some of the animation. "You couldn't have done it at a better time. When did term start at Saint Hildy's? Mum, you'd better ring Mrs. Cutting today."

"I've done it," Selena said coolly. "She was the first person I called after I cleaned the pond muck off my feet. She said she'd be delighted to have me back."

"The woman's a masochist," Rose said. "You were an absolute torment to her—I can't believe she's begging for more."

"You just rang Mrs. Cutting, and announced you were coming back?" Rufa was impressed. "God, I'd never dare."

"You're a wimp," Selena said, not unkindly. "You never know which rules you can break, so you obey every single one."

"Do I? Well, Ma Cutting was always nicer if you were clever—and I wasn't honors-board material."

Rose found something a little distant, a little forced about Rufa's satisfaction. Selena returning to school was her final dream come true, so why was she not in transports of delight? What was wrong with her? She looked more beautiful than ever, if possible. But there was a definite and unsettling change. Rose recalled, with a sinking heart, the way Rufa had looked and behaved when in love with the frightful Jonathan. Rufa and love were a combustible mixture. Sexiness (there really was no other word) melted Rufa's edges and lit her from within. She had never looked like this with Edward.

Rose said, "By the way, how's Tristan?"

Rufa laughed. She came to life; she practically caught fire. "Wonderful—and working hard, at last, because the alternative is picking tomatoes. He says he'd be happy never to see another one in his life."

"Pity he's at the other place," Rose said, seemingly offhand. "He's just the right age for Selena."

Rufa winced angrily. There were ten years between her and Selena. She saw right through her mother's pitiful attempt at offhandedness, and was determined to surrender nothing. "He's quite a bit older, actually. Nearly twenty-one."

"Oh, there's not such a yawning gulf between twenty and seventeen." Rose left the rest of the sentence—concerning the larger gulf between just twenty and nearly twenty-eight—to reverberate silently.

"He's very old for his age," Rufa said coldly, knowing he was the exact opposite. "I sometimes think he's more mature than I am." She stood up. "I must go."

"Wait—" Something made Rose leap up after her. She hugged her daughter fiercely. "Come back soon, won't you, darling? Please don't leave it so long next time." She could not shake off a sense of having lost her. Rufa bent to kiss her without a word, and almost ran to her car.

Later, when Selena was reading a story to Linnet (she had always been a surprisingly patient reader-aloud), Rose poured herself a medicinal gin and tonic, and brooded. She was afraid she would have to blame herself for letting Rufa go through that sacrificial marriage. All her instincts had been against it. Had she ignored them because they were so desperate for the money? If she had kept her eyes open, would she have seen this coming?

Oh God, she thought, please start existing, so I can believe in you and open our relationship with an urgent prayer: Please let me be wrong about Ru—but in case I'm not, please look after her.

Chapter Nine

S o the board voted to extend the scholarship," Mrs. Cutting said. "The *Vogue* cover probably helped. I certainly didn't need to beg very hard."

"Thank you," Rose said fervently. "Thank you so much."

The headmistress of Saint Hildegard's had called at Melismate directly after the governors' meeting, to bring Rose the news that despite Selena's awful behavior over the past year, her scholarship was safe. Rose was weak with relief—the way things were at the moment, she had dreaded having to beg Edward for the fees.

She had been very surprised, and rather alarmed, to find Mrs. Cutting on her doorstep. Selena's headmistress was not a formidable woman, but Rose could not shake off a memory of her own stormy school days. This had always colored her relationship with the authorities at the girls' school. In the past, she had left the business of charming them to The Zed. Now, she had to fight an impulse to apologize for the state of the house, as if Mrs. Cutting had summoned her out of a class to explain.

Apologies were, in any case, no longer called for. Selena—radiantly and unrecognizably virtuous—had shown her headmistress and her mother into the drawing room. This room made Rose uncomfortable. For the past ten years it had been a bare box, without carpets, curtains, or furniture, flooded with a permanently wintry white light. They had never used it, and it made Rose feel like a stranger, in a strange house. The Zed would not have recognized it.

It had been a long-standing ambition of Rufa's to give Melismate the drawing room she felt it deserved. During the great restoration, she had installed curtains of thick Indian silk, mended various tattered Persian rugs, and lined the alcoves with books. She had cleaned and reframed the unsaleable family portraits, and badly painted Hasty ancestors gazed down from the walls: an eighteenth-century Hasty, amateurishly daubed on wood like a pub sign; a late-Victorian Hasty apparently depicted in several shades of gravy; a 1930s Hasty in coarse pastels. Rufa had picked her way through the heaps of decay, panning for anything with one glint of rescuable quality. She had bought an enormous Knole sofa and two armchairs, which now stood before the fireplace. To Rose's amazement, Selena had built and lit a small log fire, to ward off the chill of autumn. The room was still chilly, however, and their voices echoed.

Rose thought Mrs. Cutting looked far more at home in the new drawing room than she did. She was a handsome woman in her fifties, with a tidy cap of straight brown hair. She wore a soft blue shirt under a Fair Isle waistcoat, and black shoes with high heels. Rose, in her usual baggy sweater and balding corduroys, felt rebuked ("Rose Darrow, you are a disgrace to this school!"). She had just stepped out of her Wellingtons when Mrs. Cutting arrived, and she was annoyed to notice now that her big toe was poking through a hole in one sock. She covered it discreetly with her other foot.

"You've been wonderfully kind and miraculously patient," she said. "I really don't think she'll blow it this time. I can't get her to tell me exactly what she got up to in London, but she's so much happier since she came back."

"I wanted to keep faith with her," Mrs. Cutting said seriously. "It was perfectly obvious why she was so difficult last year. It was her response to the loss of her father."

Rose sighed, suddenly acutely lonely for The Zed—so not here, so left out of all their plans. "I did my best, but I found it impossible to reach her. The silences were awful—worse than the rudeness. I sometimes thought she wanted to retreat into herself until she disappeared."

"Mrs. Hasty, I'm not saying any of it was your fault. I know you've all had a hellish time."

"Do call me Rose."

Mrs. Cutting smiled again. "Why should I, when you refuse to call me Theresa?"

"Give me time," Rose said, smiling back gratefully. "I'm still half expecting you to tell me she's been caught smoking in class again."

Both women laughed. Mrs. Cutting said, "Selena and I have been through all that, and come to a very good understanding. She's focused and motivated, and I'll be astonished if I can't get her into Cambridge. She's one of the ablest girls I've ever taught."

The door opened. Selena herself came in, carrying a tray of tea. She set it down on the antique chest on the hearthrug, and Rose tried to look as if this sort of thing happened all the time. Selena had made real tea, in a teapot, and unwrapped the new cups and saucers Rufa had bought at Heal's. Gravely, she poured the tea. Rose watched her, with the eyes of a stranger—this poised, graceful, and entirely presentable teenager. It astonished her to see her daughters remaking themselves. The Zed would not have recognized the green shoots that were springing from the ruins of his family.

"I'll go now, if you don't mind," Selena said to Mrs. Cutting. "I promised I'd read to Linnet."

"Of course I don't mind. What are you reading?"

"*The Phoenix and the Carpet.*"

"Ah, Nesbit, how splendid—you really do have excellent taste. Is she enjoying it?"

"Adoring it."

"Well, don't let me stop you. See you in school on Monday." When the unrecognizable paragon had left the room, Mrs. Cutting turned back to Rose. "Do you know who she reminds me of, now those frightful studs have gone? I'm constantly remembering Rufa at the same age."

Mrs. Cutting was fond of Rufa. Her affection for The Zed had shriveled when he talked his firstborn out of university. Since then, she had regularly employed Rufa to cook for her dinner parties, and she had unsettled all the girls by turning up at her wedding.

"Yes, I suppose there is a resemblance," Rose said thoughtfully. It had not struck her before—until now, she had thought of Selena as an elongated version of herself and Lydia. But there was a definite echo of Rufa in the set of her head, and the coltishness of her long limbs. "She has the same inbuilt ability to do things properly—I may as well tell you, that fire hasn't been lit since the Relief of Mafeking, and she didn't even use firelighters."

"How is Rufa?" Mrs. Cutting asked pleasantly.

"Fine!" Rose declared, with a shade too much enthusiasm.

"It must be lovely for you, having her settled nearby."

"Oh, yes. Lovely!"

"What's she doing with herself these days? Will she carry on with the cooking?"

"She—she's still trying to decide," Rose improvised. She had not seen Rufa for ages. She did not telephone above twice a week, and her calls were vague and hurried. What was she doing with herself? What, indeed? Rose could hardly tell her daughter's old headmistress that she strongly suspected Rufa of having a rip-roaring affair with her husband's nephew by marriage.

Mrs. Cutting said, "Rufa was the one I worried about most when your husband died. They were extraordinarily close, weren't they? I was afraid she wouldn't be able to cope with the shock."

You were right there, Rose thought; you know her better than I do; she had me fooled for months.

"But she seems to have pulled herself through it really well," Mrs. Cutting went on. "I've never seen such a stunning bride—and I've seen a good few brides, as you can imagine. I have to be quite selective about invitations, or I'd never have a single free Saturday in the summer months. But Rufa's wedding was a special symbol of renewal. I wouldn't have missed it for anything."

Outside the window, beyond the padded folds of Indian silk, they heard the sound of wheels crunching the gravel. Rose wriggled off the unfamiliar sofa to look out into the deepening dusk. "Rufa's car," she said happily. "Now you can ask her yourself."

It was not Rufa. If Mrs. Cutting had not been reflected in the window-pane, Rose would have shrieked aloud. Edward. What was Edward doing here, when everyone assumed he was still in The Hague? And why was he alone? There was not enough light to see the expression on his face, but Rose read tension and anger in every line of him. As she told Lydia and Selena afterward, "The bottom fell right out of my stomach—I knew something was wrong."

She heard him thumping on the heavy door. She heard Lydia, in the kitchen, calling, "I'll get it."

And, far too soon, Edward was in the room with them. He was sharp and clean and rigid, in his dark suit and regimental tie.

Mainly for the benefit of Mrs. Cutting, Rose kissed his cheek. "Edward, how terrific to see you—when did you get home? You know Theresa Cutting, I'm sure."

Edward's dark gray eyes had a dangerous glitter. He did not acknowledge Mrs. Cutting: a very bad sign in such a punctilious man.

"I think you know why I'm here," he said. "I want to speak to Rufa."

"To Rufa?" Mindful of Mrs. Cutting, Rose struggled to sound breezy. "She's not here, I'm afraid. Wasn't she in, when you got home?"

Edward said, "Please don't lie to me, Rose."

"Why would I be lying? I haven't seen her for weeks. Do sit down."

He did not sit down. He did not move from the doorway. He fixed Rose with his furious eyes. "I arrived back at the farm about half an hour ago," he said. "There was a note on the kitchen table. Rufa's left me."

"What?" This time, Rose did shriek aloud. "Oh God, no! Oh God, that idiotic girl!"

Mrs. Cutting, her face a mask of discretion, quickly stood up. "I must be off. So nice to see you." She hurried out, without shaking hands or looking back.

"I saw it coming," Rose groaned. "Why didn't I say something to her? Darling, I'm desperately sorry. All I can say in her defense is that she's probably lost her mind." She kept her eyes on the rug, unable to look at him. "What did the note say?"

"Basically, that she was leaving me. And that she was sorry. I think I'm at least entitled to an explanation. Where is she?"

Rose scrabbled in the pocket of her trousers for cigarettes and matches. She lit one, throwing the spent match angrily into the fire. "For the last time, Rufa is not here."

"You know where she is," Edward said.

"Not for certain—she hasn't told me a thing," Rose said. "I assume she's wherever Tristan is." She glanced up at him, and realized she had shocked him profoundly. Incredibly, he had not even suspected—what the hell was the matter with the man?

"Tristan?"

"Look, I don't know anything for certain. But I saw them together. It was pretty obvious."

His voice was quiet, simmering with fury. "I don't believe it."

"Well, let's hope I'm wrong."

"But he's a boy!"

"He didn't look like a boy to me." Rose's tone sharpened. "He looked like a young man—a rather arrogant young man."

"All his fault, is it?" Edward suddenly blazed. The roar of his voice made

Rose stagger back defensively. "What about her? What about betraying me?"

"You practically begged her to," Rose snapped back at him. "What did you expect, for God's sake? You bugger off abroad, leaving her alone in the house with a gorgeous young man—what did you bloody well expect?"

"I trusted her. The rest of you have the morals of alley cats, but I thought she was different. She's The Zed all over again—it's coming back like a nightmare."

"It's normal to fuck!" Rose screamed, touched on her wound. "For everyone else in the world except you, it's the most natural thing in the world! Oh, dear God—" She pressed both palms into her cheeks, forcing herself to be calm. "Sorry. Sorry. This is stupid. Why am I shouting at you? It must be the monumental embarrassment."

Edward was bewildered. "Why should you be embarrassed?"

"Oh, come on. She's chiseled a fortune out of you. Of course it's her fault. And mine. I let her marry you, when I knew she was clinging on by her fingernails. Oh God, what a mess."

His anger had retreated. The whole room tasted of his anguish. "I knew it too," he said. "She's been having nightmares about Rufus. She rang me two days ago, crying and begging me to come home. I pulled every string to get away—and I was too late."

"The thing is, she does love you. She must have hated running off. She must have lost her mind." Rose took a step toward him, awkwardly touching his arm. "Come into the kitchen and have a drink."

"How obvious was it? Is the whole countryside laughing at me?"

"Nobody's laughing."

"Jesus, they're all sorry for me." Edward winced, as if swallowing brambles. "Is there any whisky?"

"Yes. I'll pour you a huge one." She pushed him out of the drawing room—Rufa's dream—thankfully closing the door behind them. The situation seemed just as ghastly in the kitchen, but easier to digest. Fortunately, the kitchen was empty. Lydia, lately developing a most un-Hastyish tact, had withdrawn upstairs to keep Selena and Linnet out of the way. The house reeked of crisis. Rose poured herself a large gin. She poured Edward a whisky so enormous that he smiled bleakly when she put it into his hand.

"Medicine," he said.

"It helps." Rose sat down at the table. Edward dropped into a chair opposite, dazed with shock. There was a silence that seemed to stretch on for ages.

Rose sighed heavily. "Edward, I'm sorry—but did you really not suspect something was going on with Tristan?"

"No." He frowned. "That makes me a fool, I suppose. But I can't get my head round it. Any other woman in the world—but not Rufa. Never Rufa."

"Why not? She's only a woman, not an angel. Sleeping with a gorgeous young man who's in your house is a very understandable, ordinary sort of crime."

"Hmm." He glanced up at her. "Is Tristan gorgeous? I can't see past his youth. He's a child to me."

"And you're fond of him," Rose suggested sadly.

"Yes. You remember how Alice adored him. He was only a little boy when she died."

"Our babies grow up," Rose said. "And then they show us everything we did wrong. I leaned too hard on Ru after The Zed died—what with her reputation for being the sensible one. I somehow didn't leave an opening for her to talk through. And she got into the habit of never being listened to properly. Except by you. Only by then it was too late, and she didn't know how to scream for help."

"Is running off with Tristan her scream for help, then?" Edward snapped.

His pain wrung the blood from Rose's heart. She searched for words to cushion the truth. "It was more like a dreadful teenage infatuation. When I saw them together, she was acting as if she'd just discovered sex—perhaps," she hastened to add, "because she missed you."

"Crap," Edward said softly. "We've done it once, as I daresay she told you."

"She didn't, but I had wondered," Rose admitted. There was no satisfaction in being right. "I couldn't think of any other reason for her to betray you, practically on her honeymoon. What was the problem? I know it's a rude question, but she can't have turned you down—Ru's the soul of duty."

"That's just it," Edward said. "I couldn't do anything when I even suspected she was acting out of duty."

She nodded sympathetically. "Rather a turnoff. I had wondered how you'd get over that one. A vainer man than you would have managed to convince himself she was begging for it."

He smiled grimly. "Was that a compliment, Rose? Steady on."

She smiled back. "I meant it. You're a boundlessly good man; one of the best I ever met. You're also incredibly good-looking. Any woman in her right mind would jump at the chance to sleep with you. It doesn't seem fair that you should be rendered impotent by your inbuilt decency."

"I am not impotent—bloody hell." He was not annoyed now. He was even slightly amused by her tactlessness.

"Well, I'm sorry. But as far as I know, you haven't so much as shared a washcloth with anyone since Alice died. It did cross my mind that you couldn't do it."

Edward drained his glass. "I don't know why on earth I want to tell you this, but I have had sex since Alice died. Of course I have. Not on my home turf—mainly because Rufus would have taken it as competition."

"Definitely," Rose agreed. "You'd have been crazy to tell him. There could only be one lion in this jungle."

"And it would have been—well—awkward."

Rose said, "My God, don't tell me you took up with Prudence again! Please don't!"

He winced angrily. "Yes, all right. I have been having a sort of relationship with Prudence."

"What the hell does that mean?"

"I didn't think it was particularly serious between us. We saw each other when she was between marriages."

"Did you tell Rufa?"

"I told her we'd had an affair after Alice died." He was defensive.

"That was years ago," Rose said. "What about the sequel?"

"Look, it really wasn't serious—certainly not on my side. Pru never wanted me hanging around all the time. And she rather went off me when I left the army."

Rose was white with anger. "No wonder the old bitch wouldn't come to the wedding. I suppose you went to Paris to break the news?"

"Yes," Edward said warily, startled to find himself knocked off the moral high ground.

"And she was furious with you, wasn't she? And she cried and screamed and accused you of betrayal."

"Yes." Edward let out a heavy sigh. "I shouldn't have been surprised, I suppose. But I was, Rose—please believe that. I honestly thought it had been over for months. I thought Pru had given me my marching orders just before Rufus died. I wasn't prepared to be treated as if I'd broken some kind of understanding."

"Oh, come on, look at it from her point of view," Rose said. "Dear, reliable old Edward, always good for dinner and a screw, turns out to be just like all the others—he buggers off with someone twenty years younger."

There was a silence.

Edward said, "You think I'm an idiot."

"No, I just think you're a typical man. Or you would have told poor Ru the whole story."

"I didn't think there was anything to tell."

Rose exhaled gustily. "So you invited the bloody woman to her house."

"Pru invited herself. I couldn't think of a reason to refuse. I assumed, because I was finally married—"

"Well, I bet Rufa found out," Rose said. "She might be barmy, but she's not stupid. Think how it must have looked to her. She fails to have sex on her honeymoon, then her husband invites his old squeeze to stay."

Edward winced again. "But it wasn't like that! I might have fallen in love with Prudence when we first got it together after Alice died. But that didn't work out, and the next time was completely different. Pru made it quite clear that she only wanted a shoulder to cry on—someone who understood her—I'm sure she'd never have told Rufa."

"I'm not," Rose said, with a surge of bitterness. "I remember what she was like when she dropped you for The Zed—she couldn't stop rubbing my nose in it. It was the only time we ever rowed over one of his lovers." She regretted saying all this when she saw the agony rake across his face. Pain upon pain. She lit another cigarette, tears trembling in her eyes. "I don't understand you, Edward. I don't understand why you keep coming back for more. First The Zed runs off with Prudence, and then his daughter runs off with her son. This family has completely screwed you—I don't know why you don't get a sledgehammer and smash this whole house down. You'd be completely within your rights."

He understood that she was serious, and answered her seriously. "I think it must be because I love you all so much."

"Because you love Rufa." Rose sniffed. She dug in her sleeve for a hard piece of old tissue.

"All of you. You've been a family to me—everyone needs some very annoying relations. Let's say I liked being annoyed. It stopped me dying of loneliness." He had never made such an admission to Rose. Suddenly made awkward by the intimacy, he stood up. "May I have some more? I'll pay you back."

"Please, don't talk about money," Rose said. "If I hadn't been so obsessed with bloody money, we wouldn't be sitting here now. Pass the Gordon's."

Edward returned to the table with a fresh glass of whisky, and passed the green bottle of gin to Rose. "I'm going to get very drunk," he announced gravely. "I'm going to get as drunk as I was that Boxing Day when Rufus glued up Bute's ass. Then I'm going to sleep here, on the strangely hideous new sofa Rufa chose for your drawing room."

Rose giggled, wiping her nose. How she admired a man who arranged his behavior with efficiency—who could get drunk without involving the emergency services. "You're very welcome. I'll even crack out new sheets for you. Much better than going home to the farm." The farm where he had lost two wives: one dead and one temporarily mislaid. The gin was beginning to cauterize.

He took a dose of whisky. "Tomorrow I'll go to Oxford to fetch Rufa."

"Hang on. She may not want to be fetched."

"I owe her another chance," he said. "Part of the fault is mine. I was obtuse about Prudence. I didn't owe her anything, and I should never have let her make me feel guilty. I'm going to apologize, and offer to start all over again."

Rose, without knowing precisely why, did not like the sound of this. "You're saying you've decided to forgive her?"

"Of course."

"Please, Edward, don't—" She stopped.

"Don't what?" he asked irritably. "How could I possibly behave better?"

Rose said, "Please don't forgive her too hard."

Chapter Ten

Tristan's father had bought him a small house in the part of Oxford known as Jericho. It was squeezed into the middle of a terrace of two-story houses, each with a bay window overlooking a tiny front garden. The front door was painted scarlet. Dusty evergreens drooped in the window boxes. There was a cheerful, tattered air of well-heeled studentry.

Edward stood on the other side of the street, staring at the house. He could not connect it with Rufa. Suddenly, he was sick with longing for her. He cursed himself for never daring to tell her how passionately he had loved her at a distance, in the years after leaving the army. He had not properly made her understand how deeply he loved her now. His guilt over Prudence, coupled with his ridiculous pride, had caused all this mess. Minutes away from facing Rufa, he knew he was prepared to go down on his knees and beg. He could not imagine any other way to prise her from the arms of her triumphant young lover.

In his rational mind, he did not hate Tristan—the baby Alice had adored, the winning little boy, the callow oaf who had heedlessly blasted his marriage apart. He had already decided, while driving to Oxford, that there was no point in being heavy with Tristan. He would be reasonable, and wrestle down any unreasonable flashes of fury.

He crossed the road, feeling that the blank white windows were staring at him, trying not to picture Tristan and Rufa within, twined in each other's arms. He pressed the tarnished brass bell, moving aside a heap of plastic-wrapped telephone directories with one foot. His pulse thudded in the back of his throat. He had crouched in shell holes under fire, and not felt as nervous as this. None of the things he had intended to say seemed right now.

There was movement inside the house. Edward tensed, and was taken aback when the door was opened by—apparently—a round-faced little girl of about twelve. The top of her head came up to his breastbone. Her brown eyes were solemn behind round spectacles.

"Yes?"

"I—er—is Tristan around?"

The little girl was cautious. "He sort of is, and he sort of isn't."

"I'm his uncle," Edward said. Grimly relishing the enormity of the lie, he added, "I'm sure he'll want to see me, and I can't come back later. I'm only in Oxford for the morning."

"Oh, well," she said. "That's different. Do come in."

Edward followed her past two bicycles in the hall, into a narrow kitchen overlooking a rank, neglected patch of garden. The kitchen was new, cheap, and incredibly untidy. There was a small table pushed against one wall, with two rickety chairs. Edward sat down on one of these, to take up less room.

"I'm Clytie," the girl said.

"You're—what?"

"It's my name, I'm afraid—Clytemnestra Williams. My dad teaches classics."

"Oh. I'm Edward Reculver." He waited to see if she would react to his name.

She only asked, "Would you like some tea?" She knew her duty toward all parentish figures. "There's peppermint or chamomile. Or ordinary, of course."

Edward could not help smiling at her. "Ordinary, please. How do you know Tristan?"

"Well, I live here," Clytie said. She took two dirty cups from the draining board, and briskly rinsed them under the tap. "I'm his lodger."

He adjusted her age upward. "What college are you at?"

"Somerville. I'm reading English, like Tristan."

She knew what he had been about to ask, Edward thought morosely, because all old people asked the same questions. He did not know how to demand an audience with Tristan and Rufa. He was afraid of what he would find.

She asked, "Do you take milk?"

"Please."

Clytie went to the fridge, which was covered with magnets, photos, and scrawled notes. The inside of the door was jammed with cartons of milk, some with cheesy yellow encrustations. She sniffed two or three cartons before selecting one and shutting the door. She made tea slowly, as if for a board of examiners. Edward felt as old as Everest, and oddly moved by her freshness. She sat down opposite him. Their knees touched under the table.

"I suppose I should tell him you're here," she suggested.

Her trustfulness alarmed Edward. No wonder The Zed had been so neurotic about his daughters—it must be hellish, he thought, to turn your little girls out into the world, when you knew what men could do to them.

Then he noticed the photograph, on the door of the fridge. It was a view of the valley at home, taken from the edge of his farm. In the bottom left-hand corner, with her dark red hair pouring over one shoulder, sat Rufa. He could see the ecstatic abandon of her smile from across the room. He had one moment of piercing desolation. Clytie was curiously following his gaze. It was not fair to take advantage of her ignorance.

He spoke gently. "I'm Rufa's husband."

In any other circumstances, it would have been comical to see Clytie's mouth drop open. She was dismayed. "You? Oh, God—he'll kill me! I don't think I was allowed to let you in!"

"I'll leave, if you like."

"No, that's just silly." She was recovering. "I thought Rufa's husband would be old, you see. And you're quite young. You—you haven't come to kill him, or anything, have you?"

He smiled, in spite of himself. "No."

"Well, I think you should stay. He'll have to face you sooner or later. And you seem perfectly all right to me."

Edward mentally wrote a letter to Clytie's classical father, begging him to warn her about men who seemed perfectly all right. "Thanks. As you see, I'm unarmed. And more or less in my right mind. I only want to talk to them."

Her dismay rushed back. "Them? Oh—no—she—" Clytie made an obvious attempt to improvise, then foundered. "Look, I won't say a word. It's not my business. I'll take you upstairs."

305

Rufa was not here. Edward found himself bitterly disappointed, and suddenly enraged with Tristan. Without the presence of Rufa to control him, he wanted to flay the little bugger alive. Grimly, he followed Clytie up the newly carpeted but stained stairs, to a small landing.

She knocked softly on a closed door. "Triss!"

A voice within snapped, "What?"

"There's someone here to see you."

"Tell 'em to fuck off."

"I can't," Clytie said. "It's Rufa's husband."

A leaden silence fell behind the door. After a long moment, there were sounds of a chair being dragged across floorboards, and footsteps. Edward stiffened, his hands automatically rolling into fists.

The door opened. He was gazing into Tristan's blue eyes, on a level with his own. He looked ghastly. His face was pasty and swollen, his long hair lank and unwashed. There were bluish smudges in the hollows above his cheekbones. He was the incarnation of misery. Edward saw that he had been crying himself blind, and felt a twinge of foreboding. The two of them faced each other hopelessly, neither knowing what to say.

"I'll leave you," Clytie announced, rather regretfully. "Under the circumstances, I really think you ought to make it up." She went downstairs.

Edward asked, "What circumstances? Why is she being mysterious? Where's Rufa?"

"Come in," Tristan said. There was a hint of sullenness buried in the depths of his misery. "Make your scene. I know exactly what you're going to say." His gaze dropped. He turned back into his room, and sat down at a littered desk beside the window.

Edward suppressed an urge to smack Tristan's head. "Where's Rufa?"

"Gone," Tristan said.

"Gone? What are you saying?"

Tristan swiveled his chair round to face Edward, not meeting his eye. "It's over. She doesn't want me anymore. She's left me."

Edward struggled to process this. He had expected to find a lovers' bower, yet here was Tristan, as deserted and sorrowful as he was. It made no sense. "Look, what has been going on?"

"I can't talk about it."

"Force yourself," Edward said shortly—how dared Tristan behave as if his sorrow was higher up in the pecking order of sorrows?

At last Tristan looked up at him properly. "We had a row."

"Are you telling me she walked out after a lovers' tiff? I don't believe you."

"Well, you'd better," Tristan shouted. His words ended on a dry sob.

Edward sighed. The last thing in the world he wanted was a shouting match. His frail dignity had suffered enough. "If you don't tell me the truth, I'll start to think she's under the floorboards."

"It wasn't my idea," Tristan blurted out desperately. His reddened eyes filled. "I didn't make her run away. Yes, I fell in love with her. Yes, I had an affair with her. But as far as I knew, I was leaving her at the farm. I hated it, I begged her to arrange our next meeting—and she wouldn't. She acted as if she never wanted to see me again." He looked away, withering under Edward's searchlight glare. "She turned up here, out of the blue, the day before yesterday." His lower lip buckled pathetically. "Everything was different, because she—she'd found out she was pregnant."

Edward dug his fists into his pockets, gritting his teeth to stop himself roaring aloud. This was as cruel as death. He had lost a chance to have a child, as well as losing his wife. "And what did you have to say to that?"

His tone made Tristan wince. "I freaked out."

There was a charged silence. Tristan waited for Edward to sketch out the rest.

Edward said, "You told her to get rid of it."

"No, I wouldn't do that." He sounded doubtful. "Honestly. I just assumed, you know—it just never crossed my mind that she wouldn't get rid of it. I mean, how can we cope with a baby? Does she honestly think I want to miss my finals because I'm sitting in a maternity ward? God, it's a nightmare."

The longing to deal him a mighty sock on the jaw, like Gary Cooper in a film, was so intense that it was almost erotic. Edward struggled to restrain his anger. "Presumably that wasn't quite the reaction she'd hoped for."

"No. She seemed to think I'd want to get married, or something." Tristan rubbed his eyes wearily. "Then she went cold on me. She said I didn't love her enough. I got scared, and started swearing I loved her, and I'd do any- thing for her. But it was too late. She said I was making her choose between me and the baby."

"And of course she chose the baby," Edward said. "You don't know her at all, do you? And she realized she didn't know you."

Tristan nodded. He began to cry. "She said she was an idiot to fall in love with me, because the man she loved had never really existed—she saw me properly now. And that was it. She went." Another sob shook him. He swiveled his chair around toward the desk, and buried his head in his arms.

Edward's mind was in a state of chaos. He looked for somewhere to sit. There was only the bed, heaped with damp folds of duvet. He sat down. "Where did she go?"

"I don't know." Tristan's voice was muffled. "If I knew, I'd be there, begging her to forgive me. I'd force myself to put up with the baby, if she'd just come back."

Edward ignored the part about begging forgiveness. He knew Rufa. This was something she would never forgive. Tristan was no longer dangerous. "Do you have any idea?"

"No."

"London. Of course." Edward sprang up, reaching for the phone on the desk. He punched in Wendy's number, learned by heart during his engagement.

Wendy answered, and was fluttered to hear him—he had never been able to get much sense out of the woman. Rose had probably been on the phone since dawn, telling the whole world that Rufa had bolted. He asked about her as neutrally as possible, and ended the call abruptly as soon as Wendy told him Rufa was not there.

Anxiety gnawed at him. Rufa was somewhere in the world, pregnant and alone. She had run away from her husband, she had been rejected by the father of her child. The fearful surrounding darkness had come to claim her at last. He had to find her.

In the meantime, here was Tristan, weeping in the burned-out ruins of his great passion. Edward found his anger had evaporated. Tristan would survive, because he was mourning something that was finished. It would never be finished for him, until he had rescued his runaway bride.

He touched Tristan's shoulder awkwardly. "Come on, think. Think of everything she ever said to you. Where would she go? Was she afraid I'd be angry?"

Tristan raised his head. "She was angry with you. You hurt her."

"Me? What the hell had I done?"

"You told Prudence about your sex life. Or rather, the inexplicable lack of it." Tristan was rallying, now that he had something to fling back at the wronged husband.

Edward exhaled heavily, reining in another spasm of fury. "And Prudence told you."

"Of course. What did you expect?"

Well, of course, Edward thought. He should have remembered not to trust Prudence with anything that could be used against him in the future. He should never have let her coax and flatter and flirt him into confiding in her. The temptation to confide in someone had overwhelmed him. Now Rufa would be thinking he had betrayed her; and she would be right.

"Every single man she's ever loved has let her down," he said. "God only knows what she's going through now."

Tristan sat up. "Edward—"

"Mm?"

"I'm sorry."

"You're apologizing to the wrong person. But I forgive you, anyway."

"Thanks." Tristan blew his nose, limp with relief. "And sorry about the car."

Edward almost laughed. The smashed car was ancient history, ridiculously irrelevant. Edward's main reaction at the time, hearing about the accident, had been exasperation. Since his return, he had thought of nothing except his smashed marriage. The fact that Tristan could mention the car in the same breath as the marriage was yet another painful reminder of his youth. "Doesn't matter. I'm glad you emerged in one piece."

They stared at each other uncertainly, testing the atmosphere.

"Thanks," Tristan whispered.

God, he looked so young. "Don't let all this mess up your work, Triss," Edward said, on an impulse. "You will get over it—it won't always feel this humiliating. One day you'll look back on it, and realize what a complete little shit you were. And then you'll probably write a novel." He rubbed Tristan's hair, affectionately and slightly contemptuously. "So put it all down to experience, is my advice." He left the room.

Clytie was hovering in the kitchen. She caught Edward as he struggled past the bicycles in the hall, laying her nail-bitten hand on his arm. "Please," she murmured, "please don't be too angry with him. I think his heart is broken."

Bitterly, Edward wondered what on earth this child knew about broken hearts.

Chapter Eleven

In Rufa's dream, The Zed called to her. She saw herself, sitting beside the window of her bedroom at Melismate. At the same time she could see The Zed in the downstairs sitting room, holding his head with his two hands. Rufa could not make the self in her dream get up to mend it, though she knew he needed her. She sat and sat; The Zed called and called.

She was suddenly awake, her face awash with tears. The woman on the other side of the little table eyed her sympathetically over the top of her copy of *Good Housekeeping*. Rufa straightened in her seat, and turned toward the window. Outside, the undulating gray fields—the standard view from any train window in England—were darkening in the dusk. She saw her pale, wild-haired reflection in the carriage window, superimposed upon the landscape. She turned away from it, to fish a tissue from the bag on the seat beside her.

"I kept an eye on it for you," the woman opposite said.

"Sorry?" It took Rufa a few seconds to realize she was being addressed.

"Your bag. You want to be careful, when you fall asleep."

"Thanks." Rufa sketched a smile.

The woman's lips twitched several times before she found an outlet for her curiosity. "I'm just popping to the buffet—can I get you a cup of tea? You don't look well."

Rufa dredged up a laugh, grimly thinking this must be the understatement of the year. "Oh, I'm fine—it's just—" The woman looked kind. Her face was made of pillowy, interlocking buns and upward curves. She was as motherly and comforting as Mrs. Noah. On impulse, testing the sound of it, she said, "I'm pregnant."

Here was a perfectly satisfying explanation—one that even covered sobbing on a train. The woman smiled, relieved.

"Morning sickness? Oh dear. Isn't it hell? A good cup of tea is just what you need, then." She stood up briskly, grabbing a businesslike handbag and smoothing her tweed skirt. "It always worked for me."

"I'd love one," Rufa said, grateful to be accepted as normal. "You're very kind."

"I remember how it feels."

Left alone, Rufa took off the smile, which was painful. She would bet this woman did not know how it felt to run away from a husband and a lover, carrying the lover's child. She thought how odd it was that she had cried for The Zed, when she had not yet shed a single tear over the wreckage of her hopes.

Calm enough, at last, to look over the smoking ruins, Rufa thought back to the beginning of her descent into nightmare-land. It had been gradual at first; though the signs had been there, if she had only had the sense to read them.

The dreamlike heat wave had ended overnight. The lovers had woken one morning to a solid downpour. Rufa, who needed only Tristan's presence to be completely whole and happy, had built a crackling log fire in the drawing room. And—incredibly—Tristan had not wanted to make love to her in front of it. Still more incredibly, he had announced that he was feeling "claustrophobic," and suggested they drive over to Melismate. He had refused to understand why this was out of the question. There had been a quarrel. Not a life-threatening row, but a scratchy, bickering, irritable quarrel—mostly on his side, since he had very quickly reduced her to tears. Alarmed, but also gratified, to find that he had this much power over her, Tristan had repented and consoled. They had renewed their lovers' vows naked, in front of the fire, as Rufa had wanted all along. Now, she wished she had paid attention to his inability to face the future, and admitted that it lay between them. At some level, she thought, I knew perfectly well what was happening.

The nightmares had begun again that night, while she slept in Tristan's arms in the cramped spare bed (her refusal to sleep with him in her own bed had been another thing he did not understand). She had dreamed that she knelt on the floor of the small sitting room at Melismate, sweeping the fragments of something precious into a dustpan. The voice of the unseen Zed had been around her, assuring her that she could fix it. Rufa, in her dream, had known this was something she could never fix. She had woken in tears, and, at the moment of awakening, had felt a pang of disappointment that Tristan was not Edward.

Tristan had been sweet, but his comforting was not up to the standard of Edward's. During Rufa's halting description of the dream, he had fallen asleep. At the time, she had reminded herself that he was young, and innocent of death—never having experienced death close to him, he could not see that it applied to him even remotely. She reproached herself, not Tristan. How could she have risked driving him away with these dismal specters from her subconscious?

Throughout the following (also rainy) day, she had made great efforts to keep the atmosphere as light as gossamer. She had coaxed and flirted, until Tristan had been unable to help falling back into enchantment. The magic bubble had been sealed again. She had stopped time, and pushed away all thought of Edward. But she had been moving toward a hope—really, little more than a fantasy—that Edward would forgive her, and allow her to start again. The prospect of life without Edward had started to seem seriously frightening.

On her last full day with Tristan, the sun had returned for a final bow. It was less hot this time, with a freshness that blew in the outside world. Tristan's ability to ignore the future was extraordinary, but even he had accepted that he must return to Oxford. They had taken last walks in their lovers' haunts, and he had suddenly panicked. He had begged Rufa to come with him, stay with him, live and die with him.

Wistfully, Rufa had wondered aloud if she ought to apply for a place at a college. Tristan had reacted with white blankness, giving her the buried message that he did not consider this a good idea, and she did not mention it again. She had been too moved by his appeal to spoil it.

The question was, would everything have been different if she had gone with him to Oxford? And would he have been less horrified by her pregnancy if they had discovered it together?

Useless to speculate, of course. At the time, she had thought it important to take formal leave of Edward, as if on her deathbed. Or as if asking for permission to desert him.

Perhaps, she thought now, I was hoping he would find a way to save me, and keep me.

Rufa and Tristan had both, in an agonized sort of way, enjoyed their *Brief Encounter* parting at the station. They had clung together, shedding delicious tears. Rufa still did not understand why she had wept on the phone to Edward later, pleading with him to come home. Those tears had not been delicious at all. They had sprung from a momentary terror of the surrounding blackness, and when Rufa was calm again, she had marveled at her own baffling behavior.

With Tristan gone, the clocks had started again. Rufa had distracted herself by catching up with the duller aspects of shopping (washing powder, bleach, J-cloths), which she had neglected during her idyll. At Boots she worked her way down each shelf methodically, filling her basket with toothpaste, shampoo, soap, and some attractive washcloths that were on special offer.

And then she had paused, as she always did, in front of the sanitary products. With her hand upon a packet of tampons she had found herself wondering—with a sudden freeze of panic—when she had last had a period. Normally, she marked the onset of each period in her diary.

The next few moments ran in her mind with the awful clarity of a film. She never would forget her stillness, as she had put down the basket, and taken her diary from her handbag. She had turned the pages back, gagging with panic, to find that she was nearly two and a half weeks late. Time did pass, apparently, even when you kidded yourself it was standing still. She had bought a pregnancy test, and struggled to take in the incredible, unreal fact that she was pregnant.

After that, there had been only one course of action open to her. She had decided that regrets for Edward were irrelevant because they had come far too late. For better or worse, she belonged now to Tristan—and that was all that had stopped her going out of her mind. She had felt such warmth, such love and joy about Tristan, and the beautiful child who would enter the world in the little house in Jericho. She had been awed by the vastness of the new love that opened out before her, when she thought about her baby.

Perhaps it would be a boy, to fill the vortex in her heart left by the death of The Zed.

The kind woman was swaying back up the aisle between the seats, carrying a small paper bag. Rufa found it restful to observe the comfy way she sat herself down and unpacked her searing plastic cups and tiny drums of milk.

"I got you two milks," the woman said, "because one is never enough. And a couple of ginger biscuits."

"Thanks so much, but I honestly don't think—"

"You might not think you fancy them," the woman interrupted firmly, "but the minute you get one down you, you'll feel heaps better."

Rufa smiled, pulling the cellophane packet toward her. "Did this work for you too?"

"When I was expecting my daughter, they were all that kept me from keeling over. I was teaching a class of eight-year-olds at the time, and I ate so many they used to call me Mrs. Gingernut."

Rufa politely took a sip of railway tea, and a bite of railway biscuit. To her surprise, they made her feel better. The giddy, weak feeling passed, and she felt ready to start thinking properly.

"Told you," said Mrs. Gingernut. Smiling and tactful, she picked up her magazine.

The windows were black mirrors, reflecting a cozy image of the lighted carriage. Rufa felt she now had nerve enough to start tackling the enormous mess she had made of her life since her marriage—since the death of The Zed. All roads wound back to that. She wondered where she had been; what had driven her to forget herself so drastically.

For Tristan to overlook the unromantic question of contraception was understandable, if not forgivable. He was young, and had assumed that she would take care of it. But, until now, Rufa had taken a serious pride in her perfectly ordered life. Nancy or Lydia might go out in laddered tights or chipped nail varnish; Rufa never. The Zed had been quite capable of arranging a picnic and forgetting the food, and Rufa had been the stage manager, contriving sandwiches behind the scenes. Rose, as a slip of a girl, had considered contraception an irrelevance. Rufa—who owed her existence to this foolishness—had always faintly scorned her mother for flinging herself straight into passion without thinking of the consequences. She was now ashamed.

What a starchy little cow I've been, she thought; fancying myself for virtuous self-control, and condemning the others for their weakness.

She could hardly bear to contemplate that previous self, so scrubbed and righteous. So blind, repressed, inhibited. She wanted to wipe herself right off the face of the earth. Facing them all would mean having that unbearable self reflected right back at her. She was not strong enough to have her nose rubbed in her sordid fall from grace.

When she ran away from Tristan's house, she had managed to get herself and her suitcase to Oxford Station and onto a London train. She had intended to take refuge at Wendy's. She had been on her way there, kneading her fingers in anguish in the back of a taxi, when she suddenly realized she could not face Nancy, Wendy, or Roshan. They would tell Edward, and Rose. It could not be endured—their eyes would strip her like acid. Impulsively, she had told the driver to take her to King's Cross; the only mainline station she could think of through the internal tempest.

At King's Cross she had stopped at W. H. Smith's, to buy a postcard and a book of stamps. She did not want people to worry too much—she would tell them where she was when she got there, and it would be very, very far away. She would have some time, before they caught up with her.

This train, to Edinburgh, had been on the point of leaving. Rufa thought Edinburgh had a sonorous, historical ring to it, which she liked. She remembered a dinner-party customer of hers, who had a house there. This amiable and well-connected lady might be a useful contact—she would need to work again. Her account was full of money at present, but it was Edward's money. He would be bound to stop her allowance now. And if he did not, Rufa would be obliged not to touch it. She would kill the pain with hard work, and atone for her stupidity by building a life for her baby. It was oddly comfortable to be worrying about work and money again.

The postcard was a photograph of Buckingham Palace, yellow as butter under a turquoise sky. Rufa spent a long time tapping her chin with the end of the pen, struggling to find the words that contained least of her stupid self. She wrote: "I am very sorry." (She thought of "Please don't hate me," but immediately rejected this as too whiny.) "Please tell everyone not to worry, I am fine. Love Rufa." She addressed the card to Nancy in Tufnell Park—Nancy being the least likely to judge her harshly.

The countryside was giving way to lighted buildings. A mass of lights and houses leaped up around them. The wheels dragged as they pulled into Durham. The kind woman in the opposite seat had pulled on her coat, and neatly stowed her belongings into various neat bags. She had been sitting, fully gloved, for the past half hour.

The train stopped, and she stood up. "Well, good-bye," she said, smiling. "Good luck."

Rufa held out the card. "If it's not too much trouble, could you possibly post this for me? It's got a stamp, and everything."

"Well, of course. No trouble at all."

"Thank you," Rufa said. The parting smile she gave the woman was not painful. She was reeling with euphoria, stunned by her own dastardly cunning. Nancy would receive a postcard from Durham, and they could search every corner of Durham without finding her. She would be invisible, in Edinburgh. For the first time in her life, nobody would know where she was. How frighteningly easy it was, she thought, to disappear.

Waverley Station was a maelstrom of lights and people. Rufa, a lonely speck in the crowd, considered what to do next. It was late. She was tired in a new way, to the core of her bones. She had an urgent longing to lie down—the baby was giving the orders now. Impressed by her own presence of mind, she accosted one of the guards and asked for the nearest hotel.

The man looked her up and down, taking in her Mulberry suitcase, her Prada handbag, the jewel on her wedding finger, and directed her to the Balmoral. Rufa found his accent a little hard to understand, but gathered she would not need a taxi. She hefted her case out into Princes Street. The Balmoral Hotel was impossible to miss. Fortunately, she was too exhausted to worry that its solid opulence was unsuitable for a Fallen Woman.

At the gleaming desk, she showed her gold credit card. She had no idea how to avoid giving them her real name, and signed in as Mrs. Reculver. How very lucky, she thought, that she had posted the card at Durham—it would surely be ages before anyone thought of checking hotels in Edinburgh.

The room was wondrously comfortable. The moment she had tipped the porter a pound and shut him out, Rufa shrugged off her coat and collapsed on the firm, fatly quilted double bed. The relief of it made her head swim. She devoutly hoped it was not going to be like this for the whole nine months. Tomorrow she would think about finding herself a flat. She would buy a local paper, and scour the job columns. She would phone Diana Carstairs-McSomething, informing her that she was available for dinner parties.

Her hand strayed to her stomach. She laid her palm over her flat belly. She closed her eyes. For the very first time she visualized a real baby, and was ambushed by a fierce, pagan joy that refused to take into account The Zed's death, Tristan's hideous inadequacy, or Edward's anger. The baby overrode them all. The soft little creature would nestle in her arms, and open its tender little mouth to her aching breast. She would feel its downy head against the crook of her arm, and it would make her strong enough to laugh at her misery, and the misery she had caused to all the others. She began to sing to it, with The Zed's voice in her mind, singing her to sleep in some lost, primeval era.

Chapter Twelve

Rufa had always heard Edinburgh described as a beautiful city. The view from her window the next morning was bleak and forbidding. Roofs and spires were clustered around the hem of the Castle Rock, with the gray Castle carved into its summit. In the foreground the statue of Sir Walter Scott sat in his Victorian gothic space rocket, gazing thoughtfully toward Holyrood. She could see the shops along one side of Princes Street, facing perished gardens and a railway line that ought to have been a river. Autumn had arrived here ages ago, unpacked its bags, and settled in permanently.

The radiator under the window was hot, and made her hair crackle, but the glass was cold. The people in the street below wore thick coats, and bent their heads against the wind. Rufa put on her cream cashmere sweater, soft and warm as an embrace, and went down to breakfast.

She was still tired, but the sickness had receded. She ate porridge, bacon, eggs, a sausage, and two racks of toast. The waitress looked surprised, and Rufa did not blame her—she was surprised herself. These attacks of giddy hunger had started before she knew she was pregnant. You just had to hurl food at them, by the bucketload.

Once her stomach was full, she could think more rationally. She had been amazingly silly yesterday, going through that pantomime with the postcard from Durham. Edward would know exactly where she was as soon as he saw her credit-card statement. If she were serious about hiding, she would have to take out a big wedge of cash, and live anonymously on that until she found work. The priority was a flat. Rufa had never rented a flat, and had no idea how you went about it. Timidly, she asked the young woman at Reception.

She could see that the girl was puzzled by her urgency—why would this cashmere-clad Englishwoman want a cheap flat in a hurry? The girl gave her a local newspaper, in which there was a page of advertisements for letting agencies. Rufa chose the agency with the largest advertisement, and ordered a taxi. She returned to her room. In the gleaming white bathroom, she plaited her hair. She applied a light shield of makeup. Her lipstick tasted of soap, and she had to swallow several times to subdue the queasiness. These attacks could be handled, with enough strength of mind. She had only lost control once, at Tristan's.

It was like remembering a terrible dream. Quite apart from the pain, there had been the humiliation of looking such a fool—turning up on the doorstep with a suitcase and a smile, ridiculously sure of her welcome. Tristan had opened the door to her. For a noticeable moment, he had looked more shocked than pleased. A second later, they had fallen into each other's arms.

He had murmured: "It's been agony—I've been longing for you—out of my mind with wanting you—"

In the kitchen, he had proudly introduced her to a girl eating cornflakes. "She's here! It's Rufa!"

The sweet-faced girl had, evidently, heard amazing things about Rufa. With a gleeful show of tact, she had taken her cornflakes out of the room. Tristan had kissed Rufa again, his hand caressing her thigh. Rufa sighed and arched against him, but noticed that her body was not responding to him in the usual way; possibly because of the eternal and unromantic queasiness. The private language of their intimacy did not contain a word for queasiness.

And then Tristan had asked, "So what are you doing in Oxford? How long can you stay?" That was the first sign of the distance between them. Foreboding had pinched at Rufa's heart. He had left her with the whole, heavy task of explaining that she had come to Oxford because it was the only place left to her, and she would be staying indefinitely.

Rufa began to tidy the hotel bathroom, neatly folding towels and laying out her small, immaculate collection of Chanel cosmetics. There was, unfortunately, no easy way to tell a man he had made you pregnant. In old films, the man always reacted with clumsy, endearing tenderness: fussing rather comically and making his wife sit down. Tristan's reaction had been blank disbelief, growing into horror.

After that, it had all come crashing down around her with terrifying speed. The man she adored changed before her eyes, into a cold stranger she did not recognize. He had mentioned clinics, and friends who had used them. He had been relieved to hear that Edward did not know.

"Thank fuck for that—if we're quick enough, he'll never find out."

That was the point at which her stomach had risen in protest. Everything had gone misty. She had gasped that she was going to be sick, and Tristan had roughly pushed her to a terrible lavatory stained like a smoker's teeth. She had vomited copiously, feeling she was throwing up every hope and dream, every fantasy and illusion.

The housemate had been kind. She had heard the sound of retching, and run downstairs to make Rufa peppermint tea. Her kindness had only underscored the fact that Tristan was not being kind at all. He had been stiff and defensive, as if she had done him an injury.

Perhaps I had, Rufa thought now. He was too young to cope with any of this. Her miraculous, gilded youth had turned out to be a scared, selfish boy. Everything he said had hammered home the realization that the great passion was dead. He expected her to kill their child.

"You shouldn't think of it in such emotional terms," he had said. "It's not a child, it's a cluster of cells."

Rufa counted the cash left in her purse, thinking that Tristan had not been entirely without heart, and that this had made the pain worse. The moment he sensed her love had died, he had wept and begged her not to reject him. By then it had been far too late. Rufa, through her anguish, had understood that there was to be no support, no rescue. Though she had not expected this—would have died if she had foreseen it—she was alone. It was a fiendishly appropriate punishment for the inventor of the Marrying Game. The booby prize, the Single Mother Game.

The telephone beside the bed rang. Rufa jumped, and backed nervously against the wall. She picked it up with a shaking hand. "Yes?"

It was not Edward. It was the girl at Reception, telling her the taxi had arrived. Rufa was ashamed of her disappointment. How stupid to be disappointed that it was not her furious, mistreated husband. She must learn to be independent; to get by on her own without running to Edward every five minutes. It was going to be a hard habit to break.

Outside the hotel, the wind pounced on her like a tiger, stinging her eyes.

The air smelled of burned toast, edged with the aftertaste of an acidic belch. The taxi carried her through streets of unrelenting gray stone and small windows staring in high, blank walls. There was not one shred, one sprout of green. No trees, no parks, no window boxes. No tufts of grass clinging to cracks in walls, no moss bubbling up between the paving stones. Nature was powerless against the stones. The sterile chill of the city made her ache for the fat fields at home.

The letting agency was an office, in a depressing row of shops. Anxious-looking people waited on orange plastic chairs. There was a long counter, a line of scuffed filing cabinets, and several elderly computers. Phones shrilled continually. Rufa found that nobody was interested in hearing what kind of flat she wanted. Once she had mentioned her price limit, she was handed a sheaf of typed papers.

She sank into a chair to study them. She had decided that she needed a small garden flat, in a quiet area not too far out of town—when she started doing dinners again, she would need to be central, especially when the baby came. Her spirits plummeted when she read the descriptions of flats available. They seemed fantastically expensive, and, though she did not know Edinburgh, were obviously ghastly.

She took the papers back to the counter. "I'm awfully sorry, but these all seem to be shared. I was looking for something self-contained."

The woman at the counter looked (or Rufa imagined she looked) scornful. "You'll need to pay more, I'm afraid."

"How much? Never mind. Could you show me some details, please? I don't need more than one bedroom, but I would like my own kitchen and bathroom."

The woman turned her back before Rufa had finished stammering out her wish list. She yanked open a filing cabinet, and pulled out another sheaf of papers.

Rufa returned to her chair. She was glad she was sitting down when she saw the prices. Ye gods, could flats in this grim fortress of a city really cost this much? The cheapest place was in the North Bridge area, supposedly near Arthur's Seat. Rufa had seen pictures of Arthur's Seat, set in a sweep of green, and vaguely imagined somewhere like the outskirts of Cheltenham. It might be just about bearable—she was aware that she had been, by most people's standards, outrageously spoiled. The lady of the manor would have to adjust her ideas downward, as part of the price of her shame.

She asked to see the flat, and the woman at the counter gave her an address.

When she got there, she was to contact a Mrs. Ritchie on the ground floor. Rufa hailed another taxi. It rattled her through flinty, dreary gray streets, and stopped in the dreariest. She asked the driver to wait.

There were no bells outside the house. She pushed open the heavy door, and found herself in a dark communal hall, painted in a shade of bottle green that reminded her depressingly of her old games kit at Saint Hildegard's. There were warring smells of cooking and disinfectant. On the wall at the bottom of the stairs was a faded wooden plank, on which was painted STAIR ROTA. A disc hung from a peg, with the figure 2 peeling away into obscurity.

Rufa rang the bell on the nearest door. Mrs. Ritchie answered it. She was a pleasant young woman. She was chewing, and a radio chattered behind her. Rufa fought back a piercing, urgent pang of hunger. Mrs. Ritchie led her up echoing brown stairs. Over her shoulder, she cheerfully explained the wooden plank. English people, she said, were sometimes surprised to learn that, in Scottish flats, everyone was expected to clean the stairs and hallways once every six weeks.

Rufa had already decided there were far too many brown stairs, and was appalled at the prospect of cleaning them. The flat was small and incredibly nasty and reeked of damp. She could not possibly live here without killing herself. She could not think of bringing her baby into the world in a place like this.

Faint and dispirited, she returned to the letting agency. This time, the woman at the counter looked at her more closely. If Rufa was prepared to take a short-term let of three months only, she said, she had something that might be more her style. The rent she mentioned was enormous, but just about manageable. Rufa knew it was expensive and impractical, but no longer cared. If the place was halfway decent, she would be buying herself three whole months of not having to face them all at home.

The flat was in a four-hundred-year-old court off the Royal Mile, fifty yards below the Castle. The walls were three feet thick, and it was as cold as a dungeon in the Bastille. It had a kitchen, bedroom, and bathroom, all tiny. The only nearby shops sold nothing but tartan key rings and Monarch of the Glen T-shirts. In her first week, Rufa was woken three times by twenty-one-gun salutes up at the Castle.

She liked being near the Castle. Its stony solidity made her feel safe. The sentries said good-night when she wandered past them. Sometimes she walked past on purpose, just to hear a friendly voice. She was desperately unhappy. I might have known, she thought, that Edward only meant to give me the money—not himself.

He belonged, in that sense, to Prudence. He was heavily embroiled in an ancient relationship, and had not felt he had the right to have a full marriage with his legal wife. She now knew why their single night of sex had felt vaguely illicit—Edward had felt he was committing adultery. She hated herself for her stupidity. She hated herself for throwing such a tantrum about Melismate that Edward had felt compelled to rescue her.

She stayed in the flat until she could not bear the cold and the silence, then went for long walks through the steep streets of the blackened, beautiful, monumental Old Town.

She could not help spending Edward's money, though she tried to pay for everything in cash to make herself harder to find. The only certainty she clung to in the chaos was that she did not want to be found. It was not just a matter of her pride. She felt the pain she had inflicted upon Edward as a dagger in her own heart.

She was very tired, and could have slept all day. Merely keeping herself washed and ironed was a huge effort. Little by little, however, she began to drag herself out of the slough. Diana Carstairs-McInglis, the kind hostess for whom she had cooked in London, would not be visiting her Georgian house in the New Town until next spring, but she had promised to recommend Rufa to her Edinburgh friends. One of these telephoned soon afterward, to engage Rufa for a large dinner party. She lived in a castle about an hour's drive from the city, but offered to provide transport. She also told Rufa where to buy the best ingredients, though most of the menu would be meat, fish, and game from her estate.

Work proved to be the best medicine. Rufa spent a frantic day in the antiquated castle kitchen, and slept all the way home in the car. But her cooking was a success, and she rediscovered her delight in producing perfect food. She could see the point of Scotland, when she felt the quality of the beef and the salmon. Her employer had hung the grouse (as she proudly told Rufa) until the maggots had eaten through the necks and she found them on the pantry floor. Rufa threw up twice while plucking the birds and picking out the lead shot, but the result was a miracle of tenderness and flavor. She could still cook and she could still earn money. She had to earn more. She had been born owing the rest of the world a living.

There would be more dinner parties in the weeks before Christmas. Rufa could not think about Christmas. The longing for Melismate bit deeper every day. As she paced the streets, or the parquet floors of the warm National Gallery of Scotland, she mentally rehearsed phone calls to Nancy. She never made them. Nancy would make her come home, to face the awfulness of what she had done. She did not see how she could return as the old Rufa. They were all better off without her—Edward certainly was, though she was half ashamed of how cruelly she missed him. The baby, growing steadily inside her, gave her courage. There were days when she was strong enough to fight the whole world for the sake of her child. She began to promise herself that she would go home when the baby was born. It would be a kind of passport back into their good graces, she thought. They'll have to forgive me when I've got a baby.

One of her walks took her down some steps to a narrow street full of arty junk shops and boutiques. There was a café where she sometimes had a cup of tea: a noisy, youthful place, where the students from the university sat for hours. Rufa watched them, marveling at how green they were. Had Tristan really been this young when she fell in love with him?

I was pretending to be as young as he was, she thought; maybe I was trying to have the youth I missed.

The café put a notice in its steamy window for a cook. Rufa could not overlook a possibility of regular money. She applied for the job, giving Diana Carstairs-McInglis as a reference. After one exhausting night's trial she was hired, to make mountains of stovies (a delicious mess of mince, onion, and potato) for the students. The work was hard and hot, and swelled her feet. Her free days could only be spent lying on the short sofa at her flat, reading tatty classics from a secondhand bookshop in the Grassmarket. But hard work dulled her senses and pushed the hours past. It gave meaning and shape to the days. She became friendly with Amy, the energetic middle-aged woman who owned the café. There were people around her. She began to hate herself a little less.

Knives tore at her innards. Rufa was aware of the pain before she was aware of being awake. Stupid with sleep, she told herself this was the worst period pain she had ever known.

Except that it couldn't be.

She fumbled for the light. Blood was pooling on the sheet underneath her. She stared at it for ages, refusing to accept what she saw. The knives twisted, intensifying the pain. Rufa broke out in animal howls of despair.

She had not been good enough. She was still being punished. She was suspended on the very edge of the world, with no more reason to exist.

Chapter Thirteen

thought of taking out the wall between the kitchen and the scullery," Polly said. "To make one big, warm room—rather like the kitchen at Melismate, though tidier, obviously. It's the spirit of the place I want to re-create."

She came to Ran's side of the table bearing her white everyday Wedgwood coffeepot, and poured fragrant dark coffee into his deep cup of steaming milk. He grunted absently, turning a page of the *Guardian* with tremendous flapping that knocked a piece of toast onto the floor. He did not notice. Ran was incapable of doing more than one thing at a time, and reading the *Guardian* took all his concentration.

Polly stooped to pick up the toast. Rome—as she had to keep reminding herself—was not built in a day. Ran was oblivious to his surroundings, and the progress of her great renovation was painfully slow, but changes had been made. She allowed herself to feel optimistic. His squalid kitchen was, at least, clean. The table had been scrubbed, there were new chairs, china, and pans. Polly had wrestled the ancient Aga into submission, and it was gently diffusing warmth against the inconveniently bitter November chill. She must remember to light fires for tonight in plenty of time. Country people were used to freezing, thank God. Being able to see your breath over dinner was not the social doom it would have been in London.

She went on, in the deliberately sunny, positive tone she adopted when Ran needed chivvying, "And while we're about it, we really should get rid of the wall between the sitting room and what you sweetly call the parlor."

Ran, intent on his newspaper, blindly gulped coffee, and dug the end of his silver teaspoon into one ear.

"It must have been a proper drawing room once," Polly said. "The proportions will be lovely. I'm aiming for lots of light, which is the great asset of a typically early Georgian house like this." She sighed. "I do wish I had a magic wand, and I could make it ready for tonight. I've done my best, but this is still a hostess's nightmare. The state of the downstairs cloakroom cries out to heaven. That's another thing I'm going to fix before winter sets in." She sat down opposite him, folding her hands expectantly on the table.

Ran glanced across at her. "Hmmm?"

"I'm talking about the downstairs lav."

"Oh. Is it blocked again?"

Polly let out another sigh. "It needs a new sink, new lav, new door—and some of that gorgeous dark green paint John Oliver does. And I have to decide if eighteenth-century hunting prints are a classic, or a cliché."

The fog of incomprehension was clearing from Ran's dark eyes. "Hang on, Poll—this is all going to cost a bloody fortune."

She smiled, pouring coffee, enjoying the picture of serenity she made. "I know it's a huge project, but I don't want to do it in stages. I might ask Bickerstaff's to take it on. They're expensive, but worth it—that's what poor Rufa told me, only a matter of days before she vamoosed."

Ran was not ready to move on to the topic of Rufa. "It's going to cost a fortune, though," he repeated. There was that stubborn glint in his lustrous eyes.

Polly made her voice caressing. "Oh, darling, you don't have to worry about that. I'm not Christina Onassis, but one is moderately well-heeled. I can certainly afford to make a few more improvements here—I think of it as an investment in the future."

"But that's your money," Ran said. "I can't let you spend your money on my house."

Polly murmured, "Our money, surely. Our house."

His perfect brows drew together ominously. "If you want the truth, I don't fancy any more changes. I like it as it is."

"Now you're being silly." This was seriously vexing. Keeping her voice light and reasonable was an effort. "You can't possibly like all this chaos."

"I need the parlor for my meditation."

"You can meditate in the new drawing room."

"Why do you want to knock all my walls down?" Ran was plaintive. "This is my home!"

Polly's wedding dress was still hanging, in its protective blue body bag, on the back of the door. She did not think she needed to point out the obvious fact that it was her home too. She smiled into his heavenly eyes. "Sweetheart, I'm not trying to destroy your home, honestly. I know I harp on about redecorating. I was only getting flurried about tonight."

"Tonight?" Ran echoed innocently.

She let out a peal of indulgent laughter. "You've forgotten, haven't you? It's my dinner party for Hugo and Justine, and Hugo's parents."

"Oh. Right."

"I will admit, I do get into a state when I'm entertaining. I haven't cooked properly for such a long time—I'd love to have hired poor Rufa again, if only she hadn't married money and then eloped with her lover, and given up cooking. I don't know anyone else I could trust with those pheasants."

Ran folded his newspaper. With the expression of a man facing a firing squad, he said, "The thing is—I'm really sorry—but I won't be here."

Silence settled around them. The blood slowly drained from Polly's lips, leaving them white and compressed with unbelieving fury. This dinner party was meant to be her introduction to the local gentry. It was essential, when living in the country, to make oneself known to the right neighbors; something Ran's late father had never bothered to do. Hugo's parents were prominent among the squirearchy on this side of Gloucestershire. She had been fretting about the menu for weeks—how dared Ran act as if he did not know about it?

"Of course you'll be here," she said. "Where else would you be?"

He looked unhappy. "The thing is, it's November the fifth."

"And—?"

"Sorry I forgot to tell you, but Nancy's invited a few people over for a firework party."

Bloody Nancy, Polly thought wrathfully; why can't she just go back to London? "Well, she'll understand if you say you can't come."

"I have to be there," Ran said. "I promised Linnet."

"But you were over there two days ago, for her birthday. I do think you might pay some attention to me, for a change." Polly paused; it was never a good idea to whine. "After all, I did go all the way to London for that pink bicycle."

"No, I can't let them down," Ran said solemnly. "Nancy arranged the party specially, to cheer Linnet up."

"She seemed perfectly cheerful to me."

"She misses Rufa."

"For God's sake," Polly snapped. "You're always rushing over to Melismate. You practically live there. I wish you'd just accept that you don't belong to the Hastys anymore. Hanging around them just makes you look stupid."

"I'd rather hang around the Hastys than that berk Hugo," Ran said hotly.

"Oh, I know what this is really about—it's your obsession with Lydia again."

"I'm not obsessed!" This was his tenderest place.

"Just because she's joined a choir and got herself a life—"

"This is not about Liddy, all right?"

"I suppose I'll have to settle for a compromise," Polly said icily. "My mother always says that's the essence of a good marriage. Since you've made the arrangement, you'd better show your face for the first bit of the party—presumably it'll be early, because of Linnet. But you'll have to leave at seven at the latest. And please don't put on your new suit until you get back."

"I'm not coming back," Ran said, with an unfamiliar steeliness. "I'm staying for the whole party. I've bought sparklers."

"You're coming back at seven!" Polly was fierce. "I've invited the D'Alamberts to meet us as a couple. I've told them unofficially about the wedding. If you're not here, it will look ghastly."

"What fucking wedding?" Ran shouted. "I wish you'd told me about it, while you were spreading the news far and wide! When did I agree?"

She stood up, holding herself rigidly to control the shivers of rage. "Every time I do something you don't like, you try to ruin it by pretending we're not getting married. It's pathetically childish. Why else would I be spending all this money?"

"I've told you—I don't want your fucking money!"

"How very high-minded and noble of you. I'm expecting you here at seven. If you're one minute late, you can sleep on the sofa." Polly had been working toward sweeping majestically from the room, underlining the final threat with a smart slam of the door.

Ran confounded her by suddenly erupting from his chair, scattering slices of toast. "I'll come back when I feel like it! This evening belongs to Linnet—you're always trying to come between us!"

He stormed from the room, slamming the door so hard that Polly's wedding dress leaped in its blue plastic shroud.

Nancy carried the plate of sausage rolls out to the old stableyard, where Roger had built the bonfire. The fire was now a ten-foot wall of orange and scarlet flame, cracking out sparks like sniper's bullets. A lavish buffet was laid out on the kitchen table. Drinks and snacks were circulating. Everything seemed to be going well, though Nancy still had her doubts. Quite apart from the awkwardness of everyone for miles around knowing about Rufa, she had never taken sole responsibility for a party before.

She halted for a moment, missing Rufa so intensely that tears rushed to her eyes. Since Edward had brought back the news from Oxford, Nancy had shed rivers of tears. Where on earth had the silly mare hidden herself? Rose had protested that she was bound to turn up in a few days, but Nancy knew her sister better. Rufa could be horribly stubborn. She felt shame far more acutely than anyone else in her family—she would never face them until she could face herself. She would die before she came home.

Nancy had spent a night in the wine bar sobbing into Roshan's shoulder, picturing Rufa alone and in despair. She had fled back to Melismate, and insisted upon calling the police. Rufa was an adult, however, and there was nothing much the police could do. Their only hope was Edward. A week or so after the postcard from Durham, Edward had opened Rufa's credit-card statement, and discovered she was in Edinburgh. He was searching for her now, and he would let them know the second he saw her. Nancy loved him for loving Rufa. She did not see how she could have endured the anxiety, if Edward had not been on the case.

This party was an attempt to cast out fear. They were all frightened by the chasm in the family. The Zed had always responded to adversity by throwing a party, and it was his spirit they were trying to invoke. Nancy had been shocked by the amount of labor involved—the phoning, the endless shopping, the slicing, buttering, and general setting-out. Rufa had been the one who dealt with all this, somehow managing to look as if she were enjoying herself at the same time. She was a worker of miracles, a maker of magic.

But this is my party, Nancy thought; I have to do things in my own style.

Rose was wandering around the groups of guests, refilling wineglasses. Lydia and Selena had risen to the occasion magnificently. Nancy was intrigued by the changes she had found in her sisters on this visit home, and could not stop wondering whether they would have happened anyway, if Ru had not vanished. Selena, last seen sloping moodily off to photo shoots, had amazed Nancy by meeting her at the station in a neat white Golf. Since her return to Melismate she had passed her driving test, and now drove herself and Linnet to school. For the supper this evening, she had made an impressive venison casserole. She was young enough to wipe out the nightmare year, and revert to being an ornament to Saint Hildy's, almost as if The Zed had not died.

Lydia had been another revelation. She was as pastel-shaded and as gentle as ever, but no longer so soft that she was running off the plate. Her excellent cooking had made the supper possible—she had produced gingerbread men, complicated salads, baked potatoes, and vegetarian hot dogs.

"Stop thanking me," she had said earlier. "Consider this as your reward for cheering up Linnet. She hasn't let you speak in your own voice for days."

"Listen, I'd happily speak like Egbert Ressany for the rest of my life if I thought it would cheer Linnet up." It had cut Nancy to the heart to find Linnet sobbing every night for Rufa, and asking why she did not phone. She had dredged up all her storytelling powers to invent mad adventures for the Ressany Brothers, and fantastic narratives about Rufa's mythical life in Scotland, full of ingenious reasons why she had not been in touch. Nancy did not like Rufa becoming a fictional character, but Lydia swore Linnet was happier.

Watching Linnet now, Nancy decided the party had been a brilliant distraction. She had asked Terry and Sandra Poulter, who worked for Edward, and had a child in Linnet's class at the village school. Another child, from the same class, had been brought by two of Lydia's friends from the choir. Nancy smiled at the three small girls, silhouetted against the flames, quivering with glee like hummingbirds.

How long is it, she wondered, since nice, normal people like this came to Melismate parties? Selena had asked two friends from Saint Hildy's Oxbridge class. Nancy and Rose had been amused by their tidiness and respectability. Their names were Laura and Clarissa, and they were about a million miles away from the studded Neanderthals Selena had hung out with last year. With sparklers in their hands, they were as childlike as the smaller children. They wore wholesome woolly gloves, and had glossy hair. Selena was trying to write her name on the air. Her warm, laughing breath made a wreath around her head in the freezing night.

If I half-close my eyes, Nancy thought, I can nearly see him. She suddenly knew how The Zed would have approved of all this, as if he were standing at her elbow telling her so.

Lydia had made mulled wine, to The Zed's old recipe, in the battered tea urn he had rescued from a dustbin outside the church hall. She looked charming, in new jeans and an oversized scarlet sweater. She had invited a dozen people from the Cotswold Chorus, and was listening to the conductor, Phil Harding, with a rapt and radiant face.

"Look at him," Ran's voice said bitterly, next to Nancy's ear. "Smarming all over her."

"Have a sausage roll," Nancy said, thrusting the plate at him.

"Are they organic?"

"Of course not." She pulled the plate back. "Do stop glowering, Ran."

"He fancies her—it's disgustingly obvious."

"He's allowed to fancy her."

Almost to himself, Ran muttered, "No he's *not*."

"And I can't help thinking she rather fancies him."

Ran scowled. "He's just taking advantage of her."

"Go and light some fireworks for Linnet," Nancy said. "Isn't that why you came?"

"I'm not letting that mimsy singing bastard out of my sight!"

Nancy laughed, kindly but scornfully. "God, you've got a nerve. If you're that jealous, you'd better start thinking how to win her back, before it occurs to the mimsy singer to marry her."

"I just might."

"And how would your financier like that?"

Ran scowled. "Polly's not my fiancée."

"I didn't say fiancée—you heard me. Where is she, by the way?"

"At home. She has some friends over."

"Oh—how nice of her to let you come here. Why don't you circulate, instead of standing on Liddy's shoulder with a scythe and an hourglass?"

"I don't want to."

"Well, actually Ran, I don't care what you want." Nancy lowered her voice. "You were invited to please Linnet. So go and please her."

"I can't sully her with my anger."

"Then sully yourself, by pretending not to be angry. I do wish you'd pull yourself together—just for this evening would do."

Nancy left him scowling, and took her sausage rolls to the lively group around Lydia. It had to be admitted, The Zed would have laughed at some of these choir people—so clean, so polite, so crashingly harmless. Lydia, however, seemed entirely at ease among them. She stood close to Phil Harding, joining in the spotless gossip and lame musical jokes. Well, why not? Nancy was ashamed of her sneering reflex. Left to herself, Lydia evidently preferred unoriginal niceness to The Zed's alarming bohemianism. It was strange, Nancy thought, how they were all beginning to seek out their real selves, outside the shadow he had cast.

Lydia broke away from her group to pour out a mug of mulled wine, which she handed to Nancy. "Go on—you haven't had a single drink yet."

"Thanks, darling. Is it going well, do you think?"

"Wonderfully. You're a complete genius."

"At least they've all stopped standing about in silence."

"Everyone's having a fantastic time." Lydia poured another mug of wine. "Would you mind taking some over to Ran? He'll only get upset if I do it."

"Okay. Let's avoid a scene, at all costs."

They both looked at Ran, standing with his arms folded, glaring at Phil Harding. Nancy tried not to find it hilarious that he should consider the bald choirmaster a serious rival. "He's fallen out with Waltzing Matilda, hasn't he? I know the signs."

"What signs?"

"Well, he's still in the sulking stage at the moment," Nancy said, making a point of not lowering her voice. "This will gradually soften into melancholy. By my calculation, he should be bursting into tears at about half past eight."

"Cow. Don't be so mean."

"Ha! You're laughing!" Nancy pointed accusingly at her sister. To the obvious annoyance of Ran, they both began to giggle.

"He hates seeing me with my own friends," Lydia murmured. "When we were married, we always had to hang out with people he chose—joss-sticky people, who liked sitting on the floor and saying Om. He finds the friends I make for myself too threatening." Her face was full of tender affection for her ex-husband.

"Liddy," Nancy said sternly, "tell me you're not making him jealous on purpose."

Lydia smiled. "Course I am."

"Why bother? Why pay any attention to him at all?" Even as she asked, Nancy knew these were pointless questions. Her foolish sister, besotted with Ran since the year dot, had aimed her transformation entirely at him, with a single-mindedness you could only gasp at. Why did Liddy think she could handle him now? Did she imagine he would change?

Nancy took the mulled wine across to Ran. "This should lighten you up."

Ran muttered, "I'm not sulking. How typical of you not to acknowledge real pain."

"Bollocks," Nancy said, thinking this was the only reply he deserved. What was it with the Hasty girls and men? Rufa had practically arranged her own marriage of convenience, only to break her heart over Tristan. Lydia had stubbornly attached herself to the Village Idiot. Nancy herself had fallen in love with the one decent man to come their way—and Berry was in Frankfurt. Selena was their only hope, or they would all end their days as cranky old leftovers. She took the empty plate back to the kitchen, full of warmth and light after the gunpowdery darkness outside. Selena's massive crock of venison stew was keeping warm on the hot plate of the range. Nancy removed a tray of sizzling cocktail sausages from the oven.

The telephone rang. She reached for the receiver. "Hello?"

"Is that Nancy?" It was the voice of Polly, clipped and wrathful. "I'd like to speak to Ran, please. Is he still there?"

"Hi, Polly—yes, he's still here."

"May I speak to him?"

"He's outside, and it's a bit of a trek," Nancy said. With her free hand, she tipped the sausages into a bowl. "Shall I ask him to call you back?"

"Actually, I have to speak to him now. Urgently. Could you fetch him?"

"Well, if you don't mind waiting—sorry you couldn't come, by the way. It's going famously."

"You were very kind to ask me," Polly snapped. "Unfortunately, we're giving a dinner party. Ran seems to have forgotten the time."

"Silly old him." Nancy tried—not very hard—not to laugh. "I'll get him."

Taking her time, because she really could not resist keeping the Secret Australian chafing, Nancy sauntered back to the yard. Ran stood in the same belligerent attitude, a little closer to the group of choir people.

"Ran, darling, your financier's on the phone."

"Oh."

"Apparently you're expected at a dinner party."

"I hate her dinner parties," Ran said. "Tell her I'm not coming."

"Tell her yourself. I'm far too busy to get involved in your sordid domestic wrangles."

He suddenly clutched at her hand, his black eyes pleading. "Don't you understand? If I turn my back for a second—look at her!—rubbing herself against him!"

Nancy gently disengaged her hand. "That's rich, considering you've rubbed yourself against half the female population of Gloucestershire."

"Please, Nance—just tell Polly I'll be along later."

She laughed. "All right, but I somehow doubt she'll keep anything warm for you."

"I know I'm in deep shit, and I don't care. Please!"

"I said all right." Only slightly ashamed of herself for relishing the job, Nancy returned to the kitchen and took the phone. "Hello, Polly?"

"At last!" Polly hissed. In the background, Nancy heard clinking glassware and well-bred laughter. "Is he on his way? It's past eight o'clock—the guests are here—push him into his car and send him over, before I go insane!"

"Sorry, he won't come to the phone. He says he'll be along later."

"Later! What the hell does that mean?"

"I really do have to go, Polly, if you'll excuse me—duties of a hostess, and all that. Bye!" Nancy hung up. She found that she felt mildly sorry for the redoubtable bossyboots. Polly had burned all her boats, only to discover that Ran was not nearly as malleable as he seemed. For the sake of this idiot, she had voluntarily given up Berry, the best man in the entire world. There was some comfort in the knowledge that even people who considered themselves experts at the Marrying Game could fall on their fannies at the last hurdle.

❀ ❀ ❀

"Liddy—" Ran plucked urgently at her scarlet sleeve. "For the love of God, I have to talk to you!"

"In a minute," Lydia said. "Have you had something to eat?"

"No. I don't want anything."

"Are you sure? The stew's delicious."

"How long are you going to keep this up? Oh, please!"

The kitchen was packed. Lydia, Selena, and Nancy had just finished a production line of plates. Roger was making a dozen mugs of tea. Rose, her eyes glazed with elation, darted from group to group refilling glasses. There was a solid roar of conversation.

"I can't just walk away," Lydia said reasonably. "I ought to keep an eye on the girls, and make sure they eat something besides chocolate fudge." Her sweet, three-cornered smile lit up her delicate face as she looked over at Linnet and her two friends, sitting around Linnet's miniature table on tiny chairs. The Ressany Brothers, who normally dined with Linnet, had been relegated to the dresser. The girls were streaked with soot, giggling wildly, and shrieking witticisms that contained the word *bum*.

"They're fine," Ran said. "Please, Liddy—I really need to talk to you."

The moment had arrived. Lydia felt surprisingly comfortable and calm. Ran was, at last, beginning to see that her transformation was more than skin-deep. She had put herself through a painful course of thinking. To put it crudely, she had tested the market and ascertained her true worth. Ran did not know she had already turned down poor Phil Harding—worth ten of her ex-husband, by anybody's reckoning. Yelling at Polly, on the humiliating afternoon of the Hotel Dinnerware, had crystallized something in Lydia's mind. It had shown her how low she had fallen. She had seen herself with the eyes of a stranger—a tattered, soggy little loser. How could a man as simpleminded as Ran desire such a pathetic creature? She had decided then to take a turn at playing the Marrying Game by giving the loathsome Polly a run for her money. It was worth an effort, when so much happiness was at stake.

She asked, "Can't we talk in here?"

"No!"

"Well, okay." There were people in the kitchen, the drawing room, and the Great Hall. "We'd better go upstairs. Make it quick, though." She led him up the uneven wooden staircase. "I don't mind missing the next lot of fireworks, but we'll be singing straight afterward."

Ran hurried to keep up with her. "Singing?"

"We've been practicing some madrigals."

"Hmm—I suppose that was Baldy's idea."

"No," Lydia said serenely, "it was mine. I'm sure you'd prefer some ritual chanting from the rain forest, but I love singing madrigals. Phil says the acoustic in the Hall is perfect." She stepped into her bedroom, flicking on the lamps. "So talk."

Ran was bewildered. He had not been inside Lydia's bedroom since long before the renovation of Melismate. Unconsciously, he had expected the familiar peeling walls and heaps of frayed clothes. He was unprepared for this charming, chintzy, lamplit boudoir.

"I don't know you anymore," he said plaintively. "What's happened to you?"

"Nothing. I was always like this, if you'd ever bothered to find out. I like beautiful music and nice things. I like getting up in the mornings at a reasonable time, and sending Linnet to school in decent clothes."

Ran paced distractedly across the polished boards and flowered rugs. "You never liked all that stuff when you lived with me."

"I loved you enough to put up with not having it."

"Possessions? Since when were you into possessions?"

"Well, it's not just that," Lydia said. "It's not things, exactly. It's having the same standards as other people."

"Stop it," Ran said wretchedly. "You sound like Poll."

"She's taught me a lot, actually. She doesn't wait for permission."

"This isn't you!" There were lines appearing on his beautiful face, and threads of gray at his temples. Like The Zed, he could not fight time. Every year, he became slightly less flawless.

Lydia had made a firm and conscious decision not to let him turn into The Zed. She sat down on the bed. "I'm sorry you don't like all the changes. But you don't have any right to object to them."

"I do when they affect my daughter," Ran said.

Lydia had been expecting this line of reasoning, and was prepared. "Linnet's never been better," she said calmly. "She's settled and secure. She's making proper friends at school, instead of being treated as a peculiar little outcast. If you're thinking of criticizing the way I'm bringing her up, fuck you."

Ran's eyes widened. Lydia never, never said things like this.

She waited for him to see the height of the mountain he had to climb. There was a silence, which she refused to be the one to fill. Laughter and voices drifted from the party downstairs. Ran stopped pacing. He was pale, and suddenly looked years older.

"Nobody asked her home to play," Lydia said. "Partly because her mother was a ragged depressive who lived in a dump. And partly because her father was a sex maniac—who also lived in a dump. Her only real friends in those days were the Ressany Brothers."

"Sex maniac?" In his trance of astonishment, Ran could only echo the key words. His gentle Lydia had never spoken as if his behavior could be judged by ordinary standards.

She sighed. "You were the one who wanted to talk, and I'm doing all the talking. Sorry."

"You should have told me about Linnet," he said softly.

"What would you have done?"

"I don't know." He dropped to his knees on the rug. "Tried to make things better. It kills me when she's unhappy. I hate myself for letting Polly come between us. Why am I such a stupid shit?"

She smiled. "You grab things you fancy, without thinking of the dangers. Like Linnet chasing swans."

He was neither tearful, petulant, nor windily self-justifying. "I wish I could turn the clock back," he said quietly. "I've made some incredible mistakes."

"Is Polly a mistake?"

"Poor thing, it's not her fault."

Lydia repeated, "Is Polly a mistake?"

"Yes," Ran said humbly. "Oh God, it's awful. You should see what she's done to the house. She thinks she's bought me. I can't make her understand that I don't want to marry her."

"But will you?"

Ran reached to take her hand. "No. I'm not marrying Polly. I got it into my head that I was in love with her—well, you know what I'm like."

Lydia's hand tensed inside his. "So are you going to tell her?"

"Yes. Even though she'll probably kill me, and squat in my house till I can pay her back all the dosh she's spent on it. I don't care. It's still better than hurting my baby." Ran groaned gently, and laid Lydia's hand against his cheek. "I've got myself into a huge mess this time, eh? And I look at you, and see what a bloody great fool I am for ever letting you go. I'm sorry I got angry tonight, but if you will go round looking so incredibly beautiful—and bombarding me with psychic messages that I can't ignore—"

"If you want me now, you have to want me forever," Lydia said. "And if you want me forever, the rules have to be different. You know what I mean." She was breathless, forcing herself to make the speech she had rehearsed in her head so many times. "You made me desperately unhappy when we were married. The first time you cheated on me, I thought I'd die. You told me I'd get used to it—"

"Oh, God!" Ran winced. "I didn't, did I?"

"But I never got used to it. Each time was another death. I never stopped hoping you'd want me again." She swallowed hard. Tears brimmed in her eyes. "Maybe it wouldn't be so important, if I didn't love you."

The years melted from him. For the first time that evening, he smiled fully. "Do you still love me?"

"I don't know how you can ask me—I've never stopped loving you for a second—" Lydia's voice was fractured with sobs.

Ran sprang up, to sit beside her on the bed and gather her into his arms. Tenderly, he drew her head down to his shoulder. He whispered, "Liddy, please forgive me and start again. I'm a stupid shit, but at least I've learned that I can't be happy without you. Or Linnet. I want my family back."

❋ ❋ ❋

Nancy ended the evening rather seriously irked with Lydia. She had disappeared during supper, leaving her sisters to entertain the choir people and pretend to be delighted when they suddenly started singing madrigals. They had obviously been puzzled by Lydia's absence, and Nancy had concocted a feeble story about a sudden migraine. They all believed it, and had left with many expressions of concern.

The party was in its final stages now, the last drinkers amiably helping with the clearing up. Linnet and her remaining friend, Lauren Poulter, were slumped on the sofa in the drawing room, watching *The Little Mermaid* through drooping eyelids. Rose and Nancy were scraping leftovers into the bin and stacking the dishwasher. Selena was at the sink, attacking the pans.

In the middle of all the activity and confusion, it took Nancy a few minutes to notice Polly. She stood, taut with fury, among the rough jerseys and grimy hands of the last guests. She wore a new Barbour over a black velvet cocktail dress. A single diamond glittered at her throat.

"I've come for Ran." She was too angry to care who heard her.

Nancy tossed potato skins into the bin. "Ran? I thought he left ages ago. Isn't he at your place?"

"I know he's here, Nancy," Polly said. "And if I can't see him immediately, I'm never seeing him again."

"Hold on, no one's trying to hide him." Nancy touched Rose's shoulder. "Mum, have you seen Ran?"

"No, and I haven't seen that wretched Lydia either—how dare she leave us high and dry? I didn't know where to look during those madrigals. What bollocks." Rose had reached her brutal-honesty level of tipsiness.

Polly's neat blond face was a Japanese Noh mask of outrage. "He left me to handle the whole dinner party by myself. I've never been so humiliated in my life. And I refuse to wait at home till he deigns to come back."

"Well, do feel free to have a search for him," Rose said kindly. "Do you fancy a cup of tea while you're here?"

"No—thank you." Polly strode purposefully toward the sound of laughter out in the Great Hall. In the doorway she snorted impatiently, and veered off toward the stairs.

Rose and Nancy watched her, with detached sympathy.

Rose said, "She might as well see for herself. He'll never manage to tell her."

Nancy sighed and rolled her eyes. "I do think Liddy's a bit of a gumby. Why couldn't she seduce someone else?"

"Because she married him," Rose said. "Unlike Ran, she knew a marriage is not biodegradable—especially when there's a child. He's had to learn that there is no such thing as a Disposable Marriage. Your father always knew it. That's why he always came back."

Nancy was surprised. She had never heard her mother taking this faintly critical tone about The Zed. "You were the love of his life."

"Yes, because I married him and stuck it out. But it wasn't easy. Why d'you think I looked so old and wrinkled, and he didn't? I was his portrait in the attic." She had sobered up, and now she caught Nancy's surprise. "Oh, darling, I didn't mind. There were huge compensations. It's what I chose, and what Liddy's chosen. And two people who have a child as perfect as my Linnet ought to be bloody well chained together." She darted forward to snatch her wineglass. "Quick, another tipple, before I turn into a guardian of public morality."

Polly, with a white face and blazing eyes, stalked into the kitchen.

Rose asked, "Did you find him?"

Polly did not reply. She swept the room with one withering look, then stormed out of the back door like the Bad Fairy at the christening.

Nancy knew it all half an hour later, when she carried a sleeping Linnet upstairs. The door to Lydia's room stood slightly open. Lydia and Ran lay fast asleep in the rumpled bed, blissfully clasped in each other's arms.

Chapter Fourteen

Rufa waited at the crossing outside the Caledonian Hotel, bracing herself against the wind. Daily life in this city was an endless, hand-to-hand battle with the wind. It scoured the gray stones, drove the crowds of shoppers along Princes Street, roared through the Georgian canyons of the New Town. Hard flecks of snow stung Rufa's face. The cold was unbelievable. Her hands ached inside her gloves.

Then, on the point of weeping, the strange and not unpleasant feeling of dislocation stole over her again. The thundering traffic, the harassed crowds, the lighted Christmas windows—everything was unreal and two-dimensional, like a picture. Rufa tried to reconnect to it, enough to remember how to go about the effort of getting back to the flat. She should have stayed there, swaddled in her overcoat and the rented duvet.

But she had to find a present for Linnet. This was a large project. The tea set she had bought for Linnet's birthday had involved hours of glassy-eyed wanderings around toy departments. She had then had to find wrapping paper, a card (with badge—"6 Today!") and a Jiffy bag. In the olden days, she could have accomplished all this in an hour. These days, everything seemed to take amazing amounts of energy. She had fainted in the queue at the post office.

The faint had been very embarrassing. The place had been thronged with nosy old ladies collecting their pensions, and it had been a struggle to get away. They had wanted to call an ambulance, but were distracted when Rufa lied that she was pregnant. Being pregnant seemed to explain away all kinds of medical horrors. Your head could fall off and roll into the gutter, she thought, and if you said you were pregnant, everyone would say, "Och, no worries, then."

She had probably fainted because she was not eating. It was not that she disliked food—simply that it did not seem to have anything to do with her body. Bushes of broccoli, mats of meat, blankets of bread, plates of white china, steel forks—they were all the same to her. The huge effort of pushing things into her face made her exhausted. This morning it had taken her a good hour of the *Today* program to eat a single slice of toast. She had kept looking down at her plate, to find the toast exactly the same size—Fortunatus's piece of toast, doomed never to get any smaller.

She was fine, however, if she did not think too much about the wrong things. Such as the painful Christmas decorations, which pulled her heart toward home. The home she longed for no longer existed. She wanted the old Melismate, all grimy and chaotic and crumbling, where she could find The Zed in the kitchen with Linnet on his knee—Rose in her drinking chair—the girls up in the old nursery. She had ruined the nursery, painting it white and stowing the junk in the stable loft. The destruction had been paid for with Edward's money. She had wanted to save The Zed's home, and she had raped it.

Thinking of Edward made her warm. She had recently noticed these rushes of warmth, which muffled all noise and turned the ground beneath her feet to sponge. Very distantly, Rufa saw that the green man had appeared on the crossing. The people around her surged across the road. The red man appeared before Rufa remembered that she had intended to cross too. Why was everything happening so fast?

There was a hand on her upper arm. "Rufa? I thought it was you."

She turned her head, and saw—of all people—Adrian Mecklenberg.

Adrian reacted with the impeccable consideration one would expect from a man dedicated to the pursuit of perfection. It was as if he were following instructions in some arcane book of etiquette—*How to Behave When a Lady Known to You Faints in Princes Street.*

He took Rufa into the Caledonian Hotel, and rapidly installed her in a room like a carpeted football pitch. He arranged for a private doctor to be sent. It took him no more than fifteen minutes, then he departed for his meeting in George Street. The rational part of Rufa was mortified. To Adrian, a faint would be nearly as offensive and distasteful as a loud fart—the unwanted attention, the fuss, the sheer lack of control.

The doctor was a young woman, no older than Rufa herself. She prefixed every question with "And."

"And how long is it since you miscarried?"

"Nearly five weeks." They were drinking a pot of excellent strong leaf tea, and Rufa leaned forward to refill the doctor's cup.

"Thanks. And was there much bleeding?"

"Tons. It went on for ages. But it's stopped now."

"And has there been any other discharge?"

What a question—thank God Adrian did not have to hear it. "No."

"How long did the pain last?"

Rufa had to think about this. It was hard to distinguish between different types of pain: to tell where one ended and the other began. "Well, it comes and goes. It's manageable."

The doctor nodded. Her bedside manner was still a little solemn and unsure, Rufa thought; perhaps she had not been a doctor for very long. "Did your GP give you anything for it?"

"I don't exactly have a GP," Rufa said apologetically. "I haven't been here for long, and I never got round to it."

"But you must have seen someone when you had the miscarriage?"

"I didn't see the point," Rufa said. "What could anyone have done?"

The doctor looked disapproving, then consciously tactful. "You should always get help for something like that."

"I take Nurofen," Rufa offered.

"And are you eating?"

"Oh, yes." It was true. She worked hard at eating. She looked out of the window, at the steely sky, while the doctor wrote something in a little note-book.

"You're anemic," she announced. "I'm prescribing you some iron. And it looks as if you have an infection, so I'm giving you a short course of antibi-otics—but for God's sake, get yourself looked at properly. You might need a D and C, and I can't tell without a full examination." She tore the prescrip-tion out of her book.

Rufa smiled, glad that the session appeared to be over. Her one free day was melting away. She held out her hand.

The doctor said, "Actually, I have to give this in at the desk. Mr. Mecklenberg's instructions."

"Why?"

"It's a private prescription," the doctor said gently. "He's arranged to have it collected and paid for. Nothing for you to worry about."

Rufa was impressed. "Isn't he efficient?"

The interrogation was not quite finished. The doctor asked, "And how are you feeling now?"

A baffling question. "Well, I don't know. Fine."

"Have you been depressed lately?"

"I don't think so." What did this mean? Being "depressed" surely meant feeling very sad, and Rufa did not think she felt sad, exactly.

"That could explain why you're not eating," the doctor said.

"I told you, I am eating. It just goes on and on."

"What does?"

"You know. Life. Things. But I'm getting to grips with it now."

"Good," the doctor said, suddenly smiling. "Take it easy for a day or two, and try to eat a good lunch. I believe Mr. Mecklenberg is waiting for you downstairs."

Rufa went down to the dining room, wishing she had dressed with more elegance. Adrian was particular, and he would not care to be seen lunching at the Caledonian Hotel with a woman in jeans. If only she had worn the cashmere jersey—but she could get two thermal vests under her old blue guernsey, and the flat was arctic.

Adrian stood up at the discreet corner table where he had been reading the *Financial Times*. Rufa dropped a chaste peck on his clean, smooth cheek. "You've been so kind. I'm terribly sorry about all this."

He tucked her chair underneath her, and sat down. "Please don't apologize. Are you all right now?"

"Absolutely fine. I can't think what came over me." Rufa found, to her surprise, that she was rather glad to see Adrian. He was less stressful to talk to when you were not trying to marry him, and she was famished for conversation. She had not had a proper conversation for weeks.

"I have to say it, Adrian—you've been tremendously nice to me. Far nicer than I deserve."

He was, distantly, amused. "We won't go into that. I've ordered you the tournedos, because you look as if you need something substantial. You're considerably thinner than when I last saw you."

He had last seen her at Berry's, on the evening of her engagement to Edward. Rufa did not want to bring this up, and remained silent. Adrian did not expect a reply.

"You're altogether different," he said, "but you can't disguise your hair— I knew you at once. Now, have a glass of wine and tell me what you're doing in Edinburgh."

"Working, mainly," Rufa said carefully.

"Where?"

"I'm still doing my dinner parties. And I've got a job at a café just beside the Grassmarket—Nessie's, after the monster. You wouldn't know it."

One of Adrian's eyebrows moved slightly upward, indicating surprise. "A café? What does your husband think of that?"

Rufa decided he had a right not be lied to. Briefly, sipping rich red wine, she sketched in the details of her catastrophic foolishness. She tried to keep her voice light and casual, remembering how Adrian liked his stories—neat, and to the point. She only faltered once, hurrying over her miscarriage. He listened impassively.

Their first courses arrived—a delicate terrine of smoked duck. Rufa admired hers, and made a determined effort to eat it. Chew, chew, chew, swallow. How did normal, fat people manage to do this all day?

Before she had finished, a man in a suit came to the table, with a white paper bag, which he handed to Adrian. "Your tablets, sir."

"Thank you." He passed it across the table to Rufa. "You ought to begin now, I suppose."

Rufa opened the bag, taking out two plastic drums of pills. There were smooth brown ones, smelling like rusty wire. There were white capsules. She swallowed one of each. Adrian looked away disdainfully as she did so.

"I still don't quite understand," he said, "why you're here. What on earth is stopping you from simply going home to your family?"

"I can't face them," Rufa said. She knew this sounded feeble, and struggled to explain. "The house—everything in it was paid for by Edward, you see. I made him do it, in exchange for marrying me. And now I've broken the agreement. I've dishonored him."

"I seem to have missed a segment of the plot," Adrian said. "I gathered that you wanted to marry me for my money. But I also gathered it wasn't as important as I had been led to believe. It seemed embarrassingly obvious that you were in love with Mr. Reculver."

"Did it?"

"I confess I was slightly annoyed to find that I had been used as a device to bring true lovers together."

Rufa felt her face flaming. He made her sound cheap and silly, and he was right. "I know you don't like apologies, but I am sorry for the way I behaved. I look back now, and I can hardly believe it."

"So you turned out not to love Mr. Reculver after all?"

"It's not as simple as that." Rufa pushed a shred of duck around her plate, to make a new pattern with the unwanted food. "I do love him, actually. That makes it worse, doesn't it? I love him and miss him more than any-one—and look how I treated him. He's really far better off without me."

"Does he think that?"

"I expect so." She risked a glance across at Adrian, and found him looking at her with the same expression of tolerant amusement. "Please—if you see anyone from home—please don't give me away. Please don't say you've seen me. I couldn't bear it."

The amusement was, once more, edged with distaste. "Rufa, try to remember that I'm not part of your circle, and certainly not in the habit of spreading gossip. I shouldn't dream of interfering." He raised an eyebrow at a nearby waiter. "If you're not intending to eat that, I suggest you move on to not eating the entrée. I'm leaving for the airport at three."

"Ah, Berry." Adrian, still in his overcoat, stepped into Berry's shared office.

Berry jumped guiltily, horribly conscious that he had been caught in his braces and shirtsleeves, with a vacant expression on his face. He leaped to his feet. "Adrian. How did the meeting—?"

"This isn't to do with business." Adrian shifted his briefcase to the other hand. His gray eyes rested briefly on an empty crisp packet crumpled on the desk. "Or pleasure, now that I think of it. Do you still see that barmaid sis-ter of Rufa Hasty's?"

Berry felt his face turning a royal purple. "Yes. She—she works at Forbes and Gunning. I do go in there sometimes."

"Did you know Rufa had bolted?"

"Yes, actually." A week ago, when he had rushed into the wine bar hours after his return from Frankfurt, the other barmaid—seeing how crestfallen he was that Nancy was not there—had told him the whole story of Rufa's disappearance. His darling Nancy had, apparently, spent a whole night crying her lovely eyes out. The thought of this had given him actual physical pain. He ached for an excuse to take her in his arms and comfort her.

"Well, tell her I've seen Rufa. I met her up in Edinburgh today, and had lunch with her. She's working at a café called Nessie's, in a street leading off the Grassmarket. I don't know which, but there can't be many."

Berry was astonished. He tried not to gape. "Does she have a phone number?"

"She didn't give it to me," Adrian said. "She made me promise not to tell anyone I'd seen her."

"What made her change her mind?"

Adrian sighed. "She didn't. I was lying to her. She looked so dreadful, I knew I would be forced to send someone to fetch her."

"Is she ill?" This was alarming. Berry knew Adrian would never interfere unless he felt he really had no choice.

"Yes," Adrian said crisply. "When she saw me, she fainted. She has, apparently, had a miscarriage." His eyelids wrinkled with distaste. "The doctor thought she was anemic, and tried to tell me about infections and depressions—the entire experience was deeply annoying."

"Still," Berry said boldly, "it was awfully kind of you to take care of her."

Unexpectedly, Adrian's expression thawed into a wintry half smile. "Don't you dare accuse me of kindness. I've been hijacked into it, against all my better instincts. May I now consider my hands washed?"

"Yes, of course," Berry said quickly. "I'll go round to tell Nancy at once." He grabbed his jacket from the back of his chair. "And I'm sure she'll want me to say thanks."

"Tell her to send that silly girl back to her husband," Adrian said. He left the office without another word, the window he had allotted to Rufa now closed.

Berry knew the matter was urgent, but stopped in the gents on his way out, to smooth his mad hair with water and straighten his tie. It was evening, and the crowds along Cheapside were thinning. The opulent, oddly sterile glitter of the Christmas tree in the foyer of Berry's building forced his mind back a year, to the enchanted night he had first seen Nancy.

It was like remembering someone else's life. This time last year he had been living with Polly, confidently expecting to do so until one of them died.

347

He had been plump and complacent; Polly had been snugly poised to slip her page into Burke's Peerage. And that one chance meeting with Ran Verrall, last Christmas Eve, had overturned everything—his entire world, and Polly's; even Adrian's.

Nearly a year later, Polly was hiding her fury at the home of her intensely horsy parents, near Petersfield. She had caught Ran in bed with his ex-wife, and virtually stripped his house down to the brickwork as revenge (the other barmaid had supplied these details). Berry, meanwhile, had spent the year wearing himself out with unrequited passion, until he was as wiry as he had been at school. At last the ordeal was ending. The happy ending was written in the stars. Nancy had to be there this evening. Since he had finished his stint in Frankfurt the previous week, he had haunted the wine bar in vain. The other barmaid, whose name was Fran, had explained that Nancy was only doing two days a week at the moment, and spending most of her time down at Melismate. Today was one of Nancy's days. And though he knew it to be a little mean, he could not help reflecting that bringing the news about Rufa would be the perfect doorway to intimacy.

The bar was decked with silvered vine leaves, and packed with festive drinkers. In one corner, early as it was, an entire trading floor from some nearby bank had donned paper hats for the first leg of their Christmas binge. Berry saw Nancy's red head flashing between the rows of square charcoal shoulders. She was working like a Fury, cramming bottles and glasses onto trays, throwing notes into the till. Berry was tempted to return when the place was quieter, but nobly resisted—Rufa was ill, and her family needed to know as soon as possible.

He bent his head, and battered his way through the scrum. It took muscle, and he had to clutch at the rim of the bar to stop himself being forced out of his space.

Nancy beamed at him. "Hello—what can I get you?"

"Nothing—hello—I need to talk to you—"

"What?"

With one more determined push through the shoulders, he leaned right across the bar toward her. "It's about Rufa. Adrian met her up in Edinburgh today." As concisely as he could, through the roar of male conversation, Berry gave her the news headlines. Nancy listened in perfect stillness. When he got to the part about the miscarriage and the fainting and the illness, her blue eyes flooded with tears. His longing to comfort her was intense.

She said, "I must phone Edward," and hurried off without another word.

Berry gamely held his position, battered by elbows and squeezed against the mahogany. Nancy needed him. He refused to leave her now—he was all the more determined when he saw her hurrying back, wiping her eyes.

He asked, "Did you get him?"

"Yes." She smiled through the tears. "I'm glad you're still here."

Out of the corner of his eye Berry saw Simon, working in an apron alongside his troops, looking suspiciously at Nancy. "I'll order something now," he said. "A bottle of house champagne, please. And two glasses."

"Oh. You're with someone." She was—unmistakably—disappointed.

"Yes. I'm with you." Berry hoped he was keeping his voice free of unsuitable jubilation. "And you need a drink."

"I can't—we're too busy."

"When do you finish?"

"Not till eleven."

"Couldn't you take a break?"

Simon edged his way toward them. "Get a move on, Nancy—no time for you to hold court today."

"Sorry." Two more tears dripped from Nancy's lashes. Her lower lip buckled.

Berry felt a tremendous, soaring, exultant surge of power. He could have slaughtered a lion. "Excuse me—" He tapped masterfully at Simon's arm with his credit card, as he had seen other men do. "Nancy's had some bad news. Family stuff. I think I'd better take her out of all this for a minute. Is there somewhere we can go?"

Simon was taken aback, and shot a searching glance at Nancy. "Oh, right. Sorry. I can let you have half an hour—you can go in the office, I suppose."

"Thanks," Berry said.

Simon opened a wooden flap to admit Berry behind the bar. Berry swept a protective arm around Nancy's shoulders. The softness of her flesh, warm underneath her thin black cardigan, sent his heartbeat into overdrive. Wiping her eyes with the backs of her hands, she led him to a door, set deep into the bare brick cellar wall. It opened into a tiny, windowless office.

Berry shut the door behind him. He folded Nancy in his arms, drawing her face down into his shoulder. "Darling," he murmured into her hair. "My darling. It'll be all right."

Her voice was muffled in his suit. "I know this is stupid—I just can't bear to think of Ru having a miscarriage, and keeling over in front of Adrian— God, it's such a relief to know she's not dead!"

She drew away from him, sniffing loudly, and distractedly rummaging in her pockets.

Berry whisked out his handkerchief. He put it into Nancy's hand. "But she'll be fine now. You've found her, and you can stop worrying."

"I knew there was something wrong—I always do with Rufa. We're connected." She mopped at her face. "I can't get over Adrian playing the Good Samaritan."

He laughed quietly. "The rather reluctant and peeved Samaritan. Though I think he is fond of her, in his own peculiar fashion."

"It's ironic that he should be the one to find her, when Edward's been wearing out shoe leather searching for her all over Edinburgh. He's been up there three times, and didn't see a hair of her. Can I get snot on this hanky, or do you need it back?"

"Consider it yours."

"Thanks." Nancy blew her nose. "He's driving up again tonight. I don't know if I should have told him first, but he's the one who deserves to claim her. And he's so much more effective than the rest of us. He'll bring her home—oh, Berry, she'll be home in time for Christmas!"

She smiled properly for the first time: a radiant, brilliant smile that burned away the tears. She flung her arms around Berry's neck and hugged him fiercely. It was incredibly easy—and felt beautifully natural—for Berry to kiss her warm neck, her soft cheek, her ripe mouth.

He pulled his mouth away, keeping one hand on her breast. "Look, I have to tell you," he whispered, "because I can't hide it anymore—you're a goddess, you're an angel, and I've been completely crazy about you since the moment we met, when you made me look at your nipples."

"Oh, darling." Nancy's eyes were streaming, but her smile was beatific. "I've been crazy about you since the moment you told me you didn't have enough money for that stupid Marrying Game."

They fell ravenously upon each other's open mouths. Berry (who had not dared to have so much as a lubricious thought in Polly's presence until he had bought her a formal dinner) pressed his unashamed erection against Nancy's thigh. He groaned softly, and slipped his hand into the space between her breasts. "You're still very upset," he whispered. "I'll tell your boss you can't possibly do any more work, and then I'll take you home, and then I'll make love to you in every imaginable position. It might take days."

"Weeks." Her wanton hand caressed his flies.

"Months—maybe years. Actually, I'm terribly sorry, but I'm afraid I may have to keep you forever."

Chapter Fifteen

There was no mistaking Nessie's. A jaunty purple Loch Ness monster cavorted cheerfully above its window. Edward halted as soon as he saw it, almost gagging with anxiety. Suppose Rufa was not here? Suppose she was? Searching for her—with a determination that bordered on obsessive—had made her seem dangerously unreal, as impossible to catch and hold as mist.

Keeping his eyes on the expanse of lighted window, Edward tried to rub some warmth back into his hands. The sky was the color of lead, heavy with the threat of snow. He had driven to Edinburgh straight after Nancy's breathless phone call, pausing only to pass the hopeful news to Rose. He had arrived at his hotel in Charlotte Square in the small hours, after a tense, impatient drive along unending motorways. And he had surprised himself by sleeping till ten, when he had hardly had one peaceful, dreamless night since his marriage. He could not think of anything else, until he knew that Rufa was safe.

The three previous trips to Edinburgh had only hardened his determination. He had interrogated the embarrassed but helpful staff of the hotel at which Rufa had used her credit card. One girl had remembered that she had been looking for a flat. Edward had doggedly begun to work his way through every letting agency listed in the phone book, crisscrossing the city. And all that time she had been slaving here. He must have passed within a few yards of her a hundred times.

He had waited until lunchtime, wanting to catch Rufa at work, where there would be less chance of her running away from him. Bracing himself for yet another disappointment, he crossed the narrow street and went to the window of the café.

His heart almost stopped. He saw her.

Rufa, wrapped in a striped butcher's apron, was stirring a vast saucepan in a kind of open kitchen. Edward had last seen her at the airport, before departing for The Hague, and was startled by the change in her. She was far too thin. There were poignant hollows in her cheeks and dark smudges under her eyes. She was pale and exhausted, and unbearably beautiful. As it sank in that she was really, truly there, he experienced one moment of profound relief. Tears spilled down his face, instantly turning cold in the sawing wind.

She turned her head, and saw him. She froze, her eyes wide with shock. Edward blindly pushed his way into the café, strode right up to Rufa, and threw his arms around her. He could not hold her close enough. Her bones felt sharp and fragile under several layers of clothes. As if gulping in oxygen, he inhaled the scent of her hair. Then he gently pushed her away, so that he could look into her face. His hands on her shoulders, he held her in his gaze. Her eyes were tearless and bewildered.

"My darling," Edward murmured, deliberately ignoring the stares of the people around them. "Say something. Say you won't run off again. Say you're glad to be found."

Rufa said, "I lost my baby." A silent sob shook her. She flung her arms around his neck, and wept into his shoulder.

She did not cry for long. She pulled away from him, scooping the tears with the backs of her hands, scattering apologies. She insisted upon finishing her shift. Edward refused to leave her. He established himself at a corner table, pinning his eyes to her as if afraid she would fly away. She brought him over a plate of stovies, which he ate without tasting. Term had ended, and the café was not busy. He watched her moving between the saucepan and the till, smiling at customers, talking to the other woman in the open kitchen.

It was like being trapped in some bizarre dream. Occasionally she glanced over at him, doubtful and anxious. Every time she did this he smiled at her, determined to reassure her. He had not come to rebuke, or to condemn. He wanted her to know she was being rescued. Plainly, she needed rescuing. He thought she was beginning to be happy to see him. A spark of something like hope appeared in her sorrowful eyes when he smiled.

The other woman came over to Edward's table with a cup of tea. She murmured, "You're her husband, aren't you? She's told me a bit about you. I'll send her packing as soon as we've finished the hot food."

He would have liked to bombard the woman with questions, but there was no time. He had to wait until Rufa had cleaned the top of the big stove, wiped down the counter with Dettox, and folded her apron. She was very white, swaying slightly when she stood still. Edward watched, seething with impatience, as the café's owner brought out Rufa's coat, said something to her, and kissed her.

Rufa's flat was nearby. There was a shortcut to the Royal Mile, up a steep flight of stone steps. Edward walked behind her while she climbed, poised to shoot out an arm if she fell—she toiled up gasping for breath, battered by the freezing wind. Once inside her flat she stopped pretending to be fine, and collapsed on the sofa with a gasp of relief.

"Stairs," she said, trying to smile. "Everything in this town is vertical."

Since when had Rufa not been able to manage stairs? And how long did they have to pretend she was not ill? Edward bit back an impulse to lecture her about taking care of herself. He must remember he was not briefing a platoon, nor carpeting a troublesome squaddie. In civilian life, a lecturing habit drove foolish young wives away. "I'll make some tea."

"That would be lovely." She did not even try to protest about being waited on: a very bad sign.

He went into a kitchen the size of a coffin. It had a strip of window looking out over the ancient court below, where a knot of hardy Japanese tourists were taking photographs. He was dismayed to see that Rufa had not colonized the kitchen. Apart from a few rich tea biscuits, there was no food. Her precious library of cookery books lay in a careless heap on the draining board. The Rufa he knew had never been truly present here.

When he carried the tea into the sitting room, Rufa—still in coat and gloves—was fast asleep. He spoke her name softly. She did not stir. Very gently, Edward raised her legs, and put a hard cushion under her head. He found a chilly duvet in a claustrophobic bedroom, draped it over her, and sat down to wait until she woke up. Dear God, how sad she looked. She should not be in this mausoleum, without a living soul to talk to, or care if she lived or died. Not when there was someone to live and die for her, if only she would let him.

The short afternoon darkened as he watched her. When he could no longer make out her face in the shadows, Edward switched on a lamp and moved silently to draw the curtains against the winter night. Thick flakes of snow whirled in the light cast by the window.

He took his seat again, wondering if he would ever find a way to tell her how long, and how much, he had loved her. Whatever the local gossips thought, it had not happened when she was a child. As a little girl, Rufa had only been one of The Zed's tattered brood: gap-toothed, with sprawling legs like a colt. In his periods at home he had often found Rufa in his kitchen, sitting with his mother and Alice, gravely helping them to shell peas or mix cakes. Over the years, The Zed had drawn his attention to Rufa's growing beauty. Edward had noticed it in a theoretical way, but he had not fallen in love with her until he had left the army.

They had been friends at first. Rufa had seen, when the others had not, how the death of his mother had deepened his depression, his sense of dislocation from normal life—he wondered if she guessed how he had come to depend on her, through that long, bleak year. The moment of truth had come during an elaborate picnic at Melismate, arranged by The Zed for Rose's birthday. Torrential rain had interrupted the bacchanal, and everyone had dived for the nearest cover. Edward had found himself under one of the trestle tables, next to Rufa. He had stared at her wet hair and dripping, laughing profile, and had suddenly been able to put a name to what he felt for her. He had fallen in love with her, and it was already a serious case.

He brooded over her face as she slept. Perhaps it was the softening effect of the lamplight, but she seemed a little less ghastly. Some color had crept back into her lips. Edward thought, as he often did, of the one night he had lost control in Italy. He blamed the brandy. He had been sloshed, and poor Rufa had been as drunk as a skunk—without an inhibition left in the world, and barely able to stand up. He had felt ashamed of himself while he was doing it, but never in his life had passion made him so savage.

I made her come, Edward thought, and then she passed out—and I didn't stop. I have fucked an unconscious woman; I should be locked up.

The memory fired his blood, and mortified him. He had been appalled by Rufa's illness the following day. Since the death of The Zed, Edward had been profoundly disturbed by her aching vulnerability. God alone knew what the sight of her father's body had done to her. He wished he had not

355

lectured her so relentlessly about a reality she could not bear to face. He was ashamed to remember how he had told her off for making mountains of jam when she ought to have been thinking constructively about the auction of the house. Nancy—springing to her sister's defense, as she always did—had blurted out that she was doing it to pay the bloody undertakers, and Edward had chopped logs for a whole afternoon in a fury of remorse. He would never have taken advantage of her by marrying her, if the poor creature had not been so determined to marry someone else. Thank God she had not— he felt he had grabbed her on the very edge of the precipice.

Rufa sighed, and stirred. She blinked at the ceiling, and turned her head toward Edward. He was encouraged to see that the hunted expression in her eyes faded as soon as she saw him. "What time is it?"

Edward came over to her, perching on the sofa beside her feet. "Nearly seven."

"What? Oh, God—"

He put his hand on her shoulder. "Relax. I'll make you that cup of tea."

"I don't believe it. I've been asleep for three hours." She smiled up into his face. "I'm glad you're still here. Otherwise I might have thought I'd dreamed you. I have dreams about you all the time. If you're going to the kitchen could you bring me a glass of water? I have to take some tablets." She struggled up on her elbows, looking round for her bag. "It's incredible; I feel so much better."

"You look dreadful," Edward said. "And of course I'm still here. I'm not going anywhere."

"Adrian gave me away, didn't he?"

"Yes, thank God," Edward said. "He turns out to be a very decent sort."

"He was incredibly kind to me. Even though he thinks being ill is very bad manners."

"I'm not surprised you've been ill. There's not a crumb of food here, and it's freezing. Is there any way of turning the heating up?"

"I'm afraid this is as good as it gets."

"Well, stay under that duvet."

Edward made them fresh cups of tea with the last two tea bags, suppressing another lecture about thinking ahead when buying food. All this lunacy was only an outward sign of her state of mind. Nobody had put a label on it yet, but what Rufa had been through amounted to a kind of breakdown. And a good part of it had been his fault, though he had believed he was being utterly unselfish at the time.

Rufa was sitting up when he brought her the tea and the glass of water. She had removed her gloves, and made an attempt to smooth her hair. "Thanks so much. How is everyone? Is Linnet all right? I hated missing her birthday."

"Everyone's fine," Edward said, sitting down. "They'll be even more so when you tell them you're coming home."

"Am I coming home?" Rufa was bewildered, trying to remember why she could not go with him.

"Yes," he said firmly. "When I've finished my tea, I'm taking you right out of this bloody igloo."

"I don't know if I can."

"Don't you want to?"

Her eyes filled with tears. "Yes. More than anything."

Edward took one of her cold hands. "Ru, darling, it's all over. Let me look after you."

She bowed her head. "I can't. Not after what I did."

"My darling, that's all forgotten."

"Not by me," Rufa said. Tears dropped from her eyes, onto the back of his hand.

"Forgiveness doesn't even come into it," he said softly, in the tender and caressing voice very few people heard. "I haven't spent all this time searching for you because I wanted you to apologize. I should be saying sorry to you. I wasn't honest with you about Prudence." He hated talking about Prudence, because he felt it made him look so pathetic. He did not want Rufa to see him as some cringing beggar pleading for sexual favors. It was as uncomfortable, in its way, as giving evidence to the War Crimes Tribunal; but it had to be done. "I didn't tell you the whole history. I assumed it didn't matter because it was all in the past. I'd forgotten what a stirrer she can be."

"You told her about us," Rufa said, her voice pinched with the hurt of it.

"I didn't have anyone else to talk to, so I talked to her," Edward said. He sighed. "I knew it was wrong at the time. I'm sorry."

She looked up at him. "Do you swear it's really over?"

"God, yes. It was over after we split up that first time."

"After Alice died."

"Yes. When we—well, afterward, it was never the same. Love didn't really come into it. We saw each other maybe three times a year. She's never achieved a happy marriage—I think because she kept trying to marry her father, but never mind that. She relied on me for safety, and friendship."

"And you relied on her for sex."

"Yes." Edward was annoyed with himself for being annoyed by this—he couldn't exactly deny it. "I won't say it meant nothing, but it was basically a friendly arrangement."

"Prudence seemed to think it was a lot more than that," Rufa said.

"She wouldn't give in before she'd put us both through hell. I can see that now. At the time, I thought the guilt would kill me." He smiled grimly. "You know how I hate being in the wrong."

"That day you took her out to lunch," Rufa said, "she thought she was going to get you into bed again, didn't she?"

Edward was severely embarrassed. He saw now that he had handled the entire business of Prudence with spectacular ineptitude. He forced himself to look Rufa in the eye. "Yes, as a matter of fact."

"You slept with her when you went to Paris." Rufa said.

"Yes. Even though I'd just got engaged to you." He willed himself not to hide behind excuses. There were none. "I won't say I couldn't help it, because that would be ridiculous. But she offered, and I didn't try to turn her down."

She whispered, "You wanted sex."

Edward groaned softly. "Of course I did. I was desperate for sex." He clasped his hands together, to keep himself from frightening her with the force of truth unbound. "My life, over the past few years, has been one long struggle to avoid anything that made me remember how desperate I was. My arrangement with Pru kept me from going mad."

Breathlessly, Rufa asked, "Did I make you desperate?"

"Oh, God." He tried to laugh, but he could easily have wept. "If you only knew."

"I wish you'd shown me."

"I was waiting for everything to be perfect. And that was impossible, with that bloody bargain standing between us."

"We should have talked more," Rufa said. "But we never talked about sex. If I tried to drop a hint, you went outside and mended the tractor."

This was so true that Edward did laugh, though he despaired over the gulf there had been between them. "I was terrified of forcing you into anything. The idea of—of having you, when I'd paid for you—your mother decided I must be impotent."

"I thought you'd roll straight back into bed with Prudence because she was good at sex and I wasn't."

"Oh, God."

She smiled faintly. "Stop saying that."

"Sorry. I'll tell you everything I should have said at the time." Edward made himself look at her. "You were absolutely right, she made a pass at me at that lunch. I daresay it was extremely thick of me, but I was surprised."

Rufa asked, "How did she do it?"

"Must we go into detail?"

"Yes."

He gave her a painful smile. "All right. Pru said I'd made a fool of myself, by marrying you when you obviously had some kind of—" He sighed. "Look, I'll leave out the stuff she said about you. What's the point? You got your own back."

"Did I?"

"Come on, Rufa. She was furious when you took up with Triss. She says you've given him a nervous breakdown and jeopardized his finals, and I don't know what."

Rufa's lips were pale in her pale face. "I didn't mean to hurt him."

"He'll survive," Edward said dryly. "A lot of this is about family history. I knew she was angry about the money. Pru's not just greedy—there are all kinds of reasons why it matters to her to keep it in the family. As far as she was concerned, I might as well have set fire to it." This was not enough. He made himself expand. "After Alice died, I think I could have fallen in love with her quite easily. I know she considered marrying me—mainly because of her strange belief that I'm kind and easy to live with."

"You are kind," Rufa said. "You'd be easier to live with if you talked more, and admitted you were wrong sometimes."

"Thank you. As the psalm says, I acknowledge my transgressions and my sin is ever before me." Edward smiled, oddly touched by the solemn way she pointed out his faults. "Anyway, it didn't work out. Pru wasn't in love with me. I knew that when she fell in love properly, with someone else."

"Who?"

He could not look at her. "Doesn't matter. You wouldn't know him."

"It was The Zed, wasn't it?"

He sighed again. She wanted the whole truth. "Yes, of course it was. One of his greater passions. She fell in love with him, and, of course, he dumped her. I think he was the only man in the world who ever did. So when I married his beautiful daughter, Pru took it as rather an insult. But you might be glad to hear that I turned her down last time without too much difficulty. I expect she thinks I'm impotent too. She certainly thinks I'm an idiot. Perhaps I am." He reached out to stroke Rufa's cheek with the tip of his finger. "I can't give you up. I'm so madly in love with you that I'll do anything to keep you. When Nancy rang me yesterday evening to tell me you were alone and ill, and patently nutty as a fruitcake, I had to come and bring you home. You're not to decide anything, or think about anything, until you get there. And you're not to worry that I'm going to expect you to do anything, just because you foolishly agreed to marry me." He smiled, longing to comfort her. "Those are your orders."

Rufa's tired eyes brimmed with tears. "It wasn't foolish. It was the most sensible thing I ever did. I don't know how to begin to say sorry."

He sat down on the sofa beside her, gathering her into his arms. She clung to him, in a tempest of sobbing. He realized suddenly that something in the way she touched him had changed. The sense of physical reserve between them had vanished. The chip of ice The Zed's death had left in her heart was thawing. Now she pressed her face into his shoulder, as if she needed to touch him to ease some inner pain.

This whole train of thought was inconveniently arousing. Edward shifted against the cushions, so that Rufa would not notice he had an erection. He stroked the back of her head. "Stop it, Ru. I refuse to drive all the way to Melismate with you beating yourself up. I can see how sorry you are. You've nearly died of being sorry."

"I'm not ill—it's only since I lost the baby—" Rufa raised her head. "Did you tell Tristan?"

"No." Edward could not help bringing this out curtly.

"He ought to know."

"Hmm. I suppose so."

Hesitantly, Rufa asked, "Have you heard from him? Do you know how he is?"

"The last I heard, he was absolutely fine."

"I'm glad."

They were silent. Edward asked, "Is that all you're going to say?"

"I couldn't bear it if I'd made him miserable," Rufa said. "I wish I knew what got into me."

"You fell in love with him."

"I thought I was in love with him—with an idea of him, anyway. That's all finished now." She spoke calmly, but he noticed how her fingers nervously gripped the lapel of his tweed coat. "I'd like to say it was another Rufa who fell in love with Tristan. But that would only sound like Linnet saying it was Postman Pat who scribbled on the walls. God knows what was going through my mind. I thought it would kill me to be apart from him. He wanted me such a lot."

Edward winced over "he wanted me," with its implication that her husband had not. He spoke as neutrally as he could. "I went to Oxford a few days after you did. I spoke to Tristan."

"How was he?"

"Rather a mess. Said he'd do anything to get you back."

"Oh."

"Do you want to go back to him?"

"No." Rufa's body tensed in his arms. "I can't go back to the way I felt about him. It was all based on—I don't know—fantasies. I almost wanted to *be* him. And it all completely fell apart when I turned up on his doorstep."

"I heard," Edward said. "He told you to have an abortion. That and the disgusting state of his kitchen tore the scales from your eyes."

Rufa gave a brief laugh that was half a sob. "Am I that predictable?"

"I know you rather well." Edward's inconvenient erection had subsided. He gave Rufa a friendly kiss on the forehead and released her. "I know you need to be at home. So please, let's agree to forget about the past. We both made mistakes. I'll forgive you, if you forgive me."

"There's nothing to—"

"Well, good. Pack up your things, and I'll let Rose know you're on your way."

"Now?"

"Absolutely now," Edward said briskly. "You can accuse me of being a control freak if you like, but you're not fit to be alone."

Edward made Rufa stay in the flat while he went out in the wind and the snow to fetch his car. By the time he had driven from the New Town, the car was blissfully warm. Rufa lay back in the passenger seat with a sigh of pleasure that made them both laugh.

"I haven't been this warm for weeks."

He steered into a long line of cars heading toward the motorway. "Go back to sleep if you like."

She swallowed a yawn. "I keep telling you, I'm not an invalid. I feel so much better now I've got these tablets. I'll take a share of the driving later."

"You'll do nothing of the kind. Stop trying to be helpful. Do you mind if I put the news on?"

"Go ahead."

Edward switched on the radio in time for the weather. Heavy snow was predicted on the eastern side of Scotland. There had been a pileup on the motorway, which was causing long delays.

Rufa murmured, "That's our road, isn't it?"

"Yes."

"We could always go back to the flat, and leave it till tomorrow."

"I am not going back to that flat," Edward snapped. "I'd rather spend the whole night in a traffic jam." She was anxious. He made himself smile at her reassuringly. "But it won't come to that. I'm sure I can find a shortcut."

She trusted him. It felt delicious to lie back in the warmth, and let him do the worrying about the dreadful driving conditions. Her head was as light as a balloon. This was very like a dream, but part of her was intensely conscious of every detail. Edward's hands gripped the wheel. He frowned at the road ahead. The windscreen wipers made two fan shapes in the blanket of snow that was muffling the car.

Edward took it all—Christmas rush, ghastly weather, disastrous traffic— as a personal challenge. Rufa observed his strategies passively, wondering why she was so calm. Shouldn't she be in agonies of remorse? That would probably come later. The sheer relief of having Edward beside her canceled out everything else. This was the end of a nightmare, escape from an underground dungeon. At last she was able to admit to herself how bitterly she had missed him. She wished he had not hurried her out of the flat before they had finished talking. With Edward, there was never a feeling of having said enough.

There was no point trying to talk to him now. He was too busy proving himself superior to all obstacles. He left the crawling motorway, where flakes of snow whirled madly in dismal orange lights, and nosed along black lanes where there were no lights at all. They slipped silently through shuttered villages and skirted isolated small towns. Rufa watched him, thinking how lucky it was that she had run into Adrian. Thanks to Adrian (or rather, the doctor he had summoned at presumably vast expense) she now felt better than she had done for weeks. The antibiotics made her a little woozy, but that was nothing. It was even rather pleasant, after the wretched, nauseous weakness. The infection had turned her misery into full-blown tragedy.

How strange, she thought, that tragedy could boil down to something so prosaic, and be cured with pills.

The car slowed, and halted. Edward put on the hand brake, and switched off the engine. They were surrounded by blackness, studded with a few distant specks of light. The wind had risen, and it made the only sound in the desolation.

Rufa, who had been dozing in the warmth, foolishly murmured, "Where are we?"

"God knows."

"Sorry?"

"I'm lost," Edward said. "I can navigate a whole armored convoy through Bosnian hills riddled with snipers, but I can't find Berwick-on-Tweed. Give me another look at that map." He unclipped his seat belt and leaned across her, to study the map he had placed on her knees. "You were right, we should have stayed in Edinburgh. I can't think what possessed me—except that I had to take you away. Before you disappeared again."

"I've given up disappearing," Rufa said.

"How are you?" His gray eyes, veined like pebbles, met hers. "Is this killing you?"

"Not at all, I'm fine." His face was close to hers. She stroked his forehead, tracing the faint lines. "I do love you."

For a moment, he was wary. Then he tried to laugh it off. "Despite my hopeless orienteering?"

"I love you so much I don't mind being lost in a snowstorm in the middle of nowhere," Rufa said. "It's still better than being alone, without you."

"Without anyone."

"You in particular. Why don't you ever believe me when I say I love you?"

This startled him. "Of course I believe you."

"No you don't. I've tried and tried. You think I'm grateful, or something." Rufa's heart thudded uncomfortably, but she was suddenly desperate to speak the unspoken. "You've never let me show you. It's as if you didn't want me to love you—in that way, I mean. I wish you'd tell me what I did wrong. When we got married, I was perfectly willing to sleep with you."

He let out a brief, angry laugh. "Being 'perfectly willing' to have sex is not the same as wanting it. Every time I went near you, you looked as if you were at the dentist's."

"I did not!"

"That's how it felt to me. And I can't make love under those circumstances."

"You have too much pride."

"Yes."

"But Edward," she pleaded softly, "isn't it different now?"

"After Tristan, do you mean? Should I be thanking him for switching you back on?"

Rufa winced. "That's not fair."

"Whatever the problem was, he seems to have cured it," Edward said. He groaned, and drew away from her. "God almighty, what a time to tell me."

"I'm doing this all wrong," Rufa said despairingly. "Perhaps it was because of him that I—but if you'd slept with me, I would have learned it all from you."

He was angry, making an effort to rein in his voice. "Are you saying I should have forced you, until you got to like it? Is that what Tristan did?"

"No!" She was snapping now. "I thought we agreed to forget the past. Or did that only apply to me?"

"You seem to expect some sort of apology from me because I was too decent to rape you—"

"I do not!"

He gave a sigh that was half a growl. "This is stupid. This time yesterday, sitting here with you would have been my idea of perfect happiness—and now we're arguing. Rather ironically, just like a married couple."

"All I'm trying to say is that I love you," Rufa said. "And I loved it when you fucked me."

"You were drunk."

"I should have got my hands on more of that brandy, so you'd fuck me again." She smiled, a little sourly. "You really don't like it when I say *fuck*, do you?"

"Not madly. It doesn't seem necessary, and it's not like you."

"How do you know what I'm really like? You seem to have this fantasy picture of me, and it's a real pain to live up to sometimes. You wouldn't fuck me, and I thought you didn't want me."

"Well, you were wrong." Edward grabbed her hand, and pressed it against his erection. "That's how much I want you."

Rufa's head swam. Her flesh suddenly ached to be touched by him.

He moved toward her, unfastening her seat belt. He kissed her hard on the mouth. Their hands tore at each other's layers of clothes. When Edward pulled away from her, they were both breathless. She was afraid he was still angry, but he was smiling. He stared into her face for ages.

"I might have completely the wrong idea about you," he said, "but I really don't think you'd appreciate being fucked in a car."

❋ ❋ ❋

Braemar was a detached mock Tudor house, heavily stone-clad, in a street on the edge of Berwick. The snow was too wet to settle here. Fat flakes melted on the concrete drive. It was profoundly dark, except for one ghostly light above the porch. A sign in the front window said Reasonable Rates—Some En Suite—Vacancies.

"Only the best," Edward said. "Come on, let's wake someone up."

He jumped out of the car, bracing himself against the wind, and opened Rufa's door. With one arm around her, he rang the bell vigorously. It shrilled somewhere in the depths of the house, and echoed away into silence. He rang again. "Don't get cold," he said. He wrapped Rufa in his arms. They were kissing again. She was almost ashamed of the strength of her desire for him. There was a firmness and confidence in his touch that reawakened all the hunger she had once felt for Tristan, and something else that reached right down to the innermost chamber of her heart. She half-closed her eyes to concentrate on the feel of his hands, working their way under her layers of jersey to her breasts.

A door slammed inside the house. They sprang apart, hearts hammering. There was a sound of soft feet coming downstairs. A light snapped on in the porch, revealing a bulky pink figure behind the frosted glass. A woman with gray hair took a long time drawing bolts and turning keys, before she opened the door an inch. "Yes?"

"So sorry to disturb you," Edward said, "I know it's late, but my wife and I need a room."

The woman was doubtful. "We don't take people off the streets, I'm afraid."

"Please," Rufa said. "We hate to bother you, but—" She smiled up at Edward. "But we're on our honeymoon."

Edward experienced a rush of pure happiness, so intense that tears stung his eyes. He put an arm around Rufa's waist. "Yes. We've only been married a few hours."

Sympathy softened the woman's face. She pulled her pink dressing gown more tightly around her. "Oh, you poor things—and you've had this dreadful weather—well, I can hardly turn you away at this time of year, can I?" Smiling, she stepped back to let them into her hall. "I can let you have one of my en suites."

The room was large, and loudly decorated. There was a framed print of Landseer's *The Monarch of the Glen* above the fat, quilted headboard of the double bed. It was very warm, and blazing with light. Once the woman had wished them good-night, Edward switched off the monstrous chandelier. The walls melted into shadow, embracing them.

He asked, "Is this place really all right?"

Rufa whispered, "It's perfect."

"And you? How are you feeling?"

"Wonderful," Rufa said. "Do stop asking me—I'm not going to pass out this time. I'm sober and in my right mind."

"Well, I'm not—this is the most romantic thing I've ever done in my life." He took her into his arms, burying his face in her neck. "I couldn't wait to show you how much I love you."

"Show me what you wanted to do to me," Rufa whispered, "when I made you desperate for sex."

He began to peel away her clothes, and was inside her before he had reached the last layer. They sprawled half-clad on the nylon satin quilt, gasping at each of his hard thrusts. He whispered in her ear, "Ru, my darling, I love you so much—you're so ridiculously beautiful, you make me so desperate I had a hard-on at the altar—I wish I could stay inside you for the rest of my life—"

They came together, rocking the mattress beneath them, both weeping with the relief of it. Afterward, Rufa lay in a trance of happiness, holding his head between her breasts.

"I love you more than the world," she said. "And you fuck divinely."

He laughed softly. "It sounds lovely when you say it. I might even get used to it."

"You'd better," Rufa said, "because I'm never leaving you again, not for a single day. You'll never get rid of me now."

Chapter Sixteen

H is own heart laughed,'" Rose read. "'And that was good enough for him. He had no further intercourse with Spirits, but lived on the Total Abstinence Principle ever afterwards.'"

She sat in her drinking chair beside the range. Linnet, clutching both Ressany Brothers, was on her knee. Roger, Lydia, Selena, and Ran were around the kitchen table, drinking third cups of tea, and eating the iced gingerbread stars Selena had made that morning. Ran was weeping.

"'And it was always said of him that he knew how to keep Christmas well, if any man alive possessed the knowledge.'" Rose glanced up tearfully at her family. "'May that be truly said of us, and all of us! And so, as Tiny Tim observed—'" She lowered the book.

Everyone chorused, "'God bless us, every one!'"

The reading ended, as it had done so many times in the past, with nose-blowing and self-conscious laughter.

"I have lots of intercourse with spirits," Rose said. "Somebody please get me a prodigious gin." Linnet, supple as a ferret, slid off her knee. "When's Rufa coming?"

"Do stop asking, darling. The answer will be just the same."

"We've been expecting her all day," Roger said, pouring Rose a generous shot of Gordon's.

"Apparently they had to break the journey last night because of the weather."

"Well, I don't care how late it is," Linnet declared. "I'm staying till she comes. Why is she taking so long?"

"Edward said they had some shopping to do," Rose said. "Go and watch your video of *Muriel the Little Mermaid*."

"*Ariel*," Linnet corrected her, with withering scorn.

"Go and watch whatever load of pants you're obsessed with at the moment—and you can have a chocolate from the tree."

"Yesss!" The little girl danced out of the room, twirling her bears around her glossy black head. The moment she heard the drawing-room door close, Rose said, "What the hell are they playing at? I thought Edward was bringing me a distraught Niobe at death's door, and now they're going shopping. And God knows where Nancy's got to. She swore she'd be here by six."

"Listen to Mrs. Cratchit," Selena said. She and Lydia were still giggling over "Muriel."

Rose took her tumbler of gin from Roger. She was finding it difficult to sniff away her tears, but only because her heart—like Scrooge's—was laughing. Tomorrow morning, when she went to the village church to watch Linnet's performance as the innkeeper's wife in the nativity play, everyone she loved on earth would be in the pew beside her. She thought what a simple thing this was to wish for—and, at the same time, how immense.

Roger understood. While Lydia and Selena teased Ran for weeping over Tiny Tim, he gently squeezed her shoulder, murmuring, "Wouldn't he have loved all this?"

Rose could only nod. It was no longer painful to remember The Zed. The memories that came into her mind still made her cry, but they were joyful and benign, as if scattered by The Zed himself. He was present, in a way he had not been present since his death. Last Christmas they had been too raw with shock, too blind with grief, to notice him.

She could not stop marveling over the changes. This time last year, Selena had been sullen and belligerent. Lydia had been passive and despairing. Now Selena had blossomed into a confident bluestocking who cooked and organized, and briskly corrected her mother's misquotations. And Lydia—whether one entirely approved or not—was alight with the happiness of reclaiming Ran. He had stayed at Melismate for a week after Bonfire Night, until Polly had dropped his house keys through the letter box. Then he had carried his wife and child back to Semple Farm.

Polly, in her avenging fury, had removed everything removable that she had paid for. The kitchen cupboards were empty. There were three chairs and one bed in the entire house, and no crockery. Fortunately, Lydia had salvaged the Hotel Dinnerware, and Ran had stuffed the attic with items Polly had thrown away. They had returned to the early, blissful days of their youthful marriage—the dinner of herbs where love was, and bugger-all else, as The Zed had once described it. Lydia was radiant.

Rose had spent an enjoyable morning in Argos, buying her heaps of sheets and towels. It came to more than she had meant to spend on a Christmas present, but it also counted as a wedding gift. Ran had booked the registry office for the first week in April. He was as transparently happy as Lydia. Rose rather doubted they had heard the last of his amorous adventures—but at least he now had sense enough to keep his family together. She suspected Lydia was either pregnant, or expecting to be so any minute. Just as well, since Linnet had pointedly put "BABY BRUTHER" at the top of her Christmas list.

Selena said to Lydia, "I hope you're staying for supper. I've made industrial quantities of toad-in-the-hole."

"Well, if it's organic," Ran said.

"Course it is," Selena said. "When did you ever hear of a battery-farmed toad?"

"Oh, ha ha."

"We'd love to," Lydia said. She was far firmer with her once-and-future husband these days. "Linnet's determined to see Ru, and she might as well get as tired as possible now—I don't much fancy being woken at five in the morning."

Ran leaned over to kiss her, folding his hands protectively over her belly (pregnant! thought Rose). "Don't tire yourself out as well."

"I won't. Selena and I wrapped all the presents yesterday."

A shriek rang out in the drawing room. The door burst open. Linnet dashed blindly through the kitchen, screaming, "Rufa! She's come! Rufa!"

❄ ❄ ❄

The windows of Melismate glowed with golden light. The snow had an eerie glimmer in the darkness. The headlights of the car caught *Evite La Pesne* on the gates.

Rufa said, "Now I have to face them." She was very tired, giddy with the remembered bliss of her delayed wedding night, and suddenly nervous about meeting her mother and sisters. "I've caused so much trouble. I must've put Mum through hell. Even at the time, I didn't quite know why I had to run away. I'll never be able to explain."

"You won't have to," Edward said. He took his hand off the wheel to caress her thigh briefly. "They'll all be like me, simply glad to have you safe. Nobody will want to go on about it. Once they get you in their clutches, they'll never let you go."

"Well, they'll have to," Rufa said, smiling. "I live with my husband these days. And I've been longing to be back in a warm bed with you. It was agony getting up this morning."

He chuckled softly. They had slept fitfully, waking to make love every time their bare flesh touched, and they had left Braemar very early, so that Rufa could buy Christmas presents for Melismate and food for Edward's farmhouse. She had stubbornly shopped herself half to death, and she was paying for it with a swimming head and ringing ears. But she had found the love of her life: the missing half of her soul. Her appetite for sex had come rushing back last night in a way that might have been a little embarrassing, if the man in question had not been Edward. Tired as she was, recalling his lovemaking now made her pulse beat faster.

"You're exhausted," Edward said. "I've worn you out. I'm very bad for you. I did warn you, once I started I wouldn't be able to stop."

"Don't be silly, you're the best thing in the world for me." She looked thoughtfully ahead at the house, as they nosed cautiously along the snow-covered drive. "I can't help thinking how pleased The Zed is. I mean, now that he's dead—he wouldn't have been at all pleased about us when he was alive."

"And you feel we have his blessing now?" His voice was gentle.

"I know it sounds drippy. But I do."

Edward stopped the car in front of the drawing-room window, which was filled with the colored lights of the Christmas tree. They heard Linnet's squeal of joy, and the door-slamming tumult of her approach, and both laughed.

He murmured, "In that case, The Zed knows I'll fill you up with as many babies as you can possibly want. My house will be completely trashed and strewn with hideous plastic toys—and I'll love every bloody minute of it."

He dropped a light kiss on her lips. "So don't be too unhappy—look ahead, for a change. There's nothing to be scared of."

Rufa tried looking ahead—something she had not been able to do without terror for months—and found the picture painfully beautiful. More tears, from the bottomless well inside her, made her tired eyes swim. She and Edward were going to build a family. "Oh, darling—"

The great wooden door creaked slowly open, pushed by the small and impatient figure of Linnet. Energy poured into Rufa, on a huge surge of purest joy. She wrenched open her door, dropped to her knees on the snowy gravel, and clutched Linnet in her arms. Then the little girl was prized away, and Rose's arms were around her. Rufa inhaled her mother's familiar smell of tobacco and wood smoke, and felt her familiar bobbly, overwashed jersey. Rose rocked her daughter like a baby, crooning and soothing. "My darling, my petal, my silk princess, it's all right now."

"Mummy, I'm so sorry," Rufa mumbled in Rose's shapeless woolen bosom. "I'm so, so sorry—"

"Darling one, there's nothing to be sorry for."

"That's what I keep telling her," Edward said. "She's been wearing sackcloth and ashes all day."

"Well, take them off. We're having quite a party inside, and sackcloth is against our dress code." She released Rufa with a resounding kiss, to be vigorously hugged by her sisters.

Rufa asked, "Is Nancy here?" She was aching to see Nancy. They had volumes of talking to get through.

"On her way," Rose assured her. "She called this afternoon, in her Madame de Pompadour voice. So my guess is that she's been having some Christmas sex. Do you need help with your bags?"

"No thanks," Edward said crisply. "Ru's not staying here."

"Oh?" Rose's antennae were twitching.

"I'm going back with Edward," Rufa said, ridiculously shy. "We're—well, we've decided to give it another try."

"Darling!" Rose almost drove the breath out of her with another hard hug. "That's wonderful! And does that mean—?"

"Yes, Rose," Edward said, laughing and putting an arm around his bride. "Before you go into tactless overdrive, we've done it. All right?"

"I wasn't going to ask, but I would have guessed," Rose said. "How wonderfully typical of Ru, to have a steamy affair with her own husband."

"So that's what you were up to last night," Selena said, "you spotless devils."

Rose cuffed her affectionately. "Impertinent child—see what I have to put up with?" She shivered. "Ru, you look utterly knackered, and blue with cold. Come inside."

Everyone began to laugh and talk at once. Rufa found herself in her mother's drinking chair beside the range, light-headed with warmth, dazed by so much happiness. Roger made her a mug of hearty, brick-red Melismate tea. When she glanced over at Edward, she saw her happiness reflected. He looked younger than she did.

Linnet twined her arms around Rufa's neck. "You're not allowed to go away ever again. You're allowed to go to Edward's, but THAT'S IT. Do you hear?"

Rufa stroked her hair. "That suits me. I didn't like being so far away."

"Why did you go?"

"I'll tell you someday. I missed you so much." She could not stop gazing at the little girl, brooding over her.

"I live at Daddy's now," Linnet said comfortably.

"I heard."

"Smelly's gone. She found Daddy in Mummy's bed."

Rufa was too tired to make her usual attempt at a straight face, and could not help laughing. "Oh dear."

"You mean, oh goody," Linnet corrected her. "I was pleased. They're doing their marrying all over again, and I can wear my bridesmaid's dress."

"Really? You've set a date?" Rufa asked Lydia.

Lydia nodded. "April the first—and don't you dare say that's appropriate."

"Congratulations. I'll make you another wedding cake."

"We'll save the top layer for the christening," Ran said.

"Don't, Ran. It's not the right time to tell her." Lydia turned radiant, brimming eyes to Rufa. "Sorry. It's far too early to know properly, anyway."

"But you're trying?" Rufa asked. She smiled, to show she could bear the news. "Liddy, that's brilliant."

"We'll have to see who gets there first," Edward said. "May the best man win."

Ran gave him a friendly slap on the shoulder. "Welcome back to the family, Ed. You can't get away from these Hasty women—so you might as well make babies with them."

Selena presented Rufa with her plate of gingerbread stars. "I hope you and Edward are coming for Christmas lunch tomorrow. It's my debut, and I want lavish praise from someone discerning."

Rufa was impressed. "You're not doing it all by yourself?"

The elegant young lady suddenly grinned, turning back into a child. "I could use some help with the turkey."

Color flooded into Rufa's face. She revived before their eyes, like a Japanese paper flower dropped in water. "Have you got sausage meat for the stuffing?"

"Yes."

"Chestnuts?"

"Yup."

"Peeled?"

"Tinned."

"I picked up a bag of fresh chestnuts at the grocer's," Rufa said. "I knew they'd come in handy. I'll bring them to church with me. Edward, what is it? Why are you laughing?"

"You're going to make me get up at dawn again, aren't you?"

"Yes. You can sleep in on Boxing Day."

"He can't," Roger said. "What about the meet? You've got to be there, Ed. We can't let old Bute think he's beaten us, just because we've lost The Zed."

Ran said, "Count me in. I loathe hunting, and it's time I did something macho and phallic."

Edward was thoughtful. "I'm sure there's a box of his old leaflets somewhere."

Rose had another moment of intensely sensing The Zed. She listened to the three men talking about the Boxing Day meet, as if he had blown the idea into their minds. It was good to hear deep voices in the house again. She watched her girls, talking and laughing around the range. Lydia and Selena—constantly bumping into each other—were laying the table for supper, vying to tell Rufa about the defeat of Smelly. Rufa cradled Linnet in her arms, listening contentedly. Rose saw how often she glanced over at Edward, and how tenderly he glanced back at her. It was an amazing outcome, but Rose had a strong sense of things being in their right places, at last.

She had learned a lot about Edward over the past year. She had discovered that you could peel away layer after layer of his character, and find only goodness, right to the core. Rose shuddered to think where they would all be now, without his endless love for Rufa. He had ended up marrying the

373

entire family, resigning himself to the fact that they would all be in his hair forever and ever. He would throw money at Ran's doomed ventures. He would carry Selena through university, and keep the Melismate fridge filled. Once Rose had wondered what was in it for Edward. Seeing him with Rufa made it obvious. He was a man reborn.

"The toad's ready," Selena called. "Sit down."

The door into the Great Hall creaked open. Nancy burst in, loaded with paper bags, and with milky mistletoe berries pinned in her blazing hair. "Merry Christmas—where's Ru?"

"Hark, the herald angels sing, pom-pom, pom-pom, newborn king!" sang Berry. Nancy lay lushly asleep in the passenger seat, filling the car with her perfume. Berry ordered himself not to get an erection while driving. Back in the plump, cushioned life with Polly, he had sometimes fantasized about having a single night with Nancy. He now knew there was no such thing as enough, where Nancy was concerned. They had been making love every four hours for the past two days, in every conceivable position. Berry had never been so ridiculously, doltishly, beamingly happy in his entire life. When he made love to Nancy, he became a sexual swordsman, a Casanova, a king. She loved him, and life looked piercingly beautiful from the inside of her warm heart.

He smiled to himself, remembering how they had shamelessly snogged in the taxi on the way to Wendy's, that first night—he had given the driver an enormous tip. Then he had been inside her, with his lips and tongue around one pale pink nipple, coming and coming, pouring himself into her. He had proposed to her immediately afterward, and Nancy had said, "Don't worry, darling—it's on the house."

But he had not allowed her to joke about it. He had made her admit how much she loved him, without trying to laugh it off. She had not been able to hide it underneath her usual, public manner. And as soon as he knew, for certain, that he held the true, essential Nancy, he was surer than ever that he had to marry her. He had declared that he would buy her a diamond as big as the Ritz, and tell the whole world, before she could change her mind.

Nancy had said, "As if I'd change my mind, when at last I've found the world's most perfect man—a model of chivalry who can also make me come like the Flying Scotsman." They had ended up making love again after that.

The following day, oblivious to the jostling Christmas crowds, Berry had taken Nancy to Boodle and Dunthorne, in Sloane Street, and chosen her a beautiful, vastly expensive diamond ring.

"Darling, have you lost your senses?" Nancy had demanded. "What's wrong with Ratner's?"

"Please, Nancy. It's a personal thing. This ring is almost exactly twice the price of the one I bought Polly. I know it's rather mean-spirited of me—but I couldn't have been comfortable if my wife's ring had been cheaper. And anyway, she's never sent it back."

"Oh well, in that case," Nancy had said, holding out her left hand to be measured.

She had worn the ring that evening, when he had taken her round to his sister's flat in Clapham. His parents had been staying there, and he was impatient to introduce them to the future mother of his children (Berry had already decided four would be nice). Nancy had looked gloriously beautiful in the taupe jacket from the campaigning wardrobe. Annabel had muttered, "God almighty, she's sensational—what on earth does she see in you?" And his father had drawled "I say" in his Terry-Thomas voice. They had loved her.

Berry turned his BMW down the lane that led to the gate of Melismate. "We're here."

Nancy stretched luxuriously. "Mmmm. I was having such a rude dream about you."

"What was I doing?"

"I'll show you later."

"Go on, give me a clue—which parts did it involve?"

Nancy was shaking with laughter. "Wait and see."

He stopped the car in the drive, and leaned over to kiss her. "That's going to be difficult, when you're so stunning. Are you as happy as I am?"

"Absolutely delirious. I can't wait to tell Rufa." She opened her door. "Isn't it ironic? We were both ready to renounce everything for love, and we couldn't have married better if you'd paid us."

The future Lady Bridgmore had a diamond ring. Better than that, Rose thought, she was very obviously madly in love. She was electric with it; more herself than she had been since The Zed's death. For the first time in her career, Nancy had fallen for a man without first leaping into his bed. Berry, who had spent the previous Christmas Eve with his eyes pinned hopelessly to her curves, now had difficulty keeping his hands off them.

Ah, that blissful first stage, Rose thought nostalgically; the grappling and sobbing, the moonstruck passion. She had not left the house for nearly three weeks when The Zed first brought her home to Melismate. Love like that never died—it only went underground, to be endlessly re-created in the faces of the next generation.

All talking, laughing, and shouting at once, they ate toad-in-the-hole and drank red wine. Selena showed off to Rufa, producing a queen of puddings, scientifically browned and perfect in every detail.

"I've been reading Sir Kenelm Digby," she said coolly. "He made me want to experiment with traditional English cooking."

"She thinks her sisters are total fools," Nancy said. "Well, she's right. What a good thing we've all bagged husbands."

Rose said, "That cranking sound is Mrs. Pankhurst turning in her grave. Did feminism pass you by completely?"

"It didn't pass Liddy by," Ran said, his great eyes mournful. "Independence. Having her own social life. Singing in that bloody choir. Going to bloody church. Since she came back, she treats me like an inferior being."

"I like church," Linnet said. "Nancy, guess what, I'm the innkeeper's wife in the nativity play. I have to say: 'Husband, what about the stable?' Mummy sewed me a costume made of tea towels."

"Hmm," Nancy said, lazily feeling Berry's leg under the table. "I bet you're tremendous." In a deep, Ressany voice, she added, "Yes, she is, but she doesn't do a dance or show her bum."

Linnet, whose eyelids had begun to droop, giggled and snapped back into wakefulness. A Stilton was produced, smelling out the room like the essence of a thousand old socks. Roger made ten large mugs of strong tea, and a cup of juice for Linnet.

"Look," Edward said, nodding toward the clock above the range. "It's been Christmas Day for twenty minutes. Merry Christmas, everyone."

There was more kissing, more filling of glasses.

"I'm so happy I need to dance," Nancy declared. "I wish we had The Zed's party tape—he made a tape of all our favorite songs," she explained to Berry. "He used to bring it out at the drop of a hat. He'd certainly have played it now, wouldn't he, Mum?"

"God, yes," Rose sighed. "All this fabulous news would have merited 'Cum on Feel the Noyz' at the very least."

"Or even the Funky Chicken," Rufa said.

Selena stood up. "I might know where it is. All the stuff from his desk went into a box under the stairs, and I'm sure I saw it when I got out the Christmas lights."

Lydia, tipsy and giggling, went with her to search for it, in the dusty glory-hole under the main staircase.

"Anything we can dance to," Rose called after them. She got stiffly out of her chair. "*The Best of Abba* will do."

Roger bowed and kissed Rose's sooty hand. "May I have the pleasure?"

"Darling, of course—and I insist on cutting a rug with each of my sons-in-law."

"Got it." Selena and Lydia entered in triumph. Selena was rubbing a cob-webby cassette against her jersey. "The famous party tape." She slotted it into the ghetto blaster on the counter, turning up the sound. As The Zed had done, she announced, "Ladies and gentlemen, please take your places for 'Hi-Ho Silver Lining.'" She pressed the Play button.

There was a hissing sound, then a loud chord—then the music suddenly stopped.

The voice of The Zed filled the room. "Hello, girls. I hope you're playing this because you're having fun."

Selena snapped it off, as if stung. They stood in awed silence, staring at each other's white faces.

Rose whispered, "Of course, of course. I should have guessed. I knew there had to be a message."

Gently pushing Selena aside, she reached out a shaking hand, and wound the tape back to the beginning. Edward put his arm around Rufa's waist. Lydia sat down, scooping a large-eyed Linnet onto her lap. Deep silence settled around them all, as they prepared themselves to hear the voice from another world.

"Hello, girls. I hope you're playing this because you're having fun. I hope it means you're not too sad. I'm sorry about all this, and I won't give you the reasons why I have to leave you. I just wanted to tell you how much I love you all. And I'm recording over my tape because this is exactly how I want you to remember me. Only the fun bits, all right? You can completely forget the rest." There was a pause, during which they could hear him humming to himself, as he did when thinking deeply. "This feels rather like the Oscars," the voice went on, eerily close and familiar. "Rose, Rufa, Nancy, Liddy, Selena, Linnet—good-bye, my darlings—my silk princesses." His voice faltered. He cleared his throat. "And I ought to mention Rodge and Edward, because I'm expecting them to take care of you. I think that's all, and I'd better get going—oh, while I think of it, please don't play 'Seasons in the Sun' at my funeral."

Another pause. They waited breathlessly, feeling him among them.

"Forgive me, and be as happy as possible. Sorry to record over 'Silver Lining.'" His voice suddenly became brisk and humorous. "And sorry to put a crimp in whatever party you're having—I hope it's a corker. Ladies and gentlemen, please take your places for 'Wig Wam Bam.'"

The song began. The Zed had made his bow.

Rose switched off the tape. They were all mute, and all in tears. After a long silence, Rose said, "Yes, it's a corker all right."

These tears did not hurt. There was a great calm in the room.

Nancy lifted her wet face off Berry's shoulder. "Didn't you hear him? He wanted us to dance—switch it on!"

Suddenly, they were all smiling round at each other, their eyes unfocused, as if they had shared a miraculous vision and it had blessed them like the Spirit of Christmas. Selena switched on the music and grabbed Linnet's hands. Ran swept Lydia into the middle of the kitchen floor. Berry convulsed Nancy with his well-meaning, uncoordinated attempts at grooving. Rose danced extravagantly, clearing a large space around her. Edward leaned against the table, clasping Rufa protectively in his arms.

"After he did it, I thought I'd never be happy again," Rufa said. "But this is the happiest night of my life. I'm not quite sure why everything's suddenly so wonderful, when nothing much has changed. I feel as if I'd come to the end of a long, long journey—only to find myself back on my own doorstep."

He kissed the nape of her neck. "Welcome home."

Rebecca Meagher / Express Syndication

❋ ❋ ❋ ❋ ❋

Kate Saunders has written for the Sunday Times, the Sunday Express, the Daily Telegraph, and Cosmopolitan. She lives in London with her son.